Devil to Pay

Historical Fiction Published by McBooks Press

BY ALEXANDER KENT
Midshipman Bolitho
Stand into Danger
In Gallant Company
Sloop of War
To Glory We Steer
Command a King's Ship
Passage to Mutiny
With All Despatch
Form Line of Battle!
Enemy in Sight!
The Flag Captain
Signal–Close Action!
The Inshore Squadron
A Tradition of Victory
Success to the Brave
Colours Aloft!
Honour this Day
The Only Victor
Beyond the Reef
The Darkening Sea
For My Country's Freedom
Cross of St George
Sword of Honour
Second to None
Relentless Pursuit

BY R.F. DELDERFIELD
Too Few for Drums
Seven Men of Gascony

BY DAVID DONACHIE
The Devil's Own Luck
The Dying Trade

BY C. NORTHCOTE PARKINSON
The Guernseyman
Devil to Pay

BY V.A. STUART
Victors and Lords
The Sepoy Mutiny

BY CAPTAIN FREDERICK MARRYAT
Frank Mildmay OR
   The Naval Officer
The King's Own
Mr Midshipman Easy
Newton Forster OR
   The Merchant Service
Snarleyyow OR
The Dog Fiend
The Privateersman
The Phantom Ship

BY DUDLEY POPE
Ramage
Ramage & The Drumbeat
Ramage & The Freebooters
Governor Ramage R.N.
Ramage's Prize
Ramage & The Guillotine
Ramage's Diamond
Ramage's Mutiny
Ramage & The Rebels
The Ramage Touch
Ramage's Signal
Ramage & The Renegades

BY JAN NEEDLE
A Fine Boy for Killing
The Wicked Trade

BY W. CLARK RUSSELL
Wreck of the Grosvenor
Yarn of Old Harbour Town

BY RAFAEL SABATINI
Captain Blood

BY MICHAEL SCOTT
Tom Cringle's Log

BY A.D. HOWDEN SMITH
Porto Bello Gold

BY NICHOLAS NICASTRO
The Eighteenth Captain

Devil to Pay

C. NORTHCOTE PARKINSON

RICHARD DELANCEY NOVELS, NO. 2

MCBOOKS PRESS
ITHACA, NEW YORK

Published by McBooks Press 2001
Copyright © 1973 by C Northcote Parkinson
First published in the United States by Houghton Mifflin Co., 1973
First published in the United Kingdom by John Murray Ltd, 1973

Cover painting: *Capture of the Fort of Saint-Jean-d'Ulloa on
23 November 1838* by Jean Antoine Theodore Gunin.
Courtesy of Chateau de Versailles, France/Bridgemen Art Library.

Library of Congress Cataloging-in-Publication Data

Parkinson, C. Northcote (Cyril Northcote), 1909–
  Devil to pay / by C. Northcote Parkinson.
    p. cm. — (Richard Delancy novels ; no. 2)
  ISBN 1-59013-002-2 (alk. paper)
    1. Delancy, Richard (Fictitious character)—Fiction. 2. Great Britain
  —History, Naval—19th century—Fiction. 2. Napoleonic Wars,
  1800–1815—Fiction 4. Guernsey (Channel Islands)—Fiction.
  PR6066.A6955 D48 2001
  823'.914—dc21   2001037008

Distributed to the book trade by
LPC Group, 1436 West Randolph, Chicago, IL 60607
800-626-4330.

Additional copies of this book may be ordered from any
bookstore or directly from McBooks Press, 120 West State Street,
Ithaca, NY 14850. Please include $3.50 postage and handling with
mail orders. New York State residents must add sales tax.
All McBooks Press publications can also be ordered by calling
toll-free 1-888-BOOKS11 (1-888-266-5711).
Please call to request a free catalog.

Visit the McBooks Press website at www.mcbooks.com.

Printed in the United States of America

9 8 7 6 5 4 3 2 1

FOR JONATHAN

The Devil to pay and no pitch hot

The "devil" was the outboard plank of the ship's deck, the seam between it and the ship's side being wider than any other and needing more oakum and pitch when caulking and paying—hence the possibility of the hot pitch running short before the seam was caulked.

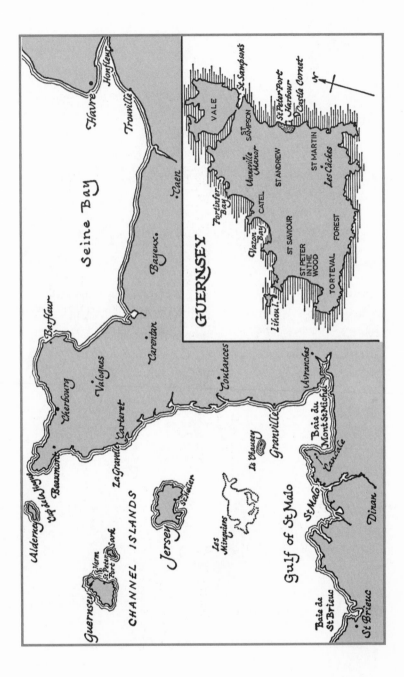

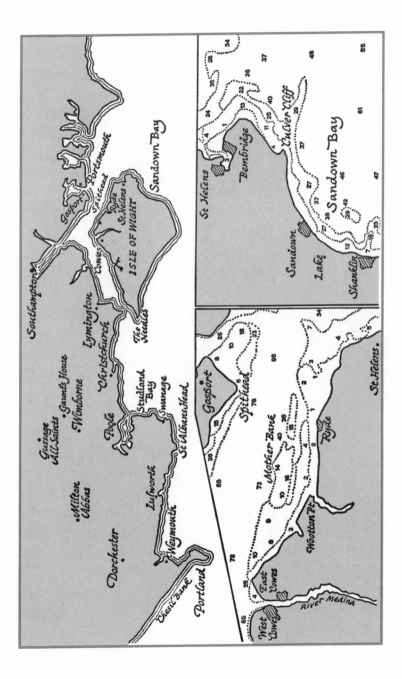

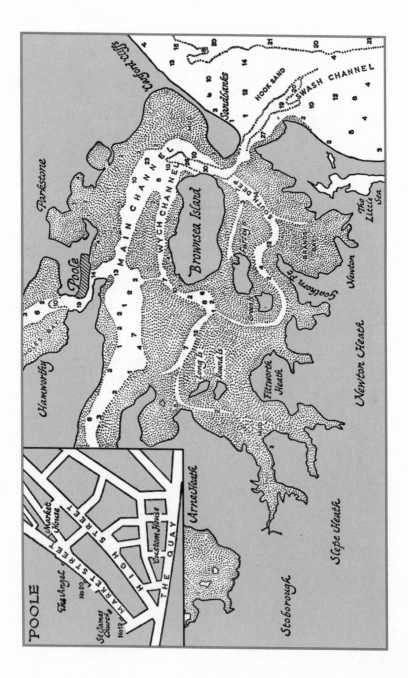

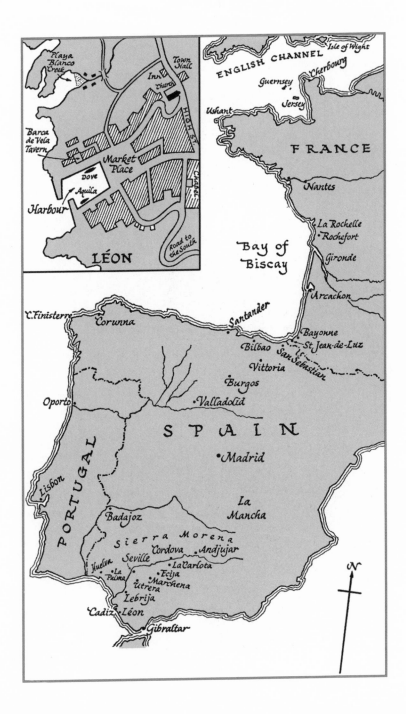

Part One

Chapter One

Under a Cloud

T HE GEORGE INN, Portsmouth, was the scene of feverish activity. Coaches rolled in and out, baggage cluttered the entrance, the inn servants bustled around and nobody took much notice of the lieutenant who had just entered from the street. It was June 3rd, 1794, and the inn parlour was full of senior officers, uniformed, gold-laced, weather-beaten and confident men, all known to each other and known to the waiters. Some minutes passed before Richard Delancey could gain anyone's attention and even then the servant he accosted was gone again in an instant. "Admiral Macbride, sir? That's his flag lieutenant on the staircase. Coming, sir!" Following the pot-boy's glance, Delancey saw an elderly officer with a portfolio under his arm talking to a still older man in civilian clothes—perhaps a dockyard official. Making his way with difficulty through the crowd, Delancey reached the foot of the stair at the moment when the two men had finished their conversation. Before the flag lieutenant could go upstairs he asked whether he might see Admiral Macbride. "And who are you, sir?" was the terse reply. Instead of giving his name, Richard Delancey presented a document, the written order his captain had received that morning from Commodore McTaggart. The flag lieutenant glanced at the paper and then again at its bearer. "Very good, Mr Delancey, the Admiral will see you. Be so good as to follow me." He led the way upstairs and along a corridor, pausing finally at the last door but one. "If you will wait here I'll see whether the Admiral is engaged." Delancey waited for ten minutes, sitting in what was probably the flag lieutenant's bedroom, and was then summoned to the Admiral's presence.

John Macbride was in his fifties at this time but looked older, being only recently promoted rear-admiral after a long career in which hard work had played a greater part than any brilliant success in battle. Grey-haired, conscientious and tired, he was working hard at this moment, his table covered with papers, his secretary at his elbow and a clerk busy in the background with tapes and sealing wax. He signed four more letters while Delancey watched, tossed them to a midshipman and then looked up to see that he had a visitor. His flag lieutenant hastened to explain: "Mr Delancey, sir, under orders to report to you." Delancey bowed stiffly and stood to attention, his hat under his left arm. Macbride looked at him in silence, wondering whether he had wasted his time in sending for the man. The officer before him was of the middle height, dark-haired, sturdily built but otherwise nondescript. If there was anything to distinguish him it was the contrast of dark hair and blue eyes. Or was there something else? He looked sullen, of course: that was to be expected. Could he be something of a dreamer, a romantic? The first impression he made was to that extent unfavourable, but one had to be fair. Who else, anyway, was available?

"Pray be seated, Mr Delancey," said the rear-admiral, taking up a document which had been placed at his elbow. It was headed "Richard Andros Delancey—commissioned 1783" and ran to half a page of notes. As Delancey sat down he felt horribly on trial. Could anything come of this interview? He told himself to expect nothing, least of all from anyone's patronage.

"I am told, Mr Delancey, that you are a native of Guernsey. Is yours a Guernsey name?"

"Yes, sir."

"Is your family one of local consequence?"

"No, sir. The Andros family—on my mother's side—held high office under King Charles II but their estates are lost now and her kinsfolk have mostly left the island."

"How old are you?"

"Thirty-four, sir."

"And you speak French like a native?"

"Like a native perhaps of the Norman coast."

"A coast with which you are familiar?"

"Yes, sir. I used to fish there as a boy."

"So you know the navigational hazards, the rocks, the racing tides. . . . No easy place, even in daylight. . . . Have you been in Guernsey recently?"

"No, sir."

Macbride rose to his feet and paced the room much as if it had been his quarterdeck. He paused finally at the window, looking out across the harbour.

"You know, I expect, that the *Artemis* has been lost, wrecked on the Seven Sisters?"

"Yes, sir."

"Then you will also have heard that Captain Fletcher was among those who perished."

"So I understand, sir."

"There has been a court of inquiry and there has to be a court martial. That is a mere formality in this case and those tried will certainly be acquitted. But one result of this affair has been to make some of us think again about the late Captain Fletcher. Some senior officers—I do not say *all*—think that last year's court martial should have ended with a different verdict. They do not think, nor do I, that the officers of the *Artemis* were justified in what they did. But there was some excuse for them at least. And any excuse that can be urged must apply more particularly to the more junior of them; the fourth lieutenant for example. In my opinion, you should be given another chance. That is why I have sent for you, Mr Delancey."

"Thank you, sir."

"You have been in the *Grafton* receiving ship since the time of the court martial?"

"Yes, sir."

"It is time you went to sea again. There is no likelihood of your being posted to a ship of the line, still less to a frigate. You could be

sent, however, on a special service and one for which you seem to be
well qualified. Success in this could lead to a better posting and even—
who knows?—to promotion. But are you the man to send? That is what
I have to decide and the decision cannot even wait until tomorrow.
Two things I must make clear from the outset. First, I cannot order
you to accept the mission I have in mind. Second, I can give you no
more than a temporary posting, one which will end when the task has
been performed."

"Am I to know, sir, what the task is?"

"Not until the eve of the operation."

"Then I have only this to say: I shall accept the chance if it is offered
to me."

"Very good, Mr Delancey. I shall ask you now to wait in the parlour for perhaps an hour. You shall hear then what I have decided."

When Delancey had left, the rear-admiral turned to his flag lieutenant and asked, simply, "Well, Mr Rymer?" That officer shook his
head and replied:

"I question, sir, whether he is the active man you need for what I
suppose to be a hazardous mission. He has spent the last eight or ten
months in the *Grafton,* much as if he had spent that time ashore. Before
that—the *Artemis* affair. He does not impress me favourably, sir. I
should judge him to be unreliable."

"What do *you* think, Wainwright?" asked Macbride, addressing his
secretary.

"Well, sir, I can but admire his courage. He agreed to accept a mission which—for reasons of secrecy—you could not describe. Not every
man would have done that."

"I take your point. Or is not that proof that he is desperate?"

"But who else is there?" asked Wainwright. "You are asked to find
a not-too-senior lieutenant who speaks French, knows the enemy coast,
is in Portsmouth now and has no berth in a seagoing ship. We were
fortunate, sir, to find *anyone* answering to that description. I can certainly think of no other."

"Have we been sufficiently thorough in our inquiries?" asked the flag lieutenant. "Why not ask at the Admiralty?"

"Because there isn't *time*," replied the secretary impatiently. "Lord Moira's plan has to be put in execution immediately. The officer chosen must sail tonight."

"Very true," said the rear-admiral, "I too have my doubts about Mr Delancey but there are only two courses open to me. Either I send him or else I inform Lord Moira that we cannot give him the assistance for which he has asked. I am loath to confess that a mission must fail for want of activity on our part. No, my decision is made. Make out the necessary orders, Wainwright, and you, Mr Rymer, see that Delancey sails in the *Cormorant* by this evening's tide. He is to report, on arrival, to Captain the Prince of Bouillon."

While the orders were being written and signed Delancey was in the parlour below. He had expected to find himself among strangers, too junior for the company and looked at askance. Many of the senior officers had gone, however, since his first arrival at the George and he was surprised to recognize an old lieutenant with whom he had some slight acquaintance, a one-legged man called Harris who was third in command of the *Warspite,* another hulk at permanent anchor. Harris was a useful officer in his way but cynical, a man embittered by disappointment. It was a relief, nevertheless, to find someone there with whom he could pass the time of waiting. They exchanged greetings and Harris sent the pot-boy for two tankards of porter.

"And what errand has brought you here, Mr Delancey?"

"Admiral Macbride sent for me, sir. There is some possibility of my going to sea again."

"You? Possibility be damned. You were finished when you gave evidence against Fletcher at the court martial. No other captain will have you. You'll serve in the *Grafton* until she sinks or the war ends, same as me in *Warspite*. Could be worse, y'know, could be worse! Your health, sir, and confusion to the French!"

"But it's not the same for me as it is for you, sir. With a leg shot

off in battle you are very well posted and nobody could ask why you
are not on more active service."

"I'll tell you a secret, young man, but don't repeat it along the quayside. I lost my leg in the after hold of the Norwich, crushed by a barrel
of salt pork. I was only in action twice—in the last war, you'll understand—and came away without a scratch. But keep that to yourself."

"Aye, aye, sir."

"And I'll give you a piece of advice. Don't accept any posting that
you may be offered. If you are chosen for a mission you may depend
upon it that the Admiral could find no one else. It will be one of those
affairs in which you are bound to fail, whatever you do being wrong
and failure to do anything being worse. If there were any prospect of
success some favourite would have been sent for, the Admiral's son-in-
law or the Commodore's younger brother. The mission they offer you
was rejected—mark my words—by everyone above you in the list. It
will end only in death or disgrace or both. In the *Grafton* you'll at least
stay alive."

"'Til we're aground on the beef bones we throw over the side."

"You'll be safer then for she can't even sink at her moorings."

"Here's a health then to the heroes of the harbour watch. Waiter!"

Over half an hour passed in idle talk, Delancey being glad of company. There was too much truth, he knew, in what Harris said. It would
be folly to expect anything to come of the interview he had attended
on the floor above. No favour would ever be shown to a man suspected of disloyalty. Captain Fletcher's acquittal had implied the
condemnation of all who had testified against him as a seaman or as
an officer. Upholding Fletcher against his lieutenants in the name of
discipline had cost George III another ship and the lives of nearly two
hundred men. Fletcher had been a lubberly, useless blackguard and his
officers were all on the beach for telling the truth about him. The truth?
They had told only a quarter of the truth. It was enough to ruin each
one of them, though. What a fool he had been! But he was younger

then and too easily led. He had learnt his lesson but it was now too late to apply it. . . .

It was all very well for Harris to tell him to stay in the *Grafton* or go ashore. But what else was there to do? There was no home to which he could go, no other trade he knew, no money with which to set himself up in business. His father had died, content with the knowledge that he, Richard, had been placed on the quarterdeck. It had been all and more than the family could afford. His sister had married and left the island and both his brothers were thought to be dead, the elder certainly and the younger most likely. There were Guernseymen with whom he had been at school but none he could name as a special friend. Some of the fishermen might remember him but his schoolfellows had thought him awkward and shy, more to be teased than liked.

"Mind you," Harris broke in on his thoughts. "I don't deceive myself into thinking that an admiral has an easy life. They have more work to do than you or I, and Macbride, for one, must be working like a brewer's dray-horse. By the time all his transports are collected and the troops embarked he'll be ready to quit the service."

"I know about the transports," said Delancey, "but where are the troops?"

"In camp at Netley. There are several infantry regiments with more, I hear, on the way. Some cavalry marched in yesterday and some artillery the day before."

"And they are going overseas?"

"The rumour is that they are destined for Flanders. God knows whether that is true but a big expedition is planned, you may depend on it. Look at the tonnage that Macbride has collected! They say that Lord Moira is to command but he seems to have gone; perhaps back to London. He was in Portsmouth last week, though—I saw him here with Macbride."

"I recently heard a story that the French are planning something too, with troops collected at St Malo."

"S'death—I never heard that. They'll lose their enthusiasm when they put to sea and find Lord Howe waiting for them!"

At this point Lieutenant Rymer interrupted the conversation, hurrying across to them from the stairs.

"Mr Delancey, I have orders for you. Collect your gear from the *Grafton* and go on board the *Cormorant* sloop now at Spithead but due to sail by this evening's tide. You will be a supernumerary, on passage merely to Guernsey, where you will report to Captain the Prince of Bouillon. Here are your orders to that effect with a covering letter to the Port Admiral. Here is a letter to the captain of the *Grafton* and another to the captain of *Cormorant*. They both need the Port Admiral's signature. Ask at his office for Lieutenant Watkins and give him this note with my compliments. And here, last of all, is a letter to His Highness which you will deliver to him in person. Do you clearly understand what you have to do?"

"Aye, aye, sir."

"Goodbye then—and good luck!" The flag lieutenant was gone again in a minute, leaving Harris to stare at Delancey with surprise and disbelief.

"Wonders will never cease! So you *are* going to sea! But remember what I said. Look out for squalls! If there was any credit to be got out of your mission the job would have been given to someone else. Keep a sharp look-out! Be ready to cut and run!"

Richard Delancey was on board the *Cormorant* before sunset, outwardly calm but secretly thrilled to be at sea again and on active service.

The sloop was ship-rigged, of eighteen guns, a sister-ship to the *Amazon*. She was a smart ship with white decks, new paintwork and every rope in its place. There were all the signs that her captain was an artist in his way, even to paying for gold leaf on the scrollwork. The breeze sang in the rigging and the ship was alive under him, a racehorse impatient to start. This passage to Guernsey, to his birthplace, was nothing in itself but it could lead on to fortune. What Harris had said was merely envious. Damn the fellow! There might be something in his confounded suspicions but he put the thought aside. He was an officer chosen for a special mission and one from which he might return with his reputation made. This could be—no, it *must* be!—the big opportunity of his life, the turning point of his career. After seeing a hammock slung in his borrowed cabin he came on deck to report for duty. He moved over to the lee side of the quarterdeck as Captain Bastable appeared, uncertain what duty, if any, would be expected of him.

"Good evening, Mr Delancey."

"Good evening, sir."

"Welcome aboard. Your orders, I gather, are to report to Philip D'Auvergne. You will find him ashore at St Peter Port. If this wind holds we should be there tomorrow before noon. I shan't ask you to stand watch but you will probably want to see the ship sail."

"Aye, aye, sir."

Delancey was secretly relieved. His fear had been that he would be told to take charge of the deck, out of practice as he was after nearly a year in harbour. But Bastable had his own reputation to think about and wanted no mishap at Spithead, not even in a failing light. He took the ship to sea himself.

Delancey found that it all came back to him, the sequence of orders for weighing anchor and making sail.

"All hands up anchor! Ready there forward? Heave away! Keep step—stamp and go!" Then came the sound of the fiddle and the groan of the capstan, the sound of footsteps together and then the cry, "Anchor's a-peak, sir!"

The next task was to make sail and Delancey could see that the topmen were ready along the topsail yards.

"Let fall!" came the order and the great sails dropped and filled in an instant with the thunder of cannon and the sudden quiet as they took on their classic curve.

"Sheet home! Hoist away! Brace up forward!"

The anchor was now at the cathead and hooked and the captain gave the quartermaster his course, "South-west by west—Steady!" The voyage had fairly begun and the captain sent the port watch below, handing over the deck to Lieutenant Saunders. The ship leaned over to the breeze, the bow wave frothed back from the stem and the stars came out among the rigging. A sailor again, Delancey stayed to watch the moonrise, pacing the quarterdeck with Saunders.

"Have you been in St Peter Port recently?" he asked.

"Three weeks ago."

"Can you tell me then about the Prince of Bouillon? Is he a French émigré?"

"No, Mr Delancey, he is not. He comes of a well-known family in Jersey. He joined the Navy and was commissioned during the war with the American Colonies. When the *Arethusa* was wrecked near Ushant in 1778 D'Auvergne was taken prisoner and remained in France until exchanged."

"And came back a *prince?*"

"The Dukes of Bouillon have D'Auvergne as their family name and the late Duke—who died two years ago—had no proper heir. He adopted this British officer as his son."

"Were they, in fact, related?"

"Oh, yes, distantly. So the experts say."

"And the Duchy of Bouillon is or was an independent principality?"

"More or less. But the D'Auvergnes have, or rather had, an even bigger estate in France. It centres on the Castle of Navarre, near Evreux. Marshal Turenne was their great man, back in the reign of Louis XIV."

"I am fortunate to find you so well-informed."

"D'Auvergne has been the talk of Guernsey. All I have told you could be heard in the market-place."

"And what ship does D'Auvergne command?"

"I can't say. He has some small craft and gunboats, used for gaining intelligence and helping the French émigrés. D'Auvergne himself is to be found on shore."

"I am most grateful to you, sir. I think I had best turn in now and look forward to meeting the Prince tomorrow."

"Goodnight, Mr Delancey."

Next morning was sunny with a stiff breeze from the east. Alderney was sighted and the *Cormorant* entered the Russel under all canvas. From the quarterdeck Delancey watched as the Guernsey coast came in sight. First there was the flat land north of the bridge at St Sampsons, the separate island called the Vale. Vale Castle was seen next with the colour flying over its batteries, and finally the sloop came abreast of Castle Cornet and saluted the flag.

As the gunfire re-echoed from the cliffs and aroused the screaming of the gulls, Delancey was looking afresh at the town in which he had been born. In the foreground were the breakwaters which enclosed the harbour, beyond these the red-roofed warehouses which lined the shore and beyond them again the roofs which surged up the hillside to Hauteville, the higher and newer part of the town. There was the tower of the town church and further along to the north he could identify the very garret window of the room he had shared with his two brothers, Mathew and Michael (Rachel's room had been on the other side, facing the street). Yes, he was home again and felt the warmth of recognition and the return of boyhood memories. There was none left of his family in Guernsey and hardly even their names would be recalled but this was all the home he had. Here were the same fishing boats in the harbour, the same sunlight on the granite walls and now, suddenly, on his left, came the booming reply from the saluting battery on the castle. By the time the gulls had finished their renewed protest, the sloop was at anchor in the roads at St Peter Port, her sails furled and her gig lowered. *Cormorant* remained only long enough to land her passengers, leaving again for Falmouth as soon as the gig had returned. Delancey looked about him and thought that there was twice the activity he had ever seen in St Peter Port before. There were ships in the harbour, more in the roads, with boats going to and fro and goods being carted into the warehouses. A longshoreman took his gear on a barrow and Delancey walked behind it to the watch-house where his belongings could be left in safety. He inquired about the whereabouts of the Prince and was given directions to a warehouse fronting the harbour. As Delancey passed the town church, a column of infantry made its way up High Street; Guernsey was evidently at war.

The Prince of Bouillon's headquarters were marked only by the sentry who stood guard at the entrance. Delancey was shown a ladder by which he reached the first floor, finding himself at a door which opened on a temporary office. The opening above the quayside to which bales and barrels would normally be hoisted had been roughly boarded over, leaving only a makeshift window from which the harbour could be seen. Facing it, seated at a kitchen table, was a young officer of his own rank. There were a few more chairs and a map nailed on the wall. There was no other furniture save the paper and ink on the table and a telescope placed on the top of a barrel. Delancey made his bow and introduced himself. "I have a letter here for His Highness," he reported formally, "and I must deliver it to him in person." The Prince's staff officer was called Bassett and seemed a cheerful young man. "The Prince should be here within the next few minutes," he assured his visitor. "Pray be seated and tell me your errand."

"I should tell you with pleasure if I had myself been told," said Delancey. "My orders were merely to report here."

"My guess," said Bassett, "is that you are to have temporary command of the cutter *Royalist*. Am I right, sir, in supposing that you speak French and are familiar with these waters?"

"I am a Guernseyman, sir, and no stranger here."

"You are the very man we need then. If you come to the window I will point out the vessel you are to command." The cutter was alongside the quay and seemed to be the centre of feverish activity.

"She should be ready for sea tomorrow, rigged, armed and provisioned for one month. You will have a master's mate, boatswain, midshipman, cook and carpenter's mate, with a corporal of marines as well. These are picked men, you will understand, not the cutter's regular crew."

"And what do I have to do?"

"The captain would rather tell you that himself. He'll be here presently. There is to be a conference here tomorrow, by the way, at which you will have to be present. The lieutenant-governor will be there—General Small—and with him General the Lord Moira."

"Lord Moira? *Here?*"

"He arrived the day before yesterday."

"Did he, though? Did he come in disguise?"

"No, and he'll be at tomorrow's review."

"A review?"

"Yes, it's His Majesty's birthday."

"So it is. I had forgotten that. So all the world (Robespierre included) will know that Lord Moira is here. Might not the French conclude that something is being planned?"

"That they may guess but they won't know what the plan is. That secret has been well kept." There was some movement on the floor below and Bassett added, "I think that will be the captain." A minute later he and Delancey stood to attention as D'Auvergne entered. "Lieutenant Delancey reporting for duty," said Bassett and Delancey presented the captain with his sealed letter from Portsmouth. D'Auvergne sat at the table, breaking the seal and quickly glancing through the contents. He was middle-aged but vigorous, with good features, stern expression and the intolerant and humourless look of a fanatic.

"Sit down, Mr Delancey," said D'Auvergne. "And welcome to my squadron. I am glad to have you aboard." He smiled briefly, looking more human for a moment and then asked:

"Do you know the French coast and would you dare approach it after dark?"

"Yes, your Highness."

"That is the mission for which you have been chosen."

"Aye, aye, sir."

"You will have the temporary command of the cutter *Royalist*. With her you will enter a small French harbour, which will have been captured by our friends, and land there a British agent. More of that tomorrow. In the meanwhile you shall take command of the *Royalist*. I will say a few words to the crew and tell them that you are to lead them on special service. Mr Burrows, master's mate, will meet us on board with a muster list of the seamen and marines and a summary of the stores. Where is your own sea-chest?"

"At the watch-house, sir."

"Good. Mr Bassett, you will see to it that Mr Delancey's gear is sent on board the *Royalist*."

"Aye, aye, sir."

"And now, Mr Delancey, when your immediate work has been done I should like you to dine with me at the Golden Lion. There are some matters we shall have to discuss and some other officers I want you to meet. Two o'clock, then, at the Inn. Tomorrow you must be here at midday for the conference at which the details will be settled. You will have a few days after that during which you can exercise your men. In the years to come this may well be described as the turning point of the war. The role you are to play is of the highest importance and can make all the difference between victory and defeat. You will do well, Mr Delancey, of that I am sure."

Chapter Two

THE ROYALIST

THE DINNER in a private room at the Golden Lion was a pleasant and convivial occasion. The other guests were Major Moncrieff of the 7th Regiment, Lieutenant Bassett and a French émigré, the Vicomte Pierre de Mortemart. At one stage Moncrieff asked the prince about his property in France. There followed a description of the Castle of Navarre and the surrounding forest of Evreux, a hundred thousand acres of woodland with great lakes and islands and exotic birds. D'Auvergne also spoke of the Elysium, a garden which was planned round a single perfect statue, a nude masterpiece representing the Goddess of Youth. He described the scene when his adoption as heir was announced, the moment when he was girded with the sword of Turenne, the moment when the trumpets sounded a fanfare, when the guns fired their salute from the terrace. It had seemed so real at the time! It seemed, in retrospect, a mere fairy story. If true, it related (surely) to some other and forgotten world. In all likelihood the castle and its magic garden would by now have ceased to exist. The prince himself was like no man that Delancey had ever met. With his air of authority went an extraordinary aura of romance, and he held them all spellbound for as long as he talked. Delancey realised with a shock that the Revolution must have destroyed the prince's inheritance, probably for years and quite possibly for ever. Then a turn in the conversation revealed the prince in a different role, the rescuer of French aristocrats, the centre of a system for gaining intelligence. In some complex way he was fighting a war of his own, a war of wits instead of guns, a war which would not end so much with a British victory as with restoration of the monarchy in France.

Back in the *Royalist* and trying to sleep that night, Delancey thought

25

over the conversation at dinner. How strange it all seemed! But even
St Peter Port was not the place he had known in his younger days. It
was now bustling and alive, with troops and seamen everywhere, with
nobles and priests who had fled from France, with concerts and assembly balls—yes, and a theatre as well. As a centre for gaining intelligence
from France it would be hard to improve upon. It must, for that matter, be as useful to the French for gaining intelligence about Britain.
But were these French-speaking islanders loyal to George III? That was
hard to say. It was easier to assess their reaction to Robespierre. Many
of the Guernseymen were devout followers of Mr John Wesley. They
might trade with the enemy but they would do nothing directly to help
the cause of the ungodly.

After a restless night Richard Delancey was awakened by bugles
sounding the reveille. He guessed that the sound came from Castle
Cornet and that the garrison would stand-to at daybreak. It was still
dark when he came on deck but with a lightening of the sky beyond
the island of Herm. It was the King's birthday and there was to be a
review, he remembered. Afterwards he would be told what he had to
do. . . . He shivered, not entirely because of the cold, and wondered
whether this was the last week of his life. Ought he to write his will?
He dismissed the idea for he had practically nothing to leave. He was
well chosen for a perilous mission, he reflected, for he would be missed
by no one. He doubted whether the same could be said of Moncrieff,
a red-haired Scotsman from what he suspected was a noble family. He
liked Moncrieff, however, and envied him his resolute and carefree
manner. What he could not understand was the choice of the Vicomte
de Mortemart for a supposedly dangerous mission. That young man
had seemed nervous, ill at ease, longing only to hear that the mission
had been cancelled. He might feel the same himself but he had not,
he hoped, allowed his feelings to become so obvious. That was something he had learnt as a midshipman or even before that at school. He
paced the deck until it was almost daylight and then went below for
breakfast in his cabin. This was his first command of anything larger

than a ship's boat and he resolved to make the most of it. He had at least the privilege of breakfasting alone.

He now had the leisure to inspect the *Royalist* from stem to stern. She was a lovely craft built at Dover in 1778, originally called *Diligent* but renamed—obviously by the prince. She measured 151 tons, mounted ten 6-pounders and was established for a crew of 55. Her lines were beautiful, her mast raked at a dashing angle, her paintwork black and cream, her sails almost as white as when new. She had rather the look of a Post-Office packet—that hint of the thoroughbred—and her only fault, according to the boatswain, was a little too much weather helm. By the carpenter's account she leaked hardly at all. Looking along her deck and seeing the guns exactly in line, he thrilled to realise that he was the captain. The paint had flaked off a hatch coaming and he told the carpenter to see to it. The jack had wrapped itself round the jackstaff and he sent a boy to unravel it. He examined the cutter's trim from the other side of the harbour and made a mental note to look at her hull when the harbour dried out. The success of some future operation—and the survival of all his men—might depend upon what he did (or forgot) while the cutter was in harbour. There was much to do and all too little time, he suspected, in which to do it.

The town church clock was striking twelve as Delancey entered D'Auvergne's office overlooking the harbour. Bassett, Moncrieff and Mortemart were already there and D'Auvergne arrived soon afterwards, accompanied by a mousy and ill-dressed civilian he introduced as "Mr A." Without ceremony he told the others to sit while he uncovered a map of France which was pinned to the wall. As contrasted with his role of the previous day he was now merely a captain in the navy, his manner that of an officer on duty.

"What I have to tell you, gentlemen, is strictly secret, not to be revealed to any living soul outside this room. The French Republicans have an army of some twenty thousand men at St Malo, collected there for an attack, we believe, on Jersey. Lord Moira has nine thousand men here and as many again at Portsmouth, with a fleet of transports under

Admiral Macbride. The French royalist forces north of the Loire—the men of the Resistance we might call them—are believed to number about fifty-five thousand, mostly in the vicinity of Angers. . . ." (He pointed to the area on the map). . . . "They would be in still greater strength if they had not been defeated last December at Saveney. Now, our enemies might expect us to reinforce the garrison at Jersey, remembering how that island nearly fell to the French during the last war. But the King's ministers have decided, instead, on a bolder stroke—with, of course, His Majesty's approval. Their plan is to capture Cherbourg with the help of the insurgents. Once that port is in our hands we can land there the cannon, the muskets, the powder and shot which the royalists need. Once their forces join ours, making (say) a hundred thousand in all, we shall be able to reconquer France and restore the monarchy. The success of this masterstroke—and it is nothing less—must depend in the first instance on us, on the men in this room. We have two tasks to perform and each is vitally important. First, we have to contact the French royalists and concert with them the capture of Cherbourg. That task will fall to you, Major Moncrieff. Second, we have to hinder the march from St Malo of the enemy army we know to be there—a force which will be sent, we assume, to recapture Cherbourg. We leave this second task to our friends near St Malo to whom we have already sent the necessary arms and explosives. It will be for you, M de Mortemart, to tell them what to do and when. On the day arranged they will blow up the bridges, fell trees across the road and offer battle as and when they can. A march which, unopposed, might take fourteen days will require three weeks or more. By then our base at Cherbourg will be secure."

"May we know, sir," asked Moncrieff, "for what day the landing is planned?"

"On June 12th. I tell you that, gentlemen, in strictest secrecy."

"So my task," said Moncrieff, "is to ensure that the insurgents capture Cherbourg before the 12th?"

"On the night of the 11th, to be exact. You'll deliver this despatch," said D'Auvergne, handing it over, "to a royalist leader called 'C' and you will explain to him the importance of attacking on the exact day. You will then remain with the royalist forces, relying on Mr Delancey to keep you in touch with me."

"And I suppose," said Pierre de Mortemart, "that I am to land near St Malo?"

"Yes," replied D'Auvergne. "You will proceed to Jersey in the schooner *Daphne*. You and Mr A will then use a smaller craft for the actual landing. You will deliver this despatch to a royalist leader called 'B.' Both landing places will be held by our royalist friends who have already had their instructions from Mr A."

"May we know," asked Delancey, "what landing places are to be used?"

"You will land Major Moncrieff at La Gravelle, a cove halfway between Carteret and Pointe du Rozel. Mr A will give you more precise directions."

"Any further questions?" asked D'Auvergne. After a pause he went on: "Very well, then. The *Daphne* will sail by tonight's tide and Mr A will complete his arrangements when he reaches Jersey. The *Royalist* will sail tomorrow for Alderney, where the other part of the operation will be rehearsed."

There followed a half hour spent on maps, charts and diagrams, with signals and passwords described. It ended with the arrival of the lieutenant-governor, Major-General John Small, and with him Major-General the Lord Moira. They presented a sharp contrast; Small being an old soldier, straightforward, benevolent and much beloved; Moira, a young man, astute and supercilious, a born aristocrat and as much a politician as a soldier. Tired after reviewing the garrison, Small had little to say beyond uttering words of encouragement. Adding a few words, Moira assured those present that the success of Moncrieff's mission would be followed up with vigour by a landing in force on June 12th. The operation would be covered by an inshore frigate squadron commanded by Sir James Saumarez, a Guernseyman to whom the coast was familiar. Sir James was already cruising between Guernsey and Jersey. Lord Moira then invited questions.

"I have one question, my Lord," said Moncrieff. "What will you do if I fail to reach the insurgents—if we find the landing place in enemy hands?"

"I shall countermand the whole enterprise," said Lord Moira. "For success we *must* have a seaport. If our friends in Normandy can't give us Cherbourg we can't give *them* what they most need—artillery. God knows we've had trouble enough over our field pieces and gunners. We've barely sufficient for our purpose. I'd never attempt landing them over an open beach."

The conference ended on that note but Lord Moira remarked as he left that he would mention his plans, in broad outline, at the coming banquet. D'Auvergne protested about this breach of security but was told that only senior officers would be present and that they'd be told to keep the information to themselves. He looked far from happy about it but said nothing more. The meeting broke up and Major Moncrieff and Delancey left together, walking down to the quayside with the ostensible object of visiting the *Royalist*. They really wanted the chance to talk.

"There's something about this affair that I don't understand," said Moncrieff. "Why was that fellow Mortemart chosen for a dangerous mission? He is plainly terrified. Why tell secrets at a banquet, with the risk of rumours being spread before the officers are sober again?"

"Why indeed?" Delancey agreed. "And why should we trust 'Mr A'? I thought him a dubious-looking fellow, as likely to be against us as for us. All the arrangements depend upon him but I have seldom seen anyone for whom I have felt a more instant dislike."

"I wouldn't trust him a yard," replied Moncrieff. "I like D'Auvergne, though. I should have thought him too good an officer to be employed ashore."

"He seems an ideal choice, though, for the work he has to do."

"That's true enough. And I'm glad that we are to work together, you and I. We'll succeed at La Gravelle even if Mortemart gives himself up or is betrayed by 'Mr A.'" Delancey warmly agreed, reflecting that his own liking for Moncrieff had been immediate. He felt instinctively that they could rely on each other.

"You said just now, Major," said Delancey, "that there is something about the operation that you don't understand. I was just about to say the same thing in almost the same words. I wish to God the whole thing were over and done with."

"So do I, in a way. But it's our chance to make a name for ourselves. You are more fortunate, no doubt, but I haven't yet been in battle."

"There will be no battle for me provided that all goes well. If the plan miscarries, however, we are both likely to be captured and executed as spies."

"Not in uniform, surely?"

"Don't be too sure of that, sir."

"Anyway, it will be an adventure."

"Now, about this rehearsal," said Delancey, "I think we must do it three times at least, once in daylight and twice in the dark. . . ."

Delancey took the *Royalist* to sea with a caution which might not have impressed the experts watching from the breakwater. He cast off at the beginning of the ebb, passed the pier head under his jib alone, hoisted the mainsail a few minutes later and let fall the square topsail only when he was in the roads. The cutter handled beautifully, however, and he soon began to gain confidence. Under a light breeze, he sailed slowly past Herm and set a course for Alderney, not then visible owing to a mist which cleared later, allowing him to head for the west side of the island, avoiding the Swinge and keeping well clear of the Coque Lihou and the Noire Roque. With the wind dying away he brought the cutter into Longy Bay and dropped anchor there with a mild sense of achievement. He could remember these waters well enough, he found, and had recognised the hanging Rock at a glance. Could he have done it on a moonless night? Possibly, but he was not so sure.

After due warning to the garrison of Fort Essex and Raz Island, Delancey staged his exercises at the Nunnery. For the second daylight rehearsal he assumed that the enemy had been warned and had laid an ambush. The exercise was one involving a withdrawal under fire. In view of this possible contingency the longboat mounted a three-pounder gun in the bows. There was a separate exercise and target practice in which this weapon was fired as the boat was rowed out stern-foremost. Then the exercise was done once more but firing grape shot with a half charge of powder, the enemy being represented by a few empty barrels. In the final phase the exercises were repeated at night, sentries ashore being told to report any sounds that they heard. "This must all be done in *silence*," Delancey insisted. "Our lives may depend upon it!" He and Moncrieff were hard to please but the point was reached when even they were satisfied. Delancey found then that he was even beginning to gain confidence as a leader. Convincing his men that the work was vital he had forgotten to wonder what they were thinking of him. Moncrieff was a tower of strength on every occasion, quick to learn, confident and level-headed, always firm and never angry. Delancey was supremely fortunate, he realised, in his military colleague. He was lucky again in having an independent command. Had there been a more senior officer present, and one with a poor opinion of Delancey, he might have gone to pieces before the night of the actual landing. As things were he became more resolute every day. Because Moncrieff believed in him he was beginning to believe in himself. He had also established his authority over Burrows, the master's mate, Rankin the boatswain and Warren the midshipman. For the first time in his life he felt that he was really in command.

On the evening of the 7th the last preparations were completed, arms inspected and stores checked. Delancey then told his men what they had to do. "Our task is to land Major Moncrieff at a small French harbour called La Gravelle. The place should be in the hands of French loyalists who are our friends and who expect us. We shall not be fired upon if all goes well. But we can't be quite sure of that. When our boats go in, therefore, our guns will be ready to cover their withdrawal and we ourselves will be armed and ready to defend ourselves. Don't shoot without orders, though. Our plan is to do what we have to do in silence and be gone again before daylight." All hands were now given a double rum issue and then, after dark, the capstan was manned and the orders given to heave away. As soon as the anchor was a-peak Delancey called out, "Hoist the mainsail!" The men toiled on the halyards and the great sail rose and filled. "Hoist the jib!" was the next order, followed by another to the topmen, "Let fall! Sheet home!" The topsail filled in its turn, the cutter answered the helm and headed out of the bay with the waves breaking over the rocks on either side. Alderney disappeared from sight in a matter of minutes and they were alone in the darkness. Under easy sail in a light breeze, the *Royalist,* towing the longboat, slid silently through the water. It was pitch dark and Delancey had the leadsman at work as soon as he had lost sight of Alderney. Approaching the enemy coast he should have felt nervous but the mere complexity of his problem kept him from thinking of any but navigational dangers. He had about 23 miles to cover and he calculated that a westerly wind and flood tide would enable him to make his landfall at about two next morning. The breeze tended to die away before midnight but freshened later. Presently the lookout in the bows reported that he could see land. It was another half hour before Delancey could see anything himself, but the dark shape of the land looked as it should do and the water was shoaling gradually as might be expected. This was La Gravelle—he felt certain of it—and a deepening of the water showed that he was in the channel. "Breakwater ahead!" said the lookout quietly and Delancey gave orders to drop the anchor. This procedure was unavoidably noisy and would certainly be audible to anyone ashore who might be awake. So Delancey ordered the man with the lantern (concealed until now) to make the signal as arranged. There was no signal in reply. As against that, there was no alarm given either. There could have been starshell lighting the target and a volley of small-arms. Delancey did not expect artillery fire, however, because the hamlet was

not on a proper road. . . . After a tense five minutes he gave orders to
man the longboat. This was done quickly and silently with six seamen
at the oars and two forward with the three-pounder. There were four
marines, two of them forward. In the sternsheets were Delancey himself, Major Moncrieff, and—in charge of the boat—Mr Warren. With
muffled oars the boat silently approached the jetty, passed along its
landward side and found the steps just where they were shown to be
on Mr A's diagram.

At this moment there was a hail—not a challenge—from the jetty.
A man there said that he was a friend, adding "Vive le Roi," to make
his position clear. Delancey gave the password "Navarre" but it was not
returned correctly. Uneasy about this, Delancey nevertheless led the way
ashore, followed by Major Moncrieff and two marines. He then ordered
Mr Warren to push out and keep the boat three fathoms clear of the
jetty. The Frenchman, meanwhile, explained to Moncrieff that his landing was expected. He mentioned Lord Moira by name and said that he
was the guide who would lead them to where their friends were gathered. No light was shown but the party reached the end of the jetty
without mishap and followed a path inland. After a hundred yards or
so the path curved to the left and descended to a stone bridge which
evidently crossed the stream at a point some distance above the harbour, into which it evidently emptied. The path led uphill on the far
side, flanked by trees, and the guide went up to a cottage which stood
alone on the right of the track. He knocked at the door, the sound
being evidently pre-arranged (rap—rap-rap) and then waited, motionless and silent. At that moment Delancey heard someone trip over a
stone. The sound came not from the cottage but from the bridge they
had crossed. There was no going back but Delancey felt in an instant
that he and his party were trapped. All but silently they had been followed, and now their escape was cut off—or was this fear groundless?
He and Moncrieff drew and cocked their pistols.

The cottage door opened and light shone across the path. The man
who was their guide motioned to them to enter, which they did, but

Delancey paused for a moment while he told the two marines to stay outside. The interior of the cottage was candlelit and there were a dozen men there, armed and in enemy uniform. One in the centre, evidently in command, levelled his pistol and said, "Englishmen, you are prisoners." At that instant Moncrieff shot him dead. Delancey, who was in the doorway, turned on the guide, shot him at close range and saw him fall. It would seem that the object was to take them prisoners for their fire was not at once returned. Several voices called on them to surrender but Moncrieff shouted, "Surrender yourselves!" He fired his other pistol and then drew his sword, calling to Delancey, "Run for it!" Delancey had drawn his sword at the same time but Moncrieff had fallen before Delancey could help him. Both marines then fired into the room, allowing Delancey to run past them in the smoke. "Follow me!" he shouted and ran down the path. He quitted it, however, so as to avoid the bridge, swerving left (upstream) and running through the trees, the two marines at his heels. There were sounds of pursuit, footsteps pounding along the path and orders being shouted, but these noises were drowned by musket shots—probably the result of the men from the cottage running into their own ambush at the bridge. Delancey himself splashed through the stream, ran uphill through some bushes, swerved right and headed for the jetty. There was enough confusion round the bridge to enable him to arrive there before the enemy. He found the longboat alongside and Mr Warren ashore with half the boat's crew. These fired a volley which checked the pursuit for the time needed for all to embark. As the longboat backed out, stern-foremost, there was a burst of firing from the jetty, a marine being killed and three seamen wounded. The three-pounder replied with a charge of grape shot which cleared the jetty. The longboat was not under fire again but a lugger in the harbour discharged her swivel guns at the *Royalist* as she made sail, doing some damage to the rigging and badly wounding Mr Burrows. Soon after daylight the cutter was rounding the Casquets and heading into the Russel. By the time she dropped anchor in the roads, Mr Burrows and one of the wounded seamen had died.

Delancey went ashore in the gig, noticing on the way that the *Daphne* had already returned and was moored alongside the breakwater. He reported at once to Captain D'Auvergne's headquarters.

"The Captain will be here in a minute," said Bassett. "What happened?"

"The enemy were expecting us. Major Moncrieff fell and I was lucky to escape. We have three others killed and two wounded."

"I feared as much when I saw the shot holes in your mainsail!"

"I see the *Daphne* is back . . . ?"

"She fared no better. M de Mortemart was captured on landing, Mr A tells us."

"And he will tell the enemy all he knows."

"They also have his despatch. Mr A informs us that the French troops at St Malo are marching to save Cherbourg. Lord Moira has countermanded his orders for the landing."

"Our failure, then, is complete."

"So complete that the French have already struck back. They have a frigate squadron heading this way and Sir James Saumarez is actually outnumbered."

D'Auvergne entered quickly at that moment and the others stood to attention.

"I'm glad to see you safe, Mr Delancey. What happened?"

"We walked into a trap, your Highness. The cottage where we were to meet our friends was held by our enemies. Major Moncrieff refused to surrender and was killed. He killed two of the enemy first—shot one and ran the other through. We had other losses, three killed and two wounded. We were lucky to save the cutter herself."

"And the despatches?"

"The enemy have them."

"You think that you were expected?"

"Oh, yes, sir."

"But how can they have known? I don't understand it, can hardly believe it. Enough of that for the moment, though. You look worn out."

"I have been on my feet for 48 hours, sir."

"Take some rest now. Report back here at midday. Lord Moira will be here then and will want to hear your own story."

When Delancey had gone, D'Auvergne asked Bassett: "How were we betrayed?"

"Perhaps in London, sir."

"But the details of the plan were not even *known* in London!"

"Perhaps at La Gravelle, then. Someone took fright and betrayed the rest."

"Could that happen at *both* places and at the same time?"

"Unlikely, sir, I must confess. There remains only the one alternative. We were betrayed here."

"Where the plan was known only to Lord Moira, the governor, to you and me, to Moncrieff and Delancey, to Mr A and the Vicomte de Mortemart. Of these eight men one must be a traitor."

"Do you think it possible that Mr A is a double agent?"

"It will be a disaster if he is. He is at the very centre of our intelligence system. He knows everything—more than I do."

"I can see no possible traitor among the other seven. There was some careless talk at the banquet, I'll admit."

"Yes, but not in any detail."

"So it has to be Mr A."

"I fear that you may be right. We've played and lost and the stakes were high. It remains to find out how the dice came to be loaded."

It was a smaller meeting at midday than Delancey had expected. There was Lord Moira, D'Auvergne and himself—no one else. The Earl was very much at his ease and only mildly interested in the reports he heard.

"So the French have both despatches?" he asked finally.

"I fear so, my Lord," said D'Auvergne.

"And their army is on a forced march from St Malo to Cherbourg?"

"We have a reliable report to that effect."

"And I hear now that Sir James Saumarez has had a partial action with their frigates, using his local knowledge to trick them. They were last seen on their way back to St Malo, looking extremely foolish!"

"So I understand, my Lord."

"On our side we lost Alan Moncrieff, a fine young officer. I shall write to his father. A pity you could not have saved him, Mr Delancey. I have no doubt that you did your best."

"I was at his side, my Lord, and would have liked to prevent the despatches from falling into the hands of the enemy. But I was also responsible for the safety of the *Royalist*. I did what seemed best, my Lord, and am only sorry that my mission should have failed."

"Your mission did *not* fail, Mr Delancey." There was a full minute's silence, broken by D'Auvergne.

"Your Lordship cannot mean that we succeeded?"

"Listen, gentlemen. What I am going to tell you is for your ears alone. It will be known to no one else, not even the governor. First, then, I owe you both a very humble apology. It has been my duty to deceive you from the beginning. There was never any serious plan for landing an army near Cherbourg. The rumour heard in Portsmouth was that my troops are destined for Flanders. Well, that is in fact the truth. That is where they are going."

"Then why, my Lord," asked D'Auvergne, "—why in heaven's name did you come here at all?"

"To prevent the French from capturing Jersey. That threat was real enough. Our reply was to make a feint against Cherbourg. The result was to make the enemy march to save that port, which we never dreamt of attacking."

"I see it all now . . ." groaned D'Auvergne.

"I want you, Mr Delancey, to see it too. You feel now that you have risked your life for nothing—that the enemy could have been tricked some other way. But I want you to learn now one of the first rules of war. It is this: we only believe the information we have gained with difficulty by our own efforts. The captured document convinces us. So does the intelligence dragged from a prisoner under threat of execution. I gave Moncrieff a despatch addressed to a real insurgent leader but almost certain to fall into enemy hands. I gave Pierre de Mortemart the verbal plans for invasion which he would certainly reveal when questioned. It was vital that Moncrieff and Mortemart should believe in the invasion and quite as essential, Captain D'Auvergne, that you should believe in it yourself. This made it certain that all the enemy agents in Guernsey would tell the same story."

"But how did the enemy come to know in advance about our two missions? Who warned them, my Lord?"

"Haven't you guessed, Captain D'Auvergne?"

"It was Mr A, I suppose."

"Exactly, Jean Prigent of St Helier, a double agent from the beginning."

"I hope to see him hanged!"

"Softly, Captain! We shan't hang Prigent. We shall use him. And when he's no longer useful we shall betray him to the French, who'll put him before a firing squad. Be patient, though. That won't happen for years."

After Lord Moira had gone, D'Auvergne sat at the table, utterly dejected.

"Here ends our attempted invasion of France!" he said bitterly. "The scheme is abandoned. More than that, the plan never even existed. It was all a feint, a gesture, a momentary phase in the war, an incident too small to merit even a line in the history book. We are used, you and I, and then tossed aside."

"Isn't that the nature of war, sir?"

D'Auvergne did not reply but, rising to his feet, he caught sight of the map on the wall, the one he had used in explaining the campaign. He stared at it for a minute as if the Castle of Navarre were actually marked. Following his glance, Delancey asked, "Shall I take this map down, sir?"

"Yes," said D'Auvergne, "take it down. Tear it up! Burn it! We shan't need it again. What chance we had is gone!"

Chapter Three

CHOICE OF WEAPONS

I N THE AFTERMATH of the landing at La Gravelle Delancey had several days' work to do; the repairs to the *Royalist,* the arranging of the burials, the writing to the relatives of the fallen, the care of the wounded and the return to store of borrowed equipment. It was while reporting to Bassett on these matters that he first heard of a sequel to the affair which he had never expected.

"I feel bound to warn you," said Bassett, "that there is talk among the military here about Moncrieff's death. Some officers are saying that he should have been rescued—that he was left to his fate by the navy—that his life was thrown away."

"It was thrown away, I must confess. But rescue was out of the question—I saw him killed."

"I know that this is the truth and I have explained this to an officer of the 42nd who told me of the feelings that had been aroused in his mess."

"But Moncrieff was in the 7th Foot."

"Yes, but he was on Lord Moira's staff. Being absent from his own regiment he had been messing with the 42nd and was very popular with his brother officers of that unit."

"That does not surprise me. He was liked, I suppose, by everyone."

"That seems to be the fact. And that is why some harsh words have been said about you."

"Does Captain D'Auvergne know about this?"

"Yes, and he has spoken with Major Simmons, presently commanding the 42nd. Their colonel is out of the island at present and Simmons is rather young to be left on his own. His Highness doubts

40

whether Simmons has much authority over his captains, several of whom are older than he and have been in battle."

"I see," replied Delancey slowly. "Strange to think that Moncrieff, had he lived, would have been perhaps my best friend. Our efforts could not have been better concerted, and now I am thought to have deserted him."

"The accusation is absurd—I know that."

"I could have landed more men and done some damage to the enemy but the probable result would have been to lose the *Royalist*. And my orders were explicit, as you know—to be away again before daylight."

"All that is perfectly true. I think it quite disgraceful that a story like this should be repeated."

"Thank you for the warning. I believe we shall meet again this evening?"

"At the Golden Lion? Yes, I am to be there and I understand that Captain Bastable will be the prince's other guest at supper. The *Cormorant* is back again from Jersey and will sail for Portsmouth tomorrow afternoon."

At supper the Prince of Bouillon was still downcast over the ruin of all his hopes. Saying nothing about the secret side of his activities, he talked generally about the situation in France.

"I begin to doubt whether the monarchy will ever be restored. A society has been torn up by the roots. Can it ever be replanted and take root again? But what nonsense the future generations will be taught! They will be told how poor peasants rose against a tyrant regime. Who will remember the thousands of poor folk who fought and died to save the regime? There have been royalist armies in the field with numbers of up to a hundred thousand. The republicans have been defeated in battle after battle. No one will remember this in the years to come. I wish I could believe that they would win. I would that it was in my power to help them."

Talk turned to the subject of Guernsey characteristics, on the local ability to reconcile smuggling with religion. D'Auvergne, as a Jersey-man, was interested in the antipathy which existed between the islands but could not explain it.

While this conversation went on, Delancey was half aware of a nois-ier party being held in the far corner of the parlour. From the glimpse of scarlet he guessed that army officers predominated and from the noise he concluded that they were fairly junior in rank. Glancing that way and half expecting some such move he saw a young ensign rise to his feet and move unsteadily towards him. He was a fair-haired youth, aged nineteen at most, with flushed cheeks and a touch of sweat on his forehead. He stood, swaying, near the naval group and made some sort of a bow, which D'Auvergne returned rather coldly.

"Ensign Watkins, gentlemen," he said, "at your service." He paused uncertainly, wiped his brow and added, "Of the 42nd Foot." It seemed for a minute of silence (the other party being quiet now, listening) as if this was the sum total of his message. Then he remembered his next lines and went on with a jerk. "Have—have—have I the honour of ad-ad-ad-addressing Lieutenant—er—Delancey?"

"You have," said Delancey briefly, rising to his feet.

"Then, sir, I have the further hon-honour of tut-telling you, sir, that you're a coward!"

Delancey, who had been expecting this, answered loudly, ensuring that what he said would be audible to the other officers present:

"And you, Mr Watkins, are a drunken and useless young puppy, of less value to your regiment than its latest recruit, a disgrace to your uniform and a sorrow to your parents. Go back to your nanny, boy, and learn how to wipe your nose!"

"I can use a pistol as well as you!"

"I doubt if you can use a chamber pot."

"That's an insult!" raged the ensign.

"Maybe," replied Delancey, "but you address me as 'Sir.'"

"I demand satisfaction—Sir!"

"Very well. Choose your seconds and ask them to arrange matters with Mr Bassett here. I hope you will agree, sir, to act for me?" Bassett nodded and Delancey sat down again, turning to D'Auvergne and resuming their conversation at the point where it had been interrupted.

"I have always thought, your Highness, that Guernsey is more fortunate than Jersey in its harbour."

"Very true, Mr Delancey. The time is coming, however, when St Peter Port will be too small. . . ."

As the discussion continued Bassett begged the others to excuse him for a minute. Knowing his purpose, Delancey said to him quietly, "He is the challenger. I choose—swords." Bassett nodded and went over to the other group.

". . . but St Peter Port has the advantage in its roadstead, sheltered by Herm in an easterly wind and sheltered by Guernsey itself when the wind is westerly."

"I am quite of your opinion, your Highness. The harbour of St Helier is on the wrong side of the island."

Bassett came back and said to Delancey, aside, "Tomorrow at daybreak—on the green near the barracks."

The conversation was resumed again but Delancey drank nothing more. To judge from his behaviour, anyone present would have thought him an experienced duellist and a man of great courage. In point of fact he was neither, having never fought before in an affair of honour and having only an average share of resolution. His heart had missed a beat when he knew that he would be challenged and he frankly dreaded the meeting that was now unavoidable. Had he been a civilian, Mr Watkins might well have changed his mind when sober and made some sort of apology. But to do that an officer would have to resign his commission. There was no future in a line regiment (or in the navy) for a man who had refused a challenge. Nervous as he might be, however, Delancey had shown presence of mind. He had noticed that Watkins spoke of pistols and this had given him his cue to make Watkins the challenger and give himself the choice of weapons. He had promptly chosen swords, guessing that his opponent's fencing skill would be rudimentary. No expert himself, he had taken lessons in his younger days and could at least remember how to stand on guard, how to lunge, how to feint and thrust and parry. Had he been a civilian, Watkins' seconds could have objected that their principal could not give satisfaction with the weapons chosen. But they could raise no such objection on behalf of a commissioned officer. If he could not use a sword he had no business to be wearing one. If Watkins had never had a lesson before—as seemed likely enough—he was going to have one now.

Delancey's other second was to be Lieutenant Saunders of the *Cormorant* whom they met after supper near the town church. He and Bassett went off to make the detailed arrangements—finding a surgeon and measuring the swords—while D'Auvergne and Bastable walked with Delancey down to the harbour.

"I don't pretend to like this business," said D'Auvergne. "That wretched boy was pushed into this folly by those other officers. I wonder if he could be persuaded to apologize?"

"I hope you don't blame me, your Highness, for acting as I did?"

"You could do nothing else. But I am distressed about tomorrow's meeting and about its probable consequences. If the colonel of the 42nd were here he would put young Watkins on picquet for the next month—and that would be that."

"I shan't kill him, sir, and I doubt whether he knows how to do any injury to me."

"Granted that the affair ends as you expect, the result is still unfortunate. You'll gain no credit from punishing that child and officers of the 42nd will still tell stories to your discredit. If you should be wounded, it is worse—you being no match for a mere schoolboy. Meeting an officer of your own age would at least have ended the matter."

"Very true, sir."

"I would prevent the meeting if I could. Look—I shall ask you, Captain Bastable, to be present as a senior officer and urge the two principals to use their swords against the French. If Watkins will withdraw his words, will you agree to withdraw yours?"

"Certainly, sir."

"Very well, then. Will you use your influence, then? I shall be very grateful to you."

"I shall do my best, sir," said Bastable, "but I am not too sanguine of the result. I should be more hopeful if young Watkins had fought in several campaigns. All would agree then that his courage needed no proof. I suspect, however, that he is newly commissioned and has never smelt powder. He has still to prove himself and to offer an apology now would be no way to do it."

"Do your best, nevertheless," urged D'Auvergne, and Bastable said again that he would.

"Goodnight—and good luck!" said D'Auvergne when they parted and Delancey, thanking him, went on board the *Royalist*. He slept badly that night and was already awake when his servant called him at four.

The infantry barracks, where the 42nd Regiment were quartered, stood on the headland to the north of St Peter Port. On a fine summer morning it was no hardship to walk up the lane to the green upon which the barracks fronted. A quarter of an hour brought them to the rendezvous, among the trees near the seaward end of the avenue. At daybreak both parties were there and Captain Bastable called the four seconds together, the two principals standing apart and out of earshot.

"As the senior officer present, gentlemen, I want to urge on you the propriety of settling our difference without resort to arms. Some story has been repeated to the effect that Mr Delancey left Major Moncrieff to be killed while he himself fled, saving his life but sacrificing a comrade. I want you all to understand that this story is totally false. Mr Delancey obeyed the orders he had received from Captain D'Auvergne. I have the captain's authority for assuring you that Mr Delancey brought the cutter away, that there was no other competent navigator present, and that the cutter without him would most probably have been lost. I must also make it clear that Mr Delancey did not escape from the French before the major had already fallen in combat. If Mr

Watkins believed a story involving cowardice on the part of Mr Delancey he was completely deceived. You must accept my word for that. I come now to the events of yesterday evening. Believing this story and having drunk, I would suggest, more than he was accustomed to drink, Mr Watkins publicly accused Mr Delancey of cowardice. Words were exchanged in anger and the result was the challenge which brings us here. What I want to say is this: If Mr Watkins, knowing that he was mistaken and knowing that he acted hastily when far from sober, should withdraw his accusation, I can assure you that his explanation will be accepted. May I add that we should none of us think the worse of him? He will quit this field with his reputation untarnished and we should all agree that he had acted like an officer and a gentleman."

Mr Watkins' seconds were Captain Henderson and Lieutenant the Honourable John Huntley. It was Henderson, the older man, who replied: "We accept all that you say, Captain Bastable, but it does not help the officer we are here to represent. Should he apologize now he would have to resign his commission and remain branded for ever as a coward. No, sir, we can't advise him to withdraw at this stage. Do you agree, Mr Huntley?"

"No question, egad, sir! Mr Watkins must stand by his words or quit the army."

"But please remember, gentlemen, that he is of an age when it is easy to be mistaken and easier still to say more than you intend. I should feel differently about this if Mr Delancey were called out by an officer of his own age, by a man who has been in battle."

"His next opponent," said Mr Huntley, "will be just such a man as you describe—Captain Hilliard."

"His *next* opponent? What do you mean, sir?"

"Mr Huntley speaks out of turn," said Henderson, frowning. "However, the damage is done. Our whole mess, 23 of us, agreed to avenge poor Moncrieff's death. All would fight Mr Delancey in turn and we drew lots to decide the order in which we should challenge him. Watkins came first and Hilliard, second. I myself came third."

"But this is a plan for murder! Who could expect to survive 23 duels?"

"It won't come to that. He won't survive the second. Hilliard used to be our fencing instructor and he is a dead shot with a pistol. He is sure to kill his opponent either way."

"So you see," said Huntley, "why Watkins *can't* withdraw." He didn't challenge Delancey because he was drunk but because there was a lottery and he lost—I mean to say, he won."

"Very well, then, gentlemen. On the subject of any further encounters, I shall report to my senior officer. Do I take it that the seconds are agreed and that no apology will be made on either side?"

"No apology, sir," said Henderson.

"No apology, sir," echoed Bassett.

"Right. You may proceed."

As the sky grew lighter, turning from grey to pink, the seconds chose a piece of level ground, inspected the swords again and agreed that the principals should face north and south. Captain Bastable, the surgeon and the surgeon's orderly stood well back under a tree. Delancey and Watkins then removed their coats, handing them to their seconds, took the swords which they were offered and were led to the positions allotted them about five yards apart.

Delancey shivered a little and hoped that nobody would notice. Then he looked across at his opponent. Watkins was white-faced, trembling and almost absurdly woebegone. Perhaps he had a headache from the night before? Perhaps he had begun the day by seeking inspiration in the bottle? His own tremors passing, Delancey felt sorry for the wretched boy he was to encounter. It was bad luck for Watkins that the fight was to take place. There had been that discussion between the seconds and Captain Bastable—it had looked as if apologies would be made and the affair end tamely. But that was not really possible, as all the seconds must have agreed. One's honour must be defended! How? By killing or wounding that miserable and stupid schoolboy? Why should the fool have picked the quarrel in the first place? Why couldn't he quarrel with someone else? At last the preliminaries were over. Two of the seconds fell back and the two more senior took post between the combatants. "Advance!" said Captain Henderson and the duellists walked towards each other until Bassett could take the two sword points and bring them into contact. "On guard!" said Henderson and the two points drew apart again. "Engage!" said Henderson and the fight began. The blades dashed warily and Delancey began to test his opponent. It was at once obvious that the boy was no swordsman. He had been taught to stand on guard and told how to lunge. That was about the extent of his knowledge and it would not save him. The danger was that he would be driven by despair into some wild attack. . . . Delancey tapped the opposing blade aside and feinted, observing the clumsy parry which left his opponent exposed on the other side. He tried to remember the disarming stroke, the sharp counter with the forte against the foible. He would keep that for later, though. What would the boy try to do in the meanwhile? Had he made any sort of plan? It seemed not, for the aimless play went on in its aimless fashion. Delancey looked at his opponent's face and tried to guess what its agonized expression foreshadowed. Yes, the grimaces seemed to suggest some desperate resolve. He was going to lunge! A few seconds later there was a clumsy feint, a moment's hesitation and then the convulsive attack, which was wide of the target and left the boy off balance. Delancey brought his left foot up to his right, straightened his sword arm and aimed at his opponent's right shoulder. In this, the elementary thrust, the swordsman acts defensively but allows an incautious antagonist to impale himself. Standing stiffly to attention, Delancey felt a slight jar up his right arm. His point had sunk about two inches into the flesh just below the collar bone. Watkins' expression changed, his angry grimace turning to childish surprise. There was a red stain spreading on his shirt and he looked down at it. A second later he dropped his sword, fainted and collapsed in a blood-stained heap. The surgeon ran forward, knelt down and produced swabs and a bandage. The seconds came forward and Bassett took the sword from

Delancey. The fight was over, having lasted about a minute and a half.

"I didn't mean to hurt the boy," said Delancey to the surgeon, much as if the whole thing had been an accident.

"He'll be none the worse," replied the surgeon with calm certainty. "You chose the right place for a flesh wound."

"Neatly done," said Saunders.

"That was soon over," said Bassett.

In the background Henderson was talking quietly to Huntley: "Watkins hardly knew how to hold a sword—let alone to use it. I'll wager he had never had a lesson in his life."

"Then you'd lose your wager, sir. Hilliard gave him a lesson this morning. I'll allow that it was his first."

"He's lucky to be alive. With pistols he would have had a chance!"

"Yes, he started practising as soon as he had drawn the ace from the pack. Hilliard took him out to L'Ancresse and said afterwards that he did fairly well."

"I heard that. It's not as easy to be steady, though, when looking down your opponent's muzzle at fourteen paces."

"Very true, sir."

Captain Bastable came up at this moment and said: "A word with you, Captain Henderson. There is to be no talk of any further consequences. . . . That is an order. I shall report to His Highness and—" Bastable was leading Henderson and Huntley away from the fallen man so that Delancey heard no more of the conversation. He realised that he was not supposed to have heard anything.

"Shall we go to breakfast?" Bassett was asking, not perhaps for the first time.

"I should like a word with Watkins first."

"You can't," said Saunders, rather urgently. "He's not conscious yet. I think we should go now."

The surgeon's orderly had been sent to the barracks and was returning with four other soldiers and a blanket.

"Very well," said Delancey. "Let's go."

Chapter Four

ON THE BEACH

L ATER THAT MORNING Delancey made his report to Captain
D'Auvergne. The duel had taken place and his opponent had been
wounded. This was no news to D'Auvergne, who had been told about
it already, but he listened patiently.

"Mr Watkins is in no danger," said Delancey, finally. "He has a flesh
wound from which he will recover in two or three weeks."

"It is all most unfortunate," said D'Auvergne. "You are in no way
to blame, however. I should say, rather, that you have behaved very
well; not least so in sparing the bellicose Mr Watkins. I question
whether you could have acted more properly in this wretched affair.
But the fact remains that the officers of the 42nd are still in an ugly
mood. Nor will they be satisfied with the result of this morning's meeting. I must do what I can to improve the relationships here between
the two services. . . ."

There was a pause and D'Auvergne rose to his feet and paced the
room for a minute or so before continuing:

"You knew, Mr Delancey, when you accepted your recent mission
that another officer commands the *Royalist*. He is an elderly man who
has seen much service but was not, in my opinion, the right man to
land in darkness on the French coast. I sent him on special duty to
Jersey and gave you the temporary command. You did very well and
Lord Moira has assured us that your mission was a success. The French
are making great efforts to improve the defences of Cherbourg. Jersey
is no longer threatened and the summer will be over before they can
pose any new threat to our territory. I had hoped to be able to reward

you for good service, having you posted to some other vessel in my squadron. This is no longer advisable, nor would it be in your best interests. I shall have vessels based on Jersey and am to move my headquarters there. Unfortunately, however, there is a company of the 42nd in Jersey and the same bad feelings would be aroused."

D'Auvergne sat down again at the table and looked almost apologetic as he came to the point: "My orders are that you return to Portsmouth in the sloop *Cormorant*. She sails this afternoon. You will go on board *at once*—that is an order—and Bassett will have your seachest and other gear sent over from the *Royalist*. You will remain on board the *Cormorant* until she sails. I shall give you a letter of recommendation—it is here before me—to Admiral Macbride. You have had more than your share of ill-luck, Mr Delancey, but it is my belief that you will have a successful career in the service. I wish you better luck in your next ship."

D'Auvergne signed the letter before him and called Bassett in to seal it. Delancey saw that D'Auvergne had turned his attention to the next problem, a report which had just come in, and would soon have forgotten his existence. Having pocketed his testimonial, Delancey made his bow and withdrew. Bassett came with him to the quayside and to the *Cormorant*'s boat which was waiting for him. "Good luck!" said Bassett and the coxswain pushed off.

As the gig pulled away from the stairs and headed seawards, its course led near the southern pier head where there were the usual idlers to be expected there on a fine morning. Apart from the longshoremen stood a small group of ladies out for a stroll and with them Delancey glimpsed the scarlet of military uniforms. As the gig drew nearer he recognized Captain Hilliard and Mr Huntley. An instant later they recognized him and turned to each other with openly expressed amusement. They were too distant for Delancey to hear anything that was said but their gestures were plain. He was seen to be running away! The story would be round St Peter Port by midday, round the island by the evening and would have reached Jersey and the mainland within

the next two or three days. Technically he had received no other challenge but gossip would have it that he had refused to fight. There was
only one remedy. He must go ashore again and appear publicly at the
Golden Lion. His best plan would be to invite Captain Bastable to dine
with him before the ship sailed. The thought of the probable sequel
made him feel slightly sick but no other course was possible. This time
it would have to be pistols. . . .

Delancey was greeted at the gangway by Saunders who
said, "Welcome aboard." Determined, however, to do the right thing
before his courage failed him, Delancey asked at once to see Captain
Bastable. He was shown below and Bastable greeted him kindly.
Delancey asked at once for a boat to take him ashore. He had one or
two calls to make, a debt to pay, his laundry to collect.

"Unfortunately, Mr Delancey, I have strict orders that you are to
remain on board until we sail."

"But I have business ashore, sir, and hoped indeed that you would
do me the honour of dining with me."

"You can send a midshipman to attend to your business in St Peter
Port and I will put the gig at his disposal. As for your kind invitation,
I am not free to accept it. For me to go ashore with you would con-
flict with the orders I have received."

"But I am sure, sir, that Captain D'Auvergne would condone a slight
departure from the letter of his orders. He would understand a case of
necessity."

"He would understand perfectly. In case of your offering to disobey
my order I am to put you under close arrest. Is that sufficiently clear?
I hope you will spare me the trouble and embarrassment."

"Aye, aye, sir."

"Have I your word, then, that you will not attempt to go ashore?"

"Yes, sir."

"With that point settled it is now my privilege to invite you to dine
with me on board this ship. The fare may not be quite equal to what

we might have had at the Golden Lion but it will be better than I could offer you after three months at sea."

"With pleasure, sir."

The dinner was excellent and Bastable took the opportunity to drink the health of his guest. "To a notable swordsman!" Delancey bowed but protested that the toast should have been, "To a barely acceptable fencing instructor." There was no other reference to the morning's affair and the party ended on a very friendly note.

The ship sailed soon afterwards and Delancey admired the way in which the trick was done. At one instant the sloop was at anchor, an instant later she was under sail and on the right course. The wind was rising and the sea with it, the *Cormorant* being close-hauled with spray breaking over her forecastle. Guernsey slid to the windward but the features he could recognize were soon lost in the mist as the sloop headed once more for Portsmouth.

As on the outward voyage Delancey found himself pacing the deck with Lieutenant Saunders.

"What will you do now? Will you return to the *Grafton?*"

"I am no longer posted to her or to any ship. I was here on temporary duty. All I have now is a letter of recommendation addressed to Admiral Macbride."

"But didn't you know? He is no longer at Portsmouth. I hear that he has gone overseas to a dockyard appointment."

"If that is so you behold the picture of a half-pay lieutenant. Where stationed? On the beach."

"Your luck will turn, I feel sure of it."

"With the reputation of one who has refused a challenge?"

"But that is nonsense. You fought and I was your second. Captain Bastable was a witness to the meeting and you were not challenged again."

"There was another officer ready to challenge me and everyone knew it."

"You received no challenge, however, and you left the island under orders from your superior officer."

"All that is true but will the soldiers believe it? You know as well as I do what the story is going to be."

In his cabin that night Delancey asked himself where he had gone wrong. Should he have made more of a fight at La Gravelle? Should he have chosen to meet young Watkins with pistols? Should he have made the coxswain of the *Cormorant*'s gig put him ashore again? Unfair it might be but the stain on his reputation was going to be permanent. But was it altogether unfair? D'Auvergne had ordered him to leave Guernsey at once but that was an act of kindness. He knew that this was what Delancey wanted. God knows he had obeyed orders with a sigh of relief. Who wouldn't? But the real test was coming and he knew that he would fail it. Having reported back to Macbride—no, to the Port Admiral now—a real hero in his position would take the next packet back to Guernsey. He would then be a half-pay lieutenant no longer under D'Auvergne's orders. A genuine hero would go back to the Golden Lion, ready to be insulted by Captain Hilliard, ready to fight again on the headland and ready, finally, to die with a great reputation for gallantry. But Delancey knew that he would do nothing of the sort. He would rather live with his courage still in question. He might have to quit the navy but what of that? There were other ways of earning a living. He was still thinking of alternatives when he fell asleep.

Next morning the *Cormorant* came into Spithead after rounding the Isle of Wight. There was a fleet of merchantmen there awaiting convoy, smart West Indiamen having pride of place but slave ships looking rakish and fast. There were ships of every kind at anchor but the craft that caught his eye was a Post Office cutter, almost a twin of the *Royalist*, his first command—and perhaps his last. She was on her outward passage and came out through the anchorage with the sunlight on her sails and the white foam parted by her stem. Yes, that was just the way the *Royalist* had looked. He would have liked to possess a picture of her, a watercolour perhaps. Given time, he might have made a drawing himself, for he had taught himself how to use a pencil and believed that the skill of recording what he had seen was proper to his calling. There had been no leisure for that and he found himself wishing that the whole *Royalist* episode was still to come. But how could he have acted differently? Still wondering what else he could have done, he said goodbye to his friends on board the *Cormorant* and was rowed ashore soon after the ship had anchored. He took a room at the Star and Garter for the night and left his gear there before reporting to Rear-Admiral Hewett. The Port Admiral was not at his office but the prince's letter of recommendation was opened without ceremony by his flag lieutenant, a brusque young man called Fothergill.

"Captain D'Auvergne speaks highly of you," he commented, handing the letter back. "I wonder why he did not retain you on his staff."

"There was some bad feeling, sir, in the army as a result of our landing in France."

"I see. What was your last seagoing appointment before you went on this mission?"

"I was fourth in the *Artemis*, sir."

"In the *Artemis?* Under Captain Fletcher?"

"Yes, sir."

"I see. I remember now. . . . Well, I think your best plan is to apply at the Admiralty in the usual way. Your vacancy in the *Grafton* had been filled and there is no other appointment presently available on this station."

Without much hope of success, Delancey set off for London by coach. He had been to the Admiralty before and found his way without difficulty to the waiting room on the right of the approach to the main staircase. On the second day after he had sent his name in he had a brief interview with an elderly clerk who promised rather wearily to let him know of any opportunity that might offer. What was most

depressing about this visit was the sight of the other applicants. The
country was at war, ships were being commissioned each week and
officers appointed every day. Those still haunting the Admiralty were
the misfits, the drunkards, the blind, halt and lame, and he could have
wept to know he was one of them. Back in Portsmouth he found an
attic room in Ropewalk Lane. The house belonged to a shipwright
called Finch whose wife kept the place clean and whose small boy,
Ned, brought him his hot water for shaving. Portsmouth was the place
for a half-pay lieutenant, almost the only place where he would not
have to explain who he was and what he was doing.

After a few days in the dockyard town Delancey fell in with Harris of the *Warspite* who asked him into the George, where captains
again glanced suspiciously at the two lieutenants who had no business
to be there.

"Well?" asked Harris, "How did you fare with the secret mission?
Was I right about it, hey?"

"You were quite right, sir, It had 'failure' written on it from the outset. I am lucky to be alive."

"Or were you careful, hey? I heard something about you t'other
day. What was it? Some army captain called you out and you refused
the challenge. Don't blame you! I should've done the same."

"It wasn't like that, Mr Harris. I *did* fight one of them and wounded
him but I'll confess that I wasn't prepared to fight them all."

"You should have laid them all out with a capstan bar. Waiter!"

For weeks to come Delancey's mind was continually on his career.
After another year ashore he would not be a seaman. But his luck might
change. There might be a battle with heavy losses and empty berths.
He might still be promoted. But, somehow, just then, it seemed unlikely.
He was a commissioned officer in wartime but without prospects of
any kind. To the story that he had almost been guilty of mutiny was
now added a story—not entirely false—that he had since been found
wanting in courage. When news came of Lord Howe's victory his

hopes revived for some weeks but such vacancies as were caused by this battle were filled by the promotion of juniors rather than by seeking ashore for officers whose merits had so far been overlooked. The mere length of time Delancey had been on the beach would evidently tell against him.

In other circumstances Delancey would have been tempted to give up his naval career and return to Guernsey. That door was closed, however, by the presence there of the 42nd Regiment. He resolved to wait for his luck to turn and was encouraged in this resolve by a chance meeting with an old officer called Fanshawe, one of a small group of veterans who played whist together. "Study the lives of the great admirals," said Fanshawe. "Read books on shipbuilding and naval tactics. Learn all you can," he would emphasise, "and read the gazette letters, hear the gossip and study the news. Be ready to take your chance when it comes!" Delancey followed this advice, borrowed books, argued over technical problems and knew the name of every ship in port. He also made a fourth at whist whenever asked to play and found, to his surprise, that the game had a certain fascination. The day came when Fanshawe had to admit that Delancey was as good a player as any in his circle.

It was a matter, he had found, of concentration and memory and he could imagine that the same qualities of mind might often be needed by senior officers. It was at this time that he developed his small talent for painting in watercolours. He began by making copies in pencil of the illustrations he found in books of travel. Then he took to colouring them and finishing the outlines with pen and ink. He resolved, when the weather improved to make sketches from life. In the meanwhile he drew several pictures of the *Royalist* from memory. At this time he took to wearing civilian clothes so that his uniform should remain presentable. On fine days he would walk on the quayside and look at the ships in harbour, learning all he could about them. There were odd days that winter when he felt confident and almost cheerful, convinced without reason that success might still be his. On other days—on days which became more frequent as the months went by—he felt that his case was hopeless. He had been ashore for longer than he cared to remember. It looked now as if he might well be ashore for good.

PART TWO

Chapter Five

THE REVENUE CUTTER

A SMART FRIGATE was leaving Portsmouth harbour, watched by a small group of idlers collected at the Point. One of these, a well-dressed and elderly gentleman, had borrowed a telescope from a one-legged seaman who stood beside him and was watching the way in which sail was made. "What a splendid sight!" he exclaimed, finally, returning the telescope to its owner. "But a common spectacle, I suppose, in time of war." He was told by the other bystanders that the port was busy enough. As they watched, the frigate heeled to the stiff breeze, foam at her stem and her pennant streaming to leeward. A fleeting gleam of wintry sunshine lit her canvas for a moment as she passed Block House Fort. In a few minutes she vanished from sight and the shivering spectators began to disperse. It was a cold February afternoon, to be followed by a colder and stormier night.

"What ship was that?" asked the elderly gentleman but the one-legged sailor had gone. His question was answered, instead, by a much younger man in civilian clothes whose eyes had followed the frigate until the last moment.

"She is the *Thalia* of 36 guns, commanded by Captain Manley, launched at Bursledon in 1782."

"Whither bound?" asked the elderly gentleman as they turned away from the Point.

"For Jamaica, sir, as I understand."

There was something about the younger man's appearance and still more about his manner—clipped, decisive and exact—that attracted the old gentleman's interest.

"You seem to be well-informed, sir, in naval matters."

"I hold a commission, sir."

"But without an appointment, perhaps?" Delancey's grim expression was answer enough and the old gentleman tried to retrieve the situation by adding, quickly: "No offence, sir—not my intention to pry—forgive my bluntness—but I know something of the service from my nephew. Promotion is often difficult to achieve in your profession and especially for those without interest." Delancey assented briefly and his elderly acquaintance looked at him more keenly. What he saw left him still curious. Of average height, dark-haired, with dark blue eyes and a rather melancholy expression, the young man was something, he guessed, between thirty and thirty-five years old. He was rather thin and rather shabbily dressed, his overcoat made of inferior cloth, his shoes well polished but badly worn, his cravat frayed and yellow in the hem. The older man, coming to a decision on impulse, decided to introduce himself.

"My name is Grindall, sir, wine merchant of Southampton. My nephew is to meet me presently for dinner at the Star and Garter. Would you do me the honour of joining us?" It seemed for a moment that the invitation was regarded as an insult and Mr Grindall went on quickly to forestall a touchy refusal.

"I'll be frank with you, sir, and explain what I have in mind. My nephew has been offered a berth in a revenue cutter and the problem is whether he should accept it. The offer came through me—for the Collector of Customs at Southampton is an old friend of mine, known to me since boyhood. His kind offer is a very handsome one, very handsome indeed, but my fear is that Henry should miss the better opportunity of serving overseas. Your advice, if you will give it, may be of the greatest value and will leave me greatly in your debt. Come, sir, I'll take no denial!" Whether seriously meant or not, this plea for guidance had the desired effect. The naval officer's scruples over accepting charity were overcome by Mr Grindall's tact.

"In that event, sir," he replied, "I can only say that I am very much at your disposal and will accept your kind invitation with the greatest pleasure. My name is Delancey and my last service was in the cutter *Royalist*." Mr Grindall soon ascertained, by indirect means, that his first guess had been correct. Delancey was an unemployed half-pay lieutenant with neither interest nor private means; left ashore for reasons which he did not choose to explain. He could only guess at the rest of the story; but it had been a cold winter for a man who might be hungry. Mr Grindall found other topics for conversation; the sad illness and death of the *Thalia's* previous captain and the scandal over naval contracts at Plymouth. Did Delancey think that any good would come of the recent changes at the Admiralty? They chatted easily enough until the Inn was reached. Then they were able to thaw in front of the tap-room fire. With his overcoat removed, Delancey looked shabbier than ever, with threadbare elbows and cuffs. He warmed to his host's kindness, however, and was glad to be indoors. It would snow, he predicted, before nightfall. There were four or five other gentlemen in the room and they all agreed that the weather was exceptionally bad for the time of year. It was February 13th, 1795, and the winter, they all felt, had gone on long enough. Mr Grindall ordered dinner for three and took some time over the wine-list. He had scarcely chosen the claret before he saw his nephew in the street and went to meet him. After a few minutes he returned, ushering Henry before him, and called out, "Here he is at last! Mr Delancey, allow me to introduce my nephew, Mr Midshipman Fowler. Henry, I want you to meet Mr Delancey, lieutenant until recently of the *Royalist!*" He looked, beaming, from one to the other.

There was a moment of tense silence, the conversation dying away. It was almost as if two mortal enemies were suddenly face to face. Then Delancey saved the situation by saying quietly: "There is no need for any introduction in this case, Mr Grindall. Mr Fowler and I are old shipmates. We served together in the *Artemis*."

"How are you, sir?" asked Fowler and his uncle was quick to comment on the strange turn of events which had brought the two of them together again.

"If I had not chanced to fall into conversation with you, Mr Delancey, my nephew would most probably have missed seeing you. What a pity that would have been!" The kindly old man led the way into the dining room and placed his guests on either side of him near the end of the table. Young Fowler was awkward and silent at first and Delancey, conversing with his host, was able to study the youngster's appearance. He was nearly two years older than he had been when he joined the *Artemis* as a volunteer in 1793. How old had he been then? Fifteen, perhaps. He would be seventeen now, perhaps nearly eighteen, unemployed most likely since the *Artemis* was stranded. His family had no interest so far as Delancey could remember and he rather supposed that the boy's parents were dead, which would account for his uncle acting as guardian. Fowler was a young man now, less of a schoolboy and quite presentable.

"One does not like to speak ill of the dead," Mr Grindall was saying, "but I have always thought that Captain Fletcher's going down with his ship was a providential circumstance. Henry here has told me, Mr Delancey, of some of the things that poor madman said and did. It must have been a terrible situation for you and for the other officers. As I understand the matter, the *Artemis* was in the worst possible state of indiscipline, disorder and fear, a ship heading for disaster up to the point when she was actually lost. Strange are the ways of providence, Mr Delancey. But for the previous running aground both you and Henry might have been drowned. I am convinced that you were both saved by divine intervention, the result of prayer."

Fowler was busy with his knife and fork but Delancey replied without batting an eyelid: "You are very right, sir, and several of my old shipmates would agree with you."

The youngster looked up from his plate and caught Delancey's eye. A glance passed between them but the older man's face was expressionless. There was a moment of silence and then Mr Grindall called for a toast to the King. After that act of loyalty, a toast followed to the navy and, proposed by Delancey, to the wine trade. Young Fowler's toast was to a long war and quick promotion but about that his uncle thought differently.

"I drink to that for your sake, Henry. It is what every sea officer must want—you not least, Mr Delancey. But we in the wine trade have our own interests at stake. Remain at war with France and you cut off our nearest and best source of supply. French wine and brandy are all but unobtainable and even German wines will soon be costly in freight and insurance. Port wine we may still have and Madeira may be plentiful but our trade must otherwise dwindle. We had laid in stocks, to be sure, but look at the duties we had to pay!"

"Duties which some people choose to avoid," said Delancey.

"Just so," replied Mr Grindall, "but I am not one of them. I am known as an old-established wine shipper and an honest merchant. I may not have a large connection but my friends include the mayor of Southampton, the collector of customs, the sheriff and his deputy and a dozen justices of the peace. Others can engage in the free trade, as it is called, but I cannot. And this brings me to the question on which I wanted to ask your advice. I can offer my nephew here a berth in the Southampton revenue cutter but would he be wise to accept?"

"Tell me first what interest you have," asked Delancey. "Do you have a relative who is an admiral or captain? Have you a vote as a Southampton burgess? What can you do to gain Mr Fowler his commission?"

"The truth is, Mr Delancey, that I can do nothing for Henry, as he has come to know by experience. When war began I had interest enough to place him on the quarterdeck. More than that I cannot do."

"In those circumstances Mr Fowler is better afloat than ashore. He can gain more experience and—who knows?—he may make some money. The sale of smuggled goods is profitable, I believe, to the captors. What is your own conclusion, Mr Fowler?"

"I am quite of your opinion, sir. I have little to lose by serving in a revenue cutter and small hope of promotion were I in the navy."

It emerged in conversation over the dinner table that young Fowler was staying with some relatives in Portsmouth and had been trying for a berth in a frigate, so far without success. His uncle had come from Southampton to explain about the vacancy on board the *Rapid* revenue cutter. But that was not the only possibility as he now made clear.

"It so happens that there is another cutter in these waters, the *Rose*, based on Cowes. She was built for Mr William Agnew, collector in the Isle of Wight, who is presently in London. His deputy is Mr John Payne, whom I have never met. I am slightly acquainted, however, with Mr Ryder, who commands the *Rose*, a very good seaman and an honest man. I do not know that he has a vacancy but I have asked him, by letter, to join us here this afternoon. His advice, if he can come, should be of great value."

Mr Grindall had a great deal to say about the excise duties and the ways in which the revenue could be defrauded. He was not disinterested, as he had to admit, for his own goods were in competition against contraband. How could he be expected to sell at the same price? Take, for example, the claret they were drinking. Free traders could offer the same wine at two-thirds the price, bought at the back door rather than over the counter. The revenue cutters did their best but no vigilance could prevent smuggling. The most anyone could do was to add to the smuggler's expenses and so reduce the difference between prices as openly and privately charged. By the time they had reached the cheese Mr Grindall was wondering whether Mr Ryder would at least be able to join them over a glass of Madeira. Delancey remarked that it was snowing already which might have discouraged Mr Grindall's other guest, more especially if he had far to go. Looking out, they could see the snow blown horizontally, with vehicles and foot passengers moving as blurred shapes in the void. "A good day to be within doors!" said Mr Grindall, passing the Madeira round for the second time and calling for the boy to stoke up the fire. "A health to the preventive service!" Even young Fowler had cheered up sufficiently to comment on his pleasure at visiting The Star and Garter. He would never have dared go there in uniform—it was the lieutenants' place. "The Blue Posts is where I really belong!"

As young Fowler was speaking there was a confused noise from the street. A coach had driven up, the clatter of horses muffled by the snow, and raised voices could be heard, one of them calling repeatedly for a surgeon. Nothing much could be seen from the window but a waiter came in from the entrance hall and Mr Grindall asked him what had happened.

"There's a gentleman been set upon by some footpads who left him badly hurt by the roadside. He was picked up, seemingly, by the coach from Chichester. He'd have died else in this weather, sir, that's for sure."

The waiter hurried out again with a bottle of brandy while Mr Grindall expressed his surprise:

"Footpads in the outskirts of Portsmouth! I never heard of such a thing."

"Nor I, sir," replied Delancey. "It sounds to me more like the result of a tavern brawl."

"Go and inquire, Henry," said Mr Grindall. "There is maybe some help we can offer." His nephew hurried out and was gone for some minutes.

"One would as soon expect to hear a tale about highwaymen! There are a few still on the road, I suppose, but not in the approaches to a garrison town. That waiter must have been mistaken, you can depend on't."

"I'm entirely of your opinion, sir," said Delancey, returning to the fireside, where young Fowler presently rejoined them.

"I have the true story now," he said. "Four sailors recently paid off mistook this gentleman for the master-at-arms of the *Royal Sovereign,* who is one of the most unpopular men in the fleet."

"I have heard that," said Delancey, "and his captain is a martinet."

"The gentleman was badly beaten before the men discovered their error and ran off. It was one of them who stopped the coach, however, and told the driver where the injured man lay. He's lucky not to have frozen."

"Where are they taking him?" asked Mr Grindall.

"The landlord has told them to bring him in."

On hearing this Mr Grindall led the way to the front door, towards which the victim of coincidence was being assisted by a group of bystanders, some of them passengers from the coach itself. All were loud in their sympathy and comment.

"His leg is broke, Tom, that I'll swear."

"And a rib too, I shouldn't wonder."

"Best send for Mr Cartwright."

"He's out of town, I hear tell."

"There's Mr Winthrop, then."

"Aye—someone go for Mr Winthrop!"

"Say it's a case of a broken leg."

"And a rib too, seemingly."

The injured man was brought in and laid on an oak settle while the apothecary was sent for. The group of sympathisers stood back for a moment, parting enough for Mr Grindall to see who it was that had been hurt.

"Why, it's Mr Ryder!" What else he had to say was drowned by a renewed babel of conversation.

Mr Grindall now insisted that Mr Ryder should be given a bedroom at the Inn. There could be no question of taking him to his home at Cowes. He felt partly responsible for the accident, he explained, as Mr Ryder was coming there at his invitation. The landlord proved sympathetic and the injured man was carefully taken upstairs. The move had hardly begun, however, when Delancey unexpectedly took his leave.

"I am sorry to desert you, sir, but I have some business to which I must attend. I thank you for your hospitality and hope that we may meet again. I am sure that Mr Ryder is in good hands." With a few hurried words of farewell Delancey had gone, Mr Grindall wondering a little at his guest's abrupt departure. "Strange that he left us so suddenly. There is little after all, that a half-pay lieutenant has to do!" But his further reflections were interrupted by the arrival of Mr Winthrop, the apothecary, a small man with a portentous manner. He finally gave it as his opinion that Ryder had broken a rib as well as his leg, would be off duty for several months and was lucky, indeed, to be alive at all.

On leaving the Star and Garter, Delancey hurried to the Sally Port and looked around for a boat. There was none there, the weather being so discouraging, and he went back to the Point. This time he was in luck. There was a man-of-war's longboat alongside the jetty and an officer just about to embark. Lieutenant Bentley of the *Venerable* (74) was somewhat the worse for liquor, having dined ashore with the military, but he was in an amiable mood and accepted Delancey as a brother officer. The *Venerable* was at Spithead and he saw no reason why the longboat should not land Delancey at Ryde. Cowes was out of the question in an easterly wind—the boat would not return until next day—but Ryde was almost opposite where the *Venerable* was at anchor.

The boat pushed off into rough water and the coxswain steered into a darkness which was only relieved by the white foam on the wave tops. The snowstorm had passed but spray came over the bows at each plunge, slapping on the tarpaulin and forming a pool under the floorboards. The oarsmen pulled well, however, and Delancey duly landed at Ryde and, his luck still holding, he even found a farmer who could drive him to Cowes. Before ten that night he was knocking at the door of Mr John Payne's house. An impatient voice from a first floor window asked him what he wanted.

"Mr Ryder has been badly hurt and will be off duty," said Delancey briefly. "I am a naval officer and I have come to offer my services as temporary commander of the *Rose*."

It took Mr Payne some minutes to pacify his wife, put on an overcoat over his nightshirt, light a candle and wake his manservant. There was eventually the sound of the chain being unfastened and the bolts being drawn. The door finally swung open to reveal the deputy collector of customs, pistol in hand, supported by an elderly servant armed with the poker. When finally reassured about his visitor's respectability, Mr Payne showed Delancey into the study and told his man to make up the dying fire while he himself brought out a decanter and a couple of glasses. He heard the details of the affair without comment and sighed deeply before taking another sip of port. "You have had a rough passage, sir, and a cold journey," he concluded. "Why could you not have left it until tomorrow?" "Because," said Delancey, "the kind of man who leaves things until tomorrow would not be an ideal commander for the *Rose*." Mr Payne smiled briefly, nodding to himself and there was a minute's silence before he replied. "The *Rose* has had no ideal commander since she was built. William Ryder is not of the same calibre as the late commander, Francis Buckley."

"Mr Buckley commanded the previous cutter of the same name?"

"He did, sir, and with great success. Willis did almost as well with a smaller cutter, the *Nancy*. Between them they nearly brought smuggling in this vicinity to a standstill. Buckley was killed in action against a French privateer in 1793 and Ryder has recently become a Methodist. Since then the smugglers have flourished, sir; not around the Isle of Wight, to be sure, but elsewhere along the coast. Fortunes are being made from contraband and we have taken nothing for months past."

"But why should the smugglers benefit from Ryder being a Methodist? I should have thought, sir, that he was the more to be relied upon as an opponent of the liquor traffic."

"An opponent he certainly is but so much so that he gains no intelligence. Mr Buckley was often at the Rose and Crown—sometimes even at the Pig and Whistle. He met the known smugglers ashore and talked with them. He was sometimes present when they had drunk to excess. He knew a dozen informers, bad characters and go-betweens. His plans were based upon the gossip he heard. Since his conversion Ryder will not be seen in the haunts of sin. He even prevents his men from going to the alehouses which the smugglers frequent. As for the women of the town, he will never keep company with them, nor would he hear the end of it if he did. Things were different in Buckley's time. He knew what he was about."

"Well, sir," said Delancey, "will you appoint me to the command for the period of Ryder's absence? The smugglers will reckon that the coast is clear, the *Rose* in harbour and everything in their favour. That will give me the chance to surprise them."

"But how will you set about it?"

"By going, as a stranger, to the Rose and Crown. No one in Cowes has ever seen me before. No one saw me enter your house tonight. I shall appear as one who is in the trade, an agent from England."

"So far your plan is possible. . . . It seems, indeed, to offer some chance of success. Very well, sir, the appointment is yours. You will be sworn in as a deputed mariner before the *Rose* puts to sea. Make your inquiries in the meanwhile and delay our first official meeting until—shall we say?—Monday next. I shall instruct the mate, Mr Thomas Lane, to prepare the cutter for sea while letting it be known that she is not to sail in Mr Ryder's absence."

There was some further discussion about terms of employment, finally, "Thank you sir," said Delancey. "I shall do my best to show that your confidence is not misplaced. May I ask your help before I go? Can you give me the name of a free trader of some note on the mainland—a man whose agent I might be?"

"That at least is easy. Your man would be John Early of Milton Abbas near Dorchester."

"Thank you. Does he pass as a merchant?"

"No, sir. He is an attorney."

"Can you give me the name of one of his men—the shipmaster who actually handles the cargo?"

"Yes—Jack Rattenbury of Lyme Regis. He used to own a lugger called *The Friends,* that is until she was taken by the *Nancy.*"

"And where can I spend the night before joining those who have landed by the morning ferry boat from Portsmouth?"

"In your place I should seek shelter on board the cutter *Nancy* alongside the Customs wharf. She is about to be broken up but her deck will still provide some shelter."

"Good. One last favour, sir. I could find good use for a flask of brandy."

"You shall have it and of the best quality, costing no less than nine shillings a gallon at the Customs House Sales."

Mr Payne produced the flask and showed Delancey to the door. A few minutes later he was explaining to his wife what had happened to keep him from bed. "An odd sort of man, my dear, who had come to tell me about Mr Ryder being assaulted by some ruffians and seriously hurt: a sad business, it would seem, and likely to keep him ashore for some time. This will give the smugglers their best opportunity for years."

"How do you know that this man is not a smuggler himself?"

"Well, come to think on't, I don't know but what he isn't. He would gain nothing, though, by deceiving me about Mr Ryder's injury for I shall hear about it, anyway, in the morning. I think he is an honest man, though. He offers to serve without pay so as not to deprive poor Ryder of his livelihood!"

While Mr Payne went to bed, Delancey was walking down to the harbour. Snow had stopped falling earlier in the night but the wind was still cold and the going unpleasant. He had much to think about and he realized, as he walked, how little he knew about the smuggling business. He had known something about the smugglers around Guernsey but suspected that the Guernseymen were not in the same line of business as the men of Hampshire and Dorset. Their task had usually been to bring the goods from France to Guernsey—a trade which was not even illegal until war began and it meant trading with the enemy. Between Guernsey and England was a different business. He remembered hearing that some Dorset free traders—"moonlighters" were they called?—no, "moonrakers" (whatever that meant)—used big and well-armed craft and traded to Roscoff. They were laden with spirits and tobacco, their cargoes being taken inland and distributed from some suitable town—hence Mr Early having his home near Dorchester. He would be a landowner, most likely, as well as an attorney, a friend of the gentry and perhaps himself a justice of the peace. To succeed against a man like that would mean persuading someone to turn King's evidence. That would be possible only for an officer with a thorough knowledge of the smuggling art, just such a knowledge as the late Mr Buckley had possessed. Delancey cursed himself for his ignorance, realising that he must have forgotten half the facts he had been told. One thing he knew and had remembered was that the smugglers were among the best seamen in the country. They were used to bad weather and dark nights. So, presumably, were the men who served in the revenue cutters, but about them he knew next to nothing. They were exempt from impressment, as he had explained to many a press-gang, but that was almost all he knew about them. They tended, he thought, to wear red flannel shirts and blue trousers. . . .

It was still bitterly cold but the clouds had gone and he would see, by starlight, the streets of the town through which he was making his way to the riverside. There were few lights to be seen but there were distant sounds of revelry from some sailors' tavern, presumably the Pig and Whistle. He walked on briskly and was able, presently, to identify the Customs House. He racked his brains to remember the facts he knew about smuggling. There was no traffic now in tea, he thought, the stuff being unobtainable in time of war save from the East India Company itself. There was nothing to be done with silks either, the duties having been lowered. Smuggling was confined, he thought, to spirits and tobacco, the spirits being often as much as forty per cent over proof. He vaguely remembered having heard stories about the ferocious Hawkhurst Gang which had flourished long ago. Present smugglers avoided fighting, he had been told, because of the militia being everywhere in wartime. They used cunning instead of force these days, sinking their cargo when pursued and coming back for it when the revenue men had gone. There was another trick reported, something to do with the kegs being slung under the lugger's keel. Revenue men had to be clever since most of their earnings came from commission on what they seized. How long would it take him to learn the trade? Still pondering on this, he identified the Customs House Wharf with, alongside, an unrigged cutter, evidently the *Nancy*. All was quiet along the wharf and there was a gangplank in position. On tiptoe now and without making a sound, Delancey went aboard the cutter.

Slowly and quietly he made his way aft, coming at last to the companionway. He stood there listening, for a minute or two and then went below. He wondered that the hatchway should be open but remembered that the cutter was to be broken up. There would be nothing aboard worth stealing, not so much as a rope yarn or a scrap of old canvas to lie on. He paused at the foot of the ladder for his eyes to become accustomed to the dark. Looking up through the hatchway he could see the starlight overhead. Looking aft he expected to see a glimmer of light through a stern window but all was dark. Perhaps there was no stern window in a cutter of this tonnage, far smaller than the craft regularly built for the Customs Board, but there should have been a scuttle aft even then, or at least a deadlight let into the deck. It was not much of a place to sleep in but no worse than some others he had known. He wondered whether there would be rats: or would they have gone ashore when they heard that the vessel was to be broken up? Cautiously he began to make his way aft. His shoe struck against a small ringbolt underfoot and at that instant his arms were suddenly pinned to his side by a powerful grip. "Keep quiet, mate," said a rough voice. "Say one word and I'll slit your windpipe." The threat was backed up by the coldness of the steel and Delancey wisely did as he was told. There were two men there, he realized, one who had seized him from behind, the other (with the knife) in front of him. While the point was still at his throat his wrists were jerked behind him and tied with a length of rope. Only then was the knife put away so that his captor could use flint and steel. A lantern was lit and raised so that the light fell on Delancey's face.

"Who is it, Dan?" said the voice from behind him.

"Damned if I know," said the other. "I think as how our best plan will be to cut his throat."

Chapter Six

TRICKS OF THE TRADE

D ELANCEY found himself looking at a shabby individual who was obviously a landsman. He guessed that the other man, whom he could not see, was some sort of fisherman or boatman. Ratface—or Dan as the other called him—might once have been a clerk or shopman but had long since been discharged, probably for petty theft or drink or both. He might see himself as a master criminal but his was clearly not the stuff of which murderers are made. Even if evil intent were there he lacked the courage.

"Killing me," said Delancey, "won't help you find the gold."

"What gold?" asked Ratface with sudden interest.

"Gold be damned," said the other man, "don't let him gammon you!"

"I mean the gold that was on board *The Friends*. Jack told me about it. Buckley's men hid it and never told the Customs."

"Who told you?"

"Jack Rattenbury."

"You know Jack?"

"Well, I should do."

"And *he* said there was gold aboard this craft?"

"One time there was. Isn't that what you were looking for?"

"No, we weren't. But we found *this!*" Ratface pointed to a half anker (or small keg) which stood on a locker, masking the deadlight on that quarter. "We was just a-going to open it when you had to come blundering aboard. If there had been gold we should ha' found it."

"Even if lashed to the keel?"

"This berth dries out with the ebb." They were spiking the keg as they talked and Ratface was finally able to taste the contents, having spilt some into the palm of his hand. He spat it out again with an oath. "Stinkibus!"

"Spoilt, eh?" asked Delancey, who had never heard the term used before.

"Stinkibus, that's what. It's been in salt water for months, maybe for years. Stinkibus!"

"I could give you something better."

"Well, where is it?"

"Untie me first. Can't you see that I'm a moonraker myself?"

"Just because you know Jack? That's nothing. Anyone could know him who lived round Christchurch."

"I know someone else."

"Who, then?"

"I know John Early." There was an abrupt change of atmosphere and Delancey knew that he had made a big impression.

"So you know *John Early?* Why didn't you say so before? We wouldn't be wanting to offend the Squire of Milton Abbas! Not by no means! Untie his wrists, Will. This genelman is in the trade and sails by moonlight. I'll wager we can trust him." Will did as he was told and insisted on shaking hands to prove that there were no hard feelings. He was a big man, strong as a horse and without a brain in his head.

"Well, where is it?" asked Ratface. Delancey produced the bottle from his coat-tail pocket and handed it over. "I want my share, mind!" This demand was more perhaps than was reasonable for Will was born thirsty and Dan wanted something (he said) to take away the taste of stinkibus. They finished the bottle between them and went to sleep on the cabin floor.

Next day, unshaven, Delancey really looked the part being almost as shabby at Ratface himself. He felt in no way conspicuous as they walked to the Rose and Crown next morning to meet a number of their friends—whose leader seemed to be a one-eyed character called Henry Stevens. Such was the technical language used, interlarded with nicknames and local allusions, that Delancey learnt all too little. Henry was disappointed, it seemed, in the backsliding of a former colleague called Isaac Hartley. He kept returning to this theme, regretting that Ike should have turned Methodist—he of all people—and given up the trade. Stories followed of how Ike had fooled the revenue men. No one, it seemed, had been more generally useful—as Stevens himself had to admit—and no one had a cellar better hidden. It was all due to his marrying Hannah, the daughter of David Mercer. Dave was a sort of lay preacher himself—damn the fellow!—and Hannah had been brought up in that hymn-singing crowd. Henry spoke of Ike's conversion with all the sorrow that chapel-goers bestow on those who have fallen from grace. "One thing I'll say for him," said Henry. "He's never split on his old-time friends. He told me he never would and he hasn't." From subsequent remarks it would seem that Ike's silence was well-advised. "What does Ike do for a living these days?" asked Delancey of Dan. "He's a ship's chandler with a place in Hog Lane," came the reply. But Henry was still bewailing the loss of a friend. "Why, I ask *why* should he go and turn preacher? I'd rather be a loblolly boy or a Frenchie! I'll never speak to him again, the scow-bunking lubber!" More ale was called for and all agreed that Ike had been disloyal and ungrateful and that he deserved to be married to that sallow-faced Hannah.

From hours of conviviality all that Delancey could gather was that Henry's gang was relatively unimportant but that its activities hinged upon the occasional visits of a man they called Sam, probably from the mainland. He concluded that Isaac Hartley would be a useful source of general information, and that Sam (whose surname nobody mentioned) was said to be interested in a local girl called Molly Brown. Pleading unspecified business, but undertaking to meet his friends again that evening at the Pig and Whistle, Delancey slipped away while Henry was in the middle of another diatribe against preachers. He went first of all to the barber's for a shave and accepted the barber's advice about where to dine. There would be good value, he was told, at the eating house in Hog Lane. So there was and Delancey felt better after his hot-pot and cabbage. He found nearby the sign "ISAAC HARTLEY, SHIP CHANDLER," and boldly entered the shop, asking to see what boat-hooks they had in stock. Isaac was evidently in a small way of business, providing mainly for fishermen, his shop probably avoided by his old associates. He was no serious rival for George Ratsey, already well known as a sailmaker. He had time for gossip and Delancey described himself as one of the redeemed, bred up in Surrey Chapel Sunday School but sorely tempted of late by some dealers in contraband. He asked Mr Hartley whether he regarded smuggling as actually *sinful?* Isaac took full advantage of this opening. Leaving his boy to take charge of the store, he took Delancey up to his loft, where he kept his rope yarn and twice-laid, his tallow and pitch. Sitting on a bolt of canvas, he explained at length that smuggling was indeed a sin. Doubting perhaps whether his argument had carried conviction, he went on to insist that it did not even pay. Fortunes might be made in Hampshire, at least by the men who financed the trade (with hellfire as their ultimate reward), but here in the Isle of Wight the game was not worth the candle. More could be made honestly, with salvation to follow.

Delancey learnt a lot that afternoon. Isaac, he discovered, was less of a preacher than his former mates were inclined to assume. He was much under Hannah's thumb, however, and her ideas were evidently strict. In talking about his old trade, though, there was a note of nostalgia in his voice. Those, evidently, had been the days! True to his vow he would name no names but he was not averse to describing the trade as a whole. Gradually the picture was revealed of the region known to him. The men of property who financed operations were centred upon Dorchester; John Early, Esquire, being obviously the chief of them. The landing places included various creeks from Bridport to Portland and from there to Christchurch. Apart from Christchurch itself the most important smuggling centres were Abbotsbury and Poole. All Isaac's detailed information was, in fact, about Poole. Smuggling vessels were based there and traded mainly with Alderney. Few of them came near the Isle of Wight for the collector there kept two armed boats, one at Yarmouth to examine vessels passing the Needles, the other at St Helen's to examine vessels passing Spithead. Goods for the island were usually sunk, therefore, in Sandown Bay by vessels which went on to Poole. One craft did this regularly (Sam's lugger, thought Delancey) and the barrels were picked up by some local men (Henry's gang, said Delancey to himself) who only used rowing boats out of Shanklin. The lugger would then put into Cowes to collect payment, this being on her next outward passage when her hold was empty. "Did the late Mr Buckley know of this?" asked Delancey and was told that he must have done. What he could not have known was the exact night when the run would take place. There were, of course, many other clandestine activities and the *Rose's* cruising ground extended from Lyme Regis to Beachy Head. Delancey asked whether Sam ever had warning about the *Rose's* intended movements but Isaac knew nothing about that. It was several years now since he had seen the light. It could be, though, that some revenue men were in the smugglers' pay. Such cases were known and no seizure, come to think of it, had ever been made in Sandown Bay. After a long conversation, interrupted by many pious platitudes, Delancey thanked Isaac for his counsel and undertook to lead an honest life.

That evening Delancey was at the Pig and Whistle. He had originally supposed that this was the haunt of lower-deck as opposed to supervisory smugglers. He found that this idea was mistaken. The same people were there as he had met at the Rose and Crown but in a different mood and at a different hour. Clients of the Rose and Crown were all male and given to serious discussion about ways to cheat the customs and excise. By the time they reached the Pig and Whistle they were more inclined towards romance. There were women there, described by the innkeeper as his daughters and nieces, and tap-room conversation was more ribald and less technical. Voices were raised in discordant song or violent disagreement. Girls appeared, giggling, and vanished again half an hour at a time. Molly Brown was not among them at first and Delancey was not disposed to waste much time on the others. He listened for hours to Dan, Will and Henry, standing his round with nearly all he had left, but learnt nothing of any interest. While they accepted him as one of themselves, this was neither the time nor the place for talking business. They told stories and made jokes at the expense of Will, whose stupidity made him the natural butt of the others. When Molly Brown appeared she was followed by an old man with a fiddle. She sang, to his accompaniment, a rather sentimental song about a maid who died of love. Applause was perfunctory and, sensing the mood of the moment, she launched at once into a ballad entitled "The Flowing Can." It was a popular tune and she illustrated the words with appropriate, if sketchy gestures showing how to heave the lead and reef the sail. Each verse ended with a rousing chorus in which everyone joined:

> We sing a little, we laugh a little,
> And work a little, and swear a little
> And swig the flowing can!

Standing on a bench to sing, Molly made a striking figure. She was dark-haired and bright-eyed with a full figure and white skin, aged 25 or less. In vigorous action, manning the deck to clear the wreck, she displayed herself to some advantage, gaining tremendous enthusiasm over the last verse:

> But yet think not our fate is hard,
> Though storms at sea thus treat us,
> For coming home, a sweet reward,
> With smiles our sweethearts greet us!
> Now too the friendly grog we quaff,
> Our am'rous toast,
> Her we love most,
> And gaily sing and laugh:
> The sails we furl

> *Then for each girl*
> *The petticoat display;*
> *The deck we clear*
> *Then three times cheer*
> *As we their charms survey.*

The last line was given special emphasis and the company present was privileged to see rather more of Molly before joining in the final chorus:

> *And then the grog goes round,*
> *All sense of danger drown'd.*
> *We despise it to a man;*
> *We sing a little, we laugh a little,*
> *And work a little and swear a little*
> *And swig the flowing can.*

Flushed and panting, Molly jumped down from the bench, blew her admirers a kiss and vanished. Delancey, who was fond of music, endured the discordant singing and was glad only when it finished. All others were happy in the knowledge that Molly would sing again later and probably with more abandon. Some minutes after Molly's act Delancey made an excuse to leave the room. Returning from his visit to the backyard, he made to climb the stairs but found his way barred by a formidable matron who asked him where he thought he was going. "I have a message for Miss Molly," he explained. "I fancy her room will be up there."

"Maybe it is," said the frowning hostess. "And maybe it isn't. But I'll give her any message that is proper for her to receive." This was the moment, as Delancey knew, when a half guinea would have solved the problem. His fortune was now to be counted, however, in pennies, which would help him not at all. "I am here on behalf of my master," he explained. "A gentleman of great fortune and estate. He wishes to pay his respects to Miss Molly and asks whether one day next week

will serve." Met with a frankly incredulous stare, Delancey went hastily
into greater detail, making his master a baronet and a colonel, adding
to his property and giving him a town house and his own stables at
Newmarket. The pity was that so fine a gentleman should be still a
bachelor. All this might have been in vain so far as his hostess was
concerned but Delancey's voice had been heard on the floor above.
Molly appeared on the landing and asked what the noise was about.
"Here's a man, Miss, whose master, he says, wants to see you next week.
I am just about to send him about his business for I don't believe a
word of it." "But wait, cousin," said Molly, "it may be a gentleman who
has been here before." "No, alas," said Delancey, "Sir Edward has not
so far had the pleasure of your acquaintance. He wishes, however, to
make himself known to you." There was some further conversation and
Molly proved easier to convince. "Very well," she said finally. "I'll see
Sir Edward on Thursday afternoon at four of the clock." This announce-
ment alarmed the older woman who hurried upstairs, bidding Delancey
to wait. When she eventually returned it was to say that Thursday and
Friday were out of the question but that Miss would be free to receive
Sir Edward on the Monday following. Any day last week would have
served, and indeed the week before, but the coming week was more
difficult. Delancey confirmed the appointment and returned to his
friends in the tap-room. It turned into a riotous evening, enlivened by
song, and Delancey—who had no head for such revelry—was sick
before it ended. He slept that night on the tap-room floor.

After sin comes the time for repentance and the next day, Sunday,
was most suitable for this purpose. The church bells rang for morning
prayer at the chapel of ease—Cowes being at this time no more than
an offshoot of the parish of Carisbrooke. A few carriages headed in
that direction. Folk more conspicuous, however, for their piety than
for their high social position made their way on foot to one or other
of the two nonconformist chapels, one for the Independents and
the other for the Wesleyan Methodists. For Delancey the choice was
already made, for Hartley was a Wesleyan and it was after the Methodist

one else, leaving them without time in which to repent.

The discussion which followed was largely theological but Isaac early knew how cross bearings could be used to mark a position at a. He would not agree that it had anything to do with the mariner's fety. It was merely a way, he insisted, of concealing contraband. To lay any part in it was to commit a sin and, incidentally, a crime. "What would you say," he asked, "if a riding officer found you placing a lantern on Wroxhall Hill or Culver Cliff?" "Is that where I should be told to put it?" asked Delancey innocently. Isaac explained that there was a useful sandbank in Sandown Bay. It was on a bearing between Wroxhall and Culver and the other bearing was between Lake and Newchurch. "To place those lanterns and light them, to douse them and bring them away would take you from midnight to five, and all for what?" Delancey was more obstinate this time, asking how he could earn half a guinea in any other way. It was not, after all, as if there were dragoons on the island. "It is what God sees that matters!" said Isaac finally and Delancey had to admit that the deity might well have the last word. He promised to avoid even this marginal involvement in crime. A brand from the burning, he was allowed to sleep that night in the Hartleys' outhouse and was even provided with a mattress and blanket.

On Monday Mr Payne received him politely and listened with interest to his tale of espionage.

"Yes," he said finally. "You know something of the business and you have certainly wasted no time. All I can add is this: the man they call Sam is almost certainly Samuel Carter, a notorious smuggler, and comes of a well-known smuggling family in Cornwall. He lives now at Poole and owns a vessel called the *Dove* of near two hundred tons, as fast a lugger as you would ever see."

"I shall do my best, sir, to bring him to justice."

"Of that I am sure. I take leave to question, however, whether you will succeed."

service that Delancey hoped to meet him again. The
place of worship was highly conducive to penitence ar
a hangover from the previous evening, looked even mo
he felt. The sermon was long and fervent, punctuated
groans of sinners remembering their past misdeeds. Sea
the free pews at the back of the chapel, Delancey mode
penitence on that of an oldish man who might once, pe
been a receiver of stolen goods. Sighing aloud at what he h
the right moments and exclaiming, "Ah, to have seen the
"What bliss to be saved!" Delancey managed to convey his ser
and redemption and was kindly addressed afterwards by sever
bers of the congregation.

After a conversation during which Hannah asked some penet
questions, the Hartleys finally invited him to join them at dinner.
gry and penniless, he was glad to accept this invitation and that
more than one reason. He ended by wondering whether any inforn
tion had ever been bought at so high a cost.

Dinner at the Hartleys began with a long-winded grace, continued
with a detailed inquiry into his spiritual life and ended with several
more prayers and a hymn. It was only afterwards, while inspecting the
garden, that Delancey was able to question Isaac again. Once more he
professed to be in need of counsel. Granted that smuggling were a
sin—a point on which he was now convinced—he was wondering
whether it was as sinful to assist the free-trader indirectly. He was under
pressure from some friends, he explained, who wanted him to place
some lanterns in position after dark, lighting them at a certain hour
and extinguishing them again before daybreak. They were mere aids
to navigation, he emphasised, a help to the mariner when homeward bound. He could not imagine that there could be anything illegal in merely placing a lantern in a gateway and another on a rock a
third beneath a tree and a fourth beside a bridge. Could there be anything sinful in that? It was no more, after all, then saving life at sea.
Those served might be smugglers but they were as liable to drown as

"Why so, Mr Payne?"

"Because Sam Carter knows more about smuggling than you do. Indeed, he knows nothing else. So the trade will go on, I suspect, for as long as any goods are heavily dutiable."

"If you were to give me three well-manned cutters, sir, I would undertake to prevent the passage of contraband on this station."

"I daresay you might. Then the trade would shift to the east and west."

"Not, surely, sir, if others were as vigilant?"

"You are new to the preventive service, Mr Delancey. There is much you have still to learn." Mr Payne paused and took snuff, as if deciding where to begin or indeed how much it would be proper to reveal. When he finally spoke again it was with evident reluctance.

"What I am going to say is entirely unofficial, you must understand, and strictly between ourselves. Preventive men, whether seamen, boatmen or riding officers, have a living to make and families to support. Their wages are modest but they are augmented from time to time out of their share in the contraband they may seize. So their interest lies in the interception of smuggled cargoes, not in the entire suppression of illicit traffic. How would they make a living if the trade were suppressed? They would have only their daily pay and that only until their services were found to be needless."

"We could use them, sir, in the navy."

"What—in time of peace?"

"Well, no, sir. In time of war, however—"

"In time of war, Mr Delancey, the principal attraction of the revenue service lies in the fact that its men are exempt from impressment. We cannot flog men, sir, for insolence or neglect of duty but we *can* threaten to dismiss them and turn them over to a man-of-war. And that—if you'll forgive my saying so—is the one thing they dread. The idea that smuggling should be suppressed has never entered their minds but the possibility—were it mentioned—would fill them with dismay."

"I understand, sir. They expect the traffic to continue but they demand their share of the profits."

"No, no, Mr Delancey. That is too crude a description of a long-established and complex state of affairs. I am bound by my office to discountenance any illicit trade and prosecute all who cheat the revenue. Heaven forbid that I should fail in my duty! My officers and men, however—and I am speaking, remember, in strict confidence—regard their activities as a kind of game, like cricket; one in which they hope to score but one which should never involve the destruction of the opposing team. Men like yourself, Mr Delancey, depend upon the French for your employment. You find yourselves on the beach—forgive my putting it bluntly—when the French refuse to play. In much the same way, all preventive men depend for their living on the smugglers."

"Are they not tempted, then, to make a direct contract with them, accepting a regular share and agreeing otherwise to leave them alone?"

Mr Payne was genuinely shocked at this suggestion and his reply was uttered in terms of pained surprise: "Really, sir, I hope you do not regard the men of the revenue service as *dishonest?* I never heard of such an infamous agreement being made or even proposed. I would have you know, sir, that our men have a strict sense of duty. They will put to sea in the teeth of a gale. They will engage their opponents with resolution. Many have been killed in action and others, more fortunate, have lived to receive the commendation of the Board for their loyalty and courage. We have good reason to be proud, sir, of the men who are employed by the Commissioners of Customs."

Delancey hastened to assure Mr Payne that he was filled with admiration for the revenue men and that he looked forward to serving alongside them. He realized that theirs was an arduous and hazardous service and one of great importance to the realm. Mr Payne was presently mollified and induced to go into practical details. Delancey would be sworn at once, the lawyer attending for the purpose, and this was done. It was agreed that he should take over the command at midday and that he should receive an immediate advance of twenty guineas; enough at least to provide him with cabin stores. It was agreed, finally, that he should sail almost immediately for Portsmouth where he needed to collect his gear and give up his lodging. That done, he would take his cutter to sea, cruising towards Beachy Head. Delancey did not reveal his plans in detail, not even to the collector. After being shaved at the barbers he kept an appointment made for him by Mr Payne with Mr Robert Edgell, Supervisor of Riding Officers. That worthy turned out to be an ex-corporal of Dragoon Guards, surly at first but responsive to the idea of making some money. Delancey told him no more than was necessary but spoke frankly about his sources of information. "You've done very well, sir, if I may say so," said Edgell finally. "You mind me of Mr Buckley, who always knew what he was about. But how will you board the cutter without anyone seeing you?" Delancey had overlooked this problem but realized that his plan would fail if Harry Stevens was to realize that his boon companion of Saturday night was commander of the *Rose* by Monday afternoon. There was still time for Sam Carter to receive warning and make his run at another place on another night. Edgell solved the problem by lending Delancey the sort of costume a riding officer would wear; a dark cloak, spurred riding boots and a low-crowned hat to pull down over his forehead.

They went down to the quayside with Delancey carrying his own overcoat as a parcel and looking for all the world like one of Edgell's men. At the Custom House Wharf Mr Edgell saw Delancey safely into the boat and when Mr Payne appeared, a little late, handed him down into the sternsheets. The boat was pushed off and rowed down the harbour to where the *Rose* rode at single anchor, provisioned for three weeks and ready for sea.

Mr Payne boarded the *Rose* with dignity and was received by the mate, Mr Tom Lane, with the crew paraded on deck. Delancey followed a minute later, leaving his borrowed gear in the boat. He remained modestly in the background while Mr Payne addressed the crew.

"You all know, men, that Mr Ryder has been hurt in an accident and will not be on duty again for some time to come. I have decided, therefore, to appoint a temporary commander. He joins the cutter today and I present him to you: Lieutenant Richard Andros Delancey of the Royal Navy, an officer of great experience, lately commanding the cutter *Royalist*. Strictly obey his orders and this next cruise will bring you success."

Having no warning of this, the *Rose's* men were taken by surprise and Lane the mate, for one, seemed to be offended. Delancey decided to waste no time. "Hands to the capstan and halliards!" he shouted. "Prepare to make sail." Ordering Mr Lane to take charge of the deck, he saw Mr Payne over the side and said goodbye to him. As he watched the cable hauled in, the mainsail and jib set, he felt a keen sense of pleasure. The deck was alive under his feet. The wind sang in the rigging. He was at sea again! There was a stiff westerly breeze and it was cold to the point of freezing but he hardly noticed even the spray in his face. He knew all too well that the craft was new to him and that he was liable to hesitate or blunder. If the crew sensed his ignorance they would lack confidence from the outset. "Lay a course for Portsmouth, helmsman," he said to the man at the wheel. "Come below, Mr Lane, and show me the chart." In the cabin the mate produced the chart but Delancey hardly looked at it. "Now tell me quickly, Mr Mate, what is our tonnage, our draught, our armament and crew?" The *Rose*, it appeared, measured 154 tons, mounted twelve 4-pounders and two 9-pounders, carried a chest of small arms and was handled by a crew of 22 including the commander, chief mate, second mate and two deputed mariners. "Very well," said Delancey. "Who is the second mate? John Torrin? And the other two? Netley and Wansbrough? Right. Who is the man with red hair, the one with the squint, the man at the wheel, the man at the lookout?" In a matter of seconds Delancey had bounded on deck again and was giving the helmsman the exact course to clear Gilkicker Point. "Right, Wilkins, steady as she goes. What's that craft Miller—on the starboard bow? Flake down the halliards,

Jackson and Field!" He was able to give the impression of knowing every man by name even while asking Mr Torrin for the names of the rest. He set the square mainsail for the run to leeward and then struck it again in approaching Portsmouth. The men were evidently on their mettle, anxious to show a naval officer that they were proper seamen and better than would be found in a frigate. There were certainly fewer of them than would have manned a naval craft of similar tonnage. While not smart in the way that Delancey knew, they did the work quickly and quietly. There was none of that singing which naval officers deplored, the bellowing of the shanty which could be heard aboard the average merchantman. What would they be like in action? He decided to leave that test until tomorrow. For the moment it was enough to enter Portsmouth on the flood, drop anchor and lower a boat. The light was fading as he stepped ashore, followed by Davis, the man who was to serve as his steward. He picked up a longshoreman with a barrow and agreed on a shilling to be paid for his services. Delancey shivered a little in his shoddy greatcoat and walked quickly towards his lodging in Ropewalk Lane.

From his lodging Delancey sent his luggage on board the *Rose* and told the coxswain to return to the Hard at four o'clock. It was his duty, he knew, to call on Mr Ryder.

So much had happened since Delancey was last at the Star and Garter that he was almost surprised to learn that Mr Ryder was still there and unfit to be moved. Delancey was shown to the sick-room without any hesitation or argument. Ryder looked white and far from well but he thanked his visitor for calling and was glad to have news of the *Rose*. He had been told of Delancey's temporary appointment in a letter from Mr Payne. "I am obliged to you, sir, for accepting the command without pay. That fifty pounds a year is now all I have but you will have nothing until you secure a prize. There was little I ever made in that way but I shall pray for your better success. There are smugglers enough at sea. It is merely a question of finding them!"

"When will you be able to return home?"

"Next week, Mr Winthrop says."

"I am sure that will speed your recovery. It should be of value to me, in the meanwhile, if you could tell me something about the men I have to command. Tell me about Mr Lane."

"Bob has served all his time in the Revenue Service. He is a good reliable seaman and has never cost us so much as a broken spar. He knows the law and he can recognize a moonraking craft on even the darkest night. He lacks enterprise, though, and chief mate is as high as he should go."

"And John Torrin?"

"Not as careful a man as Bob but better in action. He'll command a cutter some day."

"What is a deputed mariner?"

"A seaman who has been sworn in as a deputy customs officer. There has to be one in each boat and he is usually the coxswain."

"I see. Are all the men loyal?"

"We should not employ them if their loyalty was in question."

"Let me put that question in different words. If any one of your crew were to pass information to the smugglers, which man would it be?"

"My dear sir! I should hate to think ill of any seaman under my command. There is no good reason to suspect any one of them."

"But suppose that intelligence of our plans had actually reached Sam Carter? Suppose that the facts were known and could be proved beyond all shadow of doubt?"

"Really, sir, you face me with a dilemma. . . . With great reluctance—and since you insist—I should first question Michael Williams."

"The man who has lost a finger? Why?"

"His sister is married to Nick O'Brien and Nick is cousin to Dan Palmer."

"I see."

"But please don't misunderstand me. I say nothing against Mike Williams and have heard nothing against him."

"I am glad to hear it and I hope to be able to say as much." Delancey looked round the room with a swift glance and asked whether the service at the Inn was good.

"Very good, I thank you," said Mr Ryder. "And I have had many visitors. Mr Grindall could not have been kinder and I expect his nephew to call at any moment. He has been entered as acting second mate in the *Rapid* cutter based on Southampton. The cutter is at Spithead and I understand that young Mr Fowler is ashore on some errand for Mr Madden. He will be glad to join us in a glass of wine."

Delancey explained that his visit had to be brief but he was still explaining this when Fowler arrived. They greeted each other, again with restraint on Fowler's side, and finally left together. Sensing an opportunity, Delancey asked Fowler to convey a message to Mr Madden. Walking down to the Hard, he gave a brief outline of his plans:

"All this," he concluded, "is in strictest confidence. This is Monday and I am expecting the *Dove* lugger to make a run on either Wednesday or Thursday night. If the *Rapid* will cruise on each of those two nights between the Foreland and the Nab, she will be in position to intercept. She should not be seen from the Isle of Wight in daylight. Prize-money to be shared equally."

"What if she heads the other way, sir?"

"Then we keep the prize. You can point out to Mr Madden that I am providing the intelligence upon which the plan is based."

"Very good, sir. I'll tell him. I should think he will agree."

They walked on in silence for a minute or so and then Fowler said something of what was on his mind.

"It is strange, sir, our meeting again. There are things I should like to forget. I still have nightmares and wake in a sweat, thinking I am back in the *Artemis*, or giving evidence again at the court martial."

Delancey looked keenly at the young man and asked, rather sharply: "Do you talk in your sleep?"

"How can I tell sir? Nobody has told me that I do."

"You have a cabin to yourself?"

"A small one, sir."

"It is certainly better that you should. But it might be better still if you lived ashore, away from scenes which remind you of events better forgotten."

"How can I, sir? There is only the one trade to which I have been bred."

"You would be better, then, on board a merchantman."

"Even in wartime, sir?"

"Listen, young man. You have nightmares about the experiences you had in the *Artemis,* and very distressing they were, I'll allow. But ours is not a profession for the squeamish. If the thought of these past events were to keep me awake I should not be fit to hold a commission. In the navy our trade is war. Is that the trade you ought to pursue? I beg leave to question it. You would be happier in commerce."

"I *should* be happier ashore—I know that. Thank you for your advice, sir."

They came to the Hard where Delancey's boat was already waiting, perhaps ten minutes before it had to be there. The light was failing even at this hour on that wintry day and Delancey was eager to embark. Saying goodbye to young Fowler, whose boat could be seen approaching, Delancey stepped into the *Rose's* gig and told the men to push off.

"Beg pardon, sir," said the coxswain, "one of the men has gone to get some pepper for the cook. You have come a little sooner than we expected, sir."

"You also came in sooner than you were told to do. Who is it that is ashore?"

"Williams, sir."

"I see. I shall give him five minutes."

Delancey left the gig and paced up and down on the quayside. He had to decide what to do about this breach of discipline. He was not, at the moment, in the navy. He could not expect the punctual and exact obedience on which he would ordinarily insist. Nor did he know the standards of discipline to which these revenue men were accustomed. He decided to utter no more than a word of warning. Odd, however, that it should be Williams. How easy it was to be too suspicious; how easy to make a fuss about nothing. . . . More than five minutes had passed before there came the sound of hurrying feet. The missing man, still out of breath, found himself face to face with his new skipper, still very much an unknown quantity. He quickly decided to bluff his way out of it.

"Well?" said Delancey, coldly.

"Beg pardon, sir. I was running an errand for the cook. I wasted no time, sir, and ran most of the way back."

"What was your errand, Williams?"

"To fetch some pepper, sir."

"And the cook told you to do this?"

"Yessir."

"Did you do anything else?"

"Oh, no, sir."

"Very well. Into the boat; and don't let this happen again, coxswain. Boat's crew must stay in the boat. Push off, Watson."

When the gig was alongside the *Rose* Delancey told the boat's crew to remain in the boat. Going on deck, he then sent for the cook and asked him whether he was short of pepper.

"No, sir."

"You did not send ashore for some?"

"No, sir."

"Did you send Williams on any other errand?"

"No, sir."

Delancey then ordered the boat's crew on deck and addressed them. "I don't know what sort of discipline you have had on board this cutter. It may be a new idea to you that you should obey orders. It is certainly a new idea to some of you that you should speak the truth. What I want you to know and remember is that your chance of making prize-money depends upon doing exactly what you are told. I'll not inquire further into Williams' errand ashore. But I'll have no more of it. You have your duty to do and I have mine. Set an anchor watch, Mr Lane. The remainder can turn in. We shall sail before first light."

Delancey was uncertain, in fact, what punishment (if any) he could inflict. In any case, it was better to make little of Williams' offence. It meant nothing in all likelihood (some tobacco, perhaps, or a girl) but, supposing the worst, it would be better to lull Williams into a false sense of security. There was nothing against him as yet and what information, anyway, had he to sell? He could warn Carter that the *Rose* had a new fire-eating skipper from the navy but that was nothing in itself. What would the average naval lieutenant know about free-trading? Thinking on these lines, Delancey realized, almost with a shock, that he was *not* an average lieutenant. He had begun to expect more of himself than of anyone else. In what way? After a fresh effort he decided that most men would think that a certain amount of effort, whether physical or mental, was "good enough." The question he was learning to ask was different. "Could anything *more* have been done? Could anything more be done *now?*" Well, what was the answer? It was obvious as soon as the question was asked. Something should be done to put Sam Carter off his guard. How? Why, to tell him that the *Rose* would be off Beachy Head on Thursday and Friday. Make that known in Portsmouth on the day before the *Dove* was to sail from Poole? There was not time enough, and, anyway, the *Dove* must have sailed already for Alderney. . . . Delancey unrolled the chart and began to make calculations on an odd piece of paper, placing the tide-table at his elbow. Then he tore them up, realizing that he had forgotten the central fact that the *Dove* would sail after dark. Beginning again, he guessed that she would reach Alderney on Tuesday in daylight, spend the next day in shipping her cargo, sail at about nightfall on Wednesday and arrive off Sandown Bay on——But that was all too late! Sam was to visit Molly on Thursday or Friday, which meant that he had to unload his cargo near Poole on Wednesday night after calling, earlier at Sandown Bay. This meant sailing from Poole on Sunday (yesterday) rather than today. . . . Any scheme of deception would have to wait until another time. There was nothing to be done now.

Further calculations were interrupted by the arrival of Mr Lane and Mr Torrin to join him for supper. He realized now that a cutter's commander could not live alone like the captain of a man-of-war. If this was an unwelcome discovery it was softened by the realization that the food would be fresh, with bread instead of hard tack and beer instead of grog. The meal was simple but Delancey was able to offer his mates a glass of wine to follow. They drank the King's health and "Success to the *Rose!*" and then settled down to a discussion about the cutter's sail-plan, rig and armament. One fact which soon emerged was that the crew never had target practice. No allowance was made for it by the Treasury so that gun-drill, performed at least weekly, stopped short of actually firing. Delancey was shocked by this discovery, which seemed to put the revenue men at an appalling disadvantage. Mr Lane disputed this, arguing that smugglers would be still less likely to spend powder and shot on a mere exercise. Noise was the last thing they wanted.

"Aside from that," said Mr Torrin, "these smugglers of today are not like the men who made up the Hawkhurst Gang a lifetime back. They don't commit murder for the pleasure of killing. They don't fight at all if they can avoid it. Like the rest of us, they just want to make money. So we don't expect battle and murder, not in the ordinary way. It is wartime, we know, and there's the chance that we might fall in with a French privateer. That's how we lost Mr Buckley: there was no call for him to go after her the way he did. But he was always a fighter was Mr Buckley and never counted the odds against him." Anecdotes were told about other revenue craft but Delancey brought the conversation back to the subject of target practice.

"We can fire warning shots, surely, ahead of any craft we suspect?"

"Yes," said Mr Lane, "but the guns are not usually shotted."

"But they are sometimes, then? I can log it so as to account for the powder and shot?"

"Well, I have known that done and no questions asked."

"Good. I can foresee some gunfire tomorrow. I have changed my mind, however, about sailing during the morning watch. On second thought I had rather we were seen to be heading eastwards."

"Why would that be an advantage?" asked Mr Torrin.

"Because our doubling back might come as more of a surprise."

Not another word would Delancey say on the subject but the word went round that the skipper was up to something. He might be a taut hand and it seemed most likely that he was. No one would care about that, however, if only they made a capture or two. Like their opponents, the revenue men were chiefly after money.

Chapter Seven

WINGS OF THE DOVE

"FIRE!" said Delancey and the *Rose's* starboard bow-chaser sent a nine-pounder shot hurtling toward the floating barrel that was its target. The shot went wide and Delancey pointed to the port bow-chaser and ordered "Fire!" There was another miss, short and wide, and Mr Lane was told to close the range. It was a brilliantly sunny morning, cold but exhilarating, with startled seabirds circling overhead. The standard of marksmanship was appalling and the fishing boats huddled between the *Rose* and the Sussex coast had every cause for alarm. The mere fact that they were not the target was no proof, in itself, that they were safe. They would have felt no happier had they known that they were being described in the cutter's log as suspect vessels which refused to heave-to until shots had been fired across their bows. They had been identified as Shoreham craft on their lawful occasions but they had given Delancey the excuse he needed. The target barrel being unscathed, he sailed closer so as to exercise his men with small arms. This manoeuvre brought him even closer to the fishing vessels whose nets were down and for whom escape was thus impossible. Had one of these craft been captained by a man with a guilty conscience, he might have seen the *Rose's* behaviour as an elaborate manoeuvre designed to take him by surprise.

It so happened, that one vessel among the group in sight was, in fact, captained by just such a man with just such a sense of guilt. His three-masted lugger had hidden among the others, always with another craft between her and the *Rose*. His nerve finally gave way and he ordered his men to make all sail. He fled eastward with a southerly breeze and Delancey ordered an immediate pursuit. Lane went forward with a spyglass and Delancey joined him in the bows.

"Aye," said Lane finally, "that's the *Four Brothers* out of Shoreham, commanded by Jonathan Battersby. The moonshine must be on board or he wouldn't have run like that. He meant to land it at Rottingdean, seemingly, and was waiting for dark."

"Are we fast enough to catch him?"

"Not with the wind a-beam, sir. We'll barely hold our own. Before the wind we can do better with the square mainsail and topsail, having a bigger spread of canvas than he has. We'd come up with him, sir, if the wind veered again."

"It's more likely to back. With an east wind we might trap him against the land."

"You mean, sir, that he couldn't round Beachy Head on this tack?"

"That's our best hope, Mr Lane."

As the chase continued the breeze backed more easterly and both craft, pursuer and pursued, came as close as possible to the wind. They were about a mile apart and the distance between them was tending, if anything, to lengthen. By the afternoon Beachy Head could be seen and with it the last chance, probably, of making a capture. This wind was south-easterly and backing still, the lugger's sails flapping as she tried to hold her course. At last the moment came when she was fairly taken aback while the *Rose* further seawards held her wind and was beginning to close the range. To tack would have brought the lugger across her pursuer's bows, a good target for gunfire. Rather than do that, the *Four Brothers* went clean about, turning towards the land, and headed due west with the wind nearly abaft. The *Rose* lost ground in following suit and lost more still in setting her square mainsail. Delancey knew that he should set the square topsail as well but felt that there was no time for that. He steered a converging course under square mainsail and gaff topsail and was glad to see that Lane was right. Before the wind his was the faster vessel and there was soon less than half a mile between them. Delancey ordered his men to man the bow-chasers and the starboard battery. If only their standard of gunnery were higher!

They were actually within range now but Delancey thought that the target was still too distant for the gun-crews he had. Nor did he want to damage a vessel he already classed as a prize.

Suddenly the lugger tacked, heading eastwards again, and came within easy range while doing so. The *Rose* came foaming down on her prey and Delancey dared not tack while the range was lessening.

"Look, sir!" said Torrin, "She's putting her cargo over the side!" He handed the telescope to Delancey, who saw in a flash what was happening. He was also faced with the need to make an instant decision. If he held his course he would recover the cargo, which seemed to be floating. If he tacked he might catch the smuggler but with no material proof by then that he had been smuggling. His one chance of securing both criminal and cargo was to cripple the lugger before she could escape. He altered course slightly so as to bring his broadside to bear and then ordered Torrin to open fire. "Aim high!" he shouted. "Bring a mast down!" The idea was sound but the chances of success were remote. Range and bearing were altering quickly, the sea was lively and the aim indifferent. The first scattered broadside produced holes in the lugger's sails and one or two shrouds gone. There were six guns to fire and the next broadside was hardly more effective although three guns were aimed by Torrin and the other three by Delancey himself. This time the lugger's mizen sail was fairly riddled but without more than trifling damage to the mast. The range had lengthened before they could fire again and the action ended with some last ineffective shots from the bow-chasers. As the floating kegs were recovered—the revenue men were expert in this—the *Four Brothers* disappeared round Beachy Head. Delancey's prey had escaped him.

"Begging your pardon, sir," said Lane, "You were quite right to prefer the brandy to the lugger. This way we've got something. T'other way we should have had nothing." Delancey did not encourage comment of this sort but he could not resist asking the question which worried him.

"Why didn't they fire back?"

"What good would it have done?" asked Lane. "The game was over. To cripple us would have made no difference—we couldn't continue the chase, not with this lot to pick up, and it would have done us no good if we had."

"But what if we had fired into them?"

"They'd have had to reply so as to confuse our aim. As things were there was nobody hurt, which is just as well. They'll have made no profit on this voyage, though, and we now have something to share."

"Well done, sir!" said Torrin, coming up in his turn. "The men are all asking how you knew that the lugger was there?"

Delancey decided that his reputation would grow more rapidly if they continued to wonder. "I was not born yesterday, Mr Torrin."

Within minutes of hauling the last keg on board Delancey set a course of south sou'-west by west and explained that he meant to visit Sandown Bay before sunset. With this wind they should make it easily, keeping well away from the English coast. "It may be supposed in Hampshire that we are still off Beachy Head."

Late that afternoon the *Rose* completed her sixty mile run before the wind and finally brought to and dropped anchor off Shanklin. She was right over a sandbank called Shanklin Chine and the *Rose's* crew, mystified already, were still more surprised when their eccentric commander set another barrel afloat and announced a competition between the two bow-chasers. Each would have one shot at two hundred yards and the winning crew would have a prize. Neither crew scored a hit and Delancey himself then aimed the starboard gun and shattered the target into drifting firewood. Apparently satisfied by this result, Delancey took a few bearings with his sextant and (half an hour later) made sail again to the westward, setting a course to round Portland Bill. Next day he was off Lyme Regis and Bridport and cruising slowly along the Chesil Bank. That evening, Wednesday, he set a course for St Catherine's Point from St Alban's Head. The wind was westerly again and warmer, the night was dark but clear, with starlight enough to distinguish the Needles.

Delancey paced the deck, wondering whether his calculations had been correct. If they were, Sam Carter's lugger, the *Dove*, was simultaneously heading for Sandown Bay. If Madden had responded to Delancey's suggestion, the *Rapid* was closing in from the eastward, placing the *Dove* in a trap. But what if the calculation were wrong? It all rested upon his discovery that Molly Brown was not available on the coming Thursday and Friday. He had assumed that those days were kept for Sam Carter, Thursday as the day after the run and Friday in case the run were delayed. He had next assumed that cargo would be sunk in Sandown Bay well before midnight on Wednesday so that the main consignment could be delivered at Poole in the small hours. It would not be Poole itself, he knew, but some creek adjacent (and there were any number of these, to judge from the chart). That would not affect the timing, however. The weakness of his plan derived rather from the bold guesses on which it was based. What if Molly kept Thursday for somebody else? What if Sam Carter varied the pattern by going to Poole first and to Sandown Bay afterwards? What if he had taken alarm from hearing of the *Rose's* activity? There were a score of ways in which the *Rose's* commander could be made to look foolish. In one respect he had been sensible, though— he had told nothing of his plans to Lane or Torrin. His attempt might fail without his crew knowing what had been attempted. There was some consolation in that. . . . Slowly and quietly the *Rose* was approaching Sandown Bay. She was cleared for action with guns loaded and run out. There were flares ready to light when the moment came.

"There's a craft at anchor off Shanklin, sir." It was Torrin's voice, hoarse with excitement, and Delancey sighed with relief. Perhaps the gamble had come off after all! He could at first see nothing himself but there were lights ashore in the village and they were disappearing in turn as the bearing altered. There was a dark shape between the land and the silent watchers in the revenue cutter. Higher than the lights of the village were some scattered lights further inland and further to the east. Four of these glowed red and Torrin, pointing this out, could not imagine why.

"Looks like some form of signal, sir. It's also strange that a craft should lie at anchor just there—far to the south of the usual anchorage. She is very near the place where we were at target practice only yesterday."

Delancey agreed that this was indeed an odd circumstance. He then lowered the *Rose*'s sails and allowed her to drift, waiting to see what the other vessel would do. At last came the unmistakable sounds of a vessel being pulled up to her anchor. She was about to sail and the *Rose* had crept up, unnoticed, to a point within half a mile. The time had come to identify the stranger, which was done by lighting a blue flare. By its light every detail was visible for a split second. It was enough, for Lane at once called from the bows that the craft making sail was the *Dove* of Poole.

She steered away to the east and south and the *Rose* followed on her best point of sailing. Following the trend of the land, the *Dove* then headed for the area where the *Rapid* should be waiting for her. Delancey lighted flare after flare so that Madden could see the *Dove*'s silhouette. At last he was answered by another flare to the north and knew that the smuggler was fairly trapped between two cutters and the land. She stood in for Bembridge under easy sail and finally hove to while *Rose* and *Rapid* closed in on their prey. After a minute's hesitation Delancey put on his naval uniform before rowing over in the gig, taking Torrin with him and ordering Lane to keep the lugger covered by the *Rose*'s broadside. He should, strictly speaking, have sent Lane and remained on board himself but he wanted to see the *Dove* and also her captain. There were a number of lanterns lit and he was able to see both.

Sam Carter welcomed them aboard the *Dove* with elaborate irony. He was short and stout with greying hair, a soft voice and just a trace of a Cornish accent.

"Good evening to you, Mr Torrin. I hope I see you well? And this is your new captain? Glad to make your acquaintance, sir! I did not know that we were to be honoured by the sight of the King's uniform. Captain Delancey, is it? Your servant, sir. Perhaps you would care to join me in the cabin? Mr Torrin, I fancy, has business in the hold. Why not leave him to his rummage while we have a glass of toddy? This way, Captain, and mind your head as we go below. In this lugger we have little headroom between decks."

The cabin was small but clean and tidy. There were glasses on the table with lemons, sugar, a brandy flask and a steaming jug. Delancey was offered a chair and his host did the honours with smooth formality.

"When pouring I have to remember that this liquor is above proof; purchased, of course, at the Custom House auction. Use the sugar-crusher, sir. . . . A little lemon? Now, for a toast. . . . Shall we drink to the recovery of Captain Ryder?"

Delancey barely sipped the drink but looked about him with interest. This was not the pirate ship of any ballad or story. It was all too depressingly normal.

"I was greatly relieved," Carter went on, "when I recognized the *Rose*. My fear was at first that you were a French privateer. That's why I tried to escape. You will think me foolish, perhaps? I *am* a little nervous, I must confess, but I have been fired on too often and sometimes in error. Yes, sir, I almost took you for the enemy."

"So you were naturally relieved to find yourself among friends and neighbours. I assume that Mr Torrin will find nothing?"

"We sailed, alas, in ballast."

"From Alderney?"

"From Alderney, yes. I had hoped for a cargo of seaweed there but was disappointed."

"*Seaweed?*"

"Yes. It is of value, I am told, to farmers."

"Including those round Sandown Bay?"

"No, I called at that place on an errand of mercy. A friend of mine there was worried about the health of his father, who lives in Alderney.

I was able to assure him, in a written note, that the old man is on his way to recovery."

"So you are bound now for Poole?"

"No, for Cowes."

"And so back to Alderney, perhaps?"

"That depends upon what cargo I am offered."

"No doubt. Allow me to propose a toast in my turn. To the *Dove!* May she and her crew have all the good fortune they deserve!"

"To the *Dove!* I can certainly drink to that. And some better fortune would be welcome, for the present voyage will have earned us little."

"I am sorry indeed to hear it and sorrier to suspect that it may, for all I know, have earned you nothing."

"Don't say that, sir. I may at least have earned the gratitude of my friend in the Isle of Wight."

"A thought which does you credit, Captain. And here, I think, comes Mr Torrin." There was a clatter on the companionway and Torrin joined them, accepting a glass of toddy and apologising for having given so much trouble. He reported to Delancey that the *Dove's* hold was empty.

"You will understand, sir, that I have to do my duty," he concluded, "even when the vessel is well known to us."

Carter protested that there were no ill feelings and called in his chief mate to join them. He turned out to be a slight dark man called Evans, who said very little. Then the party broke up, Torrin draining his tumbler but Delancey leaving his glass almost untasted on the cabin table. As they went on deck Carter said that he hoped they would meet again—ashore, perhaps, in Cowes.

Oddly enough, Delancey had the feeling that the invitation might have been genuine. Carter was a man for whom he had a certain instinctive liking and he felt that the liking was returned. Delancey had won the first game but this was partly because he had unexpectedly replaced a bad player, taking up the cards before his own skill had been assessed and looking privily at his opponents' cards before they even knew that he was playing. All that advantage of surprise had now gone. The next game would be on more equal terms and Delancey remembered what Mr Payne had said—that he would never succeed in bringing Sam Carter to justice.

Next morning the *Rose* was back in Sandown Bay. After taking repeated and careful bearings with the sextant, Delancey brought the cutter to anchor at a point on Shanklin Chine, the very place where the *Dove* had first been sighted the night before. "Lower the boats, Mr Lane, and search the bottom with grapnels." At this point, however, the patient chief mate felt bound to protest.

"Beg pardon, sir, but what's the good? The boatmen will have come out from Sandown while we were chasing the *Dove*. They will have done their creeping while we were off Bembridge." Delancey felt the implied rebuke in this. Following Lane's principle, he should have gone after the consignment of brandy and let the lugger go. After all, she would have jettisoned the rest of her cargo before she could be over-taken. This was what had happened and heads were being shaken in the forecastle over a navy man's ignorance.

Delancey was adamant, however. "Make a careful search, never-theless. You'll find bottom in about six fathoms."

There followed an hour or so of tedious search, the boats rowing back and forth and the seamen muttering about the futility of it all. They were kept at it, nevertheless, and the mates were quick to notice any slackening of effort. Then there came a shout from one of the boats. "Grapnels caught on something!" There was much heaving and curs-ing, the guess being that they had hooked an old anchor, but Delancey told them to row to the cutter and pass their line on board. From this steadier platform, with the capstan to help, the line was pulled in and the first keg came in sight. There was a cheer from the boats and the other kegs appeared, one after another, roped together with stone weights in between each. They were hauled on board to the number of forty. That completed the chain and ended the search. The boats were hoisted in, the anchor broken out and a course set for the

Needles and so back to base. So far Delancey's reputation was made.

Over dinner in the cabin Lane and Torrin expressed their surprise along with their congratulations. "Can't understand it, sir," said Lane. "The Sandown gang had all night to find that lot, and there it was in the morning!"

"Perhaps they looked in the wrong place," said Delancey innocently, intent on his meal.

"But the place must have been arranged beforehand. They fix it by bearings taken in daylight and then place lanterns on shore at night which give a cross-bearing on the very spot. It is merely a question of cruising around until the lights are in line, two and two. A child could do it and these are men who have done little else for years."

"How very disappointing for them," said Delancey. "The pea-soup is excellent."

"But we saw the lanterns, sir!" protested Torrin. "They even had red lights to avoid confusion with lamps or candles in the cottage windows."

"It would change the situation, of course," said Delancey thought-fully, "if someone had shifted the lights."

"But who could have done that?"

"Well, you never know. The idea might have occurred to my friend, Mr Edgell."

"The riding officer? But how would he have known where to place them?"

"Let's suppose that he had taken his dog out one afternoon and was on the hillside behind Shanklin. From there to his surprise he would see the *Rose* in Sandown Bay. When she fired three guns—almost for all the world as if it had been a signal—he could (with the help of a friend) knock in four white pegs which would be visible in the dark."

"God almighty!" said Torrin, "and all he and his friends had to do last night was to shift the lanterns from where they were to where he had driven in his pegs!"

"He could have done that," admitted Delancey, "supposing that he was out for a walk after dark. He goes out sometimes, I am told, when unable to sleep. It must be very annoying for his wife."

There can be no doubt that Delancey enjoyed this little scene, which clinched his reputation in the revenue service. But he despised himself afterwards for playing to the gallery. How easy it was to win the hero worship of these simple men! He had merely played the few cards he had in his hand and they thought him a magician. It would not be so easy another time. He reminded himself savagely that his proper career was in the navy and that his real opponents were the French. He had antagonists there of a very different calibre, as ruthless as they were cunning. His war with the smugglers was a mere game, a mental exercise. In fighting the French, by contrast, he would be fighting for his life. The whole atmosphere of war was changing. There had been a time when there was a sense of chivalry. He could remember talking with officers during the last war—or, rather, listening to them—who thought of the French as worthy opponents, as gentlemen who happened to be on the other side. Old Lord Howe must have been chivalrous towards the enemy in those days and Lord Rodney perhaps still more so. Even Sir Edward Pellow was inclined that way, it was said, but there were younger men now who thought differently. Theirs was becoming a war to the death. One could not reason with revolutionaries. One could not plan to be friends with them when war was over. They were men who had to be killed. These smugglers were almost innocent by comparison, offenders merely against the law. More than that, they were probably patriots in the last resort. A man like Sam Carter would never be an actual traitor. There would be small satisfaction in having him thrown into jail. He would some day be wanted, rather in the navy, where he would be promoted master's mate on joining and given a commission, perhaps, within a year. Sam was a man to have on one's own side.

Pacing the cutter's deck, with few paces to go in either direction, Delancey took himself to task for his complacency. How easy it was to become over-confident after even the smallest success! He was already

in a chastened mood when he went ashore at Cowes and almost dif-
fident when he made his report on Friday to the collector.

"You have done well," said Mr Payne finally. "I think you are to be
highly commended for your activity and enterprise. What do you plan
to do next?"

"I had thought, sir, of paying a visit to Poole."

"I see. . . . Perhaps I should tell you, in that case, that there was
recently an incident which has given me cause for concern. A smuggler arrested here last month had on him (I cannot think why) a letter
addressed by one Mr James Weston to Mr John Early. Early's name is
known to all but there is no Mr Weston in this vicinity. On the other
hand, the handwriting of the letter is a little like that of Mr Elisha
Withers, the comptroller at Poole. The letter contained detailed information about the military forces stationed in Dorset for the suppression
of illicit trade. It may be that there is some explanation of this. Mr
Withers might be able to explain how he came to write such an impru-
dent letter—if indeed he did so. In the meantime, be on your guard.
Even the Custom House at Poole may not be on your side. The collector there, Mr Edward Rogers, is a friend of mine but too old, I fear,
for the work. I suspect that he must leave things to others."

"Thank you, sir, for the warning. If the smugglers have their spies
and informers, even within the revenue service, it is unfortunate that
we seem to have no agents working within the smugglers' organiza-
tion. One spy well placed, a man of great ability, would be worth fifty
tidewaiters and riding officers. Given a secret service we might yet have
Mr Early facing his trial at the Assizes."

"We have informers, sometimes. They come to us after there has
been a quarrel among the smugglers themselves. There is jealousy over
the leadership, perhaps, or over a woman. But these informers are the
least intelligent of the gang and their lives are apt to be brief. For setting up a proper intelligence system we lack the money. The smugglers
are engaged in a business which is highly lucrative, so much so that
the loss to the revenue has been computed as amounting to no less

than two hundred thousand pounds a year. Out of that sum a mere one per centum would give them enough to corrupt men highly placed. The rewards *we* can offer are trifling by comparison. We shall not bring John Early to justice and if we did, his place would be taken by someone else. No, Mr Delancey, the man I should like to expose is the traitor to our own service; the man, whoever he is, who is working against us at Poole."

Delancey came away from this interview with the idea in his mind that smugglers and revenue officers must come to resemble each other in the process of conflict. If the moonrakers murdered anyone it would be one of their own number, the traitor to the gang. And the revenue men were as cool about the business, angry only at the thought of betrayal by a brother officer of the service. Mr Payne had been only mildly interested in Delancey's success. His first sign of emotion was over the thought of a possible treachery. Was his concern, even then, over another official gaining, by devious means, a higher income than his own? Delancey put that thought from him but decided to abandon any plan that would be too ambitious. To bring all local smuggling to a standstill was out of the question and apparently undesirable; the revenue officers had their livings to earn. To make an example of John Early—the spider at the centre of the Dorset web—was similarly out of the question. There was no money to pay that sort of informer.

The *Rose* was in need of some minor repairs, enough to keep her in port for two days. So Delancey resolved to revisit the Rose and Crown but this time in uniform. All talk died away as he entered the tap-room but the silence was broken by Sam Carter who greeted him in the friendliest fashion.

"Welcome aboard, Captain! I hoped to see you here while we were both in port. I hear that the *Rose* needs a new topsail yard and a new port lid for the starboard bow-chaser. Allow me to stand you the toddy you failed to finish when last we met—nay, sir, I insist! George—one of my usual for the captain here, and pour it while we watch. No short measure for the revenue service!"

The pot-man obeyed orders and Delancey could see that nothing was added. He thanked Sam and proposed a toast to the king. "God bless him!" said Carter, raising his glass without reluctance. "I should like you to meet some friends of mine—Mr Henry Stevens, Mr Will Grubb and—come over here, Dan—Mr Daniel Palmer." Dan emerged unsteadily from a corner of the room and said he was proud to make the captain's acquaintance. He looked puzzled, however, and said finally, "Haven't we met before?" "Very likely," said Delancey. "Were you ever a preventive man?" This question produced a roar of laughter. No one else recognised Delancey and the party was resumed, with a certain restraint.

"You hurt my feelings, Captain," said Sam, "when you wouldn't touch the toddy I offered you."

"I didn't know you then, Captain."

"I'll lay you didn't. We are up to all sorts of tricks in this game but I wouldn't play that one."

"Why not?"

"Why, because I have to meet you again. Here we are at Cowes. Next week it may be St Peter Port or Lyme Regis. How would it be if I couldn't look you in the eye?"

"So we play fair?"

"Why shouldn't we? We know the rules and there need be no hard feelings—not even when someone shifts a few lanterns."

"Fair it shall be; and it's for me to call the next round. George! Same again. But there's a question I'd like to ask. You drank the king's health just now. Would you have drunk the health of Robespierre? I mean, while he was alive?"

"Robespierre? No, not I. My trade depends upon the French, mind you—that can't be gainsaid. There's no fetching brandy from anywhere else but France. So I know the French coast from here to the Spanish border and have friends in every port—all in the way of business, mind you. But it's our fleet I'm backing against theirs. I want to see the

Frenchies beat! What's more, I've fought against them and would do so again."

"Were you ever in the navy, then?"

"Not me! But I'll tell you a story—one these other men have never heard. I once came upon a revenue cutter in action with two French privateers. Off Jersey it was, back in '82. Well, the cutter was in bad shape and would soon have had to strike her colours. Seeing that, I sailed in with the old *Falcon*—that was the craft I commanded then— and beat off the Frenchies. They sailed back to St Malo with their tails between their legs and glad I was to see them go. Well, that was long ago, before the revolution—but I'd do the same today. I don't like to see our enemies getting the best of it."

The evening went well after that and Carter eventually proposed that they should go on to the Pig and Whistle. Delancey drew the line at this but walked with Sam in that direction. The rest of the gang stayed where they were for the time being and Delancey, having said goodnight, doubled back to the Rose and Crown. The place was noisier now and some old man-of-war's man was singing a song of which Delancey could distinguish the words:

> Smiling grog is the sailor's sheet anchor,
> His compass, his cable, his log.
> Though dangers around him
> Unite to confound him
> He braves them and tips off his grog.
> 'Tis grog, only grog is his rudder,
> His compass, his cable, his log.
> The sailor's sheet anchor is grog.

There was loud laughter following this (perhaps the singer had fallen off the table) but the last verse was sung by everybody.

> What though his girl who often swore
> To know no other charms

He finds when he returns ashore
Clasp'd in a rival's arms?
What's to be done? He vents a curse
And seeks a kinder she,
Dances, gets groggy, clears his purse
And goes again to sea.

Delancey entered the tap-room unnoticed and stood near the door. The singer, as he had guessed, was a man-of-war's man; not a prime seaman, he guessed, but a character in his own right who could hold the attention of the room. All eyes were fixed on the singer and Delancey was able to observe without being seen. Harry and Will and Dan were in a group round a table with two others known to Delancey by sight, but they had been joined by one more—yes, by Mike Williams of the *Rose!* There was no mistaking the man and no question that he was a friend of the others. He was sitting next to Dan and resumed conversation with him as soon as the song ended and the applause died away. There was undoubtedly something furtive about his manner. There was no reason, of course, why he should not be there. He had leave to go ashore, like the rest of his watch, and there was no law to forbid his frequenting that particular ale-house. There was no reason why he should not talk to Dan—after all, they were related. But there was something odd about the meeting for all that and "furtive" was the only word to describe it. Delancey went out again, closing the door quietly, and was sure that no one had even looked in his direction. He walked back to the quayside, hailed the *Rose* where she lay at anchor and was rowed out to her. All was in good order aboard and there was a man on duty as anchor watch. Delancey went below where he found Torrin reading a news-sheet.

"There's been rough weather down at Plymouth, sir. The *Falcon* revenue cutter was all but wrecked on the west mud but Fraser got her off and she's now in dock."

"Is that all the day's news?"

"There's little else."

"Tell me then, did Mr Ryder issue any positive order to the crew about avoiding the Rose and Crown?"

"No, sir. He let it be known that it was a place to avoid and they all took the hint. They mostly go to the Worsley Arms where the landlord is an old preventive man."

"Very right too. Has the new topsail yard arrived?"

"It's on the deck, sir. We'll sway it up in the morning."

"I'll turn in then. Goodnight."

The *Rose* had her full complement next day but some men of the starboard watch were something the worse for wear, Williams especially so. Delancey spoke to him sharply and asked where he had been the night before.

"At the Worsley Arms, sir."

"Nowhere else?"

"Oh no, sir, I was with my mates."

"Try to keep sober next time."

"Aye, aye, sir."

Delancey was now virtually certain that Williams was in the smugglers' pay, but what information had he to give them?

He knew nothing of importance, so what had he to sell? Delancey realised that he now had the chance to give the local gang (and through them, Sam Carter) such false information as might suit his own plan. What was his plan to be?

Delancey had one more day to spend in Cowes and he used the afternoon to renew his acquaintance with Isaac Hartley. He called at Isaac's shop, where business was still far from brisk, and explained that he had been guilty of an innocent deception. He was the temporary commander of the *Rose* and had needed information about the local gang of moonrakers. The result had been a minor success, the *Dove* losing a cargo, of which part had been found and confiscated.

"I heard about that," said Isaac, "and I wondered who had given the revenue men the tip. So you were the thief-taker, as you might say, and you made me the informer! Do you understand the danger that now hangs over me? The gang will think that I have gone back on my word and informed against them! I was merely showing Christian kindness to a starving fellow creature, as I thought, and a man who had seen the light. If my Hannah is a widow before the week ends it will be your doing, Mr Delancey—and God forgive you!"

"I must confess, Mr Hartley, that I am not, in your sense, one of the redeemed. I am merely an officer who tries to do his duty; and one of my duties is to protect anyone who has been of service to the Crown—knowingly or even otherwise."

"But this you *can't* do!" cried Isaac in great agitation. "You can't station a riding officer before my door! Do what you will the gang will murder me!"

"These petty criminals are not as ready as that to risk the gallows. I can assure Sam Carter that you have strictly kept your word. He will believe what I tell him and you will be safe."

"But is Sam a friend of yours? How can that be?"

"You can sleep soundly at night—after I have spoken to him."

"And you will?"

"Yes, I'll speak to Sam but I want you to help me first. There are two things I want to know—"

"Look, Mr Delancey, I have given my word. I'll not betray anyone. I'll name nobody. God knows I'm in danger enough as it is. Don't ask more of me!"

"I shan't ask you for a name. What I shall ask you concerns Poole, moreover, not the Isle of Wight. What I want to know, first, is this: have the Dorset smugglers a friend in the Poole Custom House— one of the officers under Mr Rogers? I don't ask his name. All I want to know is whether they have a man there who may help them on occasion."

"You will ask nothing more of me after this?"

"I shall ask only two questions, of which this is the first. I promise to ask nothing more."

"I have your word, remember. Well, then the answer is 'yes'—or at least I think so. I would not say that I know it as a fact but I have been told that there is such a man and have reason to believe that there is."

"Thank you, Mr Hartley. My other question is this: how often do the Poole smugglers make a run?"

"How should I know? It depends on the weather and the where-abouts of the preventive men. I daresay there are six or eight cargoes a month, most of them into Studland Bay, a favourite place when the tide serves. They prefer a spring tide and a moonless night and some of them won't work on Sundays."

"Thank you again, Mr Hartley. You can depend upon me keeping my part of the bargain. We had better not meet again—it will be safer for you if we don't."

Later that day Delancey was rowing out to the *Rose* in the six-oared boat. He told the coxswain to steer close to the *Dove* and, when within hail, told the men to rest on their oars. "Captain Carter!" he hailed. "May I come aboard?" A minute later Sam appeared and hailed back, "Come aboard, Captain." Within two minutes Delancey was once more on the lugger's deck.

"Surely you are not going to rummage us *again?*" asked Sam.

"No, I just want a word with you in private."

They walked together as far as the stern, out of earshot of the other men on deck.

"You will know by now that I made some inquiries here before any-one knew that I was to command the *Rose*."

"I heard about that when it was too late."

"Well, I had some conversation with Isaac Hartley and I have seen him again today."

"So I hear. Well?"

"I want you to know that he kept his word to his former friends. He would name nobody and I am sure that he never will. Nor do I expect to see him again."

"I'll take your word for it, and I'll see he comes to no harm. Some day I may ask as much of you."

"And you won't ask in vain."

They parted again in friendly fashion and the *Dove* sailed that evening, presumably for Alderney. The *Rose* was to sail next day for Poole and Delancey paced the deck thinking what tactics to pursue. He realized again how little he knew about smuggling and how much there was to know. What would happen if he cruised off Poole until the next run was due? The cargoes would then be landed (or would they?) at Lulworth or Christchurch. But how would they know where he was? Some signal would be made, no doubt, possibly from St Alban's head. There would be some point in the hills behind there from which there was a view seawards and as good a view, in the other direction, of Poole. The place might be found but the discovery would be useless unless the signal code were also discovered. For this an informer would be needed, and what chance was there of one being found? His only hope lay in using the enemy spies he now knew to be on his own side. Through them he might convey the idea that he was going to do one thing when his intention was to do the exact opposite.

And what, money apart, would have been achieved if he actually won the trick, or even the game? The only answer must be that he would have trained himself to meet more complex problems than would usually confront a junior officer. Some day he might have an independent command or another secret mission, with doubtful allies and a changing situation. He might have to weigh the chances, assess the value of conflicting information, guess at the enemy's plan and finally stake his reputation on a single decision. The war against smugglers might be trivial in itself but he could regard it as part of his education. Once more he found himself assuming that he was something better than the average, when all his past history pointed to his being rather worse. Was this assumption ridiculous? Here he was a half-pay lieutenant with no certainty—no likelihood, in fact—of ever being employed again; and he was thinking of tactical situations in which the final decision would lie with him. . . . Absurd! Going below and drawing up a chair to the cabin table, he placed a leather-bound volume before him and under the gently swinging lamp read:

> "In the first and golden years of the reign of Nero, that prince, from a desire of popularity, and perhaps from a blind impulse of benevolence, conceived a wish of abolishing the oppression of the customs and excise. The wisest senators applauded his magnanimity: but they diverted him from the execution of a design which would have dissolved the strength and resources of the republic. . . ."

If customs duties went as far back as that, they were not going to be abolished now! Mr Pitt, like another Trajan, had reduced them at one time but since had come war and the need to supply the strength of the republic. The duties must be collected, their evasion must be discouraged and it would fall to some men to do this unending and sad but necessary work. Delancey sighed for at the moment he was one of them and this was the duty he had to do.

Chapter Eight

MOONRAKERS OF POOLE

T HERE CAN BE no doubt that many of the Poole merchants were strictly honest but the topography of the harbour did nothing to make honesty inevitable. The proper and normal approach to Poole is by the Swash Channel, which lies between North Haven Point and Brownsea Island and curves westward between mudflats bringing the homeward bound ship to the quayside at Poole, which is still dominated, very properly, by the Custom House. Nothing could be more respectable than the old town of Poole, built in a warm red brick and centred upon the Market House which had been built in 1760 by the grateful Mr Joseph Gulston, elected then for the fourth time as Member of Parliament for the Town and County. From much the same period date the handsome town houses from which the shipowners went forth each day to business. Theirs was a profitable business, the cod they brought from Newfoundland being sold in Spain or Portugal, the return cargo comprising (among other things) wine. Many of the cargoes landed were dutiable and the collector's business was to see that the duties were paid. This was Poole as seen from the Custom House windows. But Poole Harbour could be looked at from another point of view. It was and is a complex of channels and creeks, accessible to small craft manned by men with local knowledge. A vessel which happened to enter the harbour at night could turn aside from the main channel and enter the South Deep on the flood, unloading illegally at Goathorn Point or Green Island. Another, more daring, might enter the Wych Channel and land her cargo on the north shore of Brownsea Island. Good use could also be made of Studland Bay or Swanage, Lulworth Cove or Ringstead. Brownsea Island actually stands between Studland Bay and Poole, rising high enough to screen the activities which might surround a vessel in the South Deep. The professional smuggler, as opposed to the merchant skipper who occasionally yielded to temptation, found Poole Harbour almost ideal for his purpose, especially if he had set up a signal station on Nine Barrow Down. It would be wrong to say that the merchants of Poole were all engaged in smuggling but most of them knew what was going on. To have prevented it altogether, with the men available, was hardly feasible and would have been highly unpopular. The collector's policy had been to let well alone, making an occasional seizure but preferring to be ignorant of practices which were known to everyone else.

It was a fine day at the end of February when the *Rose* entered the Swash on the flood. There was an easterly breeze with a lively sea and the Needles were clearly visible in the sunlight. Delancey took his cutter up the main channel and finally laid her alongside the quay at Poole. He went ashore and reported his arrival at the Custom House. The collector was not there, being said to be unwell, but the comptroller received him politely and congratulated him on the *Rose's* recent success. Mr Elisha Withers, a red-faced convivial man, evidently addicted to the bottle, was assisted by Mr George Miller, a more sober and abstemious character, who was present throughout the interview. Miller was small and thin with a sharp nose and a continual sniff, saying little but noticing everything down to and including Delancey's cheap shoe buckles. On him, as the deputy comptroller, the work of the office had mostly fallen, Mr Withers being ineffective and the collector, Mr Rogers, being seldom there. Delancey came straight to the point by asking whether Samuel Carter was known to the Customs officers.

"Carter?" said Withers. "Carter? Yes, to be sure. He trades between here and the Channel Islands. His lugger, the *Dove,* is registered here at Poole and he lives, when ashore, at the old George Inn or rather in a building behind it which belongs to John Scaplen. Do you want to see him?"

"No, sir. I believe, however, that he is a smuggler."

"Samuel Carter? Surely not! No case has ever been brought against him."

"Would you say, then, that this port is free from illicit traffic?"

"Not entirely free," replied Withers reluctantly. "But the trade is on a very small scale as compared with that which persists, say, in Sussex. Did you hear that a hundred and fifty smugglers were caught the other day by the Newhaven riding officers and the crew of the Seaford boat? *A hundred and fifty!* We have nothing like that round Poole. A few kegs are landed sometimes by fishermen but they soon give themselves away. Our merchants are all known to us personally and have a good reputation in the County. Men in a sufficiently big way of business will scorn to save money through petty evasions of the law. Many of them, moreover, have held office as sheriff or mayor."

"I am glad to hear it," said Delancey, "but I have reason to believe that the *Dove* is being laden with contraband at this moment and that the run will take place in a few days' time."

"Where?" asked Miller, speaking for the first time.

"At Lulworth Cove, I have been told."

"You may have been misled," said Withers. "The real culprit (if there is one) may be another man, landing his cargo at some other place."

"That I accept. Should you have any better intelligence I shall be glad to act upon it."

"No, we have heard nothing," replied Withers. "And Carter's name has never been mentioned to us in this connection."

"In that event, sir, the *Rose* will appear off Lulworth Cove at the proper time. I have to request that a troop of cavalry should act in concert with me and I have further to request that you put out the story that I expect a run to be made in Studland Bay."

"A clever idea, Mr Delancey, but I think I can improve upon it. A ball is to take place tomorrow night at the Market House. I shall be glad to take you there as my guest. Among other gentlemen present there will be Captain Molyneux of the 4th Dragoons. You can talk with him there without anything being noticed. You can take the same opportunity to spread what story you like about your immediate plans. Your name is known and many will be eager to make your acquaintance."

Delancey accepted this invitation with inward dismay. He might, in other circumstances, have enjoyed the ball but he wondered whether he might not find himself unpopular. There could, he knew, be no better way of concerting measures with the cavalry—nor could there be a better company in which to plant a rumour. He would need his wits about him, though, and would be glad when the affair was over.

In the meanwhile he walked round Poole and made himself familiar with the place. His thoughts as he did so were tinged with anxiety. He had walked into the lion's den, planning the lion's discomfiture. Could he assume, however, that the lion would tamely await his first move? Was it not probable that Mr John Early, having heard of his activity, would move against him straight away? He put himself in Early's place and considered the courses that would be open to him. He could direct someone to force a quarrel on him and so prepare the way for a duel. He could provide Delancey with false intelligence. He could damage the *Rose* in a collision. He might pester Delancey with a lawsuit or bribe his seamen to mutiny. He could counter-attack in a dozen different ways but it was Delancey's guess that he would not be too drastic at first. It would not be his aim to declare a war to the death. All he wanted, surely, was for Delancey to accept the official theory that smuggling in Dorset was practically unknown.

It was while pondering the situation that Delancey nearly had a collision, not in the tideway but in the middle of the High Street. The young lady into whom he had nearly blundered uttered a little cry of dismay and dropped her parasol and gloves. With her other hand she clutched the arm of another and older woman, looking as alarmed as if Delancey had assaulted them both. He hastened to apologize and restore the parasol and gloves, seeking at the same time to find some excuse for his absence of mind. The young lady was quite attractive, a brunette in her early twenties, and he supposed the older woman to

be a housekeeper. He blamed himself for his clumsiness and hoped
that the young lady was unhurt. She forgave him prettily and admitted that she was as much to blame as he.

"I suspect, sir, that you are the naval officer in temporary command
of the *Rose*." Delancey introduced himself and learnt that the young
lady was Miss Louisa Hill. She was a little more forward than Delancey
expected, perhaps out of curiosity, and she quickly explained that she
had come from Dorchester to attend tomorrow's ball. Would Mr
Delancey be there? He replied untruthfully that he was looking forward to it and added some hint of his wish to see her again. She said
that she would keep a dance free for him but warned him not to be
jealous of her other beaux. She had a weakness, she admitted, for handsome men in naval or military uniform. She allowed Delancey to escort
her to her aunt's house, No 30 in the High Street, easily recognizable
by the door and the fanlight, both of a pattern which characterized the
taste of the previous reign.

After this encounter Delancey went on board the *Rose* and explained
the situation to Lane and Torrin. The *Dove* would attempt a run at
Studland Bay but the story to circulate was that the run would take
place in Lulworth Cove. Each officer would repeat this cover story, in
strict confidence, to one other person ashore. Going on deck after a
brief conference, Delancey spoke again about Lulworth Cove, this time
in the hearing of Mike Williams, but Lane reminded him of the need
for secrecy. He swore softly and moved out of earshot. If all went well,
the signal party would thus hear the same story from the Custom House
and from Williams, with other rumours perhaps to the same effect. The
Dove would be warned in time and would head towards Poole, there
to fall into the jaws of the *Rose*. Delancey was convinced by now that
the smugglers had an accomplice at the Custom House, but who was
it? Withers did not look the type and Rogers was evidently ailing and
old. Withers he had at first suspected because of the letter which had
been intercepted but Delancey now inclined to believe that it must
have been relatively innocent, mere gossip addressed to a local squire

whose respectable character was assumed. For present purposes it could be taken for granted that anything known to the Customs officers was soon passed on to the smugglers. When Sam Carter appeared off Durlston Head he would be advised by signal that the *Rose* was off Lulworth Cove and that Studland Bay was wide open. Thus would the trap be set.

Poring over the chart and tide-table, Delancey had now to decide on the precise date and hour. Carter was at Alderney or Guernsey. How long would it take him to ship his cargo? There were unknown factors here for the speed of loading would depend on the quayside labour available and that again on the number of other craft that might be there. But Carter's run would also require a high tide and a dark night. Weighing the different circumstances, Delancey decided that the likeliest date would be March the fourth and the probable hour would be between 1:00 and 3:00 A.M., allowing the *Dove* to be over the horizon again by daybreak. The ball was to be tomorrow, March the first, which would allow time for the cavalry to march; supposing, of course, that Molyneux was ready to cooperate. Delancey had a vague idea that horses were apt to go lame or have glanders and that cavalrymen hated to move at night.

He wondered again whether his guess was correct. Would not Sam Carter have made the same calculation, choosing the fourth as the best date—and then decided against it as the night when his run would be expected? Although this was a distinct possibility it would not pay to be too clever. Senior officers had warned him against it and he had come to see that cleverness must often frustrate itself. No, his plan was made, and he would adhere to it. The fourth should be the night and Studland Bay would be the place. If no smugglers appeared the same arrangements would be repeated on the fifth and sixth, the *Rose* to be out of sight in daylight. If and when the whole plan failed, Delancey would have to think of something else.

On the night of the ball Delancey dressed carefully and went ashore, calling as arranged at Mr Withers' house in Market Street. He was introduced to Mrs Withers, as also to Mrs Rogers, whose husband was still indisposed. He guessed that Mr Rogers had remarried late in life for the lady must have been his junior by many years. His hostess was nondescript and rather dull but Mrs Rogers was more lively and addicted, she said, to the whist table. Delancey was asked whether he knew many people of the neighbourhood and had to confess that he knew nobody. He then corrected himself and mentioned the name of Louisa Hill. "Ah—Mr John Early's niece!" said Mrs Rogers, "I heard she was in town but have not seen her yet. She is here for the ball, no doubt, and will be staying with her aunt, Mrs Waterford."

"You have wasted no time about it, Mr Delancey!" said Withers. "Miss Hill is much admired by the young men of this town. She is not Mr Early's niece, however, but a cousin, I understand, and rather a poor relation."

"She has no fortune," Mrs Rogers admitted. "And Mr Early has three sons and a daughter to provide for. But Louisa is a pretty and lively girl and quite a favourite with her aunt."

"Will Mr Early be at the ball himself?" asked Delancey but nobody seemed to know. He was a busy man, it seemed, and an active magistrate, and had small leisure for merely social occasions. He would be there, no doubt, if he could spare the time but he was the sort of man who would arrive late and leave soon. He owed his wealth to his enterprise rather than to his inheritance, and it was his business connections which brought him quite often to Poole.

When the party left the house and walked up the street Delancey was thinking quickly about the tactics he was to pursue. He had wondered what Mr Early's first move would be but he need wonder no longer. The meeting with Louisa Hill had been no accident, but what had she been told to do? To trick him into a quarrel with some other man, a known duellist and a dead shot with the pistol? Or was she merely to discover his plans or comment on his character? As regards his abilities as a tactician it was possible, though unlikely, that Sam Carter had already made a report. Delancey decided to assume that

Early knew little about him and that he could now be given the wrong impression.

"We have no Assembly rooms," Mr Withers was saying, "But the first floor of the Market House answers the purpose very well. The far end is screened off for the card-players and there is a platform for the musicians." Indeed the place was a scene of festivity. The curved steps which led up to the main doors were well lighted and there was a great bustle as the gentlefolk arrived. Urchins were earning pennies by opening carriage doors and bystanders were holding horses while the ladies alighted. Most of the town gentry arrived on foot like the Withers' party and such carriages as there were served the better to emphasise the consequence of their owners. From inside, as they ascended the steps, came the sound of music, suggestive of festivity and romance.

After cloaks had been shed and the room admired, the Withers introduced Delancey to a number of their friends. Some, like Mrs Rogers, moved at once towards the card-room. Delancey might have joined them but dared not, for fear of missing Captain Molyneux. He attached himself to a Mrs Hardcastle, a widow, whose sole concern was to watch over her young daughter for whom this ball was her very first. Delancey sat with this lady while Arabella danced and so had to listen to a mother's commentary on her child's popularity and appearance. "She is in very good looks tonight, don't you think? That blue gown suits her well and everyone must allow that she dances to perfection. The young man she is dancing with is Mr Samuels, junior partner in one of the merchant houses—one in a rather small way of business. He is rather plain too, though very well mannered, I daresay. You will see the difference, Mr Delancey, when she dances with Ensign Wadsworth, who holds a commission in the Yeomanry—a very fine young officer, almost elegant one might say and heir to a very pretty estate. Ah, the air now being played is one of Arabella's favourites. She is smiling you can see, and telling her partner that the air is one she likes. I have forgotten its name but I have heard her speak of it on many occasions. She is, I always say, a *natural* dancer. . . ."

This monologue left Delancey with the easy role of agreeing absent-mindedly from time to time while watching the new arrivals. He felt that he was excused from dancing—of which he had much to learn—by the fact that he was providing company for Mrs Hardcastle. It is true that she could as easily have addressed her remarks to the lady sitting on the other side of her. That would have compelled her, how-ever, to take her turn and listen to the other lady's comments on her own *two* daughters; which could reasonably have taken twice as long. Things were better as they were and Delancey ended with an enviably complete knowledge of Arabella's wardrobe and hair-style, her musical preferences and personal dislikes. His thoughts were interrupted by the arrival of a young officer in cavalry uniform. "This," he said to him-self, "is Captain Molyneux." This guess was quickly confirmed by Mrs Hardcastle who added that the captain was a very genteel young man, the younger son (she had been told) of a baronet and just the sort of dance partner that Arabella preferred. The uniform, she pointed out, did much to add to the elegance of his figure—did not Delancey agree?—although, she added belatedly, a naval uniform looked well, too; in, of course, a quieter style. She was sure that Captain Molyneux would ask Arabella to dance, and Mr Delancey would see then how well they suited each other.

Suit each other they might but Molyneux's first partner was not Arabella but Louisa Hill, who must have arrived at the same time. When the country dances ended Molyneux went to fetch some refresh-ment for Miss Hill. Excusing himself, Delancey went over to her and reminded her that they were already acquainted. After a few minutes of polite conversation he asked whether Mr Early was expected. "My uncle will be here later, I believe, Mr Delancey, but you won't see him on the floor. He's only interested in cards."

When Captain Molyneux returned, Louisa introduced him to Delancey with some pretty hesitation as to which was the senior. At that moment she was distracted by Mr Wadsworth asking her to dance and Delancey was able to ask Molyneux whether he could have a word with him in private. He explained quickly and quietly that he wanted help against a gang of smugglers. Where could they meet without being overheard?

"In ten minutes time at the Angel—on your right as you leave the ballroom." Saying this in a hurried whisper, Molyneux went on more loudly: "A pleasant occasion this, very. Some devilish pretty girls around, eh? Have you met Miss Hardcastle?"

They parted a minute or two later, moving in opposite directions, and Delancey brought a glass of negus to Mrs Hardcastle and then chatted with the Withers. He slipped out unnoticed when the dancing began again.

Over a glass of wine, Delancey explained the position to Molyneux. For a baronet's son the cavalryman was surprisingly businesslike. "Let's agree first on how we share what we capture. If the lugger is taken at sea, will you give us a quarter of the value of the cargo?"

"Agreed," said Delancey, "but if you find the cargo on the beach or inland, you should give us half. Remember, it is I who am providing the intelligence on which we act."

"I suppose that is fair," sighed Molyneux. "What about the lugger herself?"

"We'll give you a quarter if she falls to us and will accept a quarter if she falls to you—which is not very probable."

"Agreed—and I drink to our success! The fact is that I have been unlucky of late at cards. I am deucedly short of money and that's the truth. So you want me at Studland Bay on the night of the fourth, in two days' time?"

"The night after next, between midnight and four."

"Will one troop of dragoons be enough?"

"Quite enough. I don't suppose they will fight. The crew of the lugger number about twenty but only half of them will go ashore. The cargo handlers on land will number about 24, with as many pack-horses. That is no more than a guess."

"Ah! Will you agree that the pack-horses are ours?"

"Less a quarter—as with the lugger."

"Very well. You drive a hard bargain, though!"

"I too have been unlucky."

"Let's hope for better luck this time. Now I'll tell you what I mean to do. I've a troop of horse quartered at Wareham, about fifteen miles from Studland. It's rather under strength, with some horses lame, but I think that we can ride with about 22 in all."

"That should be quite sufficient. All depends, however, on our secrecy. I am letting it be known that the run is expected at Lulworth Cove. Would you be good enough to drop some hint of that to Miss Louisa Hill—in the strictest confidence?"

"Why Louisa?"

"She might mention it to her friends."

"Why not Cathy Neave in that case? She would tell everyone in the room."

"Then our plan would fail."

"Because the rumour would seem to have been planted? I see what you mean. Very well, then—a hint to Louisa but to nobody else. You seem to be a good hand at this sort of plot, Mr Delancey."

"If I might make the suggestion, you might consider leaving Wareham by the road which leads to Lulworth. . . ."

"That's a deuced clever notion. You mean through East Holme? It would add three miles to the distance but it might be worthwhile. I'll think it over. And now I think we should return to the ballroom before people begin to wonder about us."

The ball continued and Molyneux danced with Louisa. Delancey later did the same but the dance was new to him and the girl was glad to sit down again.

"I think, sir," she laughed, "that you are more used to the quarter-deck!" Delancey made his apologies, confessing that he had never been able to learn the steps.

"Never mind," she replied, "you'll know better what steps to take at Lulworth." These last words were uttered behind her fan as from one conspirator to another but Delancey merely looked bewildered. He had never so much as heard of the place. Was it the home, he asked, of some young lady—one he was expected to know? He begged Louisa to remember that he was almost a stranger in Dorset. She might have said something more but at that moment she caught sight of some new arrivals and exclaimed, "And here, at last, is my Uncle John! Come and meet him, Mr Delancey. He is a justice of the peace, you know, and quite as interested in smuggling as you can be!"

Delancey allowed himself to be led across the floor and presented to John Early. He was surprised to find him so little like a criminal in appearance. If he had once been an attorney, as Delancey had been told, he had lost all trace of professional character. He was tall, florid and elderly, very much the county magnate and just such a squire as might preside at any Petty Sessions. He looked Delancey over with benign patronage and asked him presently whether he played whist.

"Only for low stakes, sir."

"You must join me then for a friendly game after supper."

Delancey was uncertain whether this was more than a polite gesture but it was renewed after supper and Delancey found himself being introduced to Colonel Garland and the Reverend George Tory. All agreed to play for merely nominal stakes and the game began.

Delancey had been planning his tactics while he was at supper. His cue, he had decided, was to appear slightly drunk. He wanted Early to think of him as an insignificant opponent, indifferent as a whist player and talkative in his cups. As against that, he could not afford to lose money, not even in small silver. He had, altogether, a difficult hand to play. He had the clergyman as partner, a better player (luckily) than the colonel. Affecting to be careless and talkative, Delancey's most difficult task was to play badly, losing at first, and making his recovery seem to be a mere matter of luck. He was aware that Early was watching him closely and with all the knowledge of one whose own play was masterly. In the end he displayed his stupidity less by his actual play than by his comments after each game. "We had the worst of that, partner—and the colonel had the ace of hearts all along!" "Well done, sir—I had no idea that you were so strong in spades!" They changed partners after the rubber and Delancey now had to play with Mr Early. In the ordinary way their superiority over the other two would have been obvious but Delancey tried to make his play mediocre if not exactly stupid. It was an exhausting evening, one way and another, and Delancey was glad when the clergyman said that he was tired and must leave the table.

As they stood for a few minutes in conversation, Mr Early said to him, "After that bad start, Mr Delancey, you are lucky not to be out of pocket. But I daresay that you could win back at sea more than you lost on land."

Delancey looked rather taken aback and said, after a pause, that smugglers were not easy to catch. "It's the early bird . . ." he began and then paused in apparent confusion while his opponent went on to finish the proverb: "It's the early worm," he suggested, "that gets the bird. Or that, perhaps, is what you hope?"

The *Rose* sailed the following day and Delancey set a course for Lyme Regis. It was a long beat against a stiff westerly breeze and the late afternoon found him no further west than Bridport. He turned back at that point and spent the night on a slow cruise along the Chesil Bank. He put in next day (March the fourth) at Weymouth, where he called on Mr Hayes, the collector, and received fresh confirmation that the smuggling on that coast was directed from a centre in Dorchester. "We can't prevent smuggling," Mr Hayes, admitted, "but we can curb it." The time had come to make an example, for the evasion of the law had become too blatant of late. It was easy to catch the small men, mere fishermen and farmers. The difficulty was in seizing an important cargo owned by some man of local consequence; and even such a seizure would not lead to the exposure of the man himself. There were troops stationed at Dorchester but they seemed unwilling to assist the riding officers. The rumour was that the officers' mess was supplied with liquor at a special price.

Delancey sailed that evening after dark and cruised with a light following wind towards St Alban's Head. The dragoons should have marched from Wareham by now and would be on their way to Studland. If all went as planned the *Dove* would be caught red-handed before the morning.

The *Rose* was off Old Harry just before midnight and Delancey began a slow patrol backwards and forwards between there and Canford Cliffs. The cutter was cleared for action with guns loaded and small arms ready to issue. On the first sweep southwards Delancey took the cutter fairly close to the beach. Even on this dark night he could see the line of the breakers and the gleam of the white cliffs at the Foreland. There was no sign at first of any other vessel but a light was glimpsed about an hour later and it turned out to be placed in the bows of a six-oared rowing boat. The *Rose* was hailed by the boatmen, who turned out to be from Swanage. The coxswain carried a letter to Delancey bearing the seal of the Poole Custom House. Having delivered it, he extinguished his lantern and headed back whence he came. Delancey went below and opened the letter in his cabin. It read as follows:

Custom House
Poole.
March 3rd 1795

Urgent
Dear Sir,
I have requested H.M. Collector at Swanage to endeavour to see that this letter reaches you without delay and in time, I trust, to facilitate the interception of an illicit cargo which you formerly had reason to expect would be landed at Lulworth Cove on the night of March the fourth. It has come to my knowledge that you have now altered your plan and expect the landing to take place at Studland. From a letter which I now enclose, written by an informant whose past information has proved reliable, you

will conclude that no landing is to be expected at either Studland or Lulworth. I have to request, therefore, in the Collector's
absence, that you act on this more recent intelligence and use
your best endeavour to seize both vessel and cargo.

> I have the honour to be, sir,
> Your obedient servant,
> George Miller

The enclosure was addressed to the Collector at Poole and was
dated from Corfe Castle on March the second.

Dear Sir,

Rumour has it that a cargo is to be landed illegally at Studland
two days from now and that the *Rose* has been given orders
accordingly. I think it my duty as a law-abiding freeholder to
make it known to you that this cargo is in truth to be landed at
Mudeford near Christchurch. I also have good reason to believe
that the vessel concerned will not sail again from Mudeford before
four in the morning of March the fifth which gives me the more
reason to hope the preventive cutter will be there in time.

> I have the honour to be, sir
> Your ob't ser't
> James Weston

Delancey read these documents a second time and then more slowly
again, and the more he studied them the less he liked their contents.
The *Rose* did not, of course, come under the orders of the Custom
House at Poole so that he could ignore the request if he chose. But
should he do so? With his head in his hands he began to puzzle out
what had happened. First of all, his deception plan had failed. If the
informer knew that Studland, not Lulworth, was the place where he
expected the landing, a warning must have reached him. It seemed
likely, in that case, that the smugglers had also been warned and
that a signal would have directed Sam Carter to some other point,

probably Lulworth. But what about the signature? If Withers' signature had been forged before, might not this letter be another forgery, the work of the same hand? If so, what was the object? The *Dove* was presumably at Lulworth and would be gone before the *Rose,* beating to windward, could arrive there. But somebody still wanted the *Rose* out of the way, presumably because there was another smuggling vessel expected. The aim would be to lure the *Rose* well to leeward of the point at which this other landing was to be made. Where, then, would it be? Presumably in Poole harbour itself. All this, however, was sheer guesswork. Perhaps the *Dove's* run had been delayed for a day and would take place at Studland after all. . . . . Whatever he did now might be wrong and it would be sheer luck if his guess were to prove correct. The probability was that he would be made to look ridiculous by the morning—the keen young naval officer whose knowledge was not quite equal to his zeal. All the gossip in Market Street, Poole, would be about the way he had tried to trick the smugglers and had been tricked himself. Delancey came on deck and paced up and down for five minutes. Then, abruptly, he made his decision and began to issue his orders. "Hands to go about!" was the word and the *Rose* made a course for Poole harbour.

"Mr Lane—I shall want two boats manned and armed, with a lantern in the six-oared gig. I am going to close in with Studland Bay. Start sounding in five minutes, I want a reliable man in the chains."

"Aye, aye, sir. The ebb has begun, though."

"I know that—Mr Torrin!"

"Sir?"

"I shall want you to take the gig into Studland Bay. Show your lantern and you will be challenged by some dragoons who should be posted there. I shall give you a letter to Captain Molyneux but I want you to know the situation in case he asks questions. My guess is that tonight's run is taking place in the South Deep. I shall take the other boat in and will head for Goathorn Point. I should be greatly obliged to Captain Molyneux if he would, therefore, block the landward exit from that peninsula, covering the paths between Newton and Newton Copse." Going below with the chart and map, Delancey explained his plan in detail, allowing Torrin to believe that he was acting upon information rather than upon mere guesswork. After making contact with the dragoons Torrin was to bring the gig up to the harbour entrance and mount guard there from midnight until the other boat came out again. Mr Lane, with the *Rose* herself, was to cruise as far as Christchurch, returning to the Swash next morning to pick up the boats, together with any capture they might have made.

Torrin's boat went into Studland Bay and the *Rose,* half an hour later, was near the entrance to Poole harbour. The larger boat was lowered there and manned with eight men and the coxswain. Delancey quitted the *Rose* last, leaving Mr Lane, with the boatswain and four hands, to take her under easy sail towards Christchurch. There was little Lane could do if he fell in with any smuggling craft but Delancey hoped that the gesture was sufficient. The ebb was running fast but Delancey hoisted a lugsail on his boat and was off North Haven Point in half an hour. To enter the South Deep meant lowering the sail and rowing almost into the teeth of the wind. There was over a mile to cover and it was half past two before the water deepened and the channel curved northward. It was hard work for the oarsmen and was as difficult a piece of navigation as Delancey could remember, but the South Deep was marked by stakes and the coxswain had been there repeatedly in daylight. With muffled rowlocks the boat began its cautious approach to Goathorn Point. Downwind (thank God!) came the sound of voices, the creaking of a tackle and, just audible, the whinny of a horse.

"Quiet!" hissed Delancey, priming his pistols. The boat edged silently towards a small jetty from which came the sound of barrels being rolled along planks. Against the starlit sky Delancey could just make out the two pole masts of what was probably a lugger and certainly not the *Dove*. Slowly and gently the boat came alongside the vessel, covered by the noise of her unloading. "Four with me," whispered Delancey. "Coxswain, take the boat and land with three men at the other end of the jetty. Leave one man in charge of the boat." Silently he swung up the side of the lugger and saw that the deck was dimly lit by a lantern wedged in a corner where the light could not be seen outboard. There were five men on deck, two working a hoist and the others on the gangplank. Several more could be heard moving on the jetty, one of them whistling as he did so.

"Stop that noise!" said a voice of command and the whistling stopped.

"Is that the lot, Ned?" came another voice from the jetty.

"Only six more," came the voice again of the man who had called for silence.

Delancey realised that he had to act at once. Glancing round to see that his men were behind him, he fired a pistol into the air and called out, "Stay where you are in the king's name. You're all under arrest!" He then strode across the deck and placed himself on the gangplank, his men with him, their pistols levelled.

The smugglers' immediate reaction was so prompt and expert that it had evidently been rehearsed. Someone blew a long blast on a whistle. The lantern was extinguished. The men on the jetty ran shorewards, leading their packhorses. Of the men on deck three managed to scramble to the jetty and run after the others. Two were immediately secured, and a third was trapped in the hold. From the shoreward end of the jetty came the sound of a skirmish, where the coxswain and his men were trying to stop the fugitives. Horses could be heard cantering on the peninsula and, more distant still, came the sudden shrill note of a cavalry trumpet. So the dragoons were there.

Looking about him Delancey saw that his capture was a vessel he had never seen before. "What's the name of this craft?" he asked the man with the whistle, who replied, "The *Mary Ellen* of Weymouth—damn you." He and the others were placed under guard in the cabin while Delancey went ashore to see how his coxswain had fared. Two packhorses had been secured together with a boy who had

led one of them. The rest had escaped in the darkness, where the dragoons were presumably hunting them. Delancey had only moderate
hopes of success ashore—the smugglers would know Newton Heath
better than the soldiers could.

He walked back to the lugger reflecting on the irony of the situation. His plan to trap Sam Carter had completely failed. He had been
fooled by more experienced opponents but one of them had gone too
far, using a probably forged letter to send the *Rose* out of the way. This
move seemed quite needless, for the *Rose* at Studland Bay would have
been no real threat to the *Mary Ellen* in the South Deep. The sole result
had been to arouse Delancey's suspicions and bring him back to Poole
harbour. All Delancey's careful planning had ended in his missing the
Dove and capturing another smuggling craft—one of which he had
never heard. His main achievement had been in saving his reputation
for sagacity.

At daybreak it became possible to take stock of the night's seizure.
Captain Molyneux appeared at the head of his troop and reported the
capture of four more laden packhorses and two of the land smugglers.
The rest had scattered over the heath and vanished. As for the *Mary
Ellen,* she was a fair prize, caught with the last of her cargo still aboard,
but she was not of any great value; an old vessel patched up, not worth
a proper repair. Delancey had earned enough to live on for the next
few months. Molyneux had something towards his gambling debts. The
dragoons and revenue men were happy, having undoubtedly hidden
about half the goods they had seized. The smugglers were resigned to
their losses, knowing that seizures were bound to take place from time
to time. As for the men of the *Rose,* they looked upon Delancey as an
almost legendary hero. Less pleased with himself than the others could
realize, Delancey took the *Rose* and *Mary Ellen* into Poole with mixed
feelings. He now had some business to do ashore.

"Look, sir!" said Lane as they neared the Custom House wharf,
"There's the *Dove!*" And the *Dove* was indeed at anchor within a few
cables distance. As Delancey went ashore the first man he met was Sam

Carter. They both laughed and Delancey asked, "Where did I go wrong?" Sam was still more amused.

"Perhaps you play whist too well!" So Early had not been deceived by the acting. Once he was satisfied that Delancey was really a good player, he had disbelieved the story about Lulworth Cove. Assuming it to be the opposite of the truth he had ordered the signal to be made accordingly. Delancey's wry reflections on his failure to play his part were interrupted by Sam Carter, who added, "No ill feelings, I hope?"—to which Delancey replied, "I could wish we had been on the same side."

At the Custom House, Delancey insisted upon seeing Mr Withers alone. When Miller had reluctantly left the room, Delancey produced the letter and enclosure he had received off Swanage.

"Did you know of this letter, sir?"

"No, I was off duty that day."

"You were shown it, no doubt, on the following day and told of the action that Mr Miller had taken?"

"The incident was mentioned, I think, but I did not see the letter itself."

"Might I know your opinion of it?"

Mr Withers took up the letter again and examined it more carefully.

"Well," he said at length. "I should suppose that 'James Weston' is an assumed name—one I have heard before in some connection. Letters of this sort come to us fairly often. The writer is himself engaged in illicit trade and has quarrelled with some rival. . . . No, I am wrong there. He has an interest in that craft you captured in the South Deep and wants to lead you away towards Christchurch."

"And the handwriting, sir?"

"It is disguised."

"Now compare it, if you will, with the handwriting of Mr Miller's covering note."

After a long pause Mr Withers looked up with a dazed expression and said at length:

"I see what you mean. . . ."

"The 'James Weston' handwriting is disguised, sir, as you say, but it was done in too much of a hurry. Some letters are still alike—look at the word 'Studland' in both of the documents. Look at the capital C in Collector—here—and then at the C in Christchurch, here. I submit, sir, that James Weston—known to be in secret correspondence with John Early—is Mr George Miller."

Shaken as he was by this revelation, which he had to accept, Withers still had some resolution and dignity left. He sent his clerk to fetch Mr Miller and said nothing more until the deputy comptroller stood before him.

"Mr Miller," said Withers slowly, "the acting commander of the *Rose* received yesterday off Swanage a letter from you and an enclosure. Both, in my opinion, are in the same handwriting. Their purpose was to mislead the revenue officers and I have reason to suspect that the writer has been in regular communication with a man to whom the illicit traders look for direction." There was a tense pause and Withers concluded: "May I have your comment?"

"You may have it this instant, sir," replied Miller, handing a document over. "I have spent the last twenty minutes in writing my letter of resignation, and I now confirm before this witness that I resign my office from today."

Miller walked to the door but paused for a moment to add: "I mean to retire, sir. It is fortunate that I can afford to do so."

PART THREE

Chapter Nine

THE PRIVATEER

WHEN RICHARD DELANCEY next had occasion to appear in the High Street at Poole, he had the novel sensation of being famous. He was not exactly popular but neither was he a person to be ignored. Ladies nudged each other, glancing his way, and men of substance stared more openly, grumbling a little perhaps about young men who seemed to be too clever by half. Although aware of being the centre of attention, Delancey was far from feeling self-assured. His early successes had been due to his abilities being unknown and underrated. Now that he was thought to be ruthless and subtle his opponents would be forewarned and cautious. There would be no more accidental encounters like that with the *Four Brothers* of Shoreham. After fruitless cruising he would be back in Portsmouth by June, unemployed as before and as poor as ever.

Emerging from the stationers with his latest purchase—a copy of the *Naval Atalantis* by "Nauticus Junior" published in 1788—Delancey almost collided with Mr Withers.

"Ah, glad to see you, Captain! You must realize, I suppose, that everyone here is talking about you and that every gossip is eager for information."

"I suspect, sir, that they chiefly want to know when I am going."

"Some folk are a little apprehensive. . . . But here is a young lady who wishes to attract your attention. Heaven forbid that I should stand in her way! Good morning, Miss Hill! May I ask what has brought you to Poole?"

It was Louisa, as pretty as ever and as lacking in diffidence. "La,

Mr Withers, I came in the hope of seeing you. But I'll confess that the shops of Poole are a minor attraction, amazingly better than ours at Dorchester. Mr Delancey! How pleasant that we should meet like this! The truth is that I hoped to fall in with you, knowing that the *Rose* is in port. I wish you joy of your recent success."

"Your servant, Miss Hill—and thank you."

"I will leave you two," said Mr Withers, "but I shall be jealous if you flirt too much."

"We shall be discretion itself," replied Louisa, "for all the world knows that Mr Withers is my beau and I dare not risk losing his regard."

After Mr Withers had gone Louisa produced a letter which came, as she explained, from Mr Early. "Knowing that I was to be in Poole today, he asked me to act as messenger."

"I am vastly obliged to you, Miss Hill," said Delancey, pocketing the letter, "and as obliged again to Mr Early for entrusting the missive to so charming a bearer." Louisa dropped a little curtsey and they walked slowly on together. She looked about her as she chattered, missing nothing and glad to be seen in company with a man so much in the day's news.

"You come from Guernsey, do you not?" said Louisa at the haberdasher's door. "My cousin Harriet is engaged to an officer that was recently there—Mr Nash of the 42nd. It seems, however, that his regiment is to go overseas. Her last letter from him was dated from a transport at anchor in the Downs. He did not say so in so many words but I fancy that the regiment is going to the West Indies. Harriet still hopes that the order will be countermanded but in this she may be disappointed. His serving in the Indies may cause a broken engagement. At four and twenty, and with fifteen thousand in the funds, she can't be expected to wait for ever."

Delancey agreed in deploring long engagements. Louisa asked him what book he had bought and sniffed a little when she saw the title.

"I had thought it might be a novel. I have just read the *Mysteries of Udolpho* by Mrs Radcliffe and enjoyed it amazingly. Do you ever read novels, Mr Delancey—or only books on voyages and navigation?"

"I have read some novels but none, as yet, by Mrs Radcliffe. On your recommendation I shall hasten to procure the latest."

"Pray do so, Mr Delancey. Now I must match a ribbon for my aunt. Goodbye and do not fail to call when next you come ashore."

After parting from Louisa, Delancey opened the letter she had brought him and stood in a doorway to read it.

Dorchester,
March 9th, 1795

Dear Sir,

I write to congratulate you, first of all, on your success in attempting to suppress illicit trade on the Dorset coast. You have shown yourself to be an active officer in this temporary appointment and I am amazed to think that you have been denied the promotion in the navy to which, from your known abilities, you would seem to be entitled. Nor does it seem to me that the customs service has any great future to offer you. Had I any interest at the Admiralty I should not hesitate to exert it on your behalf. While having no such influence it happens to be in my power to serve you perhaps in another direction. I have friends in Guernsey, some of whom are partners in the ownership of a private man-of-war called the *Nemesis* of fourteen guns, built for the purpose, and commanded until recently by Mr Perelle. Having been fortunate on his last cruise, Mr Perelle has yielded to his wife's entreaty and agreed to live ashore, which he can now afford to do. There is thus a captain's vacancy and I have reason to believe that my friends in Guernsey will accept my nomination. Should you consent to serve as master of the *Nemesis* I think you will have a good prospect of success, she being fast, well-armed and well-manned. I have already written to my friends in St Peter Port, being sanguine enough to count on your acceptance. Take passage in the packet from Weymouth and call on Mr Elisha Jeremie (another whist player) at his house in St Martin's. You will be kindly received and I shall look forward to hearing that you think well of the *Nemesis*. I have entrusted this letter to my fair cousin Louisa Hill and you may care to leave your answer at No 30 in the High Street. Trusting to receive a favourable reply,

> I have the honour to remain, Sir,
> Your most obliged ser't,
> John Early.

Having read the letter once, Delancey went back over it, mentally underlining the more significant words: "temporary," "no great future," "friends in Guernsey." The letter really paid him a high compliment. As a threat to the free-traders he had to be removed and the best way to do this was to offer him a better appointment. If he refused there would be some other way of dealing with him, the easier to arrange in that his present command was merely temporary. There would be no profit for him if he remained, the goods being sent to places out-side his cruising area. As for the *Nemesis,* she clearly belonged to Early, although managed by his Guernsey agents. She was a regular priva-teer, with some captures to her credit, and the offer was genuine. Early knew all about him, that much was evident and he appreciated Delancey's skill as a whist player. On only one point was Delancey in doubt. Did Louisa mention Mrs Radcliffe's novel in order to convey some other message or was that a chance reference to Louisa's own tastes in literature? Very much on impulse, Delancey turned back to the stationers and asked for a copy of the *Mysteries of Udolpho.* One was produced at once, the stationer observing that it was much in demand, and Delancey returned to the *Rose* with books to read and a decision to make. Without much hesitation he decided to accept Mr Early's offer.

Three days later the *Rose* sailed for Weymouth. From there she sailed, without Delancey, for Cowes, bearing her acting commander's letter of resignation. Robert Lane, as acting commander, called for three cheers as the cutter left the quayside and Delancey stood for a moment at the salute. He knew that he had been a success and that he had even been popular. He felt a twinge of regret but remembered, as he turned away, that his was now to be a different trade. His career in the revenue service had come to an abrupt end, not through any failure on his part but through his being too competent. Nothing he had done would add to his reputation as a naval officer but the episode had added greatly to his self-confidence. He had seen an opportunity and grasped it. He had proved himself as a secret agent, as a commander, as a tactician. Without being uniformly successful, he had been treated by his opponents with respect. They had thought it worth their while to buy him off. The result was the prospect of a new and attractive command, the privateer *Nemesis*. He lost no time, therefore, in making his way to the packet which would sail for Guernsey that afternoon. As he watched her slip out of the harbour with the old town on one side, the wooded hillside on the other, he had the holiday sensation of leaving the seamanship to those responsible. For once he could admire the sunlight on the sail of a passing lugger without wondering about her possible activities. The sea was pale green in the light but shadowed with cloud and flecked with foam. The old packet was being held close to the southerly wind but was sagging to leeward. If the mainsail could be made to stand flatter . . . but that, for once, was not his business.

Pacing the deck, Delancey tried to remember all he knew about privateering. He recalled vaguely that Letters of Marque were issued to vessels of two distinct species. In one class were ordinary armed merchantmen, shipping a cargo, which could sail without convoy and which might snap up a prize if the opportunity offered. Far fewer in number were the real privateers, sailing without a cargo and being regularly armed and manned for war. Some of these had been designed for commerce, and especially for the slave trade, but others were designed as men-of-war and had never been anything else. Several of these were based on Guernsey and more—he had been told—on Alderney. Privateer owners and officers were often, if not always, highly respectable men. There was nothing illegal about their business, he realized, but it *could* degenerate into piracy. The commander of a private man-of-war might thus be tempted to attack ships not under the enemy flag; neutral ships or (worst of all) ships under the British flag. The fact that the temptation was there was no proof, of course, that many succumbed to it. Most privateer officers kept within the letter of the law and regarded piracy as disgraceful—and, anyway, as highly dangerous.

The passage from Weymouth to Guernsey was prolonged by adverse winds and Delancey was glad to have brought some books with him. What he would have liked was a book on privateering but none, so far as he knew, had ever been published. The works he had available were those he had bought at Poole. The *Naval Atalantis* he found to be a collection of short biographies. The flag officers and captains portrayed were many of them painted in the brightest colours. Other characters were blackened, perhaps without much reason and certainly without any particular knowledge. He had to allow, nevertheless, that some of the sketches were at least amusing. He had to smile at the reference to Admiral Digby who had retired to live in his mansion near Weymouth. "And there let us leave him in his retreat from that honourable profession in which he was never calculated to shine with any great credit to himself or his country." He was interested to note that a future flag officer had once commanded the *Guernsey*—a warship's name that was new to him. Then he hunted for the names of officers with whom he had served, if only to the point of having seen them. Rear-Admiral the Hon. J. Leveson-Gower had barely more than a page: "The haughty demeanor, ill-judged consequence and illiterate superciliousness of this officer, unhappily for him, obscure some professional virtues. . . ." That, he thought, could be near the truth. What did the author say about Macbride? He was Irish, of course, and had been a member of Parliament for Plymouth. His private hobby was cock-fighting and—what was this?—"Not less a champion in the field of Venus than in that of Mars, the gallant captain was always a welcome guest where beauty held its court, generally carrying his conquests with equal success in either field. . . ." Good heavens! This was no description of the overworked man Delancey had seen at his littered desk. Of the officers mentioned some had enjoyed a belated success, he noted, their abilities having been overlooked for years. There was Vice-Admiral Milbanke, for example, whose career provided a striking instance of "merit, when sacrificed to pique or prejudice, may long lay dormant and disregarded." That was true enough but, in his own case, did the merit exist? Did he really seek distinction in battle or did he merely want to make his fortune and live ashore? If he were to believe "Nauticus Junior" there were officers who had gained affluence in a day. There was Captain Finch of the *Porcupine* (20)—hardly more heavily armed than the *Nemesis*—who captured a homeward-bound French Indiaman "so richly laden that he was ever afterwards distinguished by the appellation of the Goldfinch, his brother Seymour being also a captain in the navy." As fortunate and more deserving it seemed, was another officer and one whom Delancey had actually met. This was Captain Henry Trollope who had commanded, as lieutenant, a cutter named the *Kite*. When war began with the Netherlands—at the end of 1780—the *Kite* swooped on the Dutch merchantmen, unaware many of them that hostilities had begun—and made a series of valuable captures. The author paid tribute to Trollope's enterprise and added that "His manners in private life are correspondent with the excellence of his public character; and that he diffuses with liberality, in the milder scenes of retirement, the ample fortune which he acquired by his professional labours."

Putting the book aside, Delancey asked himself what exactly he was trying to do. Until recently he had done no more than make a living, and that with difficulty enough. Now he was to have a command and the chance of making his fortune. If he succeeded, would that be

enough? Or would he feel that he had failed in his profession, fallen
short of what he should have achieved? At the moment he could picture himself a Guernsey landowner with shipowning interests and some
town property, a Jurat of the Royal Court, a man for everyone to greet
with respect at Chief Pleas or on market day. If that were attainable,
was that sufficient? One idea left with him from reading the *Naval
Atalantis* was based upon the example of the *Kite*. The origin of Trollope's
fortune had been a sudden outbreak of war against a new opponent.
French shipping had been adjusted to wartime conditions, having
assumed a pattern of convoys, quick passages in bad visibility, warning signals from the shore and every sort of caution. The Dutch had
been neutral, much to their own profit, carrying goods that no one
would now entrust to ships under the French flag. There was a decla-
ration of war, changing the whole picture. The new situation was known
at once in the home ports and was quickly conveyed to the cruisers
and privateers. Completely ignorant were the laden merchantmen
homeward bound from the Indies, following the usual trade routes and
keeping only a casual lookout. Their guns, so far from being loaded,
would not even be run out. Their gun-decks would be cluttered with
barrels and bales and cabin partitions. Their small arm chests would
be buried under crates and boxes. They would need half an hour to
clear for action and ten minutes (or less) would be all the time they
would actually have.

So far as war with the Netherlands was concerned, Delancey knew
that history had just repeated itself. Conquered by France, the
Netherlands had recently become the Batavian Republic, Dutch ships
being liable to seizure from February but many of them actually seized
during the previous month. For this harvest Delancey came too late,
but, apart from that, Delancey's Letter of Marque did not extend to
operations against the Dutch, who were still regarded as a friendly people suffering from French oppression. There was nothing to be done
in that direction. Spain, however, was still at peace. Now if that country were to be dragged into war on the French side, as might seem

quite probable, a privateer could do well on the Spanish coast, especially if her commander were there before war were declared. For a really dramatic success the first need was to anticipate the outbreak of war, the second need to obtain early news of it. Given those conditions anything would be possible, even the capture of a register ship with treasure enough to establish one's fortune. In a pleasant daydream Delancey saw himself as a landowner, a country gentleman, allied by marriage to the nobility. He had then to remind himself that he was just as likely to end in ignominious defeat, discredited and wounded or even taken prisoner. Privateer *owners* could be prosperous enough, or so he had heard, but how many captains ended in possession of a country estate? Fewer, he guessed, than the number killed in action.

From the *Naval Atalantis* Delancey turned to the *Mysteries of Udolpho*. He was somewhat impatient with the early chapters, turning quickly over the pages until Emily, the heroine, reached the Castle of Udolpho. If there were mysteries this was her moment to encounter them. He had to admit that the scene at nightfall was well described and that Emily had some reason to feel apprehensive. A first gateway was flanked by towers over which grass and wild plants grew, having taken root among the mouldering stones. The carriage passed through a gloomy outer court.

> "Another gate delivered them into the second court, grass-grown and more wild than the first, where, as she surveyed through the twilight its desolation—its lofty walls overtopped with bryony, moss and nightshade, and the embattled towers that rose above— long suffering and murder came to her thoughts. One of these instantaneous and unaccountable convictions, which sometimes conquer even strong minds, impressed her with its horror."

Turning over the pages Delancey realized that there was no shortage of either mystery or horror. He found himself thinking of D'Auvergne's Castle of Navarre. There was nothing Gothic about that, he supposed, and yet he felt envy of anyone who had so romantic a background. His own name was sufficiently romantic but he had never heard of any Delancey being either famous or noble. There were the American Delanceys, folk he had actually met in New York, but he had no great desire to claim them as kinsfolk. His pride of ancestry must clearly centre upon his mother's family. She had been an Andros and with that name was associated some idea of former consequence. So far as Guernsey was concerned, however, the Andros family had almost ceased to exist. He resolved, though, to make inquiries when the opportunity offered. He would not turn out to be the missing heir; of that he felt tolerably certain. He did feel, however, that a touch of the romantic would be welcome.

Once ashore again at St Peter Port, Delancey asked about His Highness, the Prince of Bouillon, only to be told that his former chief was now stationed in Jersey. When he inquired about the *Nemesis* he was told that she was in harbour. And there indeed she was, apparently under repair with nobody on board but caulkers and riggers; a fine little ship, nevertheless.

She was ship-rigged with good lines, well equipped and well maintained. She could have been a king's ship, one of the smaller sloops built in about 1780, but measured only 270 tons. But for smaller dimensions she might have been a sister ship to the *Savage* or the *Thorn*, both of sixteen guns. There was nothing smart about her appearance but Delancey's heart warmed to her at once. He felt certain that she would look lovely under sail. Leaving her with some reluctance he next learnt that Mr Elisha Jeremie was not in town that day but might be found in St Martin's parish. Deciding to leave that pilgrimage until the morrow, he took a room at the Albion Inn, hiring a porter to carry his sea-chest up from the packet. On the way there he was hailed in the street by Sam Carter:

"Good to see you, Captain!" said Sam. "Welcome back to Guernsey! I hear tell that you are now in a different line of business."

There was no mistaking the sincerity of this greeting and Delancey remembered that he and Sam were no longer opposed. They met for supper that night and drank the health of John Early, who was employing them both. From the friendly conversation which followed it was evident that the free-trader was doing well. France was in a confused state, that could not be denied, but prices were rising and trade was brisk. Sam was a mine of information on Channel shipping but was rather doubtful about the success likely to be achieved by the *Nemesis*. There were too many warships around and too few prizes of any value. Delancey and Carter agreed to act together whenever it should prove possible.

Later that evening Delancey was greeted by a Mr Le Page who remembered him as a schoolfellow.

"All the island was talking about you last year, Mr Delancey. The story was that you were called out by an officer of the garrison and that you ran him through, not so much as to kill him but enough to teach him a lesson. Or was that all mere gossip?"

"Such a meeting did take place, sir."

"Well, that's what we heard. There are a few of us can remember you as a boy and we were all on your side. These young army officers behave as if the island belongs to them. But you put one of them in his place and we were all glad to hear about it."

Delancey was surprised but pleased to find that he was something of a local hero, the fight being remembered and nothing said about his subsequently leaving the island. He later came to realize that any privateer commander was a hero in St Peter Port.

Next day Delancey set out for St Martin's and for Les Câches, the place where Mr Elisha Jeremie was said to be living. Whether he actually owned the property or not (and Delancey had heard conflicting stories about that) he was certainly in residence and expecting Delancey's visit.

The house had been built early in the century and stood back at the end of an avenue, with meadows on either side and an orchard beyond. A servant showed Delancey into the parlour where he was presently joined by Mr Jeremie. Their conversation was in French.

"Mr Delancey? Your servant sir. I was forewarned by Mr Early that you were to be expected and I am happy to welcome you to this house."

Elisha Jeremie was an elderly and pompous gentleman, short, plump and red in the face. It soon became apparent that he was the managing owner of the *Nemesis*. Like almost any other privateer she was owned by a syndicate but with one more active partner deputed to act for the rest. In this capacity Mr Jeremie took himself very seriously and behaved on this occasion as if Delancey's appointment was merely under consideration. Although privately convinced that John Early's decision had been final, Delancey assumed the role of an applicant, answering Mr Jeremie's questions with a proper humility.

"I notice, sir, that your name is Richard Andros Delancey. I would suppose from your middle name that you are related to the Guernsey family that lived here at Les Câches during the reign of George II?"

"My mother was an Andros, sir, and cousin, I believe, to James Andros, whose death I remember."

"James lived here and was colonel of the South Regiment of Militia. But the Andros family were connected over a much longer period with another place in the north of the island."

"I never heard that, sir."

"The Delancey name is not as well known."

"I should suppose not, sir."

"No, not well known at all. But you hold a commission in the navy and have spent some years at sea?"

"Yes, sir."

"You have been in action?"

"Yes, sir."

"But you have never before served in a private man-of-war, Mr Delancey?"

"No, sir."

"Then you must realize that a ship like the *Nemesis* is not like a king's ship, bound to seek the enemy in battle. Her role is different in that she is expected to yield a profit. Her owners have been to considerable expense in building, arming, equipping and provisioning the ship and they hope to see a return on their outlay."

"No doubt, sir. And I should be right to conclude, surely, that they also want to play their part in bringing the war to a successful conclusion?"

There was a minute or two of silence before Mr Jeremie replied.

"The owners are loyal to the king and his enemies are undoubtedly theirs. You must recall, however, that their means are limited. It is not to be supposed that they can pursue a naval campaign at their own cost. It is the return on each cruise that must pay for the next."

"And how can the ship's commander be certain of making such a profit?"

"It is a matter of precise calculation, sir. Let us suppose that you have sighted a ship and recognized her as French. Having made an estimate of her strength and her value as a prize, you have to set down three figures: her sale value, ship and cargo taken together; the damage *you* are likely to sustain in making the capture, and the damage *she* will sustain before she is taken. If the last two figures exceed the first, you will let her alone."

"I understand, sir."

"I realize, of course, that your estimates cannot be infallible. You can recognize her port of origin, however, and the trade for which she was designed. You can count her gun ports and you can see whether she is laden or in ballast. Your success must then depend on the nicety of your calculations and the energy and resolution you display in attacking a vessel which you have judged to be worth capturing."

"Just so, Mr Jeremie."

"Certain mistakes are too commonly made, especially by young men who are new to the business. After a cruise perhaps of months, with no prize taken of any sort, a privateer commander will sometimes lose patience and make an ill-advised attempt to capture a ship of a force superior to his own. Rather than return empty-handed he will convince himself that the attempt is justified. With what result? He returns empty-handed, as he would have done in any event, but with his sails shot to pieces, his rigging knotted or spliced, a hole or two between wind and water and his pumps barely able to keep his ship afloat. You may suppose that the owners of the ship will express their disapprobation in the strongest terms."

"With good reason, sir, I must confess."

"It is also incumbent upon the commander to remember that the noise of gunfire is often undesirable. You will seldom have the whole of the English Channel to yourself. A prolonged action may attract the attention of enemy cruisers. Worse still, perhaps, it may bring to the scene another privateer under our own flag, offering assistance but claiming a half of the prize. Where possible the capture should be made by boarding and without gunfire, no damage being done to either ship."

"Very true, Mr Jeremie."

"You have also to understand that, while your crew will be large enough to man the first prizes you take, you will be progressively weakened by your own success; one attempt too many, launched with insufficient force might lead to your own capture and nullify the results of your previous good fortune. The wise commander should know when he has done enough."

"He should indeed, sir, and I take your point."

Delancey was somewhat repelled by the strictly commercial approach to what had seemed, from a distance, a more romantic vocation. He grasped, nevertheless, that Mr Jeremie's advice was based on common sense. No conceivable victory at sea would justify a commander whose owners were left bankrupt. When his chance came to ask questions he asked about the officers already appointed; who were they and of what quality and experience? On this point, however, Mr Jeremie referred him to Mr Perelle.

"You may have heard that the *Nemesis* was highly successful on her last cruise. War with Holland had just begun and there were great opportunities. Mr Perelle made the most of them and decided to quit the sea. He is now a part-owner of the *Nemesis* and the man best able to inform you about both ship and crew. He lives at Portinfer in the Vale Parish and I suggest you call on him tomorrow."

Delancey followed this advice and found himself next day in a part of the island which was strange to him. He knew his way round St Martin's and St Andrew's. He was not entirely lost in Câtel or the Forest, but St Sampson's, like Torteval, represented a foreign territory where French was spoken with a different accent. As for the Vale proper, that other island beyond the bridge at St Sampson's, he had never been there in his life. Portinfer was not as remote as that, and he had seen the place from the sea when out fishing as a boy, but he had only a vague idea of how to reach it from St Peter Port. In the end he obtained a lift in a farm cart to Cobo and walked up the coast from there.

It was a good day for a walk, sunny at the moment but with patches of cloud and some darkness over the sea to the westward. It was a lovely stretch of coast, flat and fringed with rocks. Delancey remembered that Cobo granite was of a blue colour and valued for quoins and lintels and gateposts. He saw some quarries that were being worked but the only dwellings were four low-built thatched cottages. He was finally directed to a farmhouse which indicated a higher level of prosperity; the property, he learnt, of the man he was seeking.

Mr Perelle was a typical Guernseyman, short and sturdy, suspicious at first but soon ready to help. He spoke highly of the *Nemesis* but was rather more guarded on the subject of her officers.

"Mr Le Vallois, first lieutenant, is a good seaman but rheumatic and would have retired by now if he had not lost his money that time his house burnt down. Mr Rouget, second lieutenant, is brave in action and a fair navigator. He has been in trouble, though; not here but in England. He has always been honest with me, mind you, but I shouldn't put temptation in his way. Mr Hubert is lieutenant of marines. . . ."

"He is *what?*" asked Delancey.

"Lieutenant of marines. We sometimes give that rank to a young man who is ready to fight but knows nothing of seamanship. He leads a few landsmen who are given muskets and bayonets. Hubert is a bit wild and daren't go ashore here on account of his debts. He stays aboard as watchman. Young Duquemin, the midshipman, has also to keep out of sight, having got a St Saviour's girl with child. If he were found ashore he might be made to marry her."

"And the boatswain?"

"We call him the gunner. Will Carré is a good man when sober, none better. You'll need to see that he gets no more than his share."

From this and further conversation Delancey came to realize that a privateer was manned by men who had some special reason for going to sea. There was something to be said against all of them (himself included).

For his return journey on foot Delancey was given directions by Perelle but found them difficult to follow. Instead of following the coast back to Cobo he was to strike inland by Vingtaine de l'Epine—a great saving, he was told, in distance. The lanes and footpaths were confusing, however, there were few people to be seen and he soon lost all but a very general sense of direction. The day had begun well but the sky was now overcast and the light was failing as the afternoon went on. He met with an old man who told him to go by way of the garenne. He followed where the old man pointed but the word "garenne" was strange to him. He came, however, to an area of gorse and bracken, bounded by an artificial ditch, and guessed that this was it; a warren, in fact, reserved for rabbits. Heartened by this discovery, he pushed on, losing what little path there had been but finding a gap in a belt of trees. Passing through, he found himself moving uphill through undergrowth towards a ruinous building. There was the cawing of rooks but no sound of cattle or dogs, no sign of habitation. Looking up the hill, however, from what could have been a moat, he saw what seemed to be a crumbling battlement, a ruined tower, a gothic window.

All was overgrown and derelict but the building had been a sort of castle; no, a fortified manor house. To one side was the ivy-covered fragment of an old chapel with the graveyard covered by brambles and nettles. In that failing light the ruin looked threatening and sinister. It reminded him of something he had seen—or rather, more truly, of something he had read. . . . All was still as he came to the gothic doorway which was blocked by some rough pieces of timber. He stood for a minute, wondering what to expect—the jangling of an ancient bell, the hooting of an owl? Suddenly he remembered—the Castle of Udolpho!

As he stood, wondering at the strange chance by which he had stumbled on the place, there was a flash of lightning and a distant noise of thunder. At the same time there was a stirring of the trees and a renewed cawing of the rooks. There was clearly going to be a thunderstorm. Turning aside from the ruined building he walked up the hill to the left and presently found himself on a path which improved until he came across a cart-shed and cow-house, the outbuildings of a farm. As the first heavy drops of rain fell he turned aside for shelter. He was presently joined in the cart-shed by an old countryman who had been working in an adjacent field and was equally seeking shelter. After greeting each other, they exchanged views on the weather, each convinced that the storm would soon pass. With the rain now drumming on the thatch overhead, Delancey resolved to stay where he was until the rainstorm had passed. To pass the time he asked the old countryman about the ruins he had passed. Did he know what the building had been?

"What, the old manor house? That's Anneville Manor, sir. You saw the old doorway?"

"Yes."

"Well, that's where the tenants still meet in Chief Pleas. Yes, sir, that's the old manor and the Chapel of St Thomas, centuries old as people say."

"To whom does it belong?"

"Well, sir, the fief has always belonged to the Andros family. They have been the Seigneurs as far back as anyone can remember. But they sold the land long since and the building now belongs to Mr Mahy— that is, to *old* Mr Mahy, not to Mr Elias Mahy of Le Valnord but to his father who used to be the blacksmith. A strong place, the old house must have been; made to hold, I reckon, against the French."

"So Anneville is, by tradition, the Andros home in Guernsey?"

"Why, yes, sir. They must have owned it for hundreds of years."

"What an extraordinary story!"

"Why, sir?"

"I expressed myself badly. What is extraordinary is not the existence of this old place, known only to a handful of neighbours but the chance of one in a thousand that brought me here. Andros is one of my names. This place could easily have been my home!"

Chapter Ten

TOLD TO THE MARINES

"All hands on deck! Rouse out, there! Lively, now!" Will Carré, the gunner, assembled the crew of the *Nemesis* and checked their names against his muster-list. There were 52 men and boys in all including the eight "marines" under Mr Hubert who were drawn up in line below the break of the quarterdeck. The seamen proper clustered in the waist and were presently reported present to Mr Rouget. The presence of the marines was similarly reported to Rouget, who reported in turn to Mr Le Vallois. He then doffed his hat and bowed to the captain, Richard Delancey, who stood at the rail, facing aft. "The crew all present, sir!" Delancey, in naval uniform, turned to Mr Jeremie and bowed to him as the owners' representative. "All present sir, and the ship ready to sail." In his best suit and wig, Mr Jeremie now addressed the crew. From the glibness of his words Delancey guessed that he had often done this before and probably without much variation.

"Officers and men, you will know by now that the owners of this ship have appointed Mr Richard Delancey as captain. He is a naval officer who had had great experience in the king's service. He is also a Guernseyman and brought up in St Peter Port. Obey his orders and you will gain the approbation of the owners. More than that, you will share in the value of every capture you make. You each know to what share you are entitled and you each know that no one is forgotten and that even the cabin boy has something to gain. Do your duty, men, and see that the ship is always ready for action. Keep a sharp look-out at all times and be sure that you see the enemy before you are seen. Follow your officers bravely when the moment comes and be sure that the cowardly French will run for their lives. Bring your prizes back to this port and listen to the cheers as you drop anchor. Go ashore with money to spend and you will find once more that every pretty girl loves a seaman! Good luck to you all!"

While listening, Delancey was studying the faces of the men before him. These, he could see, were the riff-raff of the waterside; the stupid, the clumsy, the drunken and dishonest, the debtors, the hen-pecked, the useless, the sick. The *Nemesis* was at single anchor outside the harbour and the boat was alongside that would take Mr Jeremie ashore. Even here the midshipman, Duquemin, was still hiding in the cable tier, afraid to be seen on deck. Glancing round, he looked again at his officers, grouped behind him, and saw that they too were unimpressive. They wore a semblance of uniform with their brass-hilted swords, but looked more eager for loot than for battle. There was no attempt at uniform among the "marines" who looked seedier even than the sailors. Their muskets were dirty and their bayonets were dull.

Stepping forward in his turn Delancey did his best to make an impression:

"Officers and men of the *Nemesis*, I am Richard Delancey, your captain. We shall come to know each other on this cruise. In the meanwhile, I have three things to say. First, this ship is a man-of-war and should look like one. The more warlike and smart we appear, the greater is the likelihood of our enemies surrendering without a fight. Second, our lives may depend upon our guns and small arms being serviceable. Third, our further success may depend upon the way we treat our prisoners. If we are known to behave well, using no violence more than is needed, robbing no seaman of his gear, enemy merchantmen will haul down their colours before a shot is fired. But if we act like pirates, every ship we intercept under the French flag will fight to the last, leaving us with two wrecks to handle, our own ship and the prize. We must be smart. We must be ready. We must be disciplined. Dismiss the men, Mr Le Vallois. Mr Jeremie's boat, Mr Rouget. Man the side, Mr Hubert."

Delancey saw Mr Jeremie to the gangway and saluted as the boat pushed off and as Hubert's marines attempted a ragged present arms. Then he went below to where Sam Carter was waiting in the main cabin. It was to him and to him alone that Delancey had confided his plan of campaign.

He apologized for keeping Sam waiting and then shouted for his steward. "A glass of wine, Sam, to toast our success."

"Thank you, Captain. I won't say 'no.' But don't let me delay your departure."

"We are here anyway until our boat returns. Tell me, what did you think of my plan?"

"I'm sorry, Richard. I could say nothing last night at the tavern, not with all that company around. But, no, I'm sorry: it won't answer."

"Why not?"

"First let me admit that your intelligence is good and your reasoning better. If the Guernsey smugglers ship brandy which comes, some of it, from Cherbourg, the brandy must have been landed there in the first place. It is not a product of Normandy and it must have come by sea. All that is undeniable."

"Then it should be possible to intercept the ships which bring the stuff."

"Look, Richard, if it were possible the Alderney privateers would have done it. But these ships are too big for them and too well armed."

"Very true, Sam, but the *Nemesis* is bigger than those Alderney craft."

"She is not big enough."

"Perhaps you think I am poaching on your preserve?"

"No, Richard. I am trading further south these days. Your capturing the *Bonne Citoyenne* might vex some people but it wouldn't matter to me. I don't think, however, that you can do it."

"You mean that she mounts too many guns?"

"She certainly does. But, apart from that, she creeps along the coast. Suppose you go in with another ship of your own class—the *Duke of Richmond*, say, commanded by Peter Norman—"

"Not me, Sam! I would never trust him."

"Very well, then. Suppose you have a larger ship, with four and twenty guns. On sighting you, the *Bonne Citoyenne* would put into the nearest harbour, one she has visited a score of times and one where she will be covered by shore batteries. Not knowing the place, you would never dare follow."

"And I should be beaten off if I tried?"

"You'd be taken, more likely, and end in a French prison."

"But, nevertheless, *Bonne Citoyenne* would be worth capturing—agreed?"

"Oh, yes, no doubt of it. She would be a good prize, anyway, when bound for Cherbourg with wine, brandy and general goods. The same would be true of that other ship—*Libération,* I think she is called. Neither, however, would have much cargo on the southward run. But forget them, Richard, and go after something smaller."

"I most probably shall, just to give the men a little confidence. And here comes the steward with the wine. . . . Thank you, Nicolle. . . . Now then—a toast to the *Libération* of the *Bonne Citoyenne!*"

"I drink to that, Richard, but your plan is only fit for bedlam!"

"I wonder? If you think me over-confident, Sam, you should know that I have failed so far through not being confident enough. I have been thought shy and absent-minded, a dreamer, an artist. But two things have changed me and one of them happened in the last few minutes."

"What—you were moved by old Jeremie's words of encouragement?"

"No, I was looking at my officers and crew. I knew then, quite suddenly, that I am the best seaman on board the *Nemesis.* I never had that conviction in the navy and I don't think it would have been justified. But here I feel that I have the right to command."

"Of course you have, Richard! But that is a modest claim, after all. Your men are the dregs, not half as good as mine. To be the best of this lot means nothing!"

"To me, Sam, it means everything."

"What other thing has happened to change your outlook?"

"I came across the ruins of Anneville Manor."

"Well, Richard—what of it?"

"It belonged for centuries to the Andros family. I came across it by accident, walking back from Portinfer. Suddenly—there it was, like a ruined castle in a tale of romance. Some day I shall rebuild it. My aim, in the meanwhile, is to make the money."

"But you are not an Andros!"

"My mother was. I feel that this is a task which has fallen to me. . . . And now, Sam, you think me a romantic fool!"

"No, Richard, not in the least. But don't lose your life in trying to take the *Libération* or *Bonne Citoyenne*. Your only reward would be a tablet in the town church, placed there by the owners. Stay alive for the sake of your friends. Don't shake your head, Richard—you do have friends. Anyway, you have one."

"Thank you, Sam."

"And now I can hear your boat returning. You must sail and I must go ashore."

The two friends parted and the *Nemesis* was soon under way, bound in the first place for the Breton coast beyond Roscoff. Delancey felt that his officers were resentful about this, knowing that the Breton coasters were not worth the trouble of pursuit and capture. He ignored their black looks, said nothing of his plans and concentrated all his efforts on gun-drill and musketry. With unwearied patience he repeated the exercises until there were signs of improvement. Then he started competitions between the gun-crews and musketry squads, with extra tots of rum for the winners. The officers were sceptical, pointing out that a fight was the last thing they wanted. Delancey ignored them, politely relentless, and ended with two gun-crews which could load and fire with at least average speed and accuracy. The others could only be said to do their best. As for Hubert's landsmen, they were drilled to the point of exhaustion.

Weeks passed before the *Nemesis* began to seek her prey and even then Delancey did no more than sweep the Baie de St Brieux, at first by daylight and then after nightfall. He spoke with Breton fishing boats and sometimes bought from them, molesting nobody and explaining that he had no interest in small craft. As nothing of any size was to be seen on that coast the local fishermen supposed that he must be weak in the head (a theory which his own officers were inclined to share). He was almost ignored by small coastal traders, which did no more than keep their distance from him. Then, and quite abruptly, Delancey struck. He opened fire in daylight on a couple of two-masted luggers out of Portrieux, crippling one of them while the other escaped. He took this small prize into Jersey while his officers fumed at his stupidity. The *Coquette,* laden with a mixed cargo, was of trifling value and the effect of the capture was to scare all other vessels back into harbour. Delancey, however, seemed to be content with his prize while pointing out that better gunnery would have secured the second lugger as well.

The condemnation and sale of the *Coquette* gave Delancey a sum in hand out of which his crew received something on account. His own and the owners' share he spent at once on uniform clothing for his officers and "marines." He had expected to buy scarlet cloth and the services of a tailor but he soon discovered that militia uniform was to be bought ready-made. After much effort he provided Hubert and his men with marine uniforms, crossbelts and headgear. The lieutenants, gunner, and midshipman were also given naval uniform with cocked or round hats as appropriate. News of this activity reached D'Auvergne, as was inevitable, and Delancey was sent for and questioned.

"So it's *you!*" exclaimed the Prince. "I might have guessed it! And may I ask what mischief you are planning *now?*"

Delancey explained something of his plans and the Prince at once offered to help.

"You will need a commissioning pennant and a smart new ensign. I'll see what I can do. And what about canvas and paint?" Delancey accepted some material help but explained that he would do none of the painting while at St Helier. He would have to find somewhere less public.

"Chausey Island would be the place," said D'Auvergne promptly. "And one other item I should add to your list—a *drum!*"

They parted on friendly terms and the *Nemesis* was soon at sea again, bound for the Chausey Islands, halfway to St Malo.

After the anchor dropped Delancey called his officers together and explained what had to be done:

"You may have wondered, gentlemen, why I have been so particular about your appearance in uniform. You may have thought that this was the whim of a naval officer; his hobbyhorse, as people say. It is part, however, of a plan to confuse the enemy. For the next week or so the *Nemesis* is to become a king's ship; a sloop, to be exact, of twenty guns, eight in each battery and two bow-chasers. Now, this is what we must do—" He went into details about the disguise but said nothing about its exact purpose. Mystified and critical, his men had to admit that their captain at least knew what he wanted. And when the *Nemesis* sailed again, with pennant and colours flying, her drum beating to quarters, her marines in uniform and her officers looking the part, the men agreed that the disguise was effective. But what could be the object? Privateers often disguised their strength so as to look harmless and even invite attack. Whoever heard of a privateer disguised as a king's ship? They had little time to discuss this problem, however, for they were now plunged into exhausting, realistic and repeated exercises, this time in the manning and arming of boats. Off Sark there were new exercises again, this time in the boarding and capture of an enemy ship at anchor. On this cruise there seemed to be nothing but work.

It was afternoon on May 22nd, 1795, when the merchantman *Bonne Citoyenne* passed the Pointe du Rozel on the last stage of her regular passage from Bordeaux to Cherbourg. There was a fresh south-westerly breeze and she stood up the Passage de la Deroute under easy sail

and keeping a sharp look-out. There was Jersey to windward and Alderney ahead and the captain, Citoyen Carignan, a cautious man, would
breathe a sigh of relief when he rounded the Cap de la Hague. It would
have been better seamanship, no doubt, to lay a course direct from
Brest to a point west of Alderney, leaving Guernsey to starboard. He
would then, however, have been far from the friendly ports to leeward.
By hugging the coastline, on the other hand, he was always within easy
reach of St Brieux, St Malo, Granville, Reynville, Havre de St Germain
or La Gravelle. Beyond that was a stretch of inhospitable coastline ending in Cap de la Hague, with Cherbourg round the point. With this
breeze even a heavily laden ship would be safe in Cherbourg harbour
by the evening. The sun was bright, the visibility was excellent and the
lookout in the foretop had no difficulty in seeing the sail which appeared
directly ahead. He hailed the deck and the captain went halfway up
the mizen shrouds with his telescope. As soon as he reached the quarterdeck again he gave the order to clear for action, for the stranger was
clearly hostile and stood directly in his path. Citoyen Carignan would
soon have to make a choice between battle or flight. Faced by a small
privateer he would be prepared to fight his way through the passage
between Alderney and Cap de la Hague. Since he mounted 22 guns
and had a crew of seventy, he could beat off the average privateer; and
the sound of gunfire might bring out a cruiser from Cherbourg. Faced
by a frigate, on the other hand, he would run to leeward and take
refuge at La Gravelle. To sail back the way he had come could be fatal,
as he realized, for a frigate, working to windward, would certainly overtake him in a matter of hours.

"What do you make of her?" Carignan asked of his first mate, to
whom he handed the telescope.

"No frigate, Captain, that is certain."

"But a national corvette?"

"Who knows? Perhaps twenty guns, no ensign, worn sails. . . . She
looks—no, I can't make her out." He handed the telescope back and
the captain renewed his scrutiny. The distance between the two ships

was lessening but the stranger, at closer range, was still something of a mystery. As he watched, the corvette (if she *was* a corvette) tacked. She had been on the port tack when first seen, standing north-west-wards under easy sail. For a minute or two her masts were in line. Then she was on the other tack, heading towards the French coast. If both ships held their present course the enemy privateer (or corvette?) would soon cut the *Bonne Citoyenne* off from her nearest refuge at La Gravelle. Carignan would then have no choice to make, with Cherbourg his only possible place of safety, the enemy to windward of him and 45 miles to go before sunset. The two ships were now converging rapidly but Carignan made more sail and thus made sure of reaching the point of intersection before his opponent. Although within range, neither opened fire for some minutes. Then the enemy's bow-chaser boomed, the smoke billowed and dispersed and the corvette (or privateer) hoisted her white ensign and pennant. The shot was across the bows and a signal followed, presumably ordering the merchantman to heave to. Carignan hoisted the tricolour in defiance but made no other response, watching through his telescope as the enemy ship crossed his wake. She was at about three cables' distance and sharply distinct in the afternoon sun. Carignan could see the blue uniforms on her quarterdeck, the scarlet and white of her marines, the glitter of their bayonets. There came downwind the beat of the drum and the faintly heard words of command. There was no other sound and all the seamen visible were standing rigidly to their guns. As soon as she had passed the merchantman's stern, the corvette put up her helm and came almost into the *Bonne Citoyenne's* wake. Assuming her to be faster and better manned, the corvette (or sloop, as the English would call her) should be alongside in twenty minutes and Carignan would have to fight her off for the time it might take to cover ten miles. He pointed this out to his first mate and added:

"We have a very good chance."

"Yes, Captain," said the mate. "She mounts fewer guns than we do. But why didn't she fire her broadside as she passed?"

The enemy corvette was well-disciplined and well-handled but she seemed to be one of the slowest ships in her class. She gained little on her prey, her captain resorting to his two bow-chasers in the hope of crippling his opponent. The British shooting was indifferent, however, and the range began to lengthen. The *Bonne Citoyenne* came into La Gravelle undamaged and the pursuing corvette turned away, baffled. The French crew cheered as they made fast to the breakwater and Carignan congratulated himself on his victory over an enemy frigate.

"A frigate, Captain?" asked the second mate.

"Of the smallest class," Carignan admitted, privately resolving to word his report rather differently.

"And the slowest," added the mate with a puzzled expression. He would have been less puzzled, in one way, had he known that the *Nemesis* had been towing an old sail astern. He would have been more puzzled in another way, however, had he known this, for such a strange piece of seamanship might be regarded as a proof of lunacy. Nor need we wonder that the long-suffering crew of the *Nemesis* had come to the same conclusion, that their captain must be out of his mind. Weeks of training had been followed by the capture of an almost worthless prize. Then there had been all this fuss over uniforms and paintwork. And now, having waylaid a valuable merchantman, he had fired a few shots and broken off the engagement. Le Vallois was irritated although secretly glad to avoid battle. Rouget was furious, Hubert was puzzled, young Duquemin almost openly relieved. When Le Vallois knocked at the cabin door it was with a gloomy satisfaction that he announced the coming aft of a group of seamen who wished to make a complaint. "Send them in," said Delancey, and the first lieutenant ushered in a group consisting of Le Breton, Puteaux, Cluett, Tardif and Wetherall. "Well?" asked Delancey and Wetherall spoke up on behalf of the others:

"You'll recollect, sir, that we proved ourselves to be the best gun-crew on board this here ship?"

"Yes, I know."

"But the crew you put on the bow-chaser were the worst we have, the crew which never came near the target."

"I am aware of that. Good practice for them."

"But we reckon, sir, that we could have crippled that frog ship and brought her to close action."

"I daresay you might have done. But that was not what I wanted."

"Well, sir, we felt disgraced."

"Forget it. Before many hours have passed you will have reason to feel proud. For that I give you my word. And when I want to *hit* the target I shall know which gun-crew to put on the bow-chaser. You may not believe it but I know what I am doing."

When the deputation had withdrawn old Le Vallois made his formal protest:

"I feel bound to tell you, sir, that the men are discouraged. They can't understand your tactics, sir, and nor do I."

"You soon will, Mr Le Vallois. Bring the other officers in—yes, with Carré as well. Leave Mr Duquemin in charge of the deck."

Delancey walked to the stern windows and saw the French coast disappearing as the light failed. The *Nemesis* was just north of Sark, heading slowly north-westwards under topsails and jib. There was a knock at the door and his four officers entered, all looking more or less resentful.

"Pray be seated, gentlemen," said Delancey, setting them the example. "I want you to picture, if you will, the evening's events in the little port of La Gravelle. The *Bonne Citoyenne* came in on the flood tide, just beginning, and tied up alongside. Her captain is pleased with himself. He was headed away from Cherbourg by a British sloop of twenty guns but he held her off and reached port, saved by the bad seamanship or cowardice—or both—of the British captain. What does he do now? Mr Le Vallois?"

"He stays where he is for the time being."

"Just so, and then? Mr Rouget?"

"He lets one watch go ashore."

"Very true. So he does! And then? Mr Hubert?"

"He goes to the local tavern and tells the company about his victory over the Royal Navy. They all shout 'Liberty, Equality, Fraternity!'"

"I think you are right, Mr Hubert. But he has to do something else first. Mr Carré?" There was silence and Delancey had to answer his own question: "He sends a messenger overland to the senior naval officer at Cherbourg, asking for a cruiser to meet him tomorrow off Cap de la Hague. The messenger rode off an hour ago and will be there three hours hence. He will have to ride sixteen miles or so but not in vain. The corvette will sail at first light."

"How do we know that?" asked Hubert.

"Because the *Bonne Citoyenne* is bringing the wine; and she won't quit La Gravelle until sure of her escort. That confounded sloop may still be around, lurking perhaps beyond Alderney. So she won't sail tonight—as she could—on the ebb. She'll be there, it has been decided, until morning. That is her captain's intention, gentlemen. But one fact has escaped his notice—the fact that we shall capture his ship tonight." There was a gasp of astonishment and all the officers tried to speak at once:

"What—go into a French *harbour?*"

"But how, sir?"

"God—it's impossible!"

"Surely this is madness?"

Delancey listened blandly to these exclamations and continued, after a pause: "It so happens, gentlemen, that I have visited the harbour before. My plan presents no particular difficulty but depends for its success on surprise."

"Do you mean, sir, that the *Nemesis* is to sail into the harbour at La Gravelle?" Le Vallois' voice was quivering with indignation.

"Certainly not, Mr Le Vallois. We shall go in with the boats."

"What—all of us?"

"No, you will remain on board, and so will Mr Carré. Mr Rouget will take the longboat, Mr Hubert the launch and Mr Duquemin will come with me in the gig. We'll go over the details later and issue the arms. In the meanwhile—about ship! It's your watch, I think, Mr Rouget? Set a course for La Gravelle. Mr Carré, uncover the boats and remember that we must muffle the oars. Mr Le Vallois, I'll show you the chart. . . ."

By driving his men into a state of bustling preparation Delancey prevented any discussion over his actual plan. He knew, however, that the seamen had reached a sense of frustration during the afternoon's skirmish (as voiced by the deputation) and that talk of action would be to that extent welcome.

There were some feelings of opposition, however, and Le Vallois gave them full expression:

"I should be failing in my duty, sir, if I made no protest about this night attack on La Gravelle. The owners, I am confident, would never countenance so hazardous a venture. I submit that we missed our chance of capturing this ship in daylight. What you now propose is far less likely to succeed."

"Is that all you have to say, Mr Le Vallois?"

"Yes, sir. With respect, sir."

"Very well, then. I have three observations to make. First I shall comment upon the word 'propose.' I have *proposed* nothing. Instead I have given you my orders and I expect them to be obeyed to the letter. Second, the chance we missed today was of an action between two ships of almost equal force; an action which would have left them both crippled, whereas our opponent tonight will be surprised, with half his men ashore. Third, I interpret your protest as a sign of cowardice."

"Sir!"

"I repeat—cowardice!" Delancey moved round the cabin table, took Le Vallois by the neckcloth and shook him.

"And if you deny that you are a coward, fetch your sword and come on deck—*now.* I'll cut you to pieces and feed those fragments to the mackerel."

"I apologize, Captain," gibbered Le Vallois. "I swear to obey orders."

Delancey flung him back against the cabin door and finished the interview by saying, with quiet intensity:

"You'll be dead before morning if you don't . . . *Get out!*"

Alone for a minute, Delancey had a moment of almost physical nausea. He had thought himself a gentleman, a man of culture, an artist, and here he was behaving like a mad buccaneer of the last century. What else, however, could he do? Le Vallois must be made to fear his captain more than he feared the enemy, and that fear must be transmitted to the other cowards on board. He strode to the door and shouted: "Pass the word for Mr Rouget!"

That officer appeared at the double, looking thoroughly alarmed.

"I have to acquaint you, Mr Rouget, with a slight change of plan. Mr Duquemin will go with Mr Hubert and Mr Le Vallois will come with me in the gig."

"Aye, aye, sir. But who will you leave in command of the ship?"

"Old Maindonal."

"The carpenter, sir?"

"Yes," said Delancey briefly. "Tell the others and send Maindonal in to see me."

The essence of Delancey's plan was to come into the harbour at high water just as the tide began to ebb. He had been into La Gravelle before—it seemed a lifetime ago—but the navigational problem on that occasion had been simpler. He had then merely to bring the *Royalist* away. This time he had to handle a captured merchantman as well, relying on the ebb tide. But the time of high water could vary from day to day by as much as fifteen minutes. . . . He was too absorbed in calculations to think of the risks involved but the chances of failure were, he thought, minimal. As all depended upon surprise, however, he had decided to drop the anchor well out of earshot and sail in with the anchor off the ground, ready to catch when the water shoaled. This would complicate the steering but the wind, luckily, was steady in strength and direction. When the anchor caught, the *Nemesis* was very near the position as planned. The boats, towed in, were quickly manned and armed, leaving the carpenter on board with a crew of nineteen. It was a starlit night with a crescent moon, light enough to see the breakwater. The three boats were initially roped together, the gig leading, and were not cast off until the harbour mouth was reached. Then the longboat went in, followed by the launch, and were almost alongside the *Bonne Citoyenne* before they were challenged. Even then a reply from Rouget in French gained another three minutes. The merchantman was taken, in fact, with surprisingly little opposition or noise. As for Delancey, he took the gig into the steps and left her there with a boy in charge. Le Vallois with one seaman went along the quay to a point opposite the French ship's bows, Delancey with another man went to a point opposite her stern. Two ropes were cast off from two bollards and the *Bonne Citoyenne* began to drift away with the ebb. Delancey and Le Vallois walked back to the gig and had pushed off before the alarm was fairly given.

Following a distant bugle call there came the sound of running footsteps. A young petty officer appeared on the jetty, saw what was happening and shouted for help. He was presently joined by two men with muskets who fired at the *Bonne Citoyenne's* present helmsman but evidently without result. There next appeared an officer who swore loudly and told the men with muskets to aim at the gig. As they did so, missing again, the petty officer ran off to tell someone more senior. The eventual result was the tramp of a whole platoon and a volley fired seaward without any very defined target. There followed another bugle call and a lot of scattered firing and shooting but without control enough to achieve anything. By the time the soldiers had arrived the *Bonne Citoyenne* was under sail and out of range.

When the *Nemesis* stood into the Russel next day with her prize astern she still had the appearance of a king's ship, no less formidable than H.M. Sloop *Albatross* which was hove to in the roads. Delancey knew that the *Albatross* was based on Jersey and wondered, idly, why she was neither at anchor nor under way. Nearing St Peter Port, he suddenly saw the point of her manoeuvre. Her longboat had been lowered and was just overtaking a lugger which was steering for the harbour mouth. Delancey then realized that the lugger was the *Dove* and that her crew were just about to be impressed into the navy. Making a quick decision, he took the *Nemesis* into a point within hail of the *Dove* and between her and the *Albatross*. Backing his own topsails, he saw the lugger's sails come down and her crew being collected on deck. Near her wheel Sam Carter was arguing with the midshipman, whose armed boat's crew were already on board. Impressive in uniform, Delancey grabbed his speaking trumpet and hailed the *Dove*.

"*Hawke* to *Albatross*. Leave that lugger alone and return to your ship!"

The agitated midshipman looked in his direction and called back: "I am only obeying orders, sir!"

"Can't hear you, bring your boat alongside."

After some hesitation, the midshipman obeyed but had sense enough to leave his coxswain and six men in the *Dove*. His slowness over this gave time for Delancey to fetch his cocked hat and sword and pass an order to Hubert. He did not order the midshipman aboard but shouted down at him from the quarterdeck:

"That lugger is on a secret mission and her crew are not to be impressed. Leave her alone and return to your ship."

"I have my captain's orders, sir."

"I am senior to your captain and you now have my orders."

"I don't know who you are, sir." The quiver in the boy's voice showed that he was on the verge of tears.

"You'll soon find out, young man!" At this moment Hubert reported to Delancey, he too in uniform, backed with five of his men equally in scarlet.

"Mr Hubert, I shall want you to take a platoon of marines on board that lugger. Now, youngster, you have five minutes to get your men back into their boat. Or do you want to have them thrown out at bayonet point? Be off with you, sir, or you'll feel the cane on your backside." The miserable boy finally did as he was told and Delancey watched the longboat make its crestfallen return to the *Albatross,* which presently made sail for Jersey. The *Nemesis* and *Dove* had drifted closer together and Sam Carter was able to express his thanks without straining his voice.

"Thank you, Richard! Impressing those men would have ruined me. You should have been on the stage. I am distressed to think what will happen to that midshipman when he reports to his first lieutenant."

"So am I, Sam, but he deserves it. He should know by now that a lieutenant *can't* be senior to a master and commander."

"Very true, but we must give him the credit for knowing one fact of which you yourself seem to be ignorant."

"And what is that?"

"Well, he knew that only a king's ship has marines aboard. . . ."

Chapter Eleven

NEMESIS

"COME IN, come in, Captain!" said Mr Jeremie. "Pray be seated. Allow me to offer you a glass of Madeira?" Delancey took a chair and accepted some wine, thanking his host for the kindly thought.

"A pleasure, Captain, and far below the consideration you merit. Last year's campaign was a great success and we are confident that the year 1796 will bring as great a measure of prosperity."

"I am happy to think that the owners have a good return on their outlay—and that your own conservatory is the proof of it."

"Well, we look forward to having our own vines. But I am told that you are yourself a landowner these days."

"Hardly that, sir. I have bought an old ruin and the land which surrounds it."

"Your success with the *Nemesis* should turn it into a fine property some day. Perhaps you will name the residence after your ship?"

"It has always been Anneville, sir, and I should not wish to change it."

"Foolish of me—I had forgotten the family connection on your mother's side. Well now, you have the land and want only the money to build your residence. I sent for you, Captain, to give you good news on that subject. I think that a fortune is yours for the taking."

"Indeed, sir?"

"A fortune, I repeat, before the year ends. Drink up, Captain, and allow me to refill your glass."

"Thank you, Mr Jeremie. You will find me attentive."

Both glasses were refilled and Mr Jeremie looked about him to make sure that he was not overheard, looking into the entrance hall and closing the door again. Even after that precaution he lowered his voice: "What I tell you is in strictest confidence. I have had a letter from Mr Early."

"Indeed?"

"He is part-owner, as you know, of the *Nemesis,* and while he lives in Dorset he is much in Portsmouth and London, moves in the best society and enjoys the confidence of men in high office. In those circles, he tells me, the talk is of war with Spain. . . . Not a word of this to anyone."

"You can trust me, sir, to be discreet."

"Of course, of course. . . . Until recently our allies, the Spanish are to make peace with France and will soon be the subservient allies of the French Directory. To privateer owners this trend of events is of the greatest importance, but not all owners will be equally well informed. We are fortunate in having Mr Early as our partner."

"He is well-named, sir."

"Well-named? . . . Ha, I take your meaning! We plan to be early in the field, heh? Very droll! I must remember that. . . . Listen, though: there is more to this news than may strike you at first. With Spain as our enemy there will be another thirty sail of the line against us. We shall be as hard put to it as during the last war, barely able to hold our own. We shall win through, sir, no doubt of that. But the war may go against us for a year or two. And that will be the privateers' opportunity."

"What—when we are in danger of defeat?"

"Beyond question! When our fleets fall back on the Channel to save us from invasion, when our frigates are all needed to protect our trade, when the enemy's fleet is at sea and undefeated and when his cruisers are on our very coast—*that* is the time when his merchantmen venture forth without convoy, richly laden, fearing nothing! *That* is when we prosper here in Guernsey. And that will be the situation, mark my words, before this year is ended."

"So that victory, sir, is the last thing you want?"

"We want to win the war, naturally; and so we shall. But that comes later, and by that time the French privateers will be out—it will be their turn—and ours might as well be laid up or refitted for some other trade."

"You mean, sir, that privateers do best on the losing side?"

"Just so; and that is the prospect we have to face. If the Spanish fleet sails for Toulon we are outnumbered in the Mediterranean and must withdraw from there. If the Spanish fleet sails for Brest the threat is to Ireland and we must go to meet it. The king's ships will have all they can do to save us from invasion, and the interception of French merchantmen will be left to us, to the few lovers of their country who go to war at their own expense."

"I see that our patriotism does us the greatest credit."

"Indeed it does. We put to sea when things are at their worst."

"But the question is, sir—when will the Spaniards declare war?"

"Now *that* is what many folk would like to know. But Mr Early is a farsighted man—very farsighted indeed—and he suggests the Spaniards will not actually declare war until after their annual treasure fleet has reached Spain, probably towards the end of September. We shall be at war with Spain, he believes, on about October the first."

"Is a privateer commander allowed to act in intelligent anticipation?"

"Ah—that's the point I was coming to. A prize taken in time of peace will not be condemned, *unless*—mark me well—she reaches a British port *after* war has been declared. I have known an instance of a prize-master taking eight weeks to reach Plymouth from Ushant."

"The result of adverse winds."

"Undoubtedly. I have now to ask by what date the *Nemesis* will be ready for sea?"

"On about May 25th, sir."

"As late as that? But I know that you sustained some damage in March—more even than you knew at the time. You can't *always* avoid gunfire—we know that. But there is still talk along the waterfront about your capture of the *Bonne Citoyenne*. That affair remains a classic, as one might say, of privateering tactics. It certainly made your reputation in St Peter Port!"

"Beginner's luck, sir! It brought me volunteers, though, and I was able to replace old Le Vallois and a few other useless men."

"You certainly have a good crew now. Well, you know what the position is and can guess what the owners want. Be off the Spanish coast by the middle of August. In the meanwhile we suggest you cruise on the French coast between Rochefort and the Spanish border. Gain intelligence from every possible source, gain the earliest news of war with Spain and strike hard before the Spanish are ready."

"You set me, sir, an exceptionally difficult task."

"Mr Early admits that in his letter. It is a task, he says, for an exceptional commander."

It was under these orders that *Nemesis* put to sea. Delancey's was certainly a difficult mission, since early success would lessen her chances of survival. Each prize-crew detached would weaken the crew still on board; more so in officers than in seamen. Cruising in the Channel, Delancey had been able to return to base at intervals, recovering his prize crewmen or recruiting others, but men sent home from the Gulf of Gascony were lost for good. Given any ordinary measure of success the *Nemesis* would be desperately short-handed before the date when the war with Spain was expected. Delancey pointed this out before he left Guernsey, obtaining leave to enrol two more officers and ten more men. This he managed to do, strengthening his crew by one more midshipman, an ensign of marines, four more seamen and six more landsmen. With any more men aboard it would have been impossible to provision the ship for six months, as was obviously essential. His only remedy for the inevitable loss of men was to recruit from captured ships, thus diluting his crew with men he could not trust.

Mr Jeremie made his speech (the same one) to the ship's company on May 28th and Delancey put to sea that evening. He was off La Rochelle by June 16th and took his first prize a few days later.

This first success involved a long chase and the Frenchman yielded only to gunfire. Even when the chase had hove to there was some resistance to the boarding party. After a few minutes of hand-to-hand fighting the French captain finally surrendered, giving up a ship of only very moderate value. Delancey sent her home with some misgivings, doubting whether she had been worth the trouble. Two more prizes struck to him in early July, one of them fairly valuable, and then he fell in with a brig called the *Thomas Jefferson,* flying the tricolour when first sighted but with American papers of registration which were produced with a flourish after Delancey had taken possession. What she was really doing remained obscure but her disreputable crew included several Englishmen and two men (the master and mate) who claimed to be, and possibly were, American. With some misgivings Delancey enlisted seven men altogether, three of them apparently English. Of his original crew of 62 he had already lost 21. He now detached six more after battening the brig's crew below hatches. This left him with 35 men to which number he added this doubtful reinforcement. His only remaining officers were his first lieutenant and marine ensign. Short-handed even to navigate the ship, he was still less able to fight an action. He could take another prize, however, provided she made no more than a token resistance.

It was off Bilbao in early August that Delancey fell in with the British sloop *Scorpion* (16), commanded by Captain Mannering, who promptly signalled for the captain of *Nemesis* to come on board. Delancey obeyed, though not in uniform, and found himself faced by a stern-looking young officer who thought poorly, it would seem, of privateers.

"What have you taken, sir?" was his first question after the routine queries had been answered. Delancey told him and went on: "As for this last prize, the *Thomas Jefferson,* I could form no opinion as to real purpose of her voyage."

"What was her cargo?"

"Naval stores and provisions, sir; canvas, cordage, tallow and tar."

"She would be bound, in that case, for Cadiz. There is a French squadron there, blockaded by our own ships. Your prize would represent an attempt to carry French stores there under the American flag. This has been done quite frequently."

"Then the French and the Spanish are already in alliance, sir?"

"There is no treaty so far as I know but they are allies in practice."

"Dare we attack Spanish shipping, then?"

"Certainly *not,* sir. No state of war exists."

"But war might begin at any moment?"

"Undoubtedly, sir. Act over-hastily, however, and I may myself apprehend you for piracy. It is surprising to me that privateering is allowed. I shall certainly discountenance any attempt to disregard the law as it exists."

"I quite understand, sir. May I ask whether you have yourself taken anything?"

"No, I have not. We recently went in chase of a lugger but she turned out to be British. She was undoubtedly smuggling but I let her go."

"Was she the *Dove* by any chance?"

"Yes, that was her name. You know the craft?"

"Oh, yes, sir. Sam Carter's lugger."

"We saw and spoke with her off Bayonne. Smuggling, privateering, trading with the enemy! I despair sometimes of victory when I contemplate the number of my fellow-countrymen who take no part in the war."

Back in the *Nemesis,* Delancey decided to work northwards again, disappointed as he was in having no news of war with Spain. Once war had begun, he realized, the pattern of future conflict would turn on the orders given to the Spanish admiral at Cadiz. Would he sail for Toulon or Brest? What would the British Admiralty give for intelligence on that subject? He realized that couriers must be passing between France and Spain and that the despatches they carried might well give the date on which war was to be declared; as also, perhaps, the plan for cooperation between the French and Spanish fleet. These couriers would have to pass along the coast road in approaching the Spanish frontier. Had he, not Mannering, been the captain of the *Scorpion,* he would have landed a party of men and intercepted the next courier to come along. If his crew had not been so weakened, he would have been tempted to do it himself. It would be worth a fortune to know in advance when the war with Spain was to begin! It would be worth another fortune to the admiral blockading Cadiz and would even give a momentary advantage to George III. That last thought he had to dismiss, remembering that his employers were little interested in the outcome of the war as such. For all he knew Mannering might have seen the same opportunity as he had perceived and was about to seize it. Mannering was not the man to discuss his plan first with any privateersman he might chance to meet. The fact remained that there was a chance for someone to show initiative and score a considerable success. There was no such opportunity, however, for the captain of the *Nemesis.*

It was on August 19th when Delancey was summoned urgently on deck by Tracey, his young first lieutenant. Without saying anything, Tracey pointed westwards and handed Delancey his telescope. There was a sail there and Delancey had no difficulty in recognizing its type. "A French corvette," he said briefly, returning the telescope, and asked Tracey why he himself had not been called sooner.

"There was a squall, sir, and she was hidden until now."

Delancey realized that this could be true. It was blowing fairly hard towards the land with low cloud and a rising sea. It was dirty weather for the time of year and the *Nemesis* was steering almost due north under reduced canvas. To leeward was the flat coastline with a hint of white where the waves were breaking. Delancey decided at once to hold his present course knowing that he would be trapped against the land if he went in the other direction. His best hope of escape lay in the coming of darkness but many hours would pass before sunset. If the weather cleared, moreover, there would be a moon that night. As against that there might be another rain cloud and with it the chance to manoeuvre unseen. Delancey wondered whether to clear for action and decided against it. There would be time for that later. For the moment his better plan would be to make more sail. With the top-gallants set the Nemesis heeled further over and seemed at least to be holding her own. More than that was not to be expected because the French ship would be better manned. Soon afterwards she too made more sail and seemed now to be gaining.

Watching the corvette, Delancey saw her hit by another squall. His opponent was lost to view in the rainstorm and Delancey gave orders to wear ship. This was quickly done, putting the Nemesis on the oppo-site course, but the manoeuvre brought her nearer to the shore. It was something of a gamble, in any case, as there was no escape southwards, but it might throw off the pursuer and gain an hour for the pursued. As Delancey weighed the possibilities the squall came down on his ship with a shriek. She heeled over with her lee bulwarks almost under water and then slowly righted herself. Five minutes later the sky cleared to windward, revealing the corvette on the same course! Her captain had guessed correctly and the Nemesis was now in a worse position, having gained nothing. Delancey swore quietly and wondered what to do next.

The clouds had gone and the sky to westwards was bright and clear, giving every promise of a fine evening. Delancey still wanted to escape northwards but wearing again would bring him still closer to the shore. If he tacked, on the other hand, he would find himself even closer to the enemy. He was still trying to make this decision when disaster struck. Quite suddenly his mizen topmast broke just above the mizen crosstrees and collapsed in a tangle of rope and canvas. Delancey bal-anced the sail area by handing the fore-topsail and, given an hour or so, could have jury-rigged his mizen. But there was no time for that. Nemesis was crippled and her opponent was closing in for the kill.

Short-handed as he was, Delancey managed to cut away the wreck of his mizen topmast, putting the tangle over the side. Then he cleared for action, doing what he could to encourage his gun-crews. Young

Tracey was doing his best and the marine officer, Brehaut, was resolute and active, but neither, as Delancey knew, had been in battle before. His crew were a very mixed collection of men, weakened by the better seamen being chosen to man the prizes. There was no question of fighting to the death, for the men would never do it. All that anyone could do in this situation was to damage his opponent and then haul down his flag. Having reached that conclusion, Delancey thought again. He would do better to wreck the *Nemesis* than allow her to fall into enemy hands. He gave the helmsman a new course which could only end with his ship wrecked in the shallows which fringed the low-lying coast. That done, he prepared to give battle with all the guns he could man. The French corvette came up with her prey, shortening sail when nearly on the beam. At musket shot range, she opened fire and Delancey replied with a broadside from his port battery and the firing then became more or less continuous. The privateer's fire was not particularly accurate but it served to keep the corvette at a respectful distance. A proper plan for the Frenchman would have been to close the range and finish his opponent by boarding. No attempt of this sort was made and the action continued for half an hour. During that time the fire from the *Nemesis* was gradually slackening. Two guns had been dismounted, a number of men had been killed or wounded and there were finally only five guns still in action. At that point the action suddenly ended, the corvette backing her topsails. Both ships ceased fire and a few minutes later the *Nemesis* ran aground, her foremast and mainmast going over the side at the moment of impact. Delancey knew that he had finally lost his ship.

There was still a heavy sea and the privateer lifted two or three times, moving further on to the sand and coming down again with a sickening thud. The timbers gaped after this, admitting about five feet of water and beginning the process of disintegration. Waves broke heavily over the ship's waist as she sank lower and it was obvious that her hull would fall apart in a matter of hours. The corvette had anchored a half mile to seaward and the activity aboard her suggested that the

French were about to lower a boat. Seeing this, Delancey called his
men together on the forecastle, now the driest place, and thanked them
for putting up a good fight.

"Well done, men," he said. "We have cheated the French of their
prize. They will have nothing to take with them, no mast on which to
hoist the tricolour over the British ensign. They will presently send a
boat over and we shall mostly end as prisoners of war. There is a good
chance of being exchanged within twelve months but this is very much
a matter of luck. Our two larger boats are smashed, as you can see,
but the gig will float—or at least I think she will. I propose to gain the
shore, if I can, and attempt to reach Portugal overland. The chances
are that this attempt will fail. I may not reach the shore and, even if I
do, may be taken prisoner as soon as I land—or may be fired upon,
indeed, before I have landed. In the gig I can take five other men, giving preference to those who speak French or Spanish. Any volunteers?"

There was some hurried discussion and then the volunteers came
forward, seven of them. Delancey rejected two of these—one as too
young and the other too stupid—and told the rest to fetch their best
clothes and small arms. The gig was lowered and Delancey gave his
final orders to his first lieutenant. "Try to hold the attention of the
French boat's crew—give them something else to look at so that the
gig is unnoticed. We shall see to it that the Nemesis is between us and
the corvette. Good luck!" There was no time to waste, for the French
longboat was already in the water, and the volunteers tumbled into the
gig as well as they might. Delancey came last and took the helm, pushing off and steering so as not to be seen from the corvette. Even without
that complication it was difficult to keep the gig afloat for the waves
ran high and the boat was leaking. Looking back, however, Delancey
could see that Tracey and his men were trying to lower the longboat.
This was quite futile, of course, for the boat had been holed, but it
certainly complicated the problem for the corvette's longboat. The longboat of the Nemesis hung askew and Tracey could be seen waving his
arms with almost Gallic despair. The French officer was trying to bring

his boat alongside but his gestures conveyed his exasperation. From each wave crest Delancey had a diminishing view of this scene. Then the boat was in the breakers and grounding on the sand, the efforts of all being just sufficient to drag the gig out of the water and up the beach. They were all very wet by this time and Delancey set them to gather firewood so that their clothes might be dried. In a last dash down to his cabin, flint and steel were among the things he had remembered. He now chose a sheltered hollow for a camp fire and looked about him for signs of life. Seawards he could see the wreck of the privateer with her mizen lower mast still standing and, beyond it, the sails of the French corvette. Landwards there was heath and undergrowth, stunted trees and, further inland, a small wood. Either way along the sea's edge stretched the sand dunes without the least sign of habitation or human activity. Their landing had been seen by nobody and they had come to as remote a place as could be imagined. They were, he guessed, on the French side of the frontier at some point north of Bayonne. Somewhere inland of them would be the road from Bordeaux to Bayonne and so to San Sebastian, the road which provided the line of communication between the French government and their fleet at Cadiz. Whatever the other drawbacks about his present situation, Delancey could see that he was well placed to intercept the mail. How would it be if he could return to England via Portugal as the bearer of vital information?

As the others came back with their firewood and as clothes were being dried before the fire, Delancey was considering the small group of survivors from the wreck of the *Nemesis*. Who were they and why did they volunteer? It was some minutes before the truth dawned on him: they were the men who had some special reason to avoid capture and exchange. The best seaman, a quartermaster indeed, was Pierre Rigault, recruited in Guernsey. He was almost certainly a deserter from the navy, a man of some education and able to speak French with a good accent. Then there was André Bisson, a Jerseyman, a fugitive from justice and accused (it was said) of forgery. Martin Ramos claimed to be Spanish and certainly spoke that language fluently, having also some words of French (but not of English). He and Tom Manning had both been in the *Thomas Jefferson* and Ramos could be assumed to be a criminal of sorts. Manning said that he was American and a groom (of all things) by trade but Delancey put him down mentally as another deserter, probably from the British army. Frederick Hodder, enlisted at St Peter Port, spoke with a cockney accent and described himself as a locksmith. He was presumably a burglar and ripe for the gallows if caught. None of these men wanted to be listed as a prisoner of war, each of them had some good reason for avoiding public notice in any form. They could muster between them some useful talents but it was doubtful how far they could be trusted. Several, it might be supposed, would like to earn a royal pardon but Delancey was in no position to promise them that or any other reward. He had by any standards a difficult team to handle.

"Listen, men," said Delancey. "We have won the first round, being safe ashore and little the worse for a ducking. We are in France but close to the Spanish frontier. War with Spain is expected but we must be treated there, in the meanwhile, as citizens of a country with which the king of Spain is at peace. Should war have begun, however, we can try to reach Portugal, knowing that the Portuguese are still our allies. If we reach Portugal we shall owe our success to keeping the strictest discipline, and my first order to you is to accept Mr Rigault as acting boatswain. You will obey him when I am not present and your survival may well depend upon it. My plan is to move across the frontier with Spain and so towards Portugal. While in France we shall march only at night, resting in concealment by day. There will be difficulties, no doubt, over food but the distance to the frontier is not more than forty miles, as I should guess, and may be nearer 35. If we gain any useful intelligence and convey it back to England we may gain a reward and perhaps induce the king to forget about any past incidents which are better forgotten. Remember this, above all, we are not defeated yet!"

Delancey's little speech was well received but he had no illusions about the quality of his men. He knew, incidentally, that he had no recognized authority over them. His powers as a privateer commander were little more than those of any ship's master and they ended with the shipwreck. All he had to enforce his orders was a vaguely naval uniform, a bag of coin and a pair of loaded pistols. The habit of command was enough for the time being but what would happen later on? Rigault was a useful man and so, he thought, was Manning. But what about Bisson or Hodder? For the moment he needed, first of all, to give them confidence. For this purpose he issued them with some biscuit and a tot of rum apiece. He then told them to rest, reminding them that they would have a long way to go after sunset. The shore was no place to linger and their first object must be to cross the frontier. Each time they slept they would have to post one man as sentry. He would himself take the first watch, Rigault the second, Bisson the third, Manning and Ramos next and Hodder last of all. Before they slept all weapons must be dried, reloaded and oiled.

It was a fine warm night, the wind having died away since the time of the action. The moon rose early and Delancey roused his men and told them that they must march. Before quitting the point at which they landed he made them haul the boat further inland and hide it in the wood. That done, they moved eastward with more caution than speed. The coast on which they had landed was a barren country, practically uninhabited, but a mile or two inland were areas of cultivation with farms and villages. They gained the main road on their first night's march and were then compelled to make a wide circuit round the town of Bayonne. By the morning after the second night they were back on the main road and in a position to intercept the next courier bound from Paris to Cadiz. Ramos was sent that day to visit a wayside tavern and came back with the news that couriers passed on every other day. They travelled thus far by coach but would continue on horseback in Spain, where the roads were so rough. They were escorted by a couple of troopers as far as the frontier but were there met, it was said, by a troop of Spanish militia. There were brigands, Ramos was told, especially in Spain—yes, and smugglers as well—so that an officer could hardly be expected to travel alone. Having this much information, Delancey decided that their present progress was too slow. To reach Portugal before the outbreak of war with Spain it would be the better plan to intercept a courier and take his place, thus continuing with the speed of horses. There was good reason to make this interception on the French side of the frontier, partly because any subsequent hunt for bandits would be in France—the country they would be leaving—and partly because the capture of some travel documents would simplify the actual crossing of the frontier. It was, of course, a southbound courier they must intercept, one whose coming would be expected, not one whose carriage had been recently seen going in the opposite direction. Once in Spain, Delancey's party had a good chance of being accepted as French. They could make only a brief attempt at being taken for Spaniards in France. The best place for the interception, Delancey concluded, would be near a place called Bidart.

The location finally chosen for the ambush was one where the road crossed a dry watercourse with plenty of undergrowth on either bank. There were few country folk around, and little traffic on the road. If the usual routine was followed the courier might be expected some time that same afternoon, perhaps between one and two, his aim being to dine at St Jean-de-Luz and possibly reach San Sebastian by nightfall.

There was much to do in the meanwhile and the preparation included the moving of two fallen trees to points on the roadside where they could be propped up and so fall, when pushed, across the carriage way. This could not be done without attracting some attention but Ramos was briefed with a story about a trap to be laid for bandits. He told it to several rustics, one of them frankly incredulous, but none was in a position to stop the work or report his suspicions to a magistrate or other public official. Work was also interrupted by the passing of an occasional farm-cart and once by a drove of cattle, but it was nevertheless completed in time. Soon after midday Pierre Rigault walked up the road towards Bayonne and sat down to wait for the expected coach and escort.

At a quarter past two the post-chaise appeared and Rigault, standing in the road, made the driver pull up. Going to the window of the coach, he warned the courier, in fluent French, that there were bandits in the vicinity and that a coach had been robbed only yesterday. The commandant at St Jean-de-Luz was sending a cavalry escort as far as a certain crossroads and had sent Rigault to warn the courier and guide him to the rendezvous. The courier, Captain Laffray, was an elderly, red-faced and fattish officer who rather made light of the danger. He gave it as his opinion that the bandits would prefer easier prey. The sergeant who was with him in the coach looked more alarmed and began to check the priming of his pistols. After a little further discussion the captain reluctantly admitted Rigault to the coach and thanked him for the warning which the sergeant passed on to the two troopers who were following as escort some fifty yards behind. The whip cracked and the vehicle rolled on.

Ten minutes later a tree crashed across the road, frightening the four horses to a plunging halt. The coachman was too occupied with the reins to draw his pistol but the second driver, sitting beside him, had his pistol ready. Several shots were fired and Rigault whipped out his pistols just ahead of the courier and the sergeant, shooting them both. Twenty yards behind the coach another tree fell across the road, bringing the two dragoons to a momentary halt. Then they charged, both being shot at close range, one of them mortally. There was a second shot, killing the wounded trooper, and then two more shots fired inside the coach. The firing died away, the smoke disappeared and the little skirmish was over.

"Dammit," said Delancey, "I meant to take them prisoners. Why to God—?"

"How *could* we?" said Manning, "What could we have done with them?"

"This was the only way," said Hodder.

In this fashion Delancey discovered the limits of his authority. His orders had been disobeyed, almost certainly by previous agreement, and he knew that the others had been right. Hating the cold-blooded killing, he could say no more on the subject.

"Strip their uniforms off," he said, "and dig a grave over there." He pointed to a clump of trees some two hundred yards away. "There's a spade on the coach," he added and Ramos unclipped it from its place. Delancey then took the courier's leather bag and told Hodder to pick the lock.

"Won't he have the key, sir?" asked that expert, only to be told to get on with it. As Delancey knew, the key would never have been entrusted to the courier but only to the officers at either end of the route. A grisly half hour followed, for the uniforms were bloodstained, but the work was finally done. It could not be finished, however, until a bucket of water and a scrubbing brush had been borrowed from a cottage and even then the stains were visible on the ill-fitting uniforms. At last the moment came when the party could assemble, ready to proceed. Tom Manning was the coachman, with Martin Ramos as his assistant. Bisson and Hodder were dragoons, sitting their horses in some discomfort. Delancey himself was the courier and Pierre Rigault was the sergeant. From the direction of the burial place came the howling of a dog. "Shall I . . . ?" asked Rigault, but Delancey replied, "We have spilt blood enough. Let's go!" He was still feeling rather sick as the carriage rolled on.

The contents of the courier's bag proved disappointing. There were no orders from Paris for the French Admiral at Cadiz. There were letters enough but they were all dealing with routine matters. The sentence of a court martial was confirmed, the report rendered by a court of inquiry was formally acknowledged, a successor was named to the purser of the *Barras* (who had died) and the appointment was notified of a new surgeon for the *Duquesne*. There was correspondence about new canvas to be supplied to the *Censeur*, as also about the cost of repairing the *Friponne*'s rudder. There were private letters in addition,

some even from officials in the Ministry of Marine, but none shed light
on the intended movements of Admiral Richery—still less on the plans
of the Spanish Commander-in-Chief, Don Juan de Langara. Reading
through all these trivialities as the coach travelled southwards, Delancey
had a sense of failure. Had those six men been killed for nothing? No,
that was not true. The result of the skirmish had been to provide
Delancey with carriage and horses, with a useful sum in French cur-
rency, with papers of identification and means of disguise. His party
would have no difficulty in passing the sentries at St Jean-de-Luz.
The frontier lay beyond and San Sebastian perhaps seven miles further
on. They would arrive late but the failing light would be an advantage.
. . . It was late afternoon by now, buildings and passers-by had become
more frequent and there was more traffic on the road. It was obvious
that the coach was in the outskirts of St Jean-de-Luz.

It was at this point that Delancey became aware of a coming problem. He foresaw no difficulty with the sentries or guard commander
but he realized that there would have to be a change of horses. The
proper coachman would have driven straight to the coaching inn but
Tom Manning would not know where it was nor was there anyone in
the party who could tell him. Rigault could inquire but that would
seem ridiculous. Perhaps the horses would know their way to their stable? Worrying over this, Delancey told himself that the problem might
not exist. There might be only the one main street and the principal
inn might be obvious from the other coaches there. While he was still
pondering this problem the coach drew up and a soldier appeared at
the window, saluting when he saw Delancey's uniform. The sentry
merely glanced at the documents which Delancey waved, stepping back
again and telling the coachman to drive on. The coach now advanced
more slowly because of the traffic and Delancey hoped that the horses
would prove better-informed than the driver. They were not and the
coach presently came to a standstill. Stepping down from the coach
door, Delancey saw that the street forked and that Manning was at a
loss. Going forward and speaking quietly, Delancey said, "To the right,"

and so returned to his seat in the coach, hoping devoutly that his guess would prove correct. Looking out he presently saw that his choice, made at random, was almost certainly wrong. The street they were in led to the quayside and away from the centre of the town. There were ship's chandlers and sailors' taverns and more than a touch of squalor. Young women and errand boys were staring at the coach in wonder and perhaps with a hint of derision. Manning drew up and Delancey again went forward to speak with him, meaning to tell him to go back to the point where they had evidently gone wrong. Before he could do so, however, a seafaring man stepped up to him and said quietly (in English):

"Captain Delancey, I think? Perhaps you have lost your way?"

PART FOUR

Chapter Twelve

CASTLE IN SPAIN

FOR A MOMENT Delancey felt that his mission—and his life—had come to an end. For a cold instant he could feel the fetters, glimpse daybreak through the bars and hear the tramp of the firing squad. Staring at the stranger, he could not remember having seen him before. Speaking in French, he said that there must be some mistake, he had not had the honour of meeting the citizen on any previous occasion.

"In that case it would be useless to remind you of David Evans, mate of the *Dove*."

With an effort Delancey remembered that dark and insignificant figure.

"But is the *Dove* here?"

Evans shook his head. "She is due here a week hence," he replied briefly. "There are some arrangements to make in the meanwhile." So Evans was collecting the cargo, in effect, and the *Dove* was elsewhere, perhaps at Arcachon. Delancey had an idea but it had to wait. There was first the immediate problem.

"We have to change horses somewhere, Mr Evans. Can you pilot us?"

Without another word, Evans went over to Manning and gave him directions, finally joining him on the coachman's box. The coach turned, swerved into a street on the right, turned left, turned right again, coming into the main street and drawing up outside the Pomme d'Or. The ostlers ran forward and Evans joined Delancey in the parlour of the inn. Their further conversation was in French.

"Thank you, Mr Evans. Could you add to your kindness by giving Sam a letter from me?"

"Asking him to pick you up?"

"Yes, at some place near Cadiz."

Evans considered this possibility for a moment before replying. "I'll give him the letter, sir, but I'm not sure that it can be done. We complete our cargo here. Once we have done that, the men will want to sail for home."

"My hope must be that Sam can persuade them. Is there a useful small port near Cadiz—one known to you for purposes of trade?"

"Yes, there is Léon, a few miles to the south. We have an agent there called Davila, a man with whom we do occasional business."

"If Sam were to go there, when would he arrive?"

"In about three weeks time. Say, on September 15th."

"Very well then. I'll send the waiter for paper and ink, for a quill and some wine."

While Evans drank his wine, presently joined by Rigault, Delancey wrote:

23rd August, 1796.

Dear Mr Carter,

Nemesis has been wrecked on the French coast and I am on my way into Spain with five other survivors, the rest being taken prisoner. My hope is to procure some intelligence about the intentions of the French and Spanish fleets now at Cadiz. Having learnt what I can of the enemy's purposes, perhaps at Cadiz itself, I shall go to the port of Léon, hoping to be there from the 15th to the 21st September and in touch with Señor Davila. Should it be possible for you to call there at that time I should be more than grateful for a passage to Guernsey. In view of the possible value of the intelligence I hope to gain you could very properly ask any British man-of-war to cover our withdrawal. There is no state of war as yet between Britain and Spain but I have no doubt that war will be declared in the near future and of a certainty before the end of October. I am fully cognisant of

the dangers inherent in your playing a part in this operation and
would not ask it of you except as tending to the king's service.

> I have the honour to remain,
> Your former foe but present friend,
> Richard Delancey

The finished and signed letter was pocketed by David Evans who
finished his glass and walked with Delancey to the coach. "If you could
have stayed here," he said, "until the *Dove* arrived!"

"How could we?" asked Delancey, and Evans, glancing at his uniform, could guess at the dangers run until the frontier had been passed.
After a hurried farewell the coach was on the road again, leaving St
Jean-de-Luz by the road to the south. Two hours later the coach was
at the frontier and passed without hindrance into Spain.

Traffic increased as they approached the town of San Sebastian but
no particular notice was taken of the escorted post-chaise, which must
have been a familiar sight. The coach reached the main gate as darkness fell and the sentry did no more than glance at the documents
that were shown him. Martin Ramos, chatting with him for a moment,
was told that the principal inn, where senior officers lodged, was the
Réal. If that were full up the courier might try the Sancta Trinidad.
Guessing that Captain Laffray might have been known at the Réal and
might be expected there, Delancey chose the lesser inn where he was
made welcome. The coachman and spare driver were lodged with
the two troopers in the hayloft over the stable, where Ramos had the
chance to hear the ostlers' gossip. Delancey himself was given a room
and Rigault had the room next to it. Their supper was sent upstairs at
Delancey's request and then began a difficult negotiation which centred upon the cleaning—and even the repair—of uniforms. The inn
servants knew little French but they were finally persuaded to take
the soiled uniforms away, leaving Delancey and Rigault in civilian
clothes for the evening. The two troopers made similar arrangements

for themselves. All, it was hoped, would pass muster by the following afternoon.

News of brigandage on the road came to San Sebastian next morning and Ramos soon knew all about it. A peasant had found some recently buried bodies by the roadside to the north of St Jean-de-Luz. He had been attracted to the spot by a dog's howling. Finding a corpse, he had hastened to inform the gendarmes. Their investigations led them to discover five more bodies, all clearly murdered. There were no brigands, it was thought, on the French side of the frontier, and the gendarmes concluded that the criminals were Spanish. They sent word, therefore, to San Sebastian; as also, however, to Bayonne. The authorities there knew of no travellers who had gone south in that number on the previous day—except, of course, for the French courier and his party. Troops of cavalry were sent out and rewards were offered for information. Messengers came and went and rumour had it that the bandits were deserters from the French army. Who their victims were no one could say for neither travellers nor local people were missing. Could the bandits have fought each other? Hearing these rumours, Delancey knew that he would have to ask the military commandant for an escort. It was usual, he knew, and all this talk of brigandage made it seem more essential. To go on without escort would seem, in fact, highly suspicious. He decided, therefore, to call on the commandant, walking to the citadel that afternoon—as soon, in fact, as his uniform was fit to be seen.

Reporting at the guard room and giving his name as Captain Rochambeau, Delancey asked the commandant to spare a few minutes of his time. He expected to have difficulties over language but he was received almost at once by a senior officer whose French was very fluent indeed.

Colonel Diego de Altamirano listened politely to Delancey's explanation of his presence and his plans. He agreed at once to provide a cavalry escort for the journey to Vittoria. It was only then, when all had been agreed, that he asked an awkward question: "With what escort did you arrive here?"

Delancey did not hesitate to answer truthfully: "I have two dragoons with me."

"From St Jean-de-Luz?"

"No, from Bayonne."

"So you will want to return them to their unit. The routine is to collect six or eight of these men and then send them back with the next coach bound for France. We have four already and your two can join them."

"I had intended, Colonel, to keep these men with me for the present. One acts as my valet and the other as my Spanish interpreter."

"How unfortunate! Our treaty with France, concluded on August 19th, does not allow French troops to pass through Spain in uniform. Any escort you have must be Spanish. I can assure you, however, that the escort commander will have some knowledge of French and that you will need no other interpreter. Tell your two men to report here tomorrow."

Delancey had a quick decision to make. He had either to agree easily as one who cared little about it or he must fly into a rage as befitted a French officer when opposed by a mere Spaniard. He decided to give way gracefully.

"I quite understand. You do not wish to see foreign armies on Spanish soil—not even an army of two!"

"Of four, to be exact," said the Colonel blandly. "We Spaniards are often thought to be obstinate and proud. On which day, Captain, do you plan to resume your journey?"

"Tomorrow, Colonel, if that is convenient."

"By all means. The escort will be at your inn tomorrow morning— you can settle the exact hour with my adjutant. My hope is that you will have a good journey. There was recently an incident on the road— as you will probably have heard—but that was in the other direction, and on the French side of the frontier. I am somewhat mystified by that affair and am wondering still what lies behind it."

"Is brigandage so unusual then, Colonel?"

"No, sir, not brigandage as such. What is unusual is the brigand who strikes only once and then disappears."

"What else can he do while the hunt is up?"

"He still has to live. However, the brigand is my concern not yours and I don't expect him to appear on the road to Vittoria."

Delancey said farewell to the commandant but came away with the feeling that the colonel was a great deal more astute than seemed desirable. Back at the Sancta Trinidad he told Rigault about the meeting and about the problem of the two dragoons.

"Very well," said Rigault, "Bisson and Hodder will put on civilian clothes. The dragoons have deserted, leaving their horses behind."

It was a reasonable policy, and perhaps the best, but the dangers were obvious, beginning with the gossip which would circulate among the servants at the inn. Perhaps a more elaborate story would better serve the purpose; something perhaps to do with a secret mission.

Delancey's party was to leave next morning but the troop of militia cavalry failed to appear. Instead of the escort the commandant's adjutant came to the inn and asked to see Captain Rochambeau. With great politeness and regret he said that there was some unavoidable delay over the troop that had been detailed for the journey. The new time of departure would be midday and the commandant would be grateful if Captain Rochambeau would, in the meanwhile, come to the Citadel, bringing with him the two dragoons who were to join the next carriage for Bayonne. The purpose of the visit would be purely routine and the commandant did not expect to detain the captain for more than a quarter of an hour. There was a hasty conference in Rigault's room while the adjutant waited on the ground floor. Bisson wanted to make a dash for the town gate but Delancey pointed out that the doors would possibly be shut and that any attempt to leave

might end merely in their arrest. No, their only policy was to bluff
their way through. It was far from certain that the commandant had
detected their imposture and he would be very reluctant to make the
sort of mistake which would incur the wrath of the French Republic.
The king of Spain was a subservient ally of France and would willingly
sacrifice any mere colonel whose head the Directory might demand.
To be puzzled was one thing, to risk one's whole career was another.
The time was approaching when Delancey would have to lose his tem-
per and remind the colonel of what was at stake. He would be
accompanied by Rigault in his sergeant's uniform with Bisson and Hodder dressed as civilians and he would have to admit that they had come
in disguise. His difficulty would be in explaining why.

At the Citadel, Delancey and his party were shown at once into the
commandant's room. The colonel was full of apologies for the delayed
escort. He regretted having to waste the captain's time over a trifle. He
hoped that the captain would understand that routine matters, however tedious, had still to be transacted. Would the captain be seated
for a moment? Would he remove his cloak? With some reluctance
Delancey allowed the adjutant to help him off with his cloak and hang
it on a peg.

"The merest trifle, sir. These two dragoons—are they with you?"

"They are and they are not," Delancey admitted. "Their uniforms
were a disguise worn by these two gentlemen. Capitaine de Corvette
Bellanger and his secretary, M. Le Cannelier. So far a disguise has been
necessary; in Spain it is not."

"Might I be allowed to know the reason?"

"In strict confidence, Colonel?"

"But of course!"

"I may tell you then, that they have been concerned for the last
two years with a certain project. It concerns the blowing up of enemy
ships of war by use of a secret device."

"Just so."

"The Directory have decided to develop this invention for use against the British. It will transform the whole situation in a day. With me I have the experts who have brought this invention to its present state of readiness. Spies in British pay have tried to penetrate our workshop at Dunkirk. We believe they know the general nature of our project. We believe they know the names of the officers concerned. If they discovered that these two men had been sent to Cadiz, they would suspect the truth—that their fleet off Cadiz is in the greatest danger. They have travelled under false names and in disguise so as to prevent the enemy guessing our intentions."

"Very ingenious indeed, my dear captain. Who would suspect two men in dragoons uniform? I am interested also in your own part in the affair, if I may say so. If your two dragoons are not soldiers it occurs to me that you might not be a real courier."

"I think, Colonel, that I have answered enough of your questions; more, perhaps, than my government would approve."

"But of course, Captain, of course! A thousand apologies! The fact is that one has too little to discuss in such an isolated post as this. Whatever seems unusual becomes at once the subject of gossip. There is, for example, the story of the two dragoons—"

"Enough of that, Colonel. I have warned you already!"

"Please! Don't misunderstand me. I don't mean *your* dragoons. I refer now to certain men killed on the highway between Bayonne and St Jean-de-Luz—killed, it would seem, by bandits. We talked about the incident yesterday, did we not? Two of them are thought to have been cavalrymen and have even been recognized. Both their uniforms were taken with both horses and arms, headgear and boots. For all we know there are two brigands on the road disguised as troopers."

"That is quite possible."

"And you came with two of your companions in the same disguise! A strange coincidence, you must admit."

"Strange indeed. Well, Colonel, if our business is concluded, I shall beg to take leave of you and resume my journey to Vittoria and so to Madrid."

"You are naturally eager to deliver the despatches with which you have been entrusted and I, for one, would hate to be the cause of delay. Tell me one thing, though, before you go. Why do you have an Englishman as one of your staff?"

"I don't know what you mean."

"But I think you do. Your coachman has been heard to speak English and is all but totally ignorant of French."

"He is actually American."

"How stupid of me! And I suppose the smaller of your ex-dragoons is another American?"

"He is French but has lived in the United States."

"But of course. What could be more natural? But another possibility occurs to me. Suppose the British were to plan an interception of couriers moving between Paris and Madrid, where would they choose to do it? My belief is that their agents would land from the sea between Bayonne and San Sebastian. The discovery of these bodies gave me the idea that such a landing might have taken place. When I first heard of the incident I asked myself, 'Could the British have a plan for capturing the French despatches sent from Paris to Cadiz? Could they not be interested in what the Minister of Marine might say to Admiral Richery?' I think they *could* be interested, I think they *are*. Do you agree —Captain?"

"The British might attempt something of the sort but interception of messages to Richery seems to me a far-fetched idea, not characteristic of British methods. I must be on my way, sir, and you will detain me further at your peril!"

"*I* detain you, my dear Captain? That would be unthinkable. I know my duty better than that. If I dared do so, however, it would not be on account of that remote possibility, nor yet on account of the two dragoons. Were I to detain you—if I dared (and I repeat, *if*)—it would be on account of a chestnut horse, a gelding with a white mark on the forehead. Your outrider's horse has been recognized, my dear

sir; as the one ridden by one of the dragoons who died so mysteriously.
. . . No, don't draw your pistol. You are surrounded, sir, but not, please
understand, with the object of detaining you. I should never dare to
do that. Instead, I am putting you and your friends under arrest."

Delancey, looking round, saw that he and the others were covered
by pistols and that a guard had collected outside the door. There was
no chance of escape or resistance. They had walked into a trap and
the colonel, sitting still but watchful at the table, was taking no chances.
The adjutant disarmed each of them in turn, feeling for concealed
weapons, and then locked their swords away in a cupboard.

"Wait till the Directory hears of this!" Delancey thundered. "Wait
until they hear that a French officer has been placed under arrest on
the Spanish frontier! What will the Minister for War say to King Fer-
dinand? What will the king say to you? You'll be lucky if you are merely
cashiered and reduced to the ranks!"

"I daresay," replied the colonel. "I would hope to be a dragoon.
Very fashionable just now, it seems, and a uniform to be had for nothing." He went on after a pause, looking idly at the ceiling. "It might
be a little bloodstained in the lining but what of that? War is war and
bandits are not always bandits. I hope you will be comfortable here,
Captain, until we hear from your superiors. Our hospitality must be
of the simplest, you will understand, with no pretence of luxury. Let
us know, however, if there is anything you want."

At a sign, the prisoners were marched out of the room, down the
staircase and across the courtyard, into another building and along the
central corridor which divided two rows of cells. Rigault was led into
the first cell on the left, the door being shut and locked before Delancey
was pushed into the second cell on the right. To judge from the sound,
Ramos was put in the third cell on the right, and Bisson in the cell
opposite. A sentry, marching up and down the corridor, prevented them
speaking to each other but each door had a small grid-covered peep-
hole through which they could see. Delancey was thus able to view,

briefly, the arrival under escort of Manning and Hodder. He had been in an enemy fortress before but under different circumstances. He had then been a prisoner of war. He was now a spy, caught in the act and due to face a firing squad.

Rigault's first reaction was to demand paper, ink and a quill. He would write to the captain of the dockyard at Bayonne and ask for that officer's assistance. The writing materials were given him and he began to write his complaints in a proper mixture of formality and outrage. They would not secure his release—that at least was obvious—but they might obtain better treatment for the whole party while any doubt remained as to their identity. Ramos had a different reaction—he tried to engage the sentry in conversation with a view to seeing whether he could be bribed. He had little success even in making himself understood. The soldier was a Catalan, speaking some dialect of the Pyrenees, and he thought of Castilian as almost a foreign language. He merely shook his head and resumed his sentry beat up and down the stone-flagged corridor. Bisson, like Rigault, demanded writing materials and began to forge an order for his own release. There was no immediate use for it but it was good to practise one's art. One never knew what might come in useful. Manning's reaction was to go to the barred window of his cell and make a minute examination of the ironwork, which seemed depressingly sound, and of the stonework, which appeared to be almost new. As for Hodder, he began to study the lock on his cell door. With some pieces of wire, which he happened to have in his inner pocket, he felt his way gently through the intricacies which lay behind the keyhole. He could picture the key he needed but had no means of making it.

Delancey barely glanced out of his cell window before he sat down on his bed and began to think. He was very conscious of being the leader whose scheme had led them all to face imprisonment and probable execution. He had run a deliberate risk, gambling with his own life as well as theirs. Their safety, at this stage, had depended on the stupidity, which he had assumed, of the Spanish commandant. It had seemed unlikely that the Spanish would appoint a military genius to command the small garrison at San Sebastian. While Spain was France's subservient ally this frontier had no strategic importance. The routine duties of the garrison commander might well have been entrusted to some elderly nobleman, some officer passed over for promotion, some courtier banished from the royal presence for duelling or cheating at cards. He had been confronted instead by Colonel Diego de Altamirano who was neither disreputable, stupid nor old. He had been sufficiently astute to see the possible connection between different incidents. He had guessed what was happening and yet had resisted the temptation to act hastily. He had allowed his opponents to feel secure while he collected information and then, at the last moment, he had closed the trap. The colonel was no fool, so much was obvious. It was Delancey's first task to guess what the colonel would do next. What would he himself do had their parts been reversed? He would write to Bayonne and ask for the help of some French naval officer, preferably one with experience of intelligence work. The chances were that he would have long since made contact with the French at Bayonne and St Jean-de-Luz and would know whom to approach and how. With such an officer present at his interrogation, Rigault would break down at once, lacking sufficient knowledge of the French army. With the same officer (or any other Frenchman) present, he would himself break down as promptly and would be seen to be a foreigner. Neither Manning nor Hodder could pass as American and neither of them knew, for that matter, that this was expected of them. That they were a group of British spies must be suspected already and little more evidence would be needed to secure conviction before a military court. By tomorrow or the next day, the colonel's case would be complete.

Was it likely, however, that the colonel would be content to execute the spies? His first aim would rather be to discover what they were trying to do. He had seen that the French lines of communication were vulnerable at this point. He had guessed that the spies had come by sea. What he had not guessed was that their landing was accidental—the result of a shipwreck. The trouble was that each one of his party, interrogated separately, would tell a different tale. One weakness in the preparation for their march into Spain—as Delancey could now realize—was that there had been no agreed story to tell if they were captured. A more professional team would have been provided with such a story, not that it would save their lives but merely to conceal the nature of their mission. There could be no agreed story now. The best plan would be for he himself to act as spokesman and for the others to say nothing. Could he transmit that message to the rest? And would they obey him after pressure had been brought to bear? Would torture be used? It seemed all too likely. . . . People who take infants to see bloodshed in the bull-fighting arena are likely to be cruel in other ways. Delancey shuddered at the thought and found himself sweating. It lay with him to think of a plan to escape. Having led his men into a trap it was for him now to lead them out of it. The question was—how?

Chapter Thirteen

MUTINY AT SEA

FLYING THE TRICOLOUR, the lugger *Dove* put into St Jean-de-Luz on August 24th, space being found for her alongside the breakwater. She had been more than welcome on her first visit because of what she brought and now she was just as welcome because of the goods she would ship; goods for which there would be no legal outlet after war began. Acting as supercargo, Mr Evans came on board with the bills of lading. He also gave Sam Carter the letter which Delancey had written, adding a brief account of how they had met.

"He was dressed as a French army officer?" asked Sam, making sure that he had the right picture.

"Yes, he was in French army uniform and so were three of his men, one in the coach and two on horseback."

"That looks to me as if he had killed that number of French soldiers."

"He must have done."

"So he needed to cross the border before the hunt was up."

"I reckon so."

"And he won't be all that safe in Spain."

"Nor he will neither. But we are not yet at war, Sam, are we?"

"Not that I hear of. But it won't be long. In three or four weeks or even less. This voyage down to Cadiz will be none of the safest, David, and that's the truth."

"What, Sam—are you going to do it?"

"Yes, I shall do it. What choice is there? I can't leave Richard Delancey to die in Spain. He'll be no prisoner of war, not after what he's done to the French. Caught in disguise, he'll be shot. He's a fine fellow is Richard and a friend of mine. We must save him if we can. You wouldn't think that he was a good seaman would you? He seems too much of the gentleman sometimes, reading novels or writing poetry, dreaming of god-knows-what. But put him in a tight corner, face him with a knotty problem, and Richard knows what to do and does it. He outwitted *me* once, remember."

"I know that, Sam. And he saved your men from the press-gang that time only for us to lose them the next week. The men we have now, shipped in Guernsey, are not to be relied upon. They won't like the idea of heading south from here."

"Are you sure of that, David?"

"Once they have a cargo aboard they'll want to steer for home."

"More's the pity then—they can't."

The next few days were spent in shipping the cargo. Relations with the French merchants ashore were excellent and there was no trouble with the customs or police. All were perfectly aware of the *Dove's* business but some were anxious to hurry her sailing. As one old sea captain explained: "There are naval officers who don't understand business. If a national ship were to come in, we might have trouble." All was well, however, until the day of the *Dove's* departure. After a last round of drinks and good wishes Sam Carter gave the order to cast off and the *Dove* made sail. It was a foggy day, the wind was faint and the lugger was moving slowly out of the harbour, when a larger ship suddenly loomed out of the mist. There was no real risk of collision but the other ship was rather close and easily identifiable as a French corvette. An officer hailed the *Dove,* probably ordering her to heave to. Carter ignored this but heard the sounds of a boat being lowered and manned. Losing sight of the corvette he became aware of the boat overtaking him. In a minute or two the boat was alongside and he was boarded by two French officers, a lieutenant and an "aspirant" or midshipman. He was ordered to drop anchor so that his vessel could be searched. Carter decided to play dumb, all the time hoping for a slant of wind. It came at last while the argument still raged and a seaman gently unhooked the boat from the mizen chains. It drifted astern as the lug-sails filled and was lost to view in about two minutes. There was some distant shouting after that and the firing of a musket shot. Then the lugger was heading seaward and two Frenchmen were being disarmed and then hustled below to the forepeak. Without the least intending to do so, Sam Carter had taken two prisoners of war.

"Well, Mr Evans," said Sam, "I'll give you a course for Cape Finis-terre—or, better, we'll keep away from the coast, close-hauled on a course farther to the north."

"The hands are not going to like that, Captain," said Evans, too softly for the helmsman to hear. "And they'll like it still less when we steer for Cadiz. There are dangers a-plenty on the enemy's coast and it will mean going far from the places they know."

"I don't pretend to like it myself, Mr Evans, but what can I do? I can't desert Delancey. Our task is to rescue him and that is what I mean to do."

"I know that, sir, but we must look out for squalls after rounding Finisterre. The men want to see St Peter Port—not Cadiz."

"How many of them are reliable?"

"I wish I knew. Then there are the prisoners, who might inspire the mutiny. I wish to God we could put them ashore."

"And have them tell the story of their capture?"

"Oh—I know we have to keep them. The trouble is, however, that we have lost three men by desertion, two by sickness, and are reduced to nine: you and I, the boatswain, the cook and five deck hands, many of them smugglers by trade but French by descent. If the two prison-ers are released the odds might be heavily against us."

"Is the cook to be trusted?"

"I doubt it, sir."

"And young Bennett?"

"I don't know. If he isn't, there could be eight against three; with the prisoners, ten against three. These are long odds, sir."

"We must go armed at all times."

"I am, sir, and so is Tom Yates."

The *Dove* was soon under way on a north-westerly course, the wind being south-west and the sky brightening as they drew away from the coast. Their course was fair for Ushant or sufficiently so to keep the men content. At some point during the following night the *Dove* would have to tack, making the first leg of the southward passage and that would be the danger point. Sam Carter decided to talk to the doubtful men individually and then, when the time came, he would address them all. His own feelings at this stage were all too mixed. On the one hand he was a smuggler by trade, not involved in the war and intent on bringing his cargo safely into port. He knew exactly how the Guernseymen felt for his own instincts were the same as theirs. As against that, Delancey, his old opponent, was ashore and in danger and had asked for help. There was an awful compulsion in the trust which Delancey had placed in a smuggler's loyalty; or was it merely in the loyalty of a friend? Had it been any other officer Sam Carter would promptly have steered for home. Friendship apart, however, Sam could see that Delancey's intelligence could be important. The smuggling business, like any other, depended upon Britain's command of the sea. Who could smuggle anything if these revolutionaries ruled over Britain as well as France? What would happen to the special privileges of the Channel Islands? Victory at sea was needed by George III but it was just as essential to the free-traders of Guernsey and Alderney. Delancey's journey through Spain was a desperate business and could end in disaster but Sam was a part of it and unable to withdraw. He must keep faith or despise himself for the rest of his life. He could not turn back, not even in the face of mutiny.

Next day, the wind from the same quarter was blowing half a gale. The *Dove* held her course with heavy seas breaking over her forecastle and the pumps kept going to free her hold from the water that had entered through the opening deck seams. Seeing Luke Bennett on forecastle watch Sam Carter went forward and asked him whether there was much water entering at the hawse-holes. Luke thought there was not. The lugger was pitching wildly and both had to shout to make themselves heard above the noise of the wind and sea. The circumstances were not ideal for conversation but Dick gained the impression that Luke, despite his name, was very much of a Guernseyman. He spoke English with a strong accent and was sometimes at a loss for a word, perhaps because he thought in the local patois of his island. The only fact of importance to emerge was that Luke was an adherent of the late Mr John Wesley, by whose preaching (he said) his father had been saved. He gathered that Henri Nicolle was of the same persuasion, though possibly belonging to a different sect. He had a word later with Nicolle, whose galley fire was extinguished, and gained confirmation about his religious views. The other men were Protestant, he gathered, but were rarely seen in church. There had never been a Guernsey party interested in "Liberty, Equality and Fraternity" (although there had been in Jersey) and it would have been still more difficult to find any Channel Island admirers of Robespierre. Treason was out of the question, the boatswain assured him, and all the men wanted was to run their cargo back to St Peter Port. Sam ended his tour of the lugger by visiting the prisoners, who were in the forepeak, sitting disconsolately on a spare staysail. They refused to give their parole, saying "Vive La France!" and complaining bitterly about the food. Sam Carter locked them in again and returned to the quarterdeck. The gale was now moderating and died away towards evening, giving place to a moderate breeze from the south with occasional rain showers.

Just before sunset Sam Carter called the crew together at the changing of the watch. For the first time he told them the whole story as known to himself. "A naval officer called Delancey, a Guernseyman like others here and well known to us all as the commander of the *Nemesis,* is ashore in Spain and trying to discover what the French and Spanish are planning to do. When he has found out he will try to embark at the port of Léon, used by us and by other free-traders. He has asked me to meet him there and bring him away and that I have decided to do. He should now be on the road to Cadiz. As Spain is

still at peace he should have no difficulty in passing through that country. When he reaches Cadiz we shall then be ready to rescue him at a
point just south of there. That done, we can steer for Guernsey and
Poole, having saved a brave man, done good business, and played our
part in frustrating the enemy."

Sam paused while the English-speaking seamen (Nicolle and Bennett) explained his little speech to the others in French. Then he went
on but now on a note of persuasion: "I know that you would rather
head for home and safety now. So should I! But I can't desert Captain
Delancey, a fine seaman and a brave man. He was running a terrible
risk in France for he would have been shot as a spy if they had caught
him. Our risk is nothing by comparison. If captured by the French we
should be treated as smugglers or, at worst, as merchant seamen, to be
held until we are exchanged. You may wonder, however, why I concern myself with the affairs of George III. You may even think that a
smuggler should stick to his trade. That is some day what I mean to
do. But where will our trade be if France should win? What if England should be conquered? What if the customs duties were abolished
between England and France? How should we make a living? We
believe in Free Trade and we mean to have it even if we have to kill
every Frenchman in France!"

There was a laugh at that, followed by another laugh after the joke
had been translated. Sam Carter decided to end on that note. "Very
well then. We shall change course tonight and you will all know why.
Port watch and idlers can go below."

Sam was pleasantly surprised by the men's behaviour. There had
been no grumbling or muttering, no signs of hostility, not even a question. Perhaps his eloquence had won them over? On this point the
boatswain was less optimistic.

"I'd rather have heard grumbling, sir. But these men are slow
and will take time to weigh up the situation. The pity of it is that the
wind is fair for Ushant." This was the painful truth but the change of
course took place without protest and the Dove was then close-hauled

on her way to the south. Sam never left the deck all night.

The first leg of the southward course took the lugger far into the Atlantic where no other sail was to be seen. Southerly winds continued all that day but veered westerly during the following evening. With this encouragement Sam was able to tack again and steer a better course for Cadiz. Feeling happier over the progress they were making, he finally turned in, handing over to Mr Evans. Dog-tired, he fell asleep instantly and several hours passed before he awoke, suddenly alert. Something had disturbed him—footsteps perhaps or the creak of the cabin door. Before he could make a move in the darkness he felt cold iron on his forehead and heard a voice saying, "Keep still, mister, or I shoot." He followed this advice and lay motionless, listening to the intruder's heavy breathing. Then there were more footsteps and the door opened, admitting the light of a lantern. Sam was now able to recognize Elisha Domaille, who held the pistol, and Gilbert Le Page, who stood at the door.

"Stop this nonsense!" said Sam. "You'll go to the gallows for this, you fools, and you could have made money by doing your duty." Neither seaman replied and neither may even have understood. There were more footsteps, however, and voices, and presently Evans was brought into the cabin, followed by Yates. There was a careful search for weapons and Sam's pistols were removed. Then Henri Nicolle told the prisoners that they need fear nothing. "I am now master of the ship," he explained, "and will take her to Guernsey. You will remain here quietly until we reach port."

"Where you'll be hanged for mutiny!" said Sam.

"For mutiny on a smuggling craft?" asked Nicolle with real interest. "It may be possible but it would certainly be something new."

"There would be nothing new about a man being hanged for treason. Think again, Nicolle, you are making a big mistake!"

There was no further argument and the three officers were left to themselves, locked in the one cabin.

"I should have stood by you, sir, if it had come to a fight," said the boatswain, "but I'm not too sorry about this mutiny and that's a fact. The voyage down to Cadiz would have been a wild goose chase, as likely as not. How do we know that Delancey will be there? How do we know that he's not in a prison cell at San Sebastian? And what could be more of a risk than lurking round Cadiz and the enemy fleet? You had to keep faith with Mr Delancey—I see that, sir, and would be the last to deny it—and you did your best. But the men have mutinied and there's nothing more you can do. Maybe it's to this mutiny we shall owe our lives, and who will blame us?"

"My thoughts were going the same way," Evans admitted, "and my conclusion is the same. We're well out of that Cadiz affair if you ask me."

"And so we leave Captain Delancey to his fate?" asked Sam. "I could never have done that. In some odd fashion he and I have become friends. There's little I can do for him now but one thing I'll ask of you, Mr Evans. Don't offer to navigate!"

"Very well, sir. There is no one among them who knows where we are or what course we should steer."

"So they may come back to me for help."

That was not, however, what the mutineers did. They preferred to release the French prisoners, one of whom could navigate. All Sam Carter knew, however, was that the lugger was now before the wind and probably heading for the French coast. At dinner time the captive officers were brought their meal by young Bennett, followed by the surly Michel Vaudin with a pair of pistols.

"Who is navigating?" asked Sam and Bennett answered—"The Frenchie." To this Sam replied, "He will steer you into a French naval base."

"Enough of that!" snapped Vaudin, pushing Bennett out of the cabin. Sam thought it useful to have planted a doubt in someone's mind. When Bennett came to fetch the dirty plates, this time with Le Page as escort, Sam expressed surprise that the men should put their trust in a Catholic navigator. Methodists could not expect good treatment in a French prison, it stood to reason. The result of these remarks was that Sam's next visitor was Henri Nicolle in person, who asked him whether he would give his parole.

"What do you mean?" asked Sam cautiously.

"Promise not to attempt anything against us—retaking the lugger or the likes of that."

"Well, what if I did?"

"You and Mr Evans could come on deck, one at a time."

"Why do you want me on deck?"

"You could warn us if we were running into danger. Whatever the risks, you have to share them."

"That's true. I'll give my parole for the day ending at sunset and I expect Mr Evans will do the same. In return for being allowed on deck I will see that the lugger is fairly on course for Guernsey. How will that do?"

Agreement was reached on these lines and both Sam and the Frenchman took a sight at midday, fixing their latitude and course. Below again with Evans, Sam described the rough outline of a plan:

"There is no real unity in Nicolle's crew. He and the youngster, Bennett, are strict Wesleyans, detesting gambling and drink but eager to make money. The other Guernseymen are ordinary smugglers, good seamen but liking their pleasure. The two Frenchmen are intent on returning to France and we three mean to do our duty. The numbers in these four groups are two, four, two and three. If I can win over the Frenchmen we shall be five against six. If I could win over the Wesleyans as well, we should have seven against four."

Sam Carter's divisive plan began with the two Frenchmen. He expressed his sympathy with the senior, Lieutenant Jean Berthier, on being so near France and yet a prisoner. It soon appeared that Berthier's frustration was the greater in that he had just been promoted. His appointment to the *Argonaute* represented his first real chance to distinguish himself. Had he done well in that ship he would have been promoted again. Here he was a prisoner before the corvette had done anything more than drive a British privateer ashore. He was not to blame—what could he have done?—but he had failed to avoid capture. It would always be remembered against him. To be captured in battle was honourable but to be taken prisoner by some mere smuggling craft must leave him discredited for ever. The other officer, young Etienne Bignon, midshipman, was less downcast but he did not look forward to being a prisoner of war in Britain. For one thing, his chances of being exchanged would be remote. When he gained his freedom again, moreover, it would be to find all his contemporaries promoted over his head and some others as well who had been junior to him. Sam Carter expressed his sympathy and then said:

"What if we took this lugger and sailed her into Cadiz? You would be able to join your ship and with all the credit of the capture. Your admiral would release me and my friends for having aided you. We should be five against six. Given a measure of surprise, we could do it! Which do you choose—an English prison or the Legion of Honour?" Having made this suggestion, Sam walked away so as not to appear too friendly with the Frenchmen and presently went below.

It was Evans who next had a word with Nicolle. "Did you ever hear of Thomas Johnson?"

"The famous Hampshire smuggler who escaped from New Prison in the Borough?"

"That's the man. He served once as pilot to the Channel Fleet and was thanked for his services. For the next year or two the revenue officers looked the other way, allowing him to make a fortune."

"What of it? He lost his money with gambling and drink and was in the Fleet Prison for debt when I last heard of him."

"A more careful and religious man would have kept what he made. Now, if you'd held to your bargain, the revenue officers would have been blind to your doings and you would have ended as a man of wealth, likely as not. You missed your chance, my friend."

"But I was only cook, Mr Evans, and in no way to do business on my own."

"You could have had your own craft with Sam Carter's help and the revenue officers never have so much as noticed her name. What a grand opportunity you have thrown away!"

"An opportunity to see inside a Spanish prison!"

"A chance to preach in a chapel of your own building. You can never do that when the story comes out of how you left Captain Delancey to die among the Spaniards. Think again, Nicolle. You can still save yourself!"

It was then the turn of Tom Yates, the boatswain. It was his task to converse with Luke Bennett and ask him what a good Wesleyan was doing with these sinners from the St Peter Port waterside.

"You have taken a serious step, Luke, taking part in a mutiny. Where will it end? What begins as mutiny will end in piracy. And where does piracy lead? It leads to the gallows, Luke! Think what a shock that will be to your mother. Think what your family and neighbours will have to say about that! Think what the good book says about the wages of sin! You were in the way to be saved and now you are on the way to damnation. Repent while there is still time!"

"What do you mean, Mr Yates—what must I do?"

"You must help me to throw the liquor overboard. These wicked men, Domaille and Blondel and Vaudin, will commit any crime when drunk. From drinking and gambling it is but a step to piracy, from piracy but a step to the gallows. You know where the spirits are kept?"

"Oh, yes, sir. But they are kept locked and Mr Nicolle has the key."

"He lets you have it, though, when the rum is to be issued?"

"Yes, sir. I lock it and bring the key back to him."

"Today you forget to lock it. I'll see to it that the men are saved from this terrible temptation to sin. With the drink over the side we shall all be the safer."

"I do believe you're right, Mr Yates. I'll do it! But don't let anyone know that I did it on purpose."

Given the opportunity, however, the boatswain did not throw the rum overboard. Instead, he took six bottles of it and, keeping two in

reserve, gave a bottle secretly to Blondel and Domaille, to Le Page and
Vaudin. By the early evening they were all more or less drunk and
inclined to quarrel over the fifth bottle which he had told them to
share. Bennett, who had left the locker open, was told that Le Page
had found it unlocked before Yates could act. He was shocked to see
what a state his messmates were in and was now all the more inclined
to turn against them. Vaudin spoke insolently to Nicolle, who felt that
his authority was waning. He saw to it that Carter, Evans and Yates
were locked in their cabin but this was the last effective order he was
able to give. Luke Bennett unlocked the cabin after dark, bringing with
him the two Frenchmen. After a short whispered discussion they all
armed themselves with belaying pins or capstan bars. Nicolle was
quickly overpowered on deck, where he was trying to keep the vessel
on course. The drunken helmsman, Le Page, needed no more than a
tap on the head and Blondel, on the forecastle, was as easily dealt with.
Domaille and Vaudin were below in a drunken stupor and were left in
their hammocks to sleep it off. In five minutes the lugger was recap-
tured and another ten minutes saw her course altered and her passage
southward resumed. She was bound once more for Cadiz.

By the following day the lugger's proper routine had been re-estab-
lished. The drunkards of the previous evening found themselves, to
their surprise, being driven to work by the boatswain's rope-end. Nicolle
was a prisoner at first but professed to have learnt his lesson. He could
never have retained any sort of discipline over the godless men who
had at first accepted his leadership. He was allowed to return to his
galley and told that, if he behaved himself, bygones would be bygones.
That afternoon Sam Carter addressed the whole crew, appealing to their
good sense but assuring them that any further trouble from them would
lead to dreadful consequences.

"Do your duty as good seamen and I will forget about the events
of the last few days. So will Mr Evans, and so will Mr Yates. When
some of you mutinied the idea was put in your heads by a ringleader,
not Henri Nicolle but another man. I know which of you it was. To

him I say, 'Mend your ways or you'll end dangling from the yard-arm.'"
(He was looking straight at Michel Vaudin). "To the others who were
misguided by him, I say this: how would you like to serve in a man-
of-war? And how would you like such a service after the ship's first
lieutenant has been told that you are mutinous rascals in need of discipline? That could easily be your fate and you would feel in the end
that you would rather be in hell. But how was it that you came to
mutiny? How did sensible men come to listen to the advice of a useless lubber, the worst seaman among you? I think you were misled
because you thought we were running into danger on the Spanish
coast. You thought we should all end as prisoners in France. Well, I
don't deny that there *was* some chance of that. But I have made an
agreement now with these two French officers and gentlemen, our
former prisoners but now our shipmates. We shall make our run southward with French colours hoisted over British, a prize to the French
Navy. That will save us from the French or Spanish. Should we meet
the British fleet, as may seem more likely, we shall have British colours
and I have only to explain what our mission is. We were never in less
danger than we are on this voyage and never more certain of bringing
our cargo safe to port. Do your duty, men, and you'll soon be in St
Peter Port, celebrating the end of a successful run."

The mutiny had wasted time but Sam Carter decided that it was
still possible to make the rendezvous. Further to encourage him, moreover, the wind was veering from west to north-west, making for a faster
passage as it freshened. It rose next day to half a gale and the lugger
foamed through the Atlantic rollers, the wind singing through her rigging and the spray coming over the deck as she pitched. With the
Frenchman standing his watch and the crew now in a chastened mood,
Sam was able to take some rest and make some plans for the future.
It was evident that the later stages of the voyage would require finesse.
Difficulties were going to arise from the lack of a Spaniard on board—
for the lack indeed of anyone with a knowledge of Spanish. His own
knowledge of that tongue was rudimentary, a smattering picked up in

foreign parts. He could never pass as a Spaniard. Who then was to land at Léon? Sam had also a problem concerning the French officers. He had told them that he would sail to Cadiz and rely on the Spanish to release the lugger. He had told the crew that he was going to keep a rendezvous at Léon, just south of Cadiz; which was the truth. What, however, was he to do with the Frenchmen? After using them to suppress the mutiny he could not fairly treat them merely as prisoners of war. How was he to put them ashore and where? What, finally, was his reaction to be if Delancey failed to keep the rendezvous? Dare he linger on the coast for another week? And would the crew mutiny again if he did? His best plan would be to complete his cargo at Léon, making himself known there as a smuggler and local benefactor. What, however, would he give them in exchange for their local wine, whatever it was? They would probably be glad to obtain coffee, sugar, tobacco and rum but of these commodities he had no appreciable quantities to spare. He had spoken boldly to the crew about his mission being understood by any British man-of-war he might encounter but he was really none too certain about it. An admiral might believe his story but would the commander of a sloop or cutter? Might he not find himself under arrest?

There were few vessels in sight off the coast of Portugal and the *Dove* was in the latitude of Lisbon before she fell in with a French privateer brig. Sam Carter decided that escape would not be easy and that to speak with her might be useful. When they were within hail Lieutenant Berthier used the speaking trumpet to announce his own identity and explain that the *Dove* was a prize on her way to Toulon. The privateer was the *Espérance,* it appeared, Captain Duval, out of La Rochelle and cruising on the Portuguese coast where she had so far taken nothing. Berthier went over to the *Espérance* in the gig and came back with the news that Admiral Mann was no longer off Cadiz and that there were signs of the Spanish fleet putting to sea. Some of Langara's ships had their yards crossed, or so Duval had been told, and a few had moved nearer the harbour mouth.

After this polite exchange the two vessels parted company again, the *Espérance* for her home port and the *Dove* heading for Cadiz. Next day at sunrise another sail was sighted and this turned out to be a British frigate on her way to Gibraltar. She was the *Penelope* (36), Captain Moss, and Sam Carter thought at first that his worst fears were justified. A dour and jaundiced sort of man, Moss looked on him and the lugger with deep suspicion and showed little inclination to believe the story of Delancey's mission. He finally decided to put a prize crew aboard the *Dove*—six men under a master's mate. When the run southward was resumed, the lugger was very much in custody but Sam was philosophic about it. He felt sure that a flag officer would be more inclined to believe him.

On September 10th the *Penelope,* with *Dove* in company, sighted a detachment of the Mediterranean fleet. The day was sunny but with drifting clouds which threw their shadows on the green expanse of broken water. There was a stiff breeze and a touch of cold in the air, a foreshadowing of winter on its way. The squadron was cruising near Gibraltar under easy sail, five sail of the line and two or three smaller vessels, filling much of the seascape with their sunlit sails. The formation was exactly kept and the total effect, compounded of power, discipline and beauty, was breathtaking and memorable. A signal from the flagship, repeated by ships that were nearer, ordered the *Penelope* to take station on the *Goliath's* beam. Moss carried out this order, with *Dove* in his wake, and was then ordered to send a boat. After Moss had reported, the next signal summoned to the flagship the master of the *Dove*. As he was rowed over, Sam Carter was awestruck by the mere size of the *Goliath* (98) which loomed enormous over him. He had seen the Channel Fleet often enough but he had never been aboard a three-decker. He felt overwhelmed, dwarfed and nervous, barely able to return a sentry's salute. At the entry port he was met by a lieutenant who led him aft to the admiral's quarters, outside which he was kept waiting for ten minutes. Finally the lieutenant ushered him into the admiral's day cabin where a group of officers were apparently in

conference. Sam realized that Rear-Admiral Griffin must be the distin-
guished-looking man with gold braid on his coat, who sat at his desk
in the middle of the group. He had just signed some document which
his secretary was replacing by another. A young officer was at his other
elbow, flanked by a midshipman. There were two other officers
present, talking quietly to each other. After a minute or two the lieutenant who was his guide had a word with the flag lieutenant, who
murmured something to the rear-admiral. A moment afterwards that
officer had risen and was looking straight at his visitor. Sam made his
best bow, which was acknowledged, and came forward towards the
admiral's desk.

"Captain Moss tells me, sir, that you claim to be master of a lugger out of Poole and Guernsey and that you have been in touch with
Lieutenant Delancey, who is ashore somewhere in Spain. You believe,
I gather, that Delancey hopes to gain information about the intended
movements of the Spanish fleet. It that correct?"

"Yes, sir."

"How far has his mission succeeded?"

"I have no means, sir, of knowing. He went ashore near Bayonne
and plans to reach Cadiz. I would suppose, sir, that any intelligence
he can secure will come from Cadiz itself."

"He will be lucky if he is still alive. We cannot judge of his success but our inshore frigates report some movement in Cadiz which
might mean that Langara was about to sail—or might again mean nothing. We shall know more, I am confident, in a few days time. In the
meantime, how is Delancey to escape from Spain? He is too good an
officer to lose."

"I have a rendezvous, sir, on the coast just south of Cadiz. That is
the place where he hopes to re-embark."

"I am astounded, sir, at what Delancey seems willing to attempt.
We must bring him away safely if we can. Confiding in you to do your
utmost, I would suggest that you stay on the rendezvous or return
there at intervals for another three weeks after the last date. To enable

you to do this I shall detach a frigate to cover the operation, Captain Norris of the *Medusa* is familiar with that coast and I shall give him the necessary orders."

"Thank you, sir. I should be more hopeful of success if I had a Spanish interpreter."

"I'll see what I can do." The rear-admiral turned to his secretary and told him to make inquiries. He then thanked Sam Carter for his services, to which Sam replied with thanks for the admiral's help.

"I hope, sir, that Captain Delancey will be able to thank you in person after Langara has been defeated."

"I hardly know whether I shall meet that young officer. Be so good, therefore, as to give him this message from me: 'If he continues to serve with the devotion and resolution he now displays he should some day reach high rank in the navy.' There is too much reason to apprehend, however, that he is dead by now. Should he have survived, however, and should he return from his present hazardous enterprise, I predict for him an outstanding career. Tell him that, Mr Carter, and convey to him my thanks and good wishes."

An hour later there arrived on board the *Marguerite* a character called José Alvarez of Trinidad, an ordinary seaman from the *Ajax*. Spanish was certainly his first language but his grasp of English was quite sufficient for all ordinary purposes. He had been given some idea of what was wanted and made no difficulties about going ashore in Spain. All he wanted in return for this service was a discharge from the navy. Of life on the lower deck he had plainly had enough! Once on land, he confessed, he meant to stay there.

The *Dove* parted company from Rear-Admiral Griffin's squadron that evening and began a cautious night approach to the fishing village of Léon. The frigate *Medusa* kept just within sight, ready to rescue the lugger in case of need. Delancey could not as yet have reached the rendezvous but Sam Carter wanted, first of all, to establish himself locally in the character of smuggler, a process essential to the rescue. His one fear was that José Alvarez, when landed, would vanish for good. He sent for him and explained that a fortune was to be made in smuggling and that it was now José's opportunity to set himself up as a contraband agent in Léon. Were he to settle there, Sam insisted, smugglers from Guernsey and Alderney would call at regular intervals and land goods which were unobtainable in Spain. In cooperation with Davila, it would be the agent's task to warehouse the goods for England and distribute the cargoes landed at Léon. He and Davila would need, of course, to maintain a friendly relationship with the local authorities. There would be hard work at first and even, quite possibly, some moments of anxiety, but José Alvarez would end as a reputable and wealthy merchant, a better fate than becoming a mere stevedore and far better than joining the ranks of the unemployed.

Alvarez was suspicious at first and slow to convince. He had to hear each explanation at least three times, responding each time with the same objections. He agreed at last when Sam hinted that he would have a bad time at sea if he was known to have refused this opportunity.

Sam doubted, in fact, whether Alvarez had enough business experience to fill the agent's role. He had never, apparently, been more than a ship chandler's clerk at Port of Spain. He was at least literate, however, and able to do simple arithmetic and the opportunity was there for someone. Alvarez was thus given a motive for keeping in touch with the *Dove*. He would not simply vanish (Sam hoped) but would spy out the land and report progress through the channels of communication which Sam meant to set up. After studying the chart Sam had decided to land Alvarez at a point just south of Léon and to do this just before dawn. He would then sail on southwards and return the following night. If all were safe, Alvarez would make a signal to that effect and the *Dove* would enter the harbour. This would be on the 14th September, the day previous to that chosen for the first rendezvous with Delancey. There was no prearranged plan for making contact but it was obvious that Delancey would recognize the *Dove* if she were there and inquire after her if she were not. Sam had come away from the interview with Admiral Griffin in a mood of stern resolve, feeling that he was present at a possibly historic scene. If there was any chance of bringing Delancey safely away he resolved that it should be and must be done.

Alvarez was landed by boat on a rocky shore before dawn on the 13th September. It was nearly calm, luckily, or the landing might have been hazardous. Then the *Dove* sailed slowly on, with the frigate shadowing her from a distance. On her return the following night there was a light signal from the point at which Alvarez had landed and Sam sent the boat in again. Alvarez told Mr Evans that he'd made contact with Señor Davila, that there was no garrison at Léon and that the local Spaniards were eager to do business. Some bribes would have to be paid to customs officers and police but there would be no real difficulty. The *Dove,* under French colours, could safely enter harbour on the morning's tide. This decided Sam's policy but gave a new urgency to the problem that had been on his mind: what to do with his two French prisoners. He decided to tell them frankly what was worrying him:

"I realize, gentlemen, that you want to return to duty. It is right that you should do so and I have no wish to hold you as prisoners. On the other hand, you will have to account for your absence and will have to describe how you came to be captured, what treatment you have received and how you were freed or else came to escape. I cannot take you into Cadiz, despite anything I may have said about it. Tell me what you think I should do."

Jean Berthier must have been expecting this question for he eventually produced his own solution. Let the two of them escape and they would swear to report that the *Dove* had gone on to the Mediterranean. The success of this scheme would depend upon their falling in with a local craft bound for Cadiz. Sam accepted this idea, ordering his men to keep a sharp look-out for a boat that would serve the purpose. He also arranged with the captain of the *Medusa* that twice lowering the tricolour on board the *Dove* should be the signal for the frigate to give chase as if the *Dove* were hostile. When a suitable fishing vessel was sighted the *Dove* sailed to intercept her. When fairly alongside the heavily laden boat the *Dove's* crew began a pantomime negotiation over the purchase of her catch. Since the lugger was under French colours the Spanish fishermen, numbering five, were treated as allies. While the bargaining took place Sam made the prearranged signal to the *Medusa* unseen by the Spaniards who were having linguistic difficulties. The negotiations, conducted on one side in Guernsey French, were being prolonged to the point of frustration.

So absorbed was everyone in the discussion that the approach of the *Medusa* from to windward was apparently unnoticed. The frigate finally fired a gun, which produced panic aboard the *Dove*. The attention of the crew, concentrated until now on the fishing boat, was suddenly transferred to the frigate. Incoherent orders were shouted, instructions were given and cancelled and there was a general tendency to collect, jabbering and pointing, on the windward side of the lugger. Apparently unnoticed in all this confusion, the two French officers scrambled furtively, baggage in hand, into the fishing boat, offering money and pointing to Cadiz. At the same moment, the *Dove* made all sail in her southward flight, another cannon shot spurring her crew into a frenzy of activity. The lugger held her own against the frigate for speed and the scene, from the point of view of the Spanish fishermen, was that of a French vessel escaping from the clumsy pursuit of the enemy. They hoisted sail and headed for Cadiz, well content to accept money for returning to their home port as they had anyway been intending to do.

At a suitable moment the *Medusa* gave up the chase and allowed the *Dove* to pursue her voyage to Léon. Her arrival was evidently expected for a boat came out to meet her with Alvarez on board. He was able to assure Sam Carter of his welcome to a berth alongside the port's tiny breakwater. Davila and other local businessmen were delighted at the prospect of trade and contraband and the local authorities were not inclined to ask questions about the *Dove's* precise port of origin. Alvarez, who seemed to be a better businessman than Sam had supposed him to be, was full of information about the place and about the imports which would be especially welcome there. The local merchants, it seemed, were more than ready to do business.

By the evening of 14th September, Sam Carter felt that his task was all but accomplished. His vessel was at the appointed rendezvous and was well received there. He had his appointed agent at Léon who was busy making himself known to the principal inhabitants. If Delancey were to arrive on the following day, as arranged, even as a fugitive and in disguise, Davila would hear of it immediately. Delancey would be able to embark at once and the *Dove* could sail with the next tide. If there was any difficulty or need for force, the *Medusa* was there in the background. If, finally, Delancey failed to appear, the *Dove* could remain where she was for another week or more. There was plenty of scope for negotiation and exchange of samples, every excuse for bargaining and gossip. The question was whether Delancey would actually keep the rendezvous. Sam had to confess that the odds were heavily against it.

There was, in fact, no sign of Delancey on the 15th of September, no news of his exploits or rumour of his approach. When midnight came, the end of the first appointed day, Sam came to the conclusion that his fears had been justified. Delancey had been killed or captured, most probably in France and just as any sensible man might have expected. If this were so, news might come of English spies arrested near San Sebastian. The faint possibility remained that Delancey was still making a dash for safety. If he were, and whether disguised as a gypsy or a priest, the *Dove* must be waiting for him. Meanwhile, Davila was hearing rumours from Cadiz. All the talk there along the water-side was that the Spanish fleet was about to sail. Stores were being shipped, crews were being exercised, ships were moving to new anchorages and all onlookers agreed that news of war might arrive any day. When news came, Langara would sail but whether heading north or south no one could say. Sam Carter settled down to wait.

Chapter Fourteen

A LEAN AND FOOLISH KNIGHT

COLONEL Diego de Altamirano sent for Delancey on the evening of the day after his arrest. He was escorted by the adjutant and four soldiers and found himself again in the commandant's office. The conversation which followed was in French.

"Good morning, Captain. I hope you slept well. How good of you to spare time to see me! Do please sit down. I should like to have a little talk with you if that would suit your convenience. Remain with us, Pedro, but tell your men to wait outside." The soldiers went but Pedro remained behind Delancey's chair.

"Do you play chess, Captain?"

"No, Colonel. I am, however, a card player."

"A good one, I have no doubt. So I need hardly tell you that the moves in many a game can be foreseen. We can, if we choose, go laboriously through the regular phases of the game, pawn by pawn or card by card. Among good players, however, it is the custom, as you know, to shorten the process by mutual agreement. The moment comes when a player will lay his cards on the table and say, 'The remaining tricks are mine.' Only a novice will object and insist upon finishing the game by the ordinary sequence of play. As we are neither of us new to the game I propose that we lay our cards on the table." Delancey bowed but said nothing. So the colonel continued as one who assumes that agreement has been reached.

"I could at this moment send to Bayonne and ask Captain Baudin for the loan of his colleague, Lieutenant Michelet. He could have a talk with your friend who wears the sergeant's uniform and the result would be his assurance that your sergeant knows nothing about the French army. He could have a talk with you and could tell me in five minutes that you speak French as a foreigner, that you are really English. I could, meanwhile, apply a little pressure to your other friends and one of them—I think the smaller of the two you left at the inn—would presently break down and tell me that your whole party was landed near Bayonne from an English man-of-war, that you had a skirmish with a courier and his escort, that you seized his coach and assumed your present disguise, that you had all been sent on a dangerous mission and one which might have succeeded had I been more of a drunkard or less of a soldier. I do not think that the two Englishmen could tell me more than this for that, I suspect, is all they know. I do not think that the two Frenchmen could tell me very much more; nor, for that matter, your one Spaniard with the colonial accent. The one point on which they would agree is that *you* are the leader and that you are an officer in the British navy, probably with the rank of captain. With a little trouble, with a little pressure, I could obtain so much information. May I assume that all this has been done? You see, I lay my cards on the table, saving time and saving your friends from—what shall I say?—discomfort."

"It is a pleasure to deal with an officer of such distinction, intelligence and humanity. My cards, too, are on the table. I agree, Colonel, that you have won those tricks and am ready to assume that your conclusions are mainly correct."

"I am so glad, Captain, that we have been able to reach agreement over the preliminary moves. It only remains for me to ask what your object was. Remember, please, that your mission has failed and that your answer is merely of historical interest. If the operation were continuing, if some of your associates were still at liberty, I would not expect to hear more from you. You would not betray your friends, least of all any Spaniards here that might be in your employ. I do not think, however, that you had any Spanish collaborators."

"No, I did not."

"No. We are still agreed. You had with you the personal documents, apparently genuine, of a French officer, Captain Laffray. These came, I assume, from the post-chaise you intercepted? Is that officer dead?"

"Yes, he is."

"So I had supposed. Allow me to return now to the object of your mission. I am only interested to this extent that the information would round off my despatch. I wonder, sometimes, why I should report as carefully as I do—no one, I am convinced, will ever bother to read what I write—but I cannot rid myself of the habit. We staff officers are more concerned with documents than with facts, working as we do on a system which was invented, I believe, by King Philip II. I should be grateful, therefore, for your version of what you were trying to do."

"I see no reason, Colonel, why you should not be told. I am here, as you have guessed, on a secret mission. I was to discover, if I could, the destination of the Spanish fleet. But we are not yet at war and war may still be averted. I should like, indeed, to do anything I can to improve relationships between Britain and Spain. It is the belief of some of us that you will be our allies again before long. When that day comes we would rather your fleet were intact and able to cooperate with ours. We do not wish to see your fleet destroyed in battle. We do not want to see Spain annexed by France. There is a great future, Colonel, for a Spanish officer who can foresee, even now, that Spain's independence is in danger and that France, not England, is the country to fear."

"An officer who said that too loudly would be relieved of his command—which reminds me to tell you that my adjutant here, an excellent officer, is wholly ignorant of the French language. You may think this a fortunate circumstance. However—to return to the point—I am in no position to discuss the wisdom of my king's policy. Any such discussion would be most improper—and, I may add, most unwise."

"Undoubtedly. But the sound plan is to prepare for two eventualities. The far-seeing officer says nothing now against the French revolutionaries. Should the situation change, however, he is already known as a true Spanish patriot, trusted as such by Spain's new allies. You would be generously rewarded if you agreed to release me now."

"You are inviting me to join you in a plot to prevent the alliance, already concluded, between France and Spain. There is nothing I can do to influence my country's policy. The risk is too great, my friend, and the reward too problematical."

"The reward, Colonel, is certain. I learnt in conversation at the inn here that your family estate was lost through your father's improvidence and that you are the eldest son. If you were on our side that estate could be yours again."

"So you know about my family estate?"

"Only that your father had to sell it. Could you recover the estate if you had the money?"

"Oh, yes. If. . . . I believe that your offer is genuine. But I have no reason to believe that your government would make good any promise that you make on its behalf. Nor can I think of any reasonable excuse for releasing you."

"On that last point, Colonel, let me set your mind at rest. You will receive a letter from the French Directory informing you that I am in the French Secret Service. A minister will explain this in a personal letter sent to you and other garrison commanders. It is most unfortunate that the delivery of these letters should have been somewhat delayed."

"A most extraordinary error! But such mistakes *are* made, as I know too well from my own experience. What I need is assurance that this letter will be good enough to deceive me and further assurance that your promise will be respected by your treasury. I can accept a gentleman's word of honour but not a promise made by—still less *for*—a mere government. I shall do my best, however, to meet your wishes. You shall prepare this letter and I will decide whether to be deceived by it. The forgery must be perfect, you understand. If completely taken in, I shall release your companions, leaving them to their own devices, but you will remain here on parole, a hostage until I know that your government will respect the agreement we have made. Even then I shall be in doubt as to whether to accept your government's promise—not an easy decision. However, there is no decision to make until I receive this letter from Paris. You shall at least have the chance to write it."

"For that purpose I need all my companions and all our luggage."

"Very well." The Colonel rose now and spoke to his adjutant in Spanish:

"Have all the prisoners moved to Cell No 6. Provide them with a table and chairs, with paper, ink and sealing wax. Give them back their luggage but not their weapons. Lock the door and place two sentries outside. When this officer reports that their work is done, bring him back to see me."

An hour later Delancey had his party together and round the table. Outside in the corridor could be heard the pacing of the sentries. Prominently placed inside the door was a recent copy of the prison's printed regulations, signed by the adjutant and counter-signed by the commandant. The cell was double the normal size, being used perhaps for meetings between prisoners and their lawyers. There was a lantern on the table, which was necessary in the fading light, and their belongings were placed against the wall. Hodder went straight to his luggage when the door closed and reported that his skeleton keys were still in the false bottom of his leather travelling case.

"Good!" said Delancey. "Now, all of you listen carefully. Manning, stand with your back to the door so that nobody can see properly into the cell. Hodder, set to work on the door lock but without making a sound. Monsieur Rigault and Mr Bisson, talk to each other loudly enough to cover any noise that Hodder may chance to make. Ramos, make out an order in Spanish for our release and for our being provided with fast horses. I shall word the order and you will translate and write."

Working quickly but carefully, Delancey and Ramos produced the necessary orders in what they hoped was the proper form. Then Delancey replaced Bisson as conversationalist, leaving that expert to copy the heading and signatures from the notice on the door. When the orders were ready, Ramos and Bisson did the talking while Delancey and Rigault went to the table. Between them they drafted and wrote the letter from Barras, explaining that the captain, Rochambeau, was in the French Secret Service and would be deserving of Spanish help. Then they changed roles again, Bisson forging the signature as he had done before and Rigault resuming his argument but now with Ramos. It was dark before they had finished these several documents and then it was that Hodder stood back from the door and confessed his failure. "I've done my best," he said in a whisper, "and there was one moment when I thought the job was done. But I couldn't get it again. I could have sworn that it was shifting. . . . No, I can't do it. It's not the sort of lock I am familiar with."

Delancey thought quickly and came to his decision. "Manning and Bisson, I want you to quarrel, shout at each other and then fight, making noise enough for the sentries to hear but not so much as to be heard in the guardroom. Ramos will then call out to the sentries that murder is being committed. Call for help—quickly—quickly! Is that understood? Right then—quarrel!"

A realistic dispute began and turned into combat while Delancey and Rigault placed themselves on either side of the door. A sentry looked through the grill and told the combatants to be quiet. He then saw, to his dismay, that Bisson was apparently being choked to death. "Murder!" shouted Ramos in Spanish. "Murder! Quick!" The sentry hesitated, knowing that he should summon the sergeant but fearing that murder might have happened in the meanwhile. Then, taking the fatal decision, he opened the door and presented his musket at Manning, the other sentry doing the same. Before they knew what was happening their muskets were snatched from them. They were overpowered in a second and knocked on the head with chairs, their uniforms removed and their wrists and ankles tied together with luggage straps. A tense minute followed as they all waited for the alarm to be given. There was silence, however, and they remembered, hopefully, that the walls were thick. "Look!" whispered Hodder in a tone of grievance, "that hellish door was bolted on the outside!"

In five minutes Ramos and Manning were in military uniform,

properly equipped and armed. Delancey then told Ramos to go and fetch the adjutant, reporting as from the sergeant that the prisoners had finished their task and that the senior of them was ready to report to the commandant. There was some little risk of Ramos being recognized but he actually met the adjutant in the semi-darkness of the corridor, returning from the commandant's office. He delivered his message, holding the lantern in front of him, and then followed the adjutant back to Cell No 6. That officer was annoyed to find that the prison corridor, save for the other sentry, was deserted.

"Where is the sergeant?" he snapped. "Where is the guard?" At that instant he was knocked senseless with the butt of a musket and dragged into Cell No 6, where his uniform was stripped off in turn. Ramos was now promoted from private soldier to captain, the sentry's uniform being given to Bisson. When the adjutant had been tied up and gagged, like the other two soldiers, the procession formed in the corridor. Ramos led as adjutant, escorting Delancey. The other prisoners followed, Rigault and Hodder. Two soldiers, Manning and Bisson, brought up the rear. When Cell No 6 had been locked and bolted, Delancey pocketed the key and the whole party marched off towards the commandant's room. Ramos knocked and was told to enter. It was Delancey who went in first, however, and Ramos remained in the doorway, turning to give an order to the two soldiers who formed the escort.

"Come in, Captain. Pray be seated. You and your friends have worked quickly, finishing at an earlier hour than I had expected. I hope you will join me presently in a glass of wine. In the meanwhile, allow me to see the letter from Paris."

"Here it is, Colonel," said Delancey, handing the document over. "I have not sealed it, of course, but will do so later."

"Thank you, Captain. Yes, this has the right appearance . . . let's see now. . . . Yes, that reads quite well . . . Good! Quite a work of art! It might not deceive everyone but I think it could deceive me. I am merely a soldier, of course, not an expert in handwriting. I incline to accept this as genuine."

"I am relieved to hear it, Colonel. I should have hated to begin our little discussion on a note of disagreement."

Something in Delancey's tone made the commandant look up sharply. He found himself looking into the muzzle of a pistol, aimed very steadily at his throat. Glancing from Delancey towards the door, he recognized Ramos in his adjutant's uniform and guessed the rest.

"The plan we discussed is still possible," said Delancey, "on the basis that we are both men of honour. With the situation reversed, however, you will not expect to gain the same terms. I am sure, incidentally, that you will not make a false move and so compel me to shoot you. Your death would not add to the risks I run but I deplore pointless bloodshed and would prefer to have you as a friend; as my host, indeed, some day, at your castle near Seville. You have only to accept this letter as genuine and order our release, giving me your word that there will be no pursuit. My offer still holds but the alternative is now less pleasant. You have to choose between the possible recovery of your estate and the certain loss of your life. The choice is not one over which you should hesitate."

The commandant shook his head slowly. "You forget, my friend, that you have overpowered my adjutant and his guard. What will these men say when they are released? If you have killed them the situation is worse."

"No, Colonel, nobody has been killed."

"What is our story to be, then? You expect me to report that you are French agents. I have then to add that you disarmed my soldiers, stunned my adjutant and made your escape! Who will believe that story? And what will my other officers say?"

"In that case, Colonel, you will have to come with us to a point on the road to Santander. From here to the stables, from there to the citadel and town gates you will be covered by my pistol, hidden under my cloak. Any false move will result in your instant death, shot through the heart. If you don't force me to shoot, your story afterwards will be simply the truth—that we used you as hostage to aid our escape."

"Not a good story to explain to a court martial."

"No, but these things take time. If you receive a reprimand it will be next year when the whole incident is all but forgotten."

"You know our old proverb then: 'If death came from Madrid, we should all live for a very long time'?"

"I never heard that. But your death, if it should take place during the next few hours, will not have to come so far."

"No. Very well, then. I accept your terms, Captain. I won't tempt you to shoot."

"Excellent. If I were to kill you it would be with real regret."

"And now perhaps you will seal this letter from the Directory? While you do that I shall write you a safe conduct. You will need it to leave the town."

"We wrote it for you, Colonel."

Delancey's party now collected their weapons and luggage and went to the stables. Delancey followed at the commandant's heels and listened with approval to the verbal orders issued for seven good horses, saddled and bridled, and for two pack horses to carry their belongings. In the commandant's company they had no difficulty at the citadel or town gate and they came out as free men on the moonlit road to Santander. This they followed for about four miles, halting then on Delancey's word of command. Dismounting near a wayside chapel but far, it seemed, from any habitation, Delancey told the colonel that the time had come to part. With Rigault behind them and with pistol in hand he led the colonel into the chapel. It was evidently in use, with a light before the altar and the lingering smell of incense.

"Sit there, sir," said Delancey, pointing to a chair near the altar. The colonel obeyed and Rigault tied him in position by the wrists and ankles, using cords and a cassock belt taken from the tiny vestry. Delancey apologized for these precautions.

"I leave you here, Colonel, reluctantly. You will be found in the morning and are meanwhile in a place of safety, sheltered at least from wind or rain. Your horse will go with us but will be left at Santander.

I can do nothing about recovering your estate but who knows how the war will end? We may yet value your services as an ally."

"Who knows, indeed? Next time we meet it may be with you again as prisoner. So leave me able to breathe!" Rigault then gagged him but with as little discomfort as might be consistent with an enforced silence. Delancey felt that they were five or six hours ahead of any possible pursuit. Soon after leaving the chapel he found a bridle path on the left. Taking this and circling southwards he and his party ended on the high road to Vittoria. There was no rest for them, though, for Delancey pressed on relentlessly. Having succeeded so far in his mission, he was impatient to finish it. If he could gain some useful piece of intelligence and re-embark safely, his reputation would be made. He might start to think then of a naval career and even of promotion.

Before daybreak Delancey called a halt, quitting the high road and finding shelter from the wind in a small wood. It was a cold night with a hint of autumn and both men and horses were glad to rest. Delancey called Rigault and Ramos into conference.

"I doubt whether there will be any effective pursuit but we are not in a position to take any chances. I propose to reach Vittoria by this evening and then, tomorrow, travel more openly towards Burgos and so to Madrid."

That night Delancey's party was at the inn in Vittoria. Delancey himself and Rigault in French army uniform, Ramos and Manning in Spanish army uniform and the other two dressed as servants. It was at this point that Delancey decided against entering Madrid itself. It was one thing to pose as Frenchmen in Vittoria or Burgos, quite another to repeat this masquerade in a capital city. For one thing a French army officer visiting Madrid would be expected to visit the French Embassy, a failure to do so being enough to cause resentment and even arouse suspicion. It seemed likely, moreover, that the French ambassador would have some army officer attached to his staff, someone who would detect an imposter in five minutes. Delancey decided, therefore, that his own way should lie west of Madrid, the road via Medina and

Avila. To Cadiz the distance by that route would actually be less, though bad roads might prevent any real gain in time. From Avila his party would have to make its way to Toledo in New Castile and so to Ciudad Real and so across the Sierra Morena into Andalusia.

It was there, in the valley of the Guadalquiver, that the drama would have to be enacted. If he was to intercept a courier on his way from Madrid to Cadiz, that would be the place for the ambush. From Madrid the main road, along which the courier must travel, seemed to pass through the country called La Mancha, made famous by Cervantes. Could Delancey find inspiration in the adventures of Don Quixote and Sancho Panza? Would there be windmills to attack around Manjenares? Somewhere between there and Cordova there must, surely, be a place suitable for an ambush or diversion. But the courier, he thought, would not be too easily led astray. With most of the distance behind him, with Cadiz already named on the signposts, he would be eager to reach his destination and deliver his despatches. Assured at Madrid that the Spanish fleet was still in port, he would press on eagerly from Baylon, not even halting for lack of carriage or escort. The plan for an interception would need careful thought.

There was a chilly wind blowing across the high sierras that autumn and the landscape looked forbidding and bleak, stormy and dry. Days were spent in the saddle and nights in the scant comfort of the Spanish inns. These travellers were delayed by nothing, being regarded, as they passed, with cold indifference but certainly not with suspicion. At last, on September 4th they came to Andujar and glimpsed greener and more fertile land ahead. They were approaching the plain of Andalusia and Cordova would be the next town they would see.

Delancey was still without a plan but he had picked up a copy of Cervantes' masterpiece and had taken to reading it each evening. He remembered vaguely that Cervantes had served at sea and fought indeed at the Battle of Lepanto and yet his hero's adventures were all on land. As another sailor on horseback, Delancey hoped to find some inspiration in the old book, as also some practice in Spanish. All he found at first was amusement and the realization that Cervantes must have ridden the self-same roads and rested at the same flea-infested inns. He laboriously translated some of the stories for the benefit of Rigault, who thought them pointless and improbable. Ramos knew them, of course, but he had in fact little taste for literature, his bent being more political and perhaps criminal. Delancey ended by keeping the book to himself.

When the party reached Cordova on September 9th, Delancey was still without any fixed plan of campaign. He paced his room on the night of his arrival there, formulating and rejecting one scheme after another. Then there came a bitter complaint from the guest whose room was immediately beneath and Delancey had to apologize and sit still. From a habit formed at sea he usually did his thinking while at least mentally pacing his quarterdeck. He felt handicapped in a chair and so decided to defer further thought until the morning. He knew that he would be sleepless, however, if he went to bed immediately. His best remedy was to read and the only book he had to hand was his copy of *Don Quixote*. He turned the pages at random, finally opening the book at the beginning of Chapter IV.

"Aurora began to usher in the morn, when Don Quixote sallied out of the inn, so well pleased, so gay, and so overjoyed to find himself knighted, that he infused the same satisfaction into his horse, who seemed ready to burst his girths for joy. But calling to mind the admonitions which the innkeeper had given him, concerning the provision of necessary accommodation in his travels, particularly money and clean shirts, he resolved to return home to furnish himself with them, and likewise to get him a squire. . . . The knight had not travelled far when he fancied he heard an effeminate voice complaining in a thicket on his right hand. 'I thank heaven,' said he, when he heard the cries . . . '. . . for these complaints are certainly the moans of some distressed creature who wants my present help.' Then turning to that side with all the speed which Rozinante could make he no sooner came into the wood but he found a mare tied to an oak, and to another a young lad about fifteen years of age, naked from the waist upwards. This was he who made such a lamentable outcry; and not without cause, for a lusty country fellow was strapping him soundly with a girdle, at every stripe putting him in mind of a proverb, 'Keep your mouth shut, and your eyes open, sirrah.'

'Good master,' cried the boy, 'I'll do so no more; as hope to be saved. I'll never do so again! Indeed, master, hereafter I'll take more care of your goods.'

"Don Quixote, seeing this, cried in an angry tone, 'Discourteous knight, 'tis an unworthy act to strike a person who is not able to defend himself. . . .'"

At this moment Delancey stopped reading with an exclamation of delight. "Of course!" he muttered. "Of course. Why didn't I think of it before?"

Chapter Fifteen

INTELLIGENCE OF VALUE

N*emesis* had been driven ashore on the day when Spain allied herself with France by a treaty which made war with Britain inevitable. For many practical purposes war had already begun in September, when Spanish ships were being detained in British ports. It took time, however, for news of this to reach Spain. All that was known in Cordova on September 9th, the day when Delancey's party arrived there, was that the treaty had been signed. It was assumed, however, locally, and Ramos was indeed assured, that war had—well, practically— begun. The result was a deputation, Rigault asking Delancey whether he would meet the others in the stable yard of the inn at which they were staying, the Santa Clara. It was Bisson who acted as spokesman and his demand was that they make for Portugal by the shortest route:

"In Portugal we should be among friends again. Your aim, we know, is to gain intelligence about the destination of the Spanish fleet—about its strength, maybe, and the like of that. When we landed your talk was of reaching Portugal, gaining some information on the way, but you haven't led us the shortest way to Portugal. The way we are going is more towards Seville and Cadiz. That was no concern of ours while Britain and Spain were at peace. But we shall soon be in peril and would rather be out of Spain by the shortest road. There is a road from here to Badajoz. With all due respect, sir, we should like to follow it."

"Do you all agree about this?" asked Delancey, looking at each of them in turn.

"No, I don't," said Hodder unexpectedly. "I think the captain knows best. We should gain some information like he says, and do that much for King George. And if we happened to make some—well, prize-money, shall we call it?—I wouldn't refuse to share in it." The others shuffled and whispered and then Manning spoke up.

"I agree with Hodder that some prize-money would be welcome. No, sir, I wouldn't say 'no' to my share, not by no means I wouldn't. But I shouldn't want to be caught in Spain with my pockets full of gold. I should want to be over the border before the gold was missed."

"Has anyone else anything to say?" asked Delancey.

"The others agree with Bisson and Manning, sir," said Rigault. "They would rather see Lisbon than the inside of a Spanish prison."

"Very well, then. I shall draw you a map. Give me a whip, some-one." Delancey drew a map by scratching on the dirt floor with a whip handle.

"Here we are at Cordova. From here the road goes down the val-ley to Seville. There the road forks, this way to La Palma, to Huelva and Portugal; the other way, to the left, goes to Seville and Cadiz—or else to Cadiz (like *that*) without passing Seville. My plan has been to re-embark near Cadiz, where I am hoping that Sam Carter will call in for me. I agree that this is risky. War may have begun in the mean-while and Sam may not be there. It won't surprise me, therefore, if some of you—or even all of you—choose to fork right at Seville. If that is your choice, I shall bid you farewell and go on to Cadiz, per-haps with some of you, perhaps alone."

"But, begging your pardon, sir," said Manning. "Our plan was to head for Portugal from here, taking the road to Badajoz."

"I know that but it would make no sense. The distance that way to Portugal is very little less and the going is worse, with hills in between. It would take as long—in fact, it would take longer." He illus-trated this point by more scratches on the dirt floor. "Going down the valley we shall be on the flat."

There was more muttering and scratching of heads and then Rigault spoke up: "So you think, sir, that we must in any case take the road for Seville?"

"I am certain of it. I also think it possible that we may have the chance to intercept a courier between here and Seville, perhaps with information, perhaps with gold; or even perhaps with both. We are on the direct road from Madrid to Cadiz. Mr Hodder and I would like to seize any opportunity that should offer. Others may be too wealthy to be interested but we are poor men. I am, moreover, a privateer commander without a ship!"

There was some laughter over this and a general agreement to work together for the time being. Some would clearly part company at Seville but Hodder was the exception and Delancey wondered why. He was soon informed, however, by Hodder himself. That unattractive and undersized cockney was loyal, apparently, to the death.

"I'll stick by you, sir," said Hodder, "and you may wonder why. Well, the truth is that I should like to earn my pardon. If I had that—yes, with some money as well—I'd give up the game and have a locksmith's business in Cheapside. I'd be a churchwarden, too, as like as not. You'll help me, sir, afterwards, if I stick by you now?"

"That I shall and here's my hand on it!"

"Thank you, sir. It will be a great day for me when I can throw the tools of my present trade into the Thames—yes, and the opiates too!"

"Opiates? Do you carry drugs as well?"

"Only a small quantity, sir. We don't, in my business, trust entirely to people sleeping soundly. We help them a little, sir. No harm in a small dose, sir, no harm at all. It helps to keep the peace, as you might say."

"Mr Hodder, you have given me an idea. I think you have a good chance of becoming a respectable locksmith and yours will be a shop at which I shall do business. Opiates are the very thing to keep the peace and I shall hope to see you an alderman!"

Back in his room, Delancey studied the map. A banker or merchant travelling on from Cordova would go to Seville, most likely, even if he were finally bound for Cadiz. A courier, by contrast, with despatches for Cadiz, would avoid Seville, parting company with the banker at Ecija. A plan for intercepting either or both would centre upon some place like La Carlota, only about 25 miles distant. This time, however, there would be a minimum of violence. Like Mr Hodder, he would keep the peace. How odd to think that he might end with that shabby little thief as his only companion! And yet there was something about Hodder which suggested a latent patriotism. He might have hoped for a better ally but fate could easily have sent him a worse.

Delancey left Cordova next day, Ramos being instructed to gather what information he could about the couriers likely to be met with along the road. The party rode into La Carlota that evening and Ramos was able by then to report that couriers bound for Cadiz passed that way about twice a week, the next being expected on about the 10th. He would undoubtedly stay at the same inn as Delancey's party, that is the Principe Heredero. He would travel by coach accompanied by a sergeant and four troopers. Delancey decided to wait, his mind going back to Don Quixote. He had the glimmerings of an idea but one irrelevant to the immediate problem. For this all he needed was a dose or two of opiate. . . .

Before the 9th some casual inquiries had identified the room which the courier would occupy and established the fact that it would be locked at night, that the sergeant's bed would be placed across the door and that there would be a sentry at the head of the stair. Of these various obstacles the lock was the one most easily dealt with because the key was left in the lock on the previous day, allowing Hodder to make a replica of it. The door was also provided, however, with two massive wooden bolts on the inside. These were removed privily and sawn nearly through from the back and then lightly smeared with olive oil. Still looking impressive, they would snap under pressure. There was admittedly no way of securing the door again after the room had been visited, so Delancey decided to convince the courier that his room had been entered by a common thief. Money would be stolen and luggage ransacked but the leather bag containing the despatches would appear to be untouched.

The courier arrived on the expected day, turning out to be a middle-aged lieutenant with only one eye, walking with a limp and addicted to brandy. While Rigault engaged him in conversation, Delancey went to fetch drinks for the party—pausing on the way back for a word with Hodder, who deftly doctored the courier's glass and later did the same for the sergeant and the troopers. That night Delancey and Manning passed the sleeping sentry at the head of the stairs and moved the sergeant, bed and all, away from the door he was supposed to guard. Hodder then opened the door with his replica key, quietly broke the almost severed bolts and led the way into the darkened room. Bisson followed but Ramos kept watch in the corridor. The courier was sleeping soundly and it was no great problem to slide the leather bag from beneath his pillow. At that instant came the sound of footsteps. The stairs creaked and a door closed somewhere. Someone was coming quietly down the stairs from the floor above. The light from a candle was reflected in the polished floor of the landing. If it was the landlord he would see that the sergeant's bed had been moved, that the door of the courier's room stood open, that thieves were in the house. The noise would wake the courier and—without pursuing this train of thought Delancey left the room, closed the door behind him and stood face to face with a pretty maidservant whose candle was fairly shaking in her hand. He knew that his only chance was to put her in the wrong. "What are you doing?" he demanded in Spanish, signalling Ramos to join him. Taking his cue from Richard, Ramos repeated the question: "What are you doing? Why are you here? Why aren't you asleep?" An older girl might have asked in turn what Ramos was doing at that time of night. This girl, luckily, was young and confused, a fact which allowed Delancey to press his advantage. "Are you a thief?" he asked and Ramos repeated the question. "We had best call the landlord," he added. "No, no!" the girl wailed but with sense enough to weep quietly. "Go back to bed then," said Delancey, "and we'll say no more about it!" Ramos led her up to her garret leaving Delancey to wonder what would be said in the morning.

"Tell her to plead sickness," he said to Ramos, "and keep out of sight." The message was delivered but Delancey was left wondering what she would actually do. The poor child would have to tell someone, he knew, either another maidservant or the boy she had wanted to visit. What would be the result?

While this little scene was being enacted Bisson carried out a realistic burglary, slitting linings and leaving clothes all over the floor. He took away with him the courier's purse, his watch, his pistols and his gold-hilted sword, afterwards dropping the empty purse into the street and hiding the other loot (apart from the money) up the chimney. Hodder, meanwhile, took the leather bag to his room, where he opened it skilfully. Rigault then searched the bag and took from it the more promising letters, all those bearing an official seal, and handed the rest back to Hodder. The expert Hodder replaced them and relocked the bag, sliding it once more beneath the courier's pillow. He then left the room and helped Manning lift the sergeant and his bed into position before the courier's door. The whole operation took only half an hour, disturbing only that one girl and leaving all quiet again until morning. The present sentry might be relieved presently but the new sentry would see nothing unusual and would conclude that all was well.

The stolen documents numbered five and no one of them was interesting in itself. A lieutenant's resignation was accepted. The report of a court of inquiry was formally acknowledged—it concerned the recent loss of stores on board the *San Leandro*. A letter to the harbour master at Cadiz conveyed an official reprimand—something to do with a collision in harbour between a gun-vessel and a water-boat. A certain midshipman was to be dismissed from the *Neptuno,* having given a false date of birth and being, in fact, too young to serve. The only letter which seemed to deserve a second reading was from the ministry to a certain official of the dockyard at Cadiz. Its purport was obscured by its continual reference to previous correspondence, as also by the technical nature of the subject under discussion. Certain ships "those listed in paragraph 17 of the letter under reference" were to have some structural alterations, something to do with fire precautions in the magazine. Pages of description followed, with diagrams and tables of quantity and neither Ramos (translating) nor Delancey (listening) could make out what was to be done or by whom or when. It was worse than any document from the Navy Board which had come Delancey's way. By the time Ramos had reached the last pages, following the tabulated summary, Delancey sensed that the author of the document had himself lost all hope of explaining anything. He had finally turned, in fact, to another and a possibly more effective means of communication. He did this in a final desperate postscript which read as follows:

> "To avoid any possibility of confusion, Rear-Admiral de Grado, who is fully informed in the matter, will travel to Cadiz in two days time and will explain any aspects of the subject that are not fully understood. He will be provided with the means of purchasing such material as may not be found in the dockyard."

From this it seemed possible, though not certain, that the rear-admiral was to bring money as well as expert guidance. Delancey, for his part, could not imagine how anything would ever be found in a Spanish dockyard; or in a British one either, for that matter. He hoped, therefore, that a large sum would be needed. Or would the "means of purchasing" turn out to be some written authority for payment? Having finished his task of translation, Ramos passed the document over to Delancey. Glancing at the foot of the last page—before the postscript—Delancey then saw the lines which Ramos had not bothered to translate:

> "In case the fleet should have sailed a copy of this letter has been sent to Toulon."

So that was Langara's destination! No copy had been sent to Brest or Rochefort, only to Toulon. There could be only one reason for that. Delancey's search for intelligence was over. He must somehow pass the news to Gibraltar.

There was uproar at the inn next morning, the 11th, when the theft was discovered. At first light the courier was shouting for the landlord and questioning the servants. The other guests peered over the banisters, the most helpful of them being Rigault who said that he heard sounds in the small hours: the footsteps, he had supposed, of some belated arrival. Of the courier's party the most embarrassed was the sergeant, who had somehow to explain how the door he had been guarding should have been forced by intruders. A watchman had found the empty purse in the street and the magistrates of La Carlota expressed their belief that the thieves were strangers from out of town. As for the courier himself, he had no money to pay the innkeeper and was grateful for the small loan offered him by Delancey. The maid did not appear and Ramos reported that she had not come down to the kitchen. Still cursing, the one-eyed lieutenant went on his way, attributing his headache to the poor quality of the brandy he had drunk the previous night. The sergeant, who had not tasted the brandy, had much the same headache but he knew better than to complain about it. His only consolation was that the leather bag had not been touched. There was, thank God, no actual breach of security.

When Delancey's party left, going in the same direction, they bore left at Ecija and did so without anyone grumbling. With the possibility—not the certainty—of loot, the group was united again. Delancey had at least two days to prepare his trap and the place he had chosen was on the road to Cadiz rather than on the road to Seville. Just beyond Marchena was a minor turning which led to a small town called Paradas, lying perhaps two miles off the main road, which goes on to the town of Utrera, a place of some consequence. It was in this area that Delancey rehearsed his campaign for 48 hours, going over every phase, making certain purchases, and examining every inch of the ground. When confident that each man knew exactly what to do, he called them together at the Paradas Inn and ended his final instructions with these words:

"If my plan succeeds and if my information is correct, we shall end the coming campaign with a captured sum of money; not a great sum but enough to reward us for our trouble. I propose to divide that equally among us, hoping to have no dispute over it. It may well be that the division of the prize-money may have to be done hurriedly. It may well be that we may separate then, most of you wanting to reach Portugal by the shortest route through Seville and Huelva, so I shall say farewell now. I have to thank you all for your help. We have passed through some dangers together. We have undertaken a long and tiring journey. We have gained some information that may be of value to our admirals. We shall end, I hope, by making some money. It will then be our hope to leave Spain without delay, most of you into Portugal and I through a small port south of Cadiz. Good luck to you all! I trust that we shall meet again some day and that I shall see you all well and prosperous, remembering over our ale the strange adventures we have had by sea and land. Goodbye and good fortune!"

There was a chorus of farewells, the men crowding round to shake Delancey's hand. "You were a good skipper," they said. But Hodder would have no farewell, saying, "I'll stick by you, sir, like I said."

Rear-Admiral de Grado's coach had left Marchena and was heading mainly downhill for the town of Utrera, where the admiral expected to spend the night of September 14th. He was in a cheerful mood for the day was fine and the road in relatively good repair. He had cause for satisfaction because his career, which he had thought at an end, had been suddenly revived. He was known, he flattered himself, as a sound administrator if not as a fighting admiral. He had nevertheless been allowed to retire, his services seemingly unwanted. Now, however, he had been given an important mission. If he did his work well he might be given some further and higher appointment, perhaps (who could tell?) with promotion. Travelling through La Mancha during the last few days he had often, and inevitably, thought of Cervantes—who had served, after all, in the Spanish navy. He would have to address the dockyard officers soon after his arrival. Would it be appropriate, he wondered, to make some reference to Cervantes' hero? He decided to try the idea on his flag lieutenant, Pedro de Lares.

"In my speech at the dockyard I thought of making some comment on our journey through La Mancha and our passing the Sierra Morena. I might end with a reference to Don Quixote. How do you think that would be received?"

"Very well indeed, Admiral!" replied de Lares. "A further mention of Lope de Vega and Calderon might add something more to the impression you would make." Pedro wondered, privately, whether it was wise for the old admiral to draw any comparison with Don Quixote but he very properly kept his doubts to himself. A flag lieutenant is not supposed to argue but rather to assist and applaud.

"It is good to be making better progress," the admiral went on, "with the hills mostly in our favour. I can almost smell the sea already! Do you know Cadiz, Pedro?"

"No, sir."

"I have not been there for some years but I remember it as a fine old city built on what is almost an island, well fortified, with the cathedral dome rising above the ramparts. Like Venice, it has a character that is almost oriental."

"I was once there, sir," said Diego Escalante, the admiral's secretary. "It was in summer and I remember how pleasant it was as compared with the heat and dust of Seville."

"It can be quite hot enough for me," said the admiral. "But not at this time of year. It should be pleasant, I think, for our visit."

At that moment the coach stopped and the flag lieutenant looked out to see what the trouble was. There was a coach at the road junction ahead of them, blocking the highway. As there seemed to be some sort of dispute in progress the flag lieutenant resolved to investigate. "With your leave, sir," he said to the admiral. "I'll ask the coachman why he has stopped."

Pedro de Lares walked forward, learning no more from the coachman than that an arrest was being made. There were two other coaches following that in which the admiral was travelling and a troop of cavalry behind the rear one. Captain Garcia, the escort commander, rode forward at the same time. He and de Lares were surprised to see a French army officer struggling in the grip of two Spanish soldiers.

"How dare you arrest me?" roared the Frenchman. "Take your dirty hands off me!"

"You are arrested, Señor, because you have not paid your bill at the Paradas Inn. I am to take you back there for questioning."

"Damn your impudence! I broke the journey there because there was no inn on the main road. I paid the bill and am on my way to Madrid on official business. Stop me at your peril!"

The shouting match continued in a mixture of French and Spanish, the Frenchman demanding his release, the Spaniard merely repeating that he was only obeying orders. The flag lieutenant finally intervened by asking the Frenchman to give his name.

"I am Jean Pelletier," he replied, "captain in the Army of the French Republic but recently serving at sea under Admiral Richery as marine officer of the *Intrepide*. I am on my way to the French Embassy at Madrid." Pedro de Lares asked one or two more questions and then reported to the admiral that a French marine officer was under arrest for failure to pay his bill. He claimed, however, to have paid it in full.

"We cannot leave him in prison," said the admiral. "The French are our allies and this sort of affair might have the worst possible results. It could become an international incident! Tell Captain Garcia to deal with these people, using force if necessary."

"I suggested that to Captain Garcia but he was reluctant to act in that way. He would rather you accompanied Captain Pelletier to Paradas. He thinks that your influence should be sufficient to secure this officer's release and that to use force at this stage would put us in the wrong. He thinks that some mistake has been made and that a word with the mayor will clear up the misunderstanding. Paradas is only a short distance off the main road—it is almost in sight."

"A few minutes ago," said the admiral, "I should have said that nothing—but *nothing*—would have kept me from reaching Cadiz by the shortest route. A task of great importance awaits me at the dockyard. My technical knowledge is needed and I must clearly be there as soon as possible. But if there is one appeal I cannot ignore it is this—the appeal of a brother officer and an ally, unjustly accused and in danger of imprisonment. It may well be that I am destined for higher command. When I hoist my flag I want it to be known that I expect loyalty but that I too am loyal to those who serve under my command. If a man falls overboard I am not the one to make all sail. No! I'll back my topsails and lower a boat. That is what I shall do now. Tell this police officer from Paradas to go back there, taking his prisoner. Tell Captain Garcia to lead the way with his troop—a show of force may be useful. As for me, I shall see the mayor and show him where his duty lies."

Before these orders could be obeyed the Spanish army officer, the man responsible for making the arrest, came up to the admiral's coach and apologized for all the trouble he had caused. He was only obeying orders and could well imagine that a mistake might have been made. He hoped that the whole matter would be cleared up within the next hour. To this the admiral responded politely and then the Spanish army officer came up with a useful suggestion. Since the admiral was to be in Paradas for only an hour—and possibly less—there was surely no need for his other two coaches to leave the main road. If they went on slowly to Utrera they would be there, with luggage unpacked, when the admiral arrived. The horses would be less tired, moreover, and the inn would have time to prepare for the admiral's reception. Admiral de Grado accepted this common sense suggestion immediately, being assured that the main road at this point was perfectly safe and well patrolled. The result was that Captain Pelletier's coach turned back towards Paradas, guarded by the Spanish officer and his orderly, both on horseback, and preceded by Captain Garcia's troop of cavalry. The admiral's coach brought up the rear of the column. The other two coaches, one for the servants and one for the luggage, remained on the main road and presently went on towards Utrera. They might expect to be there in about two hours.

The main cavalcade, going by the minor road, crossed a wooden bridge over a deep ravine and, breasting the slope on the far side, were soon in sight of Paradas. It was at this point that the Spanish army officer's orderly found that his cloak, rolled up behind the saddle, had dropped off. He was told to go back and fetch it and went back accordingly at a canter. The cavalcade went on to Paradas and stopped outside the inn, only to discover that there had indeed been a mistake. The French officer's bill *had* been paid. The landlord had no complaint against anyone. The Spanish officer was confused and apologetic. He had misread the name as written in the order he had received—he could see now that the name was Pelissier. He expressed his abject apologies to all who had been inconvenienced, and especially to the admiral. His recent prisoner could afford to be generous and agreed that the name in the order, which he was allowed to examine, *did* look like Pelletier. He and his captor entered the inn to ask whether an officer called Pelissier had been seen there. Neither the admiral nor Captain Garcia saw them again for the immediate discussion—in the course of which the admiral was told of the mistake—was interrupted by the sound of a distant explosion. It came from the direction of the road—the only road—by which Paradas can be reached. Garcia sent a couple of troopers to investigate. They were back again in half an hour, reporting that the wooden bridge had been blown up. Completely bewildered, the admiral asked Garcia, "Why to God should anyone do that?" The cavalryman was equally at a loss:

"Why indeed?" he said, shrugging his shoulders.

"What on earth had the criminals to *gain*?" the admiral persisted.

"I can't imagine, sir—unless it was *time.* . . ."

Meanwhile, the two coaches, the first with the servants and the second with the luggage, went on to Utrera. They came into a town which had a good deal of traffic in its narrow and twisting streets. As might so easily happen in such a place, a laden cart came to separate the two coaches and then stopped dead, allowing the first to vanish round the next bend on the road. The two men on the second carriage, the coachman and his second driver, swore at the owner of the cart, who seemed to be drunk, but could find no way to pass the obstacle. They were rescued, providentially, by an army officer who appeared from nowhere, climbed up beside the driver and pointed in a peremptory way to a turning on the left. The driver readily supposed that this lane would bring them round to the Seville road, where the other coach would probably be waiting. Far from doing that, however, the lane wandered on through a poor quarter of the town and gave out, finally, in a silent and lifeless cul-de-sac. Their guide was crestfallen and apologetic, having obviously taken the wrong turning. In the deserted lane where they found themselves there was nobody to question and the best policy was probably to go back the way they had come. Another man suddenly appeared, however, and the coachman leaned from the box to ask him the way. The stranger thereupon hit him over the head with a sand-filled stocking. He tumbled into the roadway, where he was instantly joined by the equally unconscious figure of his companion who had been similarly maltreated by the officer who had proved so bad a guide. The two men were still there and motionless when the coach drove off with their two assailants on board.

"Drive on!" snapped Delancey to Hodder after the coach had been turned around. It soon left the town behind and jolted down the minor road which led to a point in the outskirts where Bisson, now sober, jumped on board. The coach presently reached the main road and there was heard soon afterwards the sound which Delancey had dreaded—

the distant note of a cavalry trumpet. With horses tired at the end of a long day there could be no question of escape. On a straight road crossing a featureless level there was no hope of concealment. The horsemen could already be glimpsed as a tiny and moving dust cloud. Something had gone wrong finally on a day when everything had seemed to go well. Had that coachman come to life again and called for help, describing his assailants and guessing somehow which way they had gone? Had there been time for that? Or had the admiral seen through the whole plot and turned back short of the bridge which led to Paradas? The one thing certain was that the criminals in this case, he and his men, would never be treated as prisoners of war. They would be lucky to be shot, not hanged. And what a way to die, within a few miles of safety! Looking back along the road, Delancey could now distinguish the horsemen and hear, from afar, the drumming of the hooves. Should he, Bisson and Hodder make a fight of it? What was the point? There must be twenty troopers at least. Would any object be served by killing three of them? None that he could see. Following a sudden inspiration Delancey told Hodder to turn the coach round. It might just possibly save them. Now he could distinguish the uniforms, the faces, the officer in the lead, the trumpeter behind him. They came nearer and nearer. . . . What had Colonel Altamirano said? "If death came from Madrid. . . ?" Here was death made visible, inescapable and swift. No swords were drawn—as yet—but what remained of his life was perhaps to be measured out in seconds rather than hours. An order was shouted and the troop came to a halt. Looking straight at Delancey, the officer bawled out a question. The words meant nothing but the sense might possibly mean "Which way—or did you see them?" or something similar. Taking a chance, Delancey shouted back "That way!" and pointed the way they were going. There was another sharp order and the troop galloped on again, hidden now in dust, the noise dwindling and finally dying away into silence. Delancey mopped his sweating forehead and told Hodder to drive on. He was never to know the explanation of this incident. At a small wood south of Utrera the coach kept a rendezvous with three horsemen. The operation had finished.

The admiral, it transpired, had not been entrusted with a vast sum. Delancey divided the silver into six heaps as the others watched, added a few other items of value to five of these and then kept the admiral's best sword for himself. "How is that?" he asked finally. "Is that fair?" The others agreed with words of thanks—remembering that the leader's share should have been at least double. "Very well then, Mr Rigault, lead the party which is riding to Portugal. Are you still with me, Hodder? Good! The rest of you, mount and ride like the devil. You have a hundred miles to go and you should do it in three days. Be off with you—and good luck!"

"Good luck to you, sir!" came their voices in chorus as the horsemen moved off.

"Take the reins, Hodder, and drive on. We want the road to Lebrija but I doubt if we shall go much further this evening. Cadiz lies just beyond and our journey ends at a point just to the south of that city. I had hoped to be there tomorrow, the 15th, but that is impossible. A few days more, however, and our work is done!"

"Well, sir, you know what my trade has been, I never thought to find myself a spy in enemy country, risking death every day. And I don't suppose that you expected to end this journey with a man like me as your only companion. How strange life is, to be sure!"

"As compared with what, Mr Hodder?"

"Well—you have me there!"

With perhaps seventy miles to go, Delancey and Hodder did well to reach Cadiz on the afternoon of the 17th. Having hidden their coach in a wood they finished their journey on horseback and found accommodation at a small inn overlooking the harbour.

Looking on the distant sea, Delancey found that he was strangely moved. Through the past weeks he had been away from his true element. In earlier years he had wondered sometimes whether he was a seaman by accident or choice. The result of being so far from the sea for so long had been to convince him, and finally, that he could have no other career. And then, somehow, the sight of Cadiz reminded him of that other navy in which he ought to be serving. There before his eyes at last was the Spanish fleet with Langara's flag in the *Principe de Asturias*. These great ships made a splendid sight in the autumn sunshine, drawn up as they were in exact formation and surrounded by ordered activity with boats and barges going back and forth. There were no French ships there, they had evidently gone. Borrowing a telescope from the innkeeper, Delancey could see that the fleet was ready or almost ready for sea, for all the topmasts had been sent up and nearly all the yards were crossed. So much would be known to the British admiral at Gibraltar, whose frigates would be somewhere outside the harbour. But how to inform the admiral that Langara was to sail for Toulon?

Chapter Sixteen

THE KING'S SERVICE

AFTER SUPPER on the evening of their arrival in Cadiz (September 17th) Delancey told Hodder that their next problem was to embark at the port of Léon. The intelligence he had gained would be of more value, taken promptly to Gibraltar, than would any further information he might hope to gain at Cadiz. He and Hodder should resume their journey as soon as possible and preferably on the following day.

"Very true, sir," said Hodder. "You put everything very clearly indeed and I am entirely of your opinion."

"I am glad to hear it. As our object now is merely to leave Spain, I felt that I should obtain your views on how to proceed. Both our lives are at hazard and I should not like to think that yours might be lost as the result of a mistake made by me. Our place of embarkation is about ten miles distant and we might well be there tomorrow. Tell me what you think should be done."

"I thank you kindly, Captain, for your consideration. The first thing, in my opinion, is for you to change into civilian clothes. That French uniform has been useful so far but it is now becoming a danger."

"I must confess that I hadn't thought of that."

"Well, sir, it will become conspicuous. Until recently Cadiz must have been full of French officers and some of them would have come here by road to join their ships. You could pass very well as one of them who had arrived too late and I as your servant. Our host here did not even trouble to ask where you had come from or to what ship you belonged. But for a French marine officer to leave here, going southwards . . . *that* must attract more attention. People are bound to ask *why.*"

"You are quite right. I was too concerned with Langara to notice any dubious looks directed at me. But you are right. Were I a French officer posted to a man-of-war that had already sailed, I should leave at once for Madrid."

"That you would, sir."

"But if I now appear as a civilian that will be still more suspicious."

"That can't be helped, sir; and the landlord knows too little French to ask questions."

"True enough. What next?"

"I think we need some muskets. Should it come to a fight, we are too poorly armed with just your sword and a pair of pistols apiece."

"I agree, but how to carry muskets unnoticed."

"I've thought of that, Captain. Suppose we sell one of our two horses and use the money to buy a small cart. We can load it with what we need, not forgetting some lanterns to use as a signal to the lugger."

"A good idea. And then?"

"We need a story to explain what we are doing. We are going fishing, perhaps, and we are wanting to hire a boat."

"Fishing with *muskets?*"

"Maybe we are thief-takers looking for an escaped prisoner."

"Escaped from where?"

"Well, sir, we need some sort of a story."

"Indeed we do, Mr Hodder, and I'll tell you what the story is. We are French agents hunting for deserters. The French fleet was here recently but some of their sailors were missing when their ships sailed."

"Will the innkeeper believe that, sir?"

"I don't see why he shouldn't. The deserters in Cadiz have all been caught by now but we think that some are hidden in the vicinity. We are going to inquire in some of the villages adjacent."

"He'll think we would be better employed at sea."

"So we should, but we have to obey orders."

"Aye, aye, sir."

On the next day Delancey completed these precautions, selling one horse and purchasing a small cart. Muskets proved unobtainable but he managed to buy two sporting guns, with ammunition, not quite as lethal as muskets would have been but more accurate and more easily explained. The purchase of lanterns presented no difficulty and Delancey also acquired some wood laths with which to make a frame to which the lanterns could be hung. To this equipment he added a well-used spyglass, a knife, an axe, a saw, hammer, nails and a ball of spunyarn. Last of all he bought, second-hand, a suit of blue cloth such as might be worn by the master of a small merchantman, not a uniform, but a costume with a nautical air and a hat with it such as might serve a boatswain ashore. He finally told the innkeeper of his deserter-hunting mission and said that he and his servant would return in two days time. He used a fellow guest as an interpreter in telling this story, his own knowledge of Spanish—which had improved of late—being too limited for this purpose although sufficient for asking the way or ordering a meal. The innkeeper was mainly concerned as was natural, with his bill being paid. Reassured on that point, he showed no great interest in Delancey's plans.

Delancey might, in fact, have escaped notice altogether had it not been for the arrival of Pierre Marigny, appointed purser of the *Duguay-Trouin*. Marigny came to stay at the inn on the Tuesday evening, missing his ship by about a week. And whereas the innkeeper found no difficulty in accepting Delancey as a Frenchman, Monsieur Marigny was suspicious from the outset. What was the army captain supposed to be doing? Tracking down deserters? But no captain would ever be detailed to do that, a task for a reliable boatswain's mate! As soon as questions began to be asked, Delancey was in danger. He could pass as a Frenchman among the Spaniards. He could even pass as a Spaniard among the French. In a mixed company of French and Spanish he was obviously an alien, and Hodder, who had to pose as stone-deaf or half-witted, was still less able to pass muster. Meeting Marigny in the parlour, with the innkeeper present, Delancey had to explain his accent by stating that he had lived for some years in the United States. He then excused himself, saying that he had to make an early start in the morning. He was conscious of being followed by curious glances as he left the room and decided to leave even earlier than he had planned.

Delancey left the inn at daybreak, having paid his bill the night before. Hodder led their remaining horse round to the livery stable from which the cart was to be collected and at which their sporting guns and lanterns were temporarily stored. Delancey's personal documents, those of a French army officer, satisfied the sergeant at the city gate and they were presently on the road to Léon. It was a stormy day, overcast, with a westerly gale and Delancey and Hodder were glad to huddle into their cloaks and pull their hats over their eyes.

"I'm glad to be out of Cadiz," said Hodder with a sigh of relief. "We might have been arrested any minute. I don't mind admitting, Captain, that I was sleepless last night, expecting a knock on the door. There was a fellow in the courtyard who kept asking me questions. I played dumb as usual but he went on and on. I was glad to escape him when I had the chance but I have an unpleasant feeling that we may be pursued. That sergeant will remember us, too. They'll be after us, sir—mark my words."

"Thank you for the warning. I think you are right. I also think we are an hour of two ahead of them with time enough to see whether the *Dove* is in the harbour. If she isn't I must ask whether she has been there and whether she is likely to return. That done, we must quit the town on the far side, leave some sort of false trail and then hide somewhere on the coast where we can signal seawards."

A drive of two hours brought them to the little town of Léon, grouped round a fishing harbour and rising to the church and town hall on higher ground to the eastwards.

The harbour was small but easily entered, with apparently enough

water for ships of average draught. It was roughly oblong, the seaward
side formed by two breakwaters. A stone-built quayside defined the
other three sides, with space for unloading between the water's edge
and the warehouses or other buildings. On the inland or eastern side
the houses and shops stood farther back, leaving an open space which
might serve as fish market or fairground. There were no stalls set up
at the moment but there were a number of boats, brought there perhaps for sale or repair. There were one or two adjacent creeks to the
north of the town, one of them with white sand and a few small boats
drawn out of the water. There was something of a surf running with
a strong wind from off the sea and waves breaking on the beach. The
better houses were in the area between the church and the harbour,
entered from the north by what was probably the high street. Delancey
drove his cart in from that direction, drew up boldly outside the principal inn and joined the few inhabitants who had already gathered
inside round the fireplace. His order for rum caused some mild con-
sternation, however, and the tapster said that he had none.

"No rum?" Delancey repeated. "In the name of God you can't have
drunk all that was landed here from the lugger!" The citizens and seamen exchanged glances and the poor tapster said that he would call
his master.

"If we have any, the master will know about it." There was a semi-
audible conference in a back room and then the innkeeper appeared
in person and admitted to knowing a few words of French.

"The señor was asking for *rum*? But that, as you must know, is
unobtainable in time of war. We have some brandy, however, which I
can recommend." There was a suppressed snigger from one of the
sailors and the innkeeper frowned in his direction.

"Strange!" said Delancey. "A friend of mine had rum here only yesterday. It was landed quite recently from a French vessel called the
Dove. . . ." There was a tense silence, broken eventually by the innkeeper
who first looked hastily around to see whether all others present were
known to him.

"You are a friend, perhaps, of Señor Davila?" This question was asked in little more than a whisper.

"He is the man I have come here to meet." The tension almost visibly ended and the innkeeper was obviously relieved.

"For any friend of Señor Davila I am pleased to produce a very special brandy." There were more smiles as he poured.

"And where is Señor Davila to be found?" asked Delancey.

"At this time of day he will be at the Barco de Vela tavern on the waterfront. He comes here only in the evening. He is a good friend of mine, señor, and well known here."

"To Señor Davila!" said Delancey, raising his glass. "And is the *Dove* in port?"

"No, señor, not today. She may be here tomorrow or the next day. Who knows?"

"Who knows?" Delancey repeated. "Señor Davila, perhaps. I am his friend but he has enemies too. It would be well not to mention my name to any who should come here asking too many questions."

"I do not know your name, señor."

"Then it will be easy for you to deny having seen me."

"Nothing easier, señor. I am singularly unobservant, as my wife always complains. But it grieves me to hear that Señor Davila should have enemies. All here are his friends."

"No doubt. But there is jealousy to be met with everywhere."

"How true, alas."

Delancey said farewell and rejoined Hodder who had been patiently holding the horse's head. "We must go down to the quayside and visit the Barco de Vela tavern. The *Dove* has been here and is expected again. I want to know *when*."

The cart drove on and made its next stop in the street of the fishmongers. Waves could be seen bursting over the breakwater and Delancey doubted whether the *Dove* would even attempt to enter until the wind abated. There was a heavy shower of rain as he walked over to the Barco de Vela tavern and asked boldly for Señor Davila. A short dark man of prosperous appearance detached himself from the group by the window and Delancey quickly claimed him as an old friend.

"Señor Davila! How good to see you looking so well! The saints have you in their good keeping, I can see."

Davila looked puzzled for a few seconds and then quickly guessed what part he was supposed to play.

"My dear friend! How good to see you and what a pleasant surprise! Join me by the fire while your cloak dries. A glass of brandy, perhaps?" Davila steered Delancey over to a corner where they could talk in French without being overheard.

"Captain Delancey? What a relief to see you! We had almost given you up for lost."

"You are working with Sam Carter, señor?"

"We are in business together and I expect him here tomorrow or whenever this gale stops blowing. The *Dove* has been here but had to put to sea again. Señor Carter was inquiring after you at a village just to the north of here. He left Señor Alvarez with me—a very useful man. He and I will look after you. I should add that it is greatly to our interest to see that you reach the *Dove* in safety. What I want to know is this: are you being followed?"

"I think it quite probable."

"Then you must go to a place I know in the country just south of here. You must go as soon as possible and remain hidden until the *Dove* returns, perhaps tomorrow, perhaps the next day."

"Very well, but how do I get there?"

"You shall have a guide."

Davila went quickly to the front door and came back with a young man called Marco.

"This is my groom and he knows the way. I shall come and visit you after dark. Go now, please, and quickly!"

Delancey and Marco hurried back to the cart and Hodder, following Marco's directions, drove out of Léon by a minor road which twisted up the hillside. They were barely in time for Marco, looking back, muttered, "Soldiers!" Delancey glimpsed a troop of cavalry drawn up on the quayside with an officer dismounted outside the Barco de Vela tavern. It looked as if the hunt was up and Delancey guessed that the rear-admiral, for one, might be in an ugly mood after the loss of his baggage. The inhabitants of Léon would be unwilling to betray a smuggler with whom they did business. They would not be as tolerant of an English spy and the place was far too small for Delancey's arrival to have passed unnoticed.

Hodder whipped the horse into a gallop when the road flattened out and an hour later took a lane, as directed, on the right which presently dwindled into a mere cart track. There were no peasants in sight and Delancey sensed that they were approaching a desolate part of the coast. The track ended at a ruined and roofless cottage, beyond which the cliffs fell steeply to a storm-swept tangle of rocks. There was a high wind still which carried with it the sound of the breakers. The hiding place was well chosen but it was not a place from which to embark. When the cart stopped, Marco told Delancey that this was a place of safety, visited by no one. It was unlikely to be safe very much longer but Delancey did not think that he had been seen on the way there, certainly not since quitting the road. A general search of the countryside would disclose his whereabouts in the course of a day but no such operation was to be expected, not at least with the small force so far available. Delancey had seen no more than a single troop, just over twenty dragoons, adequate for making an arrest but quite insufficient for scouring the country. He and Hodder were safe at least for the time being and could make themselves comfortable.

Marco said adios and left them, walking back the way they had come, and Delancey set about building a shelter for the night. Choosing a windward corner of the ruin, he and Hodder cleaned it of loose stones and rubbish. Demolishing the cart, they used its wheels for two side walls, its floor for a roof and its shafts to make a temporary stable for the horse. Finally, Delancey lashed some timbers together to make a frame for his lanterns. After dark it would be at least technically possible to signal the *Dove*. Whether any signal would be recognised was also problematical for Sam was no man-of-war's man and Mr Evans' knowledge would be as limited. Looking seaward, Delancey could see one or two sail in the distance but they were most probably fishing craft or coasters. If the *Dove* returned it would be after dark. One thing was certain, however, he and Hodder would have to embark at Léon; and yet how were they to pass through a town where their descriptions had most probably been circulated and where troops were hunting for them?

That evening Señor Davila appeared, having walked out from the town. He was accompanied by José Alvarez whom he introduced as his business partner. They brought with them meat, bread, butter, cheese and a bottle of wine. Sitting with them as they ate by their hidden camp fire, Davila drank a glass of wine and gave them the news. First of all, he said, the cavalry had been sent in pursuit of them; an officer and 24 troopers. The lieutenant was young and inexperienced and had gleaned little information at the Léon inn and nothing at all at the Barco de Vela tavern. He had told people that he had been ordered to arrest a couple of spies but the seafaring folk disbelieved him, thinking that he was really searching for contraband—of which the place had plenty. So far as the soldiers were concerned the people of Léon had seen nothing, heard nothing and knew nothing. Unfortunately, however, the garrison commander had followed up his cavalry troop by a whole company of infantry under a captain called Miguel de Passamonte. Since his arrival in the late afternoon he had taken the cavalry under command and intensified the search.

"He is not another boy without experience, then?" asked Delancey.

"Miguel de Passamonte? No, señor, he is an old soldier risen from the ranks, a man who knows his trade. His patrols are ready to ask who is known and who is a stranger. It is all most unfortunate, señor. Until today this was a peaceful town with no real difficulty over anything. A man could do business without fear of gossip. Now all is upset and we have begun to distrust each other. Passamonte is at the Barco de Vela tavern this evening and who knows what may be revealed by men who have drunk too much? You and I were seen there together, remember. Frankly, señor, I don't know what to do!"

"May I suggest that we take one problem at a time? The first one, I think, centres upon the *Dove*. Dare we bring her into port? I assume that you have the means of warning her to remain outside?"

"Yes, there is a signal arranged. I think, however, that she can enter harbour safely under the French flag. The customs officers are friends of mine and it is to them that Passamonte will address any questions he may want to ask about the *Dove*. She will be safe but Passamonte will place sentries on the quayside. The lugger will be watched, of this we can be certain."

"Very well. The next problem concerns the extent of Passamonte's knowledge. How much does he know?"

"He knows that you have been in the town. He is certain, I should say, that you are not there now. He will conclude that you are somewhere in the vicinity and he will assume that Léon is the place at which you mean to embark. His plan will be to wait and watch."

"But how does he know that I am to embark here? I might well go on down the coast and attempt to reach Gibraltar. I may yet have to do this and I should regard it indeed as the obvious plan."

"I agree, señor, but Passamonte is not concerned with what happens at Tarifa—that is another officer's responsibility. His orders confine him to this place and he must assume that this is the point at which you intend to leave Spain."

"So my best plan might be to go farther south . . . ?"

"But other garrisons will also have been warned and you would not, elsewhere, have a friend ashore."

"You think that Passamonte will look on the *Dove* with suspicion?"

"Yes, but not to the point of interference. She will be the bait, her gangplank the point at which the trap is to close."

"I wonder that she has been able to linger on this coast: visiting this port more than once, I assume?"

"She has been here three times already and her visits are profitable to me and to my friends. At sea she is protected on this occasion by a British frigate, the *Medusa*, which keeps almost out of sight."

"The *Medusa?* Captain Morris?"

"I don't know the captain's name."

"How does the frigate keep in touch?"

"The *Dove* has been lent a set of signal flags and a midshipman who knows the code. She also carries rockets and blue flares to light in an emergency."

"Good! What other ships are there in port? Anything of interest?"

"Only the *Aguila*, supposed to be fitting out as a ten-gun privateer, but the owners could never find a crew for her."

"One other question: is there another landing place, outside the actual harbour?"

"There is a sort of creek on the north side called the Playa Blanco where one can land on a calm day but it is extremely dangerous in any sort of sea—impossible, for instance, on such a day as this has been. Fishing boats are sometimes repaired there."

"Good! With the wind moderating I think that we shall be able to leave Spain tomorrow night. During the next few hours I shall try to signal the *Dove*. If Señor Carter knows that I am here he will bring the lugger into port tomorrow. When he does that I want you to go aboard, give him my kind regards, explain the situation and tell him to expect me aboard just before the beginning of the ebb. What hour would that be?"

"At half-past one in the morning."

"Then I want you to bring the signal midshipman out here, disguised as a Spaniard and bringing with him a rocket, his flags and code. I want to communicate with the *Medusa* from here."

"Very well, señor—all that is possible, even under the sentry's eye."

"Thank you for all your help, Señor Davila, and not least for the supper. The crisis should be over in two days' time and you should be back in business."

"What I have done is nothing. My reward will be to know that you
are safe. Forgive me if I leave you now."

"You can reach home without being challenged by the sentries?"

"Oh, yes, señor. I know this town well and have good friends in
every street."

"Goodnight, then, and thank you!"

"Goodnight, señor, and God keep you safe!"

After Davila and Alvarez had gone Hodder asked Delancey whether
he thought the Spaniards were to be trusted. He himself was more
than doubtful. "I don't like the look of Davila, Captain. I don't like the
look of him at all. These dagoes are all alike, sir, each one no better
than the last. He would change sides any day if he thought it would
pay him."

"I daresay; but in this case it wouldn't pay him. He is in business
here as a smuggler's agent, he and Alvarez working with Sam Carter.
Sam is therefore the man he dare not antagonise—and Sam is a friend
of mine."

"I hope you're right, sir, and I hope you regard me as a friend, too.
My life has not been all that respectable, as you know, or will have
guessed, but I've learnt something in these last few weeks, I don't
exactly know what. But I want England to win, sir, and I admire the
way in which you never waver from your purpose. You are a gentleman, sir, and can trust me as you would your own boatswain or gunner.
If we have to fight our way out of this, I'll not give in easily."

"I know that, Mr Hodder—and thank you. It's time now to signal
the *Dove*. God knows whether she is in sight!"

Delancey had hoped to find a tree from which he could hang his
pattern of lanterns, a tree which, bereft of branches, could be used as
a mast. All the trees in sight were stunted oaks, however, the best of
them effectively masked by others. In the end he chose a sturdy bush
on the very cliff top from which his frame could hang on the cliff face,
not an ideal arrangement but one which ensured that the signal could
not be seen from any other direction. He and Hodder now arranged

six of their eight lanterns in a framework, making a pattern which was
(or had been) the Channel Fleet recognition signal. The lanterns were
lit and the whole clumsy device was lowered gingerly down the cliff
at a point where projection hid it from either side. Over the next hour
or two Delancey hauled the frame up for a few minutes at a time. The
signal might or might not be understood but it would at least be recognised as a signal. Hours passed without a reply and it was not long
before dawn when Hodder called out, "Look, sir!" and pointed to a
distant blue flare which showed for an instant and vanished again.
Delancey pulled up his framework and rearranged the lanterns, adding
two more and using all eight to form the letter "D." He hoped that this
would tell Sam everything. There was an answering flare and no further signal from either side. Delancey and Hodder lay down to rest.

   They woke in broad daylight to breakfast on what remained from
yesterday's supper. Afterwards they walked northwards to a headland
from which they had a better view of Léon. The wind had dropped
and there, sure enough, was the *Dove!* She was about to enter the harbour in daylight and there, far seawards, was another sail, evidently
that of the *Medusa*. The sight of these distant sails had the emotional
impact of a miracle. To have exchanged signals in the dark had given
him reason to hope but actually to see the *Dove* again brought tears to
his eyes. He brushed them aside impatiently and then found that his
hands were trembling as he levelled the spyglass. He realised with a
sort of shock that he had not really expected to escape from Spain.
God knew that the chances were still against his survival. But there
was the *Dove* and his spyglass, when finally focused, showed her sails
being lowered as she sidled up to the farther quayside. He could just
see a rope being made fast to a bollard in the north-east corner of the
harbour. That would be Evans, that speck on the forecastle, not recognizable at this distance but placed where the chief mate should be
as the vessel was hauled into her berth. Here were petty criminals risking their vessel and their lives to rescue a friend. . . . He realised that
Hodder was talking.

"There's a sight, sir, to do me a power of good. I'm no seaman, as you know, but it's a tonic, as you might say, to see the old *Dove* again."

Delancey could not reply but turned his spyglass on the *Medusa*. There was little he could see but he remembered something about her. She was a fifth-rate of 36 guns and would measure something over 900 tons with a length of 145 feet or thereabouts on the gun-deck. She would mount eighteen-pounders, he thought, and could have been built at Buckler's Hard. Or had she been taken from the French? Morris he had heard mentioned as the previous captain of a sloop; a sister ship, he thought, to the *Calypso*. He pictured for a moment the ordered routine on board. Her crew would number 264 and Morris would have made them into seamen by now. They would just have finished holystoning and washing the decks. The brasswork would have been polished and the ropes coiled down. Now the pipes would call "Up hammocks" and soon it would be eight bells and time for breakfast. There had been a time, years ago, when he had resented the inexorable pattern of the naval day's work. Now the mere sight of these distant sails gave him a sense of homecoming. He had lacked for so long that sense of security he had derived from other men about him who knew their tasks and would do their duty. For the first time since he left the *Royalist* he was feeling homesick.

As there was nothing more to do they returned to camp where they were joined before midday by Señor Davila and José Alvarez, bringing with them some dinner and also, in disguise, the signal midshipman from the *Dove*, carrying his flags in a bundle. This youth was a red-haired character called O'Keefe, in whose presence Delancey again felt a sense of exile. Had it been weeks or months since he had spoken with a man-of-war's man? He forced himself to give all his attention to Davila who was full of news and anxiety. Handbills had been printed now with a description of the two spies as wanted men and an offer of a reward for information which might lead to their capture. There were soldiers everywhere and the *Dove* was being closely watched. Sam Carter sent his greetings and said that his lugger would be ready to

sail after dark and at a minute's notice. O'Keefe professed a knowledge
of the current system of numerical signals. To the burden of flags,
shared with Alvarez, he had added several rockets. "One wouldn't do,"
he explained, "to convey a message. Without a sequence of colour they
are meaningless."

"You address me as 'Sir,'" said Delancey.

"Beg pardon, sir," replied O'Keefe. "But the signal asking for assistance is a red and a blue. That would best serve to bring the *Medusa*
to within flag-signalling distance."

"Very well, Mr O'Keefe. Prepare the rockets for firing and get ready
to use the bush as your mast." He explained that the hoist would hang
down the cliff face, weighted by a stone.

Davila expressed his alarm: "But the rockets will be seen from Léon,
señor! We shall have the cavalry here within the hour!"

"Not if Alvarez here does his part. The time has come, Señor Alvarez,
for you to give information to Captain Passamonte. Tell him, when you
return to Léon, that the men he is hunting are at some hiding place
on the inland side of town—you don't know exactly where. When their
friends, camping here, see the vessel that is to rescue them—a schooner,
now in the offing—they will fire certain rockets. That is the signal for
the two fugitives to come here at nightfall. It is also the signal to the
schooner, which will come in after dark and send her boat into the
Playa Blanco, the creek on the north side of the harbour. Tell Passamonte that his best plan is to surround this place just before sunset,
allow the fugitives to enter and then close in on this ruined cottage at
two in the morning, capturing both the spies and their accomplices
ashore. Simultaneously he should lay an ambush at the Playa Blanco
creek and be ready to fire on the boat which comes in with the last of
the flood. If the spies are taken you claim the reward. If they should
not be caught here they will be caught at the landing place."

"But what will happen to me when the plan fails?"

"It won't entirely fail. The soldiers will find proof here that there *has* been a camp, with the embers of the fire still warm and with signal halliards still attached to this tree. And there *will* be a boat making an attempt to land at the creek you indicate. There will be proof enough that you gave the right information."

"How am I supposed to know all this?"

"From information received. This spot is known to you and you can guide the troops here."

"And what do you really intend?"

"I expect that some plan will occur to me. I shall certainly avoid being here after sunset!"

After Davila and Alvarez had gone, taking the horse with them as a farewell present, Delancey discussed with O'Keefe the messages he wanted to convey to the *Medusa*. His first object was to request her presence off the harbour mouth that night, his second to tell her about the *Aguila*, his third to ask for a feint landing at the Playa Blanco creek at two in the morning.

"Begin with the word 'submit,'" said Delancey, "for Morris is senior to me." With Hodder posted as lookout on the land side, he began to work on the problems of signalling. With some difficulty these were solved, words having to be spelt out, and finally, an hour and a half after Davila's departure, the two rockets were fired. There was only a moderate breeze and there was at first no sign of reaction from the *Medusa*. It eventually became clear, however, that she was closing the land under all plain sail and would be able to receive signals in another half hour.

"Send up the first hoist now, Mr O'Keefe," said Delancey. "It will help her to see where we are." He paced impatiently up and down, leaving O'Keefe to watch with his telescope for any response. It seemed hours before the young man was able to call, excitedly, "Signal acknowledged, sir!"

When the signals had been made O'Keefe was told to make his way back to the *Dove* and explain the situation to Sam Carter. "In his place," Delancey concluded, "I should send a boat to the *Medusa* after dark with you in it to enlarge on his written message."

Meanwhile, at the Barca de Vela tavern, Alvarez was in conference with Captain Passamonte, a grey-haired and grim-faced veteran, whose first reaction was one of skepticism.

"Why didn't you come to see me before?"

"I have only today received the information."

"From whom?"

"I promised my informant not to reveal his name."

"Why did he talk to *you?*"

"Because he knew that I would honestly share the reward with him."

"Why the secrecy?"

"My informant is engaged in other activities which he would not like to have known."

"In other words, he is a smuggler. Why should I trust him? Why, for that matter, should I trust *you?*"

"Me, Captain? I am well known here. Ask anyone! Ask the collector of customs or the harbour master. But why, anyway, should I deceive you?"

"I don't know. I won't act on your information, however, until this signal is seen, this flare or rocket or whatever it is. When that is reported, I shall be more confident."

Alvarez reflected wryly that he was trusted by neither side. He was consoled, however, by the appearance of the deputy collector of customs who looked into the parlour as if in search of a friend. Alvarez promptly hailed him and asked for his help.

"Will you tell the captain here that I am a merchant well known here and doing good business?"

"That you are, señor! You are doing as well as anyone and better than most. We all know Señor Alvarez, Captain; he is partner with Señor Davila who is highly respected in this town."

There was some further conversation and Passamonte accepted a glass of wine with a hint of cordiality. The wine itself had no effect on him at all and Alvarez guessed that another gallon of it would have left him with as steady a hand, but his air of distrust was slightly modified. It all but vanished, moreover, when news came of the rockets being seen. It was his lieutenant who brought this intelligence, having evidently run from the breakwater:

"Two rockets fired from the coast to the south of the town, sir; a red and a blue."

"Thank you, Tomas. Did you see the vessel to which this signal was made? A schooner, for instance?"

"No, sir. There is a ship out there but very distant, impossible to identify."

"Strange," commented Passamonte, "I was led to expect a schooner."

"You forget, Captain," said Alvarez, "that the rockets were fired from cliffs which rise two hundred feet above this town. Anyone posted there can see much farther than we can."

From this point Passamonte appeared to be convinced. Taking his lieutenant outside, he issued orders for the night. Of his infantry about half (that is 43) would take up positions after dark round the Playa Blanco creek. Of the remainder, twenty would patrol the outskirts of the town in groups of four and the lieutenant, with 22, would continue to guard the harbour.

"I have been given information," he explained, "that the two men we are seeking will try to embark at two in the morning from the Playa Blanco creek. That is quite possible for two o'clock marks the turn of the tide, the beginning of the ebb. There will be moonlight then and it is vital to keep our soldiers out of sight. I shall lead that party and see that the men are neither seen nor heard. I shall send the cavalry out after dark with this man Alvarez as guide. They are to surround the camp from which those rockets were fired. The spies we have been sent to arrest should be taken either there or at the Playa Blanco creek.

But I still have my doubts about this information we have received. It came too easily."

"I don't quite understand what you mean, sir."

"This information was given me. I prefer the information I have had to extract."

"Indeed, sir?"

"So I have my doubts. The story I have been told may be intended to draw us away from the harbour at the moment when these spies are to embark."

"But I shall be there, sir."

"Yes, you will be there. But I don't want you or your men to be seen. I want two sentries on the quayside, ready to give the alarm. You and your men must be hidden but at a point from which you can see the sentries. Can you do that?"

"Easily, sir. I'll use the warehouse that belongs to Alonzo Perez, ten yards up the lane from the quayside. You can almost see it from here."

"You won't see the sentries from there."

"No, sir, the men won't. But I'll be in the house at the corner. I can see the sentries from there and when I go to the other window the sergeant can see me."

"Very well. Go there after nightfall, two or three men at a time, walking as if they are off duty. Be ready to dash in if you see anything suspicious. We would prefer to have these two men alive but it won't matter too much if they are killed. Use the bayonet and don't fire unless you are fired upon. Send your orderly now to fetch Lieutenant de Garay."

By the evening all arrangements had been made and Captain Passamonte was ready to send the cavalry troop on its way, encouraged by a scout's report of the smoke being seen of a distant campfire. It was after dark before the troop marched but Alvarez, who rode with de Garay, was confident of the route. "We shall have them trapped," he explained, "between your troopers and the sea."

While Passamonte deployed his troops Delancey and Hodder lay hidden in a disused cow-house in the southern outskirts of the town. They were occupied in rehearsal. Having ascertained that Hodder had no experience of firearms, Delancey taught him the elements but then explained that he himself would be the marksman and that Hodder's task would be to reload for him. With two guns and four pistols quickly reloaded, Delancey could maintain an almost continuous fire. Hodder could not become a good shot without practice in firing but he had all the manual dexterity which went with a lifetime's experience in the picking of locks. He quickly mastered the sequence of cartridge, wad, ball, wad and ramrod, repeating the actions and improving on the time until even Delancey was satisfied. "If it comes to a fight," he concluded, "they are going to suffer some losses." If all went well, however, there was a chance of reaching the *Dove* without a battle. "If Alvarez has told his story convincingly, the dragoons will be surrounding our camp site and the infantry will be watching the Playa Blanco creek. The quayside should be almost unguarded."

"Let's hope so, Captain. But certainly that infantry officer was not born yesterday."

"Hence this little rehearsal. Shall we try it once more? I'll take this sequence: musket, pistol, musket, pistol, pistol, musket. You keep one pistol in reserve for your own defence. Right? Go!" The last rehearsal finished, they ate what bread and meat was left and lay down to rest until midnight.

When the town church clock struck twelve Delancey and Hodder began their slow approach to the harbour, planning each move from doorway to yard entry, from one shadow to the next. There was all too much moonlight for their purpose and they were alarmed at one stage by the persistent barking of a dog. Hardly had the dog forgotten them before they found themselves near a small church or chapel from which came, surprisingly, the sound of prayer. The windows were candlelit and Delancey guessed that it must be the eve of some saint's day. He was vague about Catholic ritual but supposed that mass could be said at odd hours on particular occasions. He was grateful, however, at the moment, for a pious activity which might help to explain what he and Hodder were doing in that street.

While still deciding what to do next, Delancey heard in the distance the sound he had been dreading, the marching steps of a patrol. The soldiers were coming in his direction and the church offered the only hiding place. Beckoning Hodder and walking on tiptoe, Delancey opened the church door and slipped inside, Hodder closing the door after him.

The church was very dark apart from the candles on the high altar and there cannot have been more than six people present. He realised, nevertheless, that he and Hodder had to merge with their surroundings before the patrol arrived. There was no knowing whether they would look into the church but it was the sort of thing a conscientious corporal might do. "I'll go over there," he whispered to Hodder, pointing to a confessional box. "You kneel outside it as if waiting your turn." A minute later he was ready to make his confession, muttering suitably to a priest who was not there.

But that was where he had made his mistake. A voice through the grille said, "Yes, my son?" and added the words for blessing. Racking his brains for material, Delancey began his first confession, beginning in Spanish and soon lapsing into French, half his attention on the footsteps of the patrol, which had halted at the church door. "I have grievously sinned, Father, by drinking to excess, by illicit traffic in evasion of customs duties, by looking with desire on women, even on those that are married, by—." The church door had opened quietly and a corporal stood there, looking round the church. Desperate for ideas and realising that the known sins are all too few, Delancey plunged into a story of having cheated at cards and sold a horse for more than its value, having hopes that his mother-in-law would die and failing to give what he had promised to charity. The corporal had gone and the door of the church was closing. By now Delancey was at his wits end but he could hear the patrol marching away. "I told gossip falsely against a neighbour who is sick and whom I said is with child. I spoke in anger to a young boy who had failed in his errand. I have not been to mass for three weeks. . . ."

The confession ended rather abruptly and Delancey did not hear and might not have understood what penance was enjoined. Muttering something which he hoped was appropriate he rose and walked quietly to the door.

A minute later he and Hodder were outside and approaching the town centre. One patrol was now behind them but there might be others. That there would be sentries on the quayside was certain. As they came in sight of the harbour, the town church clock struck one.

Moving very silently, Delancey reached the end of the lane he had been following and looked across the open space which fronted the harbour basin on its landward side. On the other two sides the harbour was flanked by its stone-built quay with warehouses closely adjacent. There were fishing boats in plenty and against the nearer quayside a brig of some size, almost certainly the *Aguila*. It was nearly high tide with the waves lapping gently against the stonework. On the far side with a thrill of recognition he saw the *Dove*. Two sentries paced the pavement opposite where she was tied. No light showed in any building but the moon lit the whole scene with pitiless detail.

From a merely tactical point of view Delancey did not like what he could see. The open space, probably where the market was held, seemed all too open, offering no cover at all. Several boats had been dragged out of the water and lay at the quay's edge but these were isolated and distant from where he was. If he went back and tried to circle left he might with luck come out near the *Aguila* but he would then have the harbour between him and the *Dove*. To circle right would lead him into the very middle of the town and probably into the arms of another patrol. If he could reach the boats on the harbour's edge he could find cover behind them, being halfway towards the *Dove* before he would be seen again. He hesitated, weighing the risks and vaguely disquieted by the apparent absence of the enemy. The approach appeared easy—too easy to be quite convincing. His next move was settled for him by accident. Kneeling in the shadow of a doorway, he felt his shoe clink against something that moved. Looking down he saw that it was an empty bottle. It gave him a moment of inspiration and he turned to Hodder with sudden urgency:

"Can you sing something in Spanish?"

There was a bewildered silence and finally Hodder whispered, "I know the tune all the street boys were singing in Cadiz but I don't know the words. Something about 'Hasta la vista, caro mio.'"

"Right," said Delancey. "We are both drunk but I am the more drunk of the two. Keep your gun out of sight under your cloak. Give me your right arm to prevent me falling. Ready? Then off we go!"

Waving his bottle in his right hand, Delancey staggered out on to the square. Hodder simultaneously began singing "Caro mio" and was joined by Delancey in drunken parody. They swayed together and nearly fell over, recovering sufficiently to repeat all that Hodder could remember of his song. They made a horrible row between them; enough, seemingly, to disarm the immediate suspicions of anyone placed in ambush. "Hasta la vista!" sang Delancey as they reached the middle of the market-place, and it was there that he dropped his bottle with a crash and tinkle of broken glass. "Caro mio!" roared Hodder as he once again saved Delancey from falling. Still singing and staggering, they covered another dozen paces and came at last to the upturned boats on the quayside. Sitting on the keel of the nearest, Delancey was able to look about him and see what their vocal efforts had achieved. One or two windows had opened but were closed again now that the singing had subsided.

Delancey continued to talk loudly in Spanish but, moving on to the next phase of intoxication, slid to the ground and remained there. Under cover of the boats he began to crawl silently towards the far side of the harbour, the quayside to which the *Dove* was tied. Hodder followed as quietly and they found themselves in the shadow of the last and stoutest of the upturned boats. There was another fifty yards to the angle of the basin and, once that corner was turned, a good hundred yards to the *Dove's* gangplank, with the two sentries pacing the cobbles in the foreground.

"What do we do now?" asked Hodder in a whisper. "Wait!" replied Delancey, watching the sky. The sky was not cloudless and it seemed to Delancey that it was only a question of time before the moon was hidden. Five minutes of relative darkness was all he wanted but the clouds that drifted across the sky seemed to avoid the moon of set purpose. Ten minutes passed, then fifteen, and eventually the church clock struck the half hour. At long last a useful cloud appeared on what seemed the right course. It came nearer and nearer and finally obscured the moon.

Delancey rose to his feet and set off at an ordinary walking pace, with Hodder at his heels. He was seen at the same instant by the nearer sentry who challenged him. To make matters worse, the cloud which had momentarily helped them turned out to be a tattered fraud. They were clearly visible and the sentry, taking no chance, fired his musket in their direction.

The result was a shouted order from the far side of the market-place and the rapid appearance of soldiers who shook out at once into extended order. Seeing no alternative, Delancey doubled back to the upturned boat, took cover behind it and whipped out his mus-ket. Hodder dropped beside him as in their rehearsal and the battle fairly began.

Delancey's first musket shot took effect and the advancing line wavered. His next pistol shot missed but caused hesitation again, the next musket shot hitting a man who collapsed with a groan. The whole line fell back into the shadow of the buildings, where an officer's voice could be heard, probably telling his men to load. Then there came a scattered volley, most of the bullets going high but some thudding into the boat's timbers.

There was another shouted order and a more resolute advance but Delancey's first shot would seem to have wounded the sergeant, his second only just missing the officer. Two more shots were enough to bring the advance to a halt, driving the men back to the shadows from which they had started. It looked to Delancey as if the men had never been under fire before.

While he waited to see what they would do next he heard a burst of firing in the distance. The feint landing was being ambushed, which would at least keep the other troops busy for the time being. It was bad luck having this opposition in the town centre but there were only about twenty men and a probably inexperienced subaltern. There was no further assault but his immediate opponents began to fire independently from where they were.

Delancey wondered now what the sentries were doing, well placed as they were to attack him from the rear. Looking back, he saw that they were both crumpled on the quayside, their muskets fallen beside them, almost as if killed by their friends' fire. There was no sign of life on board the *Dove,* the lugger being apparently deserted. Firing continued, both near and in the distance, but the battle seemed otherwise to have reached stalemate. Just after the church clock struck two the situation changed suddenly for the worse. The firing was desultory and mostly ineffective but one bullet hit the sternpost of the boat they were using for cover, sending splinters of wood in all directions. Hodder uttered a groan and Delancey could see that his breeches and stockings were soaked in blood. Tearing the sleeve off his own shirt, Delancey tried to bandage the wounded thigh but not very successfully. Hodder was out of action and probably bleeding to death.

"Don't worry about me, Captain," said the wounded man. "Give me your musket and I'll hold them off while you board the lugger. I'm finished anyway and your life is worth saving."

"I'll come back for you. Keep firing while I go to fetch help."

At this moment Delancey had little hope of reaching the *Dove* alive but he suddenly became aware of new developments somewhere on his right. There was the sound of cheering and a fresh outburst of small arms fire. Alongside the *Aguila* there had appeared from nowhere a ship's longboat. Men were swarming over the privateer and were already pushing her away from the quayside. The soldiers on the far side of the market-place were now firing at the captured *Aguila* although not very effectively at that extreme range. The subaltern must have realised this because he made another attempt to make them advance. He fell, however, to a shot from Hodder and his men took cover again, remaining where they were until the battle was over.

Delancey, meanwhile, seizing his opportunity, ran to the angle of the harbour basin, swerved left past the two dead bodies and sprinted down the quayside to the *Dove*. Sam Carter appeared at the gangway, musket in hand, and the rest of the crew, similarly armed, lined the ship's side, cheering, as he jumped down to the deck. They were about to cast off but Delancey stopped them, pointing back to where Hodder was still in action. "Save him!" he shouted breathlessly and led the way back to the upturned boat.

They came too late, for Hodder had been hit again and died before they could lift him up. At this moment a frantic figure pelted across the open to join them, the soldiers being evidently too surprised to stop him or even pick him off. It was Alvarez, who said, breathlessly, "Take me with you—can't stay here—not after *this!*" For their final dash to safety they divided into two parties, to shoot and to move alternatively, but it was hardly necessary, their immediate opponents being demoralised and almost silent.

As soon as they had regained the *Dove* the gangway was dragged inboard and the ropes cast off. Slowly and silently the lugger began to slip out of the harbour on the ebb, her sails gently filling to a breeze off the land.

If the *Dove* was silent, the town was a scene of pandemonium. The cutting out of the *Aguila* had not been difficult but she had few sails to set and nothing useful to hand. She was now under fire from another direction because the dragoons had returned from their fruitless mission and had marched towards the sound of battle. They were dismounted and firing from cover along the south side of the harbour basin, adding to the difficulties of the boarding party.

To the north of the basin there was a sudden outburst of firing as the infantry came back from the Playa Blanco creek and appeared along the quayside which the *Dove* had left. The crew of the lugger returned this fire as the distance lengthened, Delancey and O'Keefe both trying to pick off Captain Passamonte but without success. The *Dove* might have been badly damaged by this new fusillade but the thunder of cannon was now added to the crash of musketry. Seeing the flashes outside the harbour mouth, Delancey realised that the frigate had opened fire with her broadside to cover the withdrawal. As the southern quayside was swept by grape shot the small arms fire slackened and almost ceased. The next broadside had a similarly discouraging effect on the dragoons. Several houses were now on fire and the smoke drifted seawards, mingling with the gunpowder fumes. Some of the streets were fitfully visible in the light of the flames and Delancey glimpsed the distracted citizens, some passing buckets of water and others attempting to barricade the streets against an expected landing. Gradually the firing died away and the battle was over, the town disturbed only by the crackling of flames and the complaints of the inhabitants. The light of morning revealed an empty sea, some blackened ruins, a hundred broken windows and a score of bodies awaiting burial. Voices were raised against the British whose conduct, all agreed, was tantamount to mere piracy. Vain, however, was the search for Señor Alvarez who had vanished as if he had never been.

Amidst the uproar of the bombardment the *Dove* had slipped out without hindrance, sliding past the deserted pier head and passing under the bows of the *Medusa*, half hidden in the smoke of her last broadside. Astern of the lugger came the *Aguila* with foresail and stay-sails set, towed by the longboat and apparently undamaged. Soon after withdrawing in her turn, the *Medusa* made sail for Gibraltar with the *Dove* and *Aguila* in her wake. On board the *Dove* Delancey was sound asleep until late in the morning being finally disturbed by Sam Carter, who told him that he was wanted on board the frigate. "There was an earlier signal," he added, "but I decided to ignore it. To be more exact, I took your place."

"How can I thank you, Sam?" asked Delancey. "You ran a great risk to bring me out of Spain. It could have cost you the *Dove* or your life or both."

"What would they have thought of me in St Peter Port if I had let you die in a Spanish prison? No, Dick, we had to bring you out somehow."

"And nobly you did it. I shall always be proud to claim you as my friend."

Delancey washed and shaved, borrowed a clean shirt and had breakfast. While he did so the *Dove* went ahead of the *Medusa* and finally lowered a boat which the frigate could overtake. Delancey came in at the entry port where a marine sentry came to the salute. He touched his hat and stood for a moment to look about him. The deck was spotless, the guns exactly in line, the paintwork new, the boarding pikes glittering and the musket barrels bright. He made his way to the quarterdeck, touching his hat as immemorial custom decreed, and reported his presence to the officer of the watch. No immediate action could result for this, as he could see, was a moment when everyone else was preoccupied. The master, master's mates and midshipmen had brought out their sextants and were intent on taking a sight. The master reported when the sun reached the meridian, eight bells were struck and a boatswain's mate piped the hands to dinner. Only when the ceremonial finished could a midshipman be spared to take Delancey to the captain's cabin. Looking up at the taut curve of the sails, looking at the order maintained and at the faces of the men around him, Delancey knew that this was the service to which he belonged.

Captain Morris was known to Delancey as having the reputation of a fine seaman and a strict disciplinarian. He listened in silence while Delancey made his laconic report. "Of the party which landed with me," he concluded, "all, I hope, escaped into Portugal with the exception of Mr Hodder, who was killed in action during the skirmish at Léon. I have reason to be grateful to Mr Alvarez, without whose help I should not be here to make this report. I can also speak highly of Mr O'Keefe who behaved very well while ashore. As for me, sir, I owe it to you that I am alive and in a position to report what I know about the Spanish admiral's intentions."

Captain Morris replied thoughtfully and slowly, choosing his words with care: "I realise that what you have told me, in bare outline, is the story of an astonishing achievement, even when considered merely as a journey through enemy territory. The document you have intercepted must go at once to the commander-in-chief. It is not for me to judge its importance. Whether it prove to be vital or trivial you will have done what few other men would have dared attempt. I am proud to have had some part in covering your final escape from Spain." Captain Morris paused and took up a piece of paper which was lying on his desk. "I have here a list of our casualties in yesterday's action. We had one lieutenant, four seamen and two marines killed, one officer and nine seamen wounded, two of them seriously. I want to add this, that heavier casualties than these would not, in my opinion, have been too high a price to pay for your safety."

Delancey was too overwhelmed by this to say more than a lame word of thanks and protest.

Morris went on to deal with the wording of his gazette letter. "You will understand that my written report will cover only the cutting out of the *Aguila*. I shall say nothing about you, nothing about Mr Alvarez, nothing about the *Dove*. On these other aspects of the operation I shall report verbally to Rear-Admiral Griffin. I cannot do justice to you in any other way."

"That, sir, is well understood."

"My hope is that the Board of Admiralty will remember this dangerous mission and its successful outcome, doubly rewarding you on some future occasion for your part in some action of perhaps lesser consequence."

"Thank you, sir."

"There remains the question of your immediate posting. I know something of your recent career, being indebted for this information to Mr Carter, master of the *Dove*. I understand from him that you are at present without a berth. That being so, I am happy to offer you a lieutenant's vacancy on board this frigate, replacing Lieutenant Halsted who was killed in the recent action. I see from the list that your position will make you next in seniority to the first lieutenant. You will understand that the appointment will have to be confirmed by the commander-in-chief, Sir John Jervis, but I venture to predict that he will do so on Rear-Admiral Griffin's recommendation. May I ask whether such a posting is acceptable to you?"

"I am happy to accept your offer, sir, and I look forward to serving under your command."

"I am glad to welcome you. There remains the question of Mr Carter and the *Dove*. Would he accept an appointment as master's mate?"

"I think not, sir. He is too successful, I fancy, in his present trade."

Later that afternoon the *Dove* was to part company, heading northward and leaving the *Medusa* to make for her rendezvous with Rear-Admiral Griffin. Sam Carter had dined with Captain Morris; Rothery (first lieutenant), Delancey (second) and Maltby (surgeon) being the other guests. Over the wine the captain sent his steward out with a written message, soon afterwards bringing the party to its close. "We must not detain you longer, Mr Carter—not with the wind fair for Ushant—but we'll drink your health before you go." Farewells were said as the topsails were backed and Delancey escorted Sam to his boat. As he did so he realised that the whole crew was manning the side. As Sam stood for a moment, amazed, the boatswain called for three cheers. Quickly Sam ducked down into his boat, and stood with his hat removed as the oarsmen pulled away. While the company still manned the side and the small boat dipped to the swell on clearing the frigate's quarter, there crashed out the stately measure of a three-gun salute.

"Well!" said Rothery, replacing his hat. "He'll be the first smuggler that was ever saluted by a man-of-war."

"Perhaps we should do it more often," said Delancey. "It is useful sometimes to have a smuggler on your side."

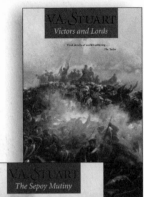

NEW! The Privateersman Mysteries

"Not content to outflank and out-gun C.S. Forester with his vivid and accurate shipboard action, storm havoc and battle scenes, **Donachie has made Ludlow the most compulsively readable amateur detective since Dick Francis' latest ex-jockey.**"

Cambridge Evening News

In this exciting new series—available now for the first time ever in the U.S. in hardcover and quality trade paperback—David Donachie re-invents the nautical fiction genre with his smart, authentic, action-filled shipboard whodunits set in the 1790s during Britain's struggle with Revolutionary France.

Donachie's hero, Harry Ludlow, is an admiral's son who was raised to serve. When he is forced out of the navy under a cloud, Harry becomes a privateersman in partnership with his younger brother James, a rising artist with his own reasons for leaving London. Together, murder and intrigue take more of their time than hunting fat trading vessels.

From the dark bowels of a troubled ship of the line to the rough-and-tumble docks of Genoa, Harry is stalked by the specter of murder. In the roiling waters of the West Indies and the Spanish colony of New Orleans, he is caught up in the intrigues of great nations and the power plays of men far from the control of their home governments.

The Privateersman Mysteries, Volumes 1 & 2

THE DEVIL'S OWN LUCK
ISBN 1-59013-003-0 • 6" x 9" 320 pp., $23.95 hardcover

ISBN 1-59013-004-9 • 5.5" x 8.5", 304 pp., $15.95 quality trade paperback

THE DYING TRADE
ISBN 1-59013-005-7 • 6" x 9" 400 pp., $24.95 hardcover

ISBN 1-59013-006-5 • 5.5" x 8.5", 384 pp., $16.95 quality trade paperback

"High adventure and detection cunningly spliced. Battle scenes which reek of blood and brine; excitements on terra firma to match."

—*Literary Review*